ALSO BY DORIS BETTS

The Beasts of the Southern Wild and Other Stories

The Astronomer and Other Stories

The Scarlet Thread

Tall Houses in Winter

The Gentle Insurrection

Heading West

Souls Raised from the Dead

The River to Pickle Beach

Doris Betts

Scribner Paperback Fiction
Published by Simon & Schuster

SCRIBNER PAPERBACK FICTION
Simon & Schuster Inc.
Rockefeller Center
1230 Avenue of the Americas
New York, NY 10020

First Scribner Paperback Fiction edition 1996
SCRIBNER PAPERBACK FICTION and design are trademarks of Simon & Schuster Inc.

Text set in Adobe Granjon
Designed by Brooke Zimmer
Manufactured in the United States of America

10 9 8 7 6 5 4 3 2 1

Library of Congress Cataloging-in-Publication Data
Betts, Doris.
The river to Pickle Beach / Doris Betts. —1st Scribner pbk. fiction ed.
p. cm.
I. Title.
PS3552.E84R58 1996
813'.54—dc20 96-28808
CIP

ISBN 0-684-81860-4

To Lowry, Lewellyn, David and Erskine Betts

With further thanks to Daphne Athas, C. Hugh Holman

"And what is the sea?" asked Will.

"The Sea!" cried the Miller. "Lord help us all, it is the greatest thing God made! That is where all the water in the world runs down into a great salt lake. There it lies as flat as my hand and as innocent as a child; but they do say when the wind blows it gets up into water mountains bigger than our mill, and makes such a roaring that you can hear it miles away upon the land. There are great fish in it five times bigger than a bull and one old serpent as long as our river and as old as all the world, with whiskers like a man, and a crown of silver on her head."

ROBERT LOUIS STEVENSON,
The Merry Men

Time the destroyer is time the preserver,
Like the river with its cargo of dead Negroes,
  cows and chicken coops,
The bitter apple and the bite in the apple.
And the ragged rock in the restless waters,
Waves wash over it, fogs conceal it;
On a halcyon day it is merely a monument,
In navigable weather it is always a seamark
To lay a course by: but in the sombre season
Or the sudden fury, is what it always was.

T.S. ELIOT,
"The Dry Salvages" (FOUR QUARTETS)

All the rivers run into the sea; yet the sea is not full; unto the place from whence the rivers come, thither they return again.

ECCLESIASTES 1:7

The River to Pickle Beach

I

Bebe Sellars

May 1968

Sunburned and stripped to shorts, Jack crossed to the bedroom wall switch. His face, hands, a V at his neck were brown from long exposure; his red torso was streaked with Bebe's cleansing cream. Bebe pulled up the sheet and closed her eyes.

As soon as the light went out, she planned to change the room to suit her. She'd wipe out the knotty pine walls first of all, think up a stone fireplace and low coals, maybe a bearskin rug, but keep the ocean's roar. She had not heard a surf like that since it beat for Irene Dunne under Dover's white cliffs.

But when Jack sat on the bed, finished undressing in the dark and then kept sitting there, she forgot. "What's the matter? Sore?"

"Don't know. Something."

In the dark, Bebe smiled. She'd heard it a thousand times. He smelled smoke when the house was not on fire. Drove as if only maniacs steered all the other cars. Expected every scratch to lead to tetanus. She reached out to pat the hot skin on his back. "A free vacation with a job offer thrown in? Looks like a piece of good luck to me."

Jack didn't trust luck. With a grunt he slid between the sandy sheets, trying to ease his sunburn gently down. Then his foot, in the signal that meant No Sex Tonight, crossed hers and hooked under the other ankle. She kissed the closest part of him, a fiery shoulder, and lazily turned her attention to the dark room. Jack liked to sleep; Bebe thought it wasteful.

Suppose, she began dreamily, this is really an old house in Cornwall with a smuggler's tunnel to the sea? She pictured it, on black and white film, a place where Ray Milland had once heard ghosts. Pressed her eyelids shut. I use the tunnel to meet a fisherman's son my family won't accept. . . . Barely did she have a plot going before Jack's foot fell loose from hers; his breath got long. Until she married Jack, Bebe had not known how far down anyone could fall, falling asleep. Nightly he dived into it, plunged, dropped to some bottom she could not remember even as a child. She threw herself onto her back without waking him and listened to the ocean grind the land. The seabreeze was so strong, the moon so high, that light as thick as milk seemed blown past the curtains, spilled over the floor. It lit up the raw pine walls and a string of coat hangers. She couldn't make Cornwall out of that.

Rolling away from his body heat made the bedsprings clash, but he never stirred. Long ago as a bride, Bebe had breathed lightly while Jack Sellars slept so deep and far away. He had been a mystery to her. Those first nights she might measure him with her flat hand laid briefly on his leg or steady chest, then touch both knobs of bone which grew below his throat. Or listen to the clock, counting. He was still mystery, although familiar, and now she made up movies while he slept. Now they were married eighteen years and when she was wakeful she could cough, flap in bed, even hum music, only to feel Jack turn as easily as a fish in water and sleep on. Sometimes he ground his teeth. Millstones.

Other times, bad times, he dreamed. The jerk of his knee would wake Bebe instantly. She could hear him some nights reciting almost wearily in the dark, "Don't do it this time. Don't do it this time." Always the same words while his body stiffened. She would start rocking him back and forth. *Wake up, Jack, all right now, it's only a dream,* hoping for once she might help him wake before the woman did it this time. Did it again. If she could change the sequence of his standard dream, who knew what else might change? And Jack would pull Bebe onto him as if she were part of the warm weight of his sleep. Sometimes, then, they made love that way. (It isn't my favorite, she thought now.) But most times he slid his prickly face against her neck and his smile lay on her skin like a wrinkle she had earned, while his muscles loosened and dropped him under sleep again.

Bebe listened now to the sea, tried to picture it and could not, almost went to the window to check. If I lived here, she wondered, could I hear the difference between high tide and low?

Will I live here? Tomorrow, Sunday, and he'd have to decide. She closed her eyes. There was some movie about a tidal wave. Burt Lancaster making love to a woman on a flat beach in the moonlight. Another filmed in green, where Jennifer Jones drowned in a storm at Land's End, just beyond reach of Joseph Cotten's hand.

She pulled up a blanket and began to drowse to the ocean's roar, some thought half forming in her mind: How easily the sea could kill us and does not.

Bebe woke in the everlasting roar.

Once, in the hall, her mother had used a varnished conch shell for a doorstop in summertime, and Bebe had braced its noisy mouth against one ear at an age when her whole skull matched its size. Now their bedroom seemed to float deep in that seashell's core. She was forty, and had grown in instead of up.

She opened her eyes and the morning window blazed. That's how the sun looked to the conch before he died. Do conchs have eyes? Bebe rolled over in bed. Jack's eyelids quivered in his sleep. He did not really like the beach.

Feeling guilty for liking it so much, she slid her foot across the grainy sheet and clenched her toes in the hairs on his leg. At least there had been no dream. Maybe the noisy sea jammed dreams the way governments could jam enemy radios.

In a normal voice she said, "Jack?" Then louder. His breathing snagged out of rhythm once and went on.

Early—the sun rose early here. Might as well get up. She sat on the mattress edge and turned to cover him with the sheet. There were pearly water blisters on his shoulder blades. He was going to peel like a katydid. That's probably what he predicted when he first walked in the ocean's edge Saturday: *I'm going to burn and peel.*

In the mirror Bebe watched herself, naked and smiling, swing out of bed and cross the pine boards. Sea air had clouded the tall mirror. Made him look like a ghost, Jack said. Bebe liked the way it softened her face and left the wrinkles out. She turned sideways. Early in the mornings her belly was flatter but the scar ran across it like a streak of chalk. She patted the line with pancake makeup to match her recent tan.

She almost went to the kitchen naked before she remembered George. It was George's beach house and already she wanted him out of it. She found yesterday's shorts on the bathroom floor and shook out the sand, put on one of Jack's old shirts. George's toothbrush lay by the spigot. I hope he's hungover.

The three of them had left the kitchen in a mess. Bebe didn't care. Like brown worms, their wet cigarettes swelled in the sink. She tossed them away and wiped her fingers on Jack's shirt. The men had stayed for a last drink while she got ready for bed, and she gazed around the kitchen for clues to what had happened. Somebody had knocked over Karo syrup in a cabinet and spilled a glassy puddle—looking for ginger ale? Its shape almost matched the map they had drawn on the plastic tablecloth. Bebe leaned closer. Ballpoint ink that wouldn't ever scrub off. Have to turn the damn thing over. Correction: Whoever lives here will have to turn it over. Was anything decided while she slept—yes or no? It wasn't written on the tablecloth.

When the coffee was hot, she carried a cup onto the screen porch, braced for the sight of that endless sea, shocked when it came. Imagine having the Atlantic Ocean in your front yard every day! Even in winter she would go out in a yellow slicker and stand at its edge. Say yes, Jack. Yes.

At home in Durham, she looked from her porch at sidewalk and street through an edging of plants which hardly showed over the grass. These were slowly growing toward Jack's fine camellia hedge, rooted from cuttings under glass, which in ten years would be green and glossy with blooms the size of saucers. If a lawn mower didn't get it by mistake. That's what I'd see there, at fifty.

But here Bebe's hedge would be water, greasy gray in the early light, trimmed perfectly even against the sky. And every day it would throw up shells and seaweed, change color, move, hold up toy ships, and make that everlasting noise.

Bebe finished the coffee. I'd like still to be watching all that when I am old.

But surely Jack had already said no, looking the gift horse in the mouth plus any other opening he could find. Getting out of the car, he had glanced at Bebe, jerking his head toward the rusty trailers propped on concrete blocks. In Bebe's mind these were already repainted and strewn with rambler roses. He said, "What do you call it?"

"Pickerel Beach," said George Bennett. "Named for the plant that grows in the marsh. You ought to like that, knowing flowers the way you do."

Jack nodded—to his knowledge of flowers, not to liking the beach. The whole visit had happened by accident. That's what he couldn't stand, what she and Jack had argued about even before leaving Durham. Bebe said one thing just led to another. Why should it? Jack had asked.

A few days before, they held a reunion of Jack's old army unit from World War II at Fort Bragg, and George Bennett came. Jack wouldn't go. So George had showed up in Durham with some other buddy—big surprise!—and next thing she knew they were at a beach George owned, on a free vacation, and George was asking Jack to manage the place for him.

"What a piece of good luck!" she'd said when they were alone in the bedroom, putting on swimsuits.

"I don't trust luck," said Jack, pushing a finger into his ear as if the ocean made him deaf.

Bebe laughed, pinched him when he bent to step into the knit trunks. "We wouldn't be married if it wasn't for luck."

"Yours or mine?" he asked.

Would it have killed him just to nod his head?

Later, standing knee deep in the waves, he had pointed out the trailers, the frame house where they were staying, the marsh across the road from which mosquitoes would fly out in clouds. "This beach is ugly." You'd think he was used to country clubs instead of a tract house that cost them nine thousand dollars. His idea of a vacation was to turn over the compost pile or use Bebe's old nylons to tie a grapevine to a fence.

Bebe just touched him lightly between the shoulder blades.

Once she had won a set of free dishes at the bank, and Jack wasn't really glad till he checked and found only one plate was chipped. After that he bought steaks to eat off them, and a bottle of wine and table candles that smelled like hyacinths. That's how he was. Bebe didn't mind it. It seemed to her when she added weight and her throat began looking slack, he had turned back into a bridegroom. As if he felt sure of keeping her then.

So she knew he wouldn't start having a good time at the beach until he settled what the drawbacks were. He was always telling her, "Bebe, don't take things at face value. That's simpleminded."

She set her coffee cup in a chair. If I wasn't simpleminded, she thought, he'd be a bachelor yet. I met him one day; on the next he said, "Come with me," and I came. Sometimes we simpleminded people do all right.

She went out into the washed, clean air. Her lungs weren't used to it, and she had to hunch in the wind to light a cigarette. Weekdays at home, she'd be walking into the café about this time, stuffing her yellow hair into a net, making herself smile at the college boys who needed coffee before they went to eight o'clock class. Those boys killed Bebe, moaning how hard school was, explaining it to waitresses they never tipped whose arches fell before those boys were born. Jack ate lunch in the café with her. In the booth she could almost see his ears flare. The noises the students made, talking of books, roared for him more beautiful than the sound of conch shells. He thought they were all smart and he envied them. It hurt Bebe to watch the envy on his face. She wanted to imitate Jack, wanted to whisper, "Don't take things at face value," but did not.

Bebe lay alone on the sand and the sun against her eyelids turned every blood vessel into a stream of lava. Like a network of the bright rivers of the world, pouring to the sea and never filling it.

* * *

While she cooked supper and talked to George Bennett, Jack crossed the highway and walked alongside the marsh matted with pickerelweed, which gave the beach its name. Bebe could see him from the kitchen window, squatting by cattail reeds at the edge of swamp, moving on. Once a small heron, dragging legs like sticks, rose from the grasses and crossed Jack's shadow with its moving one.

"What do you think?" asked George, teetering in a chair at the kitchen table. "Will he stay?" He propped his sandy feet on another chair. George was a dentist now, and claimed it had given him varicose veins, standing all day before open mouths.

"It's up to Jack."

"You leave things up to him, do you? I like that in Southern women." She said nothing. He sweetened his drink from a bottle of Jack Daniel's. "You like it here, don't you, Bebe?"

Stirring the shrimp creole, she glanced out the window at Jack pacing the marsh's edge. I like it but Jack says I'm not hard to please. "The house needs a lot of work."

"Oh, I agree. I agree. Whatever you need. Paint it up, inlay linoleum. Air-conditioning—would you like that?"

I bet the marsh stinks up close, she thought. Jack was coming toward the house now, slapping his leg with a long reed. Bet you could make a whistle out of it, like a stalk of rye.

"The property's got a funny shape, but that comes from buying it one piece at a time," George said. He bent his half-bald head over the tablecloth sketch. "I'll drain that marsh someday if the damn government doesn't condemn the whole coast for a park. Hand me some ice, will you?"

While she loosened cubes from the tray, he smoothed the wrinkled plastic map and talked about the future of Pickerel Beach: a housing development inland along dredged canals, and at the tip a pavilion where kids could come to dance, perhaps build a marina on the creek. His words made a slow film in Bebe's head. A merry-go-round spinning by the highway, as slowly as her spoon turned in the pan. She made Jack step on its colorful platform and drop off again. Out-of-state cars between which he might be walking toward them now. She grew Jack a beard that George Bennett would like, dressed him as captain of a deep-sea fishing boat, bringing home happy tourists with a big catch. Bebe hummed background music, putting ice in George's drink, setting out three plates for their supper. And that's me, in a back room, making hush puppies and dropping potato strips in a greasy basket, letting drunks pat me on the fanny. The legs are on loan from Betty Grable. The syndicate tries to break in at Pickerel Beach with gambling interests but . . .

"Jack needs to think of this as an opportunity. Why should he keep on planting bushes and mowing grass at his age? There's no future for him in Durham," George said. "Or you, Bebe."

She didn't like hearing her own arguments in George's mouth. Instantly she changed the movie and put Jack, white-smocked, inside a greenhouse surrounded by rare orchids, but the screen went blank.

Jack came up the high back steps into the kitchen and his eyes went to her first. He liked the red bathing suit, though she doubted he'd ever say so aloud.

"Smells good."

Jack was handsomer now than eighteen years ago, partly because the lines in his ruddy face made his blue eyes more astonishing than ever—even Paul Newman's eyes were second-rate. Bebe once thought if she put her own up close to them she could see halfway inside his head and watch the thoughts go round, and she wanted to, since he thought more than he ever said.

They ate hungrily, George trying to promote the beach, to recall Naples in the war, to draw Jack out. Under the table Jack rubbed her leg with his. Like *that,* is it? Bebe rubbed back. George described how Fort Bragg had grown, Fayetteville's go-go bars. He asked Bebe if she'd need more cabinets in this kitchen. Didn't Jack think copper screening would be better for the porch?

"You could try running the beach one year. Then quit if you didn't like it."

"But I couldn't get my old job back," said Jack quietly, "and I like that job."

He'd never even ask, thought Bebe. When Jack leaves a place, his life grows shut behind him and he won't go back. They were both born in the foothills of the Blue Ridge, Stone County, North Carolina, but he never went home with Bebe for a visit. She still had family living in Stoneville and Greenway, but all Jack's kin were gone except on the nights they visited him in the dream and made him beg, "Don't do it this time"; and then did it.

"George, you've talked everything but money," said Jack, pushing back his plate.

"Finish off with a drink and I'll get down to salary."

He's going to take the job, thought Bebe. Probably for me. She whispered, "It's up to you, honey," then said she would walk on the beach while the men talked.

Jack handed her his Audubon book off the refrigerator. "Might as well learn the bird life," he said. Always trying to improve her mind. She left the two men writing dollar marks on their napkins.

Beatrice Fetner Sellars had seen the ocean once before, age twenty, half her life ago. She had added fifteen pounds and twenty years of time, had married, miscarried, lost a father and a faulty uterus, slept with a clerk and a sailor and Jack (mostly

Jack); and still the sea looked to her exactly as it had to Columbus. She could not explain this awesomeness to Jack. He was the one who read books and studied nature, made fun of her weekly movies and Hollywood magazines. She did not even want to understand these feelings she got by the ocean, merely to go on having them. That wind off the water through her hair, the sound of the tide which throbbed through her whole body—outside and inside, inescapable. She wanted to live surrounded by them both, letting the breeze and the noise invade her in some way she could not express, until the sea's rhythm and her own would be vaguely the same. She could not guess what would happen then, or even if she would recognize the moment.

She stood in the sea oats on a low dune between the house and shore. If I knew more, I could say what I mean. How the sea I can't imagine an end to reaches around and makes this same noise against Africa. How all the rain ends up here. That it all goes together.

A gull cried out and swept the ocean's edge, looking for something that had died between trips. Shading her eyes against the low sun, Bebe watched it sail lower, stiff-winged, like the wooden planes her brothers had pieced together and slung off the roof while she sat in a darkened hallway, listening to the promise inside a seashell. She opened Jack's book but could not get interested in matching some bird to its picture. The gull struck water, bounced away. She walked down the beach and birds no bigger than bantams ran away from her in the foam. Jack called them sandpipers. She flipped the book's pages. Snipe? In Stone County that was a made-up bird. Curlew. Marbled godwit—pretty name. A turnstone never left one unturned, she guessed.

Let's admit it, she thought, dropping to the packed sand. Books are not for me. She lay on her back and used Audubon for a pillow, watching the sky get darker red as the sun dropped down the sky.

As soon as Bebe got quiet, a crumb of sand fell in nearby and a crab that seemed too big for its tunnel edged out sideways. It froze, seeing her there in its path like a log. Bebe kept her eye on its sandy color, knowing if she looked away she could never find it again. The crab skittered a little closer to Audubon.

She remembered the movement. The last year Grandma Fetner lived with them—when Bebe was eight—she would creep into Bebe's bedroom and drop her curled gray hand on the bed and waggle it down the blanket. She was a little childish by then. "Comes a little spider," she would say in singsong, making her fingers travel on the wool. "Comes a little spider . . ." in a slow threat, getting faster and louder. "Comesalittlespider . . . Bite 'em in the Belly!" and her claw would leap up and drive at Bebe's middle and make her scream and try to crawl up the headboard.

The crab looked now like her hand did then. Bebe felt her skin burst into gooseflesh. She slid away. In a ball, the crab rolled down its hole.

She hadn't thought about Grandma Fetner in years. Funny how everything that ever happened is saved up in your head a hundred percent, even the shiver that flies down your skin at the proper time, even the noises of Grandma's breath and your own breath, that the blanket was dark green and the headboard felt greasy from lemon oil.

She sat up and watched the sea. If I were like Jack and got a lot out of reading books, that's what I'd want to learn about. How people remember, and why. Just as I wonder now if the crab, folded and dark in the bottom of his hole, has already forgotten what it was that scared him.

Moving Day

May 15, 1968

The workmen closed the van and slouched in the yard on Mayhew Street while Jack showed them once more his diagram of what furniture was to be put in which rooms at the beach. He wore coveralls and a billed cap that said *Durham Paint Store.* "You'll beat us there by a couple hours." He handed a house key to the driver.

The man snatched it, angry about thick sand and the high back steps up which tables and bureaus had to be carried. "Be just about as cheap to buy all new stuff down there."

Except that George Bennett would pay the moving bill. Jack rattled a chain which looked too loose on the tailgate. "Wait a minute." He called Bebe to make sure they had all the big stuff and she said they did, and Mickey McCane—sprawled in the yard—agreed. Mickey had invited himself and his pickup truck to help move them from Durham to Pickerel. Mickey was another convenient leftover from that army reunion.

The Sellars house, almost empty and with every door propped open, already looked like nobody's house. A pile of dust had been swept to the front porch and left, and something shone deep in the trash, like tinsel off last year's tree. The wooden garage was bare, wide open, hung with spider webs and black rags.

In the kitchen Bebe sat on the floor, wrapping her small cups and saucers in tissue paper and stacking them inside a wooden keg. They were all colors and patterns, bought over the years and never used but kept on a whatnot shelf in the living room. She used to imagine pouring coffee into them, serving from a silver pot and using tongs for the sugar cubes. One time she dreamed she was doing that at her daddy's labor union meeting, and after everybody drained his cup each man picked up his tiny saucer and ate it like a cookie.

The empty rooms echoed and Jack and Mickey seemed to come down the hall in steel shoes. "Listen, I'm glad to do it," boomed Mickey's voice. She made a face. "I just wish somebody would offer me a soft job by the ocean, that's what I wish." That wasn't all he wished. If Mickey found one more excuse today for touching her, Bebe thought she might bite his hand.

". . . wrong with it," Jack answered, and his words bounced softer off the kitchen wallpaper: *Wrong with it. Wrong.*

She could hear cardboard boxes scrape along the floor. How did the ocean sound? Why couldn't she remember? The boxes must hold the last bedsheets, even the one with a damp spot in the center she had just taken off their bed. She began to hum a chorus of "Rolling in My Sweet Baby's Arms," and sounded so resonant in the stripped kitchen that she sat back on her heels and tried it full voice. The Fetners liked to sing. Her brother Troy could make anybody cry with his version of "The Letter Edged in Black." And one time they sat in the chinaberry tree and drew the whole neighborhood with nothing but a mouth harp. "I'll hang around the shack / Till the mail train comes back /And roll in my sweet baby's arms!" Troy had bawled, and the whole crowd bent back and forth like grass and hollered out the chorus.

From the doorway, Mickey clapped. She was embarrassed and began stuffing unwrapped china on top of the rest. "That's a good song," he said, winking an eye maybe half as blue as Jack's. "You ready for me to load that?"

"Not yet."

He clomped into the room and got behind her to look at the scum that was under the refrigerator. Her wrists grew stiff. Sure enough, he dropped one hand—the one with the Moose club ring—on her shoulder. "I don't know where you get the energy to sing with all you've done today."

Bebe leaned away from his squeezing fingers. I ought to mail his wife a sympathy card.

"You sure have got pep," he added.

His hand pushed her lopsided so she nearly dropped her favorite cup. Painted in its bottom was the curved face of an angel, smiling right into your eye at the last swallow. There was a line of stars around the rim.

"Tell Jack not to forget that box of books on the step."

"Already in the truck." He let go at last. "You never know how things will turn out, do you, Bebe?" He liked to use her name.

"Some things you know *won't* turn out."

Mickey hoisted himself on a kitchen counter, maybe to look down her dress front. She started to tuck a nylon strap out of sight but wouldn't give him the satisfaction. "You ever look back and decide you've lived your whole life by accident?"

"Not exactly." She listened for Jack's movements in the house.

"I met my wife by accident."

Like to hear her story, Bebe thought.

"And then I go back to Bragg and there's old George after all these years, and he says he's lost touch with Sellars. And who's the only one in the outfit that's seen him in Durham?"

Just from uneasiness she shouted, "Jack?" and when he answered called again, "Never mind!"

"So we show up at your house and now you're moving to the beach—what's its name?"

"Pickerel," said Bebe. Mickey must not go to the movies much, she decided. If Doris Day and Rock Hudson didn't get booked in the same hotel room by mistake, there'd be no show at all. She got up and peered into the hall until she caught Jack carrying out a load and waved him down. "What do you mean, there's something wrong with it? We don't have to go, you know."

This time he smiled, tried to shrug the armful of curtains. "You know me," he said. Yes. She leaned on the doorframe. "Heard you singing." Bebe jerked a thumb Mickey couldn't see and made a grammar school face: cross-eyes and vomit. "He wasn't my idea." She made grabbing motions at her own breasts and crotch while Jack watched. "That bad?"

"Not yet."

"Harmless," he said. "No follow-through."

Behind her Mickey asked Jack if he could manage by himself and Jack said he could manage *everything* by himself. Laughing softly with Bebe. She turned back to the china keg.

Mickey hopped off the sink. "Bebe, you've got soot on your face." The way he said it—sŭt—sounded dirtier. His white handkerchief flew at her eye, smelling of bleach and fabric softener. Mickey owned a laundromat in Harnett County and one across the line in Lee. Already he had explained how to soak her cleaning rags in an enzyme detergent. He was wiping Bebe's face just as Jack came in the back door and stopped with the screen door pressing his heel. Bebe rolled her eyes and crossed them again. The corner of Jack's mouth jumped upward once before he asked Mickey to give him a hand lifting the birdbath.

She dropped to the linoleum beside her cups. "You're not taking that heavy thing?" He was, of course. To where the whole Atlantic lapped in the backyard. Any bird that can't wash in salty water, she thought, can do without.

"It comes apart; easy to carry," said Jack, who had made it himself on Saturdays. When they first moved on Mayhew Street, he scooped out a place for a trashcan lid and the birds used that; later he dug a shallow pool and spread that with cement. When he got tired of raking leaves out of there, he learned how to mold a concrete bath on a pedestal and even shaped a bone-white rabbit and a chalky frog to sit in the shrubbery. Fifty pounds apiece. They were leaving those behind.

The next time she could get Jack alone, Bebe asked if she couldn't ride to the beach with him in the truck.

"Is Mickey really bothering you?"

Sounded like her mama, asking after a date, "Did he have W.H.?" Wandering Hands. "He'd like to."

Softly, so his voice wouldn't boom in the empty house, Jack said, "It's all brag," and bent to take water straight from the kitchen faucet. "Mickey *talks* a good fuck, that's all."

"He'll hear you." She tapped the lid shut over her cups and saucers.

"Just want you to know he's not much threat. Has trouble getting it up. Always did have trouble."

The news made Mickey interesting for the first time and even through the kitchen screen he felt Bebe's eyes run over his body. Jack asked him to carry out her wooden keg. "But be careful with Bebe's chinaware. She's got a temper." He held back the door.

She couldn't help asking, "You have any children, Mickey?"

"Two boys," he said. Got it up twice, at least. He had become very alert, perhaps from the curiosity in Bebe's face. "We're ready to roll, then," he said, carrying the keg down the back steps.

Roll. The song came back. Bebe pressed herself on Jack's back, locked her arms around his waist. She had forgotten how the ocean sounded and only felt sad to leave one place for another, move out of a room everything that ever made it hers. After eight years, she thought, her face in his shirt, there's nothing left of Jack and me here but a little dirt, the grease in the kitchen fan, some floor dents, and a million fingerprints only the FBI could find.

Jack took her two hands and hooked them together like a belt buckle on his front, and left his warm fingers resting there a minute. "We forget anything?"

He doesn't want to go. It's all for me. If things go wrong at the beach, I'll be to blame. She scraped her nose on his spine. He turned and held her. Said, grinning, "Now you behave yourself with Mickey."

"After you said that he . . . ?"

"Yeah," he said, "but don't you *cure* him," and went whistling out to the borrowed truck. Bebe was to drive their car with Mickey so he could later take his pickup home.

She waved her pocketbook till Jack drove out of sight, then sat on the warm hood of the dusty car—dusty herself—while Mickey finished in the toilet or whatever he was doing. She didn't want to be alone in the house with him.

Overhead the white oak leaves, so late to sprout, so slow to let go for the winters, were still light green for May, and small. A plastic bottle Jack hung on a limb last year had catbirds in it. The cement porch was dotted with rusty circles where Jack's plants had been growing in old oil cans. There must be thirty loaded on the truck: ligustrum, fire thorn, chrysanthemums, things he thought could stand the salt air and sea winds. One place in the yard looked like a shell hole, where the birdbath had stood, with ivy pulled loose and dropped just anywhere.

Before Mayhew Street, they had lived in an apartment house in Winston-Salem, where Jack delivered Golden Guernsey milk and drove a taxicab at night. Their rooms were on the top floor of a set of brick squares in a field of creeping Bermuda. The nearest pine tree grew a mile away. Summers, the window fan rattled all night and sucked in hot truck exhaust and pizza smells.

I guess Jack hated it; he never said. Now the scuppernongs he set are beginning to bear and I'm taking him to a place that's all sand and sea oats. She drew on the dusty car a wave, a sailboat, a blob that was meant to be a fish.

Mickey locked the front door. He came toward her with his jacket slung over one shoulder like an imitation schoolboy. He was forty-one, with black hair and furry eyebrows. In his high school yearbook he would have been handsome, a little sinister, one of those milltown boys who smiled with only half his mouth. Now he was Elvis Presley, fading, not sure why.

"Throw me the keys," he called, so there was nothing to do but let him drive the first few hours. He swung open the front door to read the sticker about when the oil was changed. As soon as Bebe got in the car she took off her shoes. He idled the engine, tried the brake a few times.

They went barreling out of the driveway so fast she cracked an elbow on the door. "Hey!" He was racing under a yellow traffic light. "Hey, where'd you learn to drive? On the track at Darlington?"

He eased off a little. "I go down there every year. George Wallace is coming to the Labor Day race; you want to go?" He whipped from lane to lane as if they were already on the interstate highway.

"I'd like to live that long."

"Relax. We'll be at the beach by the time Jack gets through Fayetteville." His thick arms had blood veins twined near the surface like clinging stems. He laughed at her with a sidelong look.

And with no warning, Bebe got gooseflesh on the inside,

low, perhaps on the lining of her stomach. She was so surprised she jerked upright and stared through the windshield and waited for it to go away. Her hands folded themselves politely in her lap.

Mickey pulled down both visors. "Sun in your eyes?"

She must be frowning. "Thanks." A little squeak ran down her backbone. She held her body very still except for the toes on the ridged rubber mat.

He started talking about their army days, playing poker, how Jack wouldn't gamble much. "George tell you he won his first piece of beach property in a poker game? It went on every night for a week at Bragg."

Bebe didn't listen. Thank God I'm not dumb and seventeen. Mickey wants me—that's all. It's in the air. And I can want that want. He's contagious. I've known people hoarse with a cold that made *me* start whispering. All right. Easy now.

She turned, drew both knees on the seat to face him. He was short, black-haired, his blue eyes watery. There were a hundred like him on the back desks at school. The boys who got sent to the principal for smoking young and carrying big sharp pocketknives and confusing dumb girls by asking how their cherries were. Bebe had never been one of the dumb girls. When Mickey was twenty, she decided, he combed his hair in a pompadour and grew a long ducktail in the back. Pegged the bottoms of his pants. Carried a leather blackjack under the dashboard of his car to show the girls.

Bebe plucked at a piece of loose upholstery. It bothered her, not being able to spot a man who's impotent from one who's not. She believed in intuition.

He dropped his right hand off the steering wheel and raked the forefinger over her knee. It felt like dry ice. "How'd you get that little scar?"

"I cut it in a wreck." Bebe decided to sit straight again.

And to go away from him. She was good at that. The long straight road with painted lines which rushed toward her eyes and seemed to pass on through her head and blow behind her like ribbons—easy to blur. She passed into that flow and was herself blurred.

She tried out a quick scene—Beatrice Sellars, young and rich, with her satin bed and by it the white French telephone seen once in *Trail of the Lonesome Pine.* Her hair in little yellow watchsprings. An ostrich hem to her gown.

Or she might make up the girl off the Morton salt box, spilling her white trail from under the umbrella; she had always seemed mysterious, old for her years.

The child walks as usual ahead of me down a lumpy street so narrow it must be a lane. Brick walls on both sides. I think we're in London. I follow her, stepping on the line of melting salt in the rain, or hurry alongside to stare at that false, sweet smile. Doesn't she know that where she salts the land nothing will grow again?

Now I'm on a pirate ship, in color, wearing boots with a soft rolled edge and a wide belt (patent leather) and I used to live on Frenchman's Creek. The pirate with me is very lean and long-faced and quiet, only shows his teeth in battle.

I'm on safari with my shorthand notebook. I work for a man who studies apes. Our guide has lived in the African sun so long he is parched like a peanut. I barely speak to him because he swears and drinks whiskey and I come from a fine Philadelphia family. Someday soon, in a tent at night, he will take off my glasses and turn me beautiful. . . .

"They got foot-long hot dogs here. You hungry?" Mickey was parking at the Tick Tock Grill. A big plywood clock on the roof with painted hands.

"Club sandwich."

He wanted to eat off a tray but Bebe preferred to go inside.

She loved club sandwiches. Like bacon and eggs, they tasted good everywhere. She hooked up the backs of her stockings and went inside sniffing; the place was clean. Grade B, it said in the picture frame. She liked B restaurants and worked in one herself. More human. She liked it when the waitress left her hairnet off; whose mother wore one? This woman was old and knew how much salt and pepper was enough. Wouldn't it be funny, Bebe thought, if later Jack stopped here and ate in this very booth? If she had a hairpin, she'd scratch her name on the wall just in case.

Knocking the plastic with his ring, Mickey flipped through the jukebox list. He tapped a lot on the steering wheel, too. He said, as though reading a song title, "You're a lot younger."

"Younger than who?"

"Than Jack is all I meant."

Bebe was forty and Jack was forty-six. It wasn't worth answering.

"Say he never mentioned me being in the army with him? We got him drunk once, did he tell you that?"

Last week he did. "That was in Germany?"

He nodded. "Jack and George Bennett and me spent nearly three years together. And he never mentioned us." Mickey turned his hand over to see if his palm was as surprised as the rest of him, then grinned. "You know what I thought? After I saw Jack in Durham a few times, I thought there was some reason he never asked me to his house. His wife was ugly or something. Plenty of times I'd tell him to drive down our way and I'd take him hunting. Bring your wife, I said."

"Jack doesn't hunt."

"That's what he said and I really was surprised. He was a good shot, nearly as good as me, and I've been around guns all my life."

Mickey pinged his Moose ring with its fake sapphire on the beer glass. "I'm not too clear what Jack did at that college where he worked. Landscaping, was it? Some kind of teacher?"

Bebe was surprised. Jack worked with the grounds crew, clipping hedges, spraying trees. She didn't know what to say and was glad when the food came, her sandwich in neat stacked triangles. She used to imagine biting down on a toothpick which would thrust like a spear straight through the roof of her mouth. A woman in Greenway had a cleft palate; Bebe and her brothers thought something like that had happened to her, and the whole dome above her upper jaws been taken out in surgery. Even now, the first thing she did with the toothpicks was draw them all out and lay them by her plate: four. All right.

Suddenly Mickey's knee hit hers like a doorknob. Again there was a spread of goosebumps but something new in it, something worse. Here was a man who couldn't screw and—if he could—she wouldn't like it. Bebe hurried with the sandwich and got him to the car as quickly as she could. For the rest of the trip she played the radio and pretended to nap.

When they got to the house at Pickerel Beach the moving van was still backed to the high steps so she didn't have to be alone with him. Her furniture was so well wrapped in comforters that nobody could tell antiques from Sears Roebuck, the workmen hollering, "Watch the door!" while they eased in a table nobody could hurt much with a hammer.

Bebe peeled off her stockings and wadded them into a shoe and worked her toes out of sight in the hot sand. She would never get tired of that feeling. Still have two arches down there; seems I haven't used them since the days I went barefoot in the pasture.

"Where do you want your cups and saucers?"

She told Mickey, "I want to carry them in myself."

Shaking his head, he lifted the keg from the car trunk. "This thing is heavy."

"They're mine. I want to carry them myself." She hugged the small barrel and for a minute they were both pulling on it before he stepped back, watched her stagger away and lean crooked up the stairs and carry it through the kitchen to the big hearth and mantelpiece.

He slouched in the kitchen door. "Don't you want to place the furniture in here first?"

Already the wooden lid was off. Each tissue wrapping went into the black fireplace to be burned. "No." The flowered cup was left from a tea set Bebe got for Christmas once. A tall one, painted with holly berries, Jack said was for people who put coffee in good whiskey. The starry rim went right in the center. You'd have to stand tall, she thought, on tiptoe and look down to see how the angel's face was bent around inside. Most people wouldn't know.

By the time Jack came, the moving men were nearly done and all Bebe's demitasse mix was set evenly across the mantel. He smiled to see it.

"Want a drink?" called Mickey from the kitchen. His voice had been sharp and his sentence short. No doubt Jack could tell that his condition remained the same.

Just so there wouldn't be any doubt, Bebe walked straight up to Jack and put her hand between his legs, all the time saying in a polite voice and smiling over his shoulder in case Mickey came in, "I thought you'd never get here. Have a good trip?"

"Pretty good," he said, trying not to laugh.

She stroked him lightly. If they could make finger rings the color of Jack's eyes, she thought, the Moose club people would really have something.

2

Jack Sellars

May, Early June

There may be something evil inside the world, always threatening to break loose, under pressure and searching out weak spots in the crust. Something inimical to human happiness.

Jack Sellars had good reason to believe that this was true. It had let him alone for a long time—since he was fourteen—and as far as he could tell it couldn't reach Bebe at all. She was color blind or tone deaf to what he meant.

Some people could hold a forked twig over the driest land and for them, and for them only, the stick would dip where the underground rivers flowed. He was like that, and heard the rumbles underneath. Even in the war he had walked over mine fields and some had blown sky high just after he had passed. He had been overseas with Mickey McCane, whose gun seemed heat sensitized and shot down strangers, and with George Bennett, who would have sold a seamless robe to the highest bidder at Golgotha; and still Jack's turn to be hurt had not come a second time.

He lived defensively, looking ahead and never back, trying to prevent and outwit the worst. He owned more insurance than anything else. Nothing must be left to chance. For all he knew, Chance was its alias.

Or maybe the ocean was its other name.

Until George Bennett took Jack and Bebe to Pickerel for a weekend, he had hardly looked at the ocean. Troop carriers didn't count. At embarkation points, it was only smelly water slapping against the piers. Off Italy, the sea had been something to ride on, then to get out of as quickly as possible and storm the Nazi guns. He saw now the sea would do exactly as it chose, beat in forever on the sand, make up its own hurricanes in its own good time. Nobody could control the waves. In the surf, Bebe playacted like Esther Williams while he stared. He was drawn to the ocean by his fear of its disregard.

Jack Sellars knew exactly why they left Durham to live in this barren place.

It was because of the brown thrasher, who came all spring to the birdbath in their backyard. Every morning he lit on the last twig of the peach tree strong enough to bear his speckled weight, and looked with a yellow eye at his picture on the water. Then he dropped to the rim of the concrete bowl and paced slowly around its edge, dipping his curved beak a time or two to make sure it still held water and not some dose of hydrochloric acid.

April mornings Jack watched him with a smile and called Bebe to the window. She was not interested in birds. "*Toxostoma rufum,*" he told her. "Watch what he does." She stood at his side, bored, anxious to scald the coffeepot.

Next the thrasher would test the depth, barely wetting his claws, and again he would circle the basin just at the water's edge. At last he waded in and spread his white-barred wings. His golden eye seemed to fix Jack through the window glass.

He dared Jack to move. Awkwardly, he stroked the water and with the broken image of himself, cleaned his rusty feathers. Bebe nodded and went back to scraping egg off the skillet.

By May he began to resent the thrasher's distrust. Each day the concrete bath was the same, the water fresh; each day the bird breakfasted nearby on the edges of their toast, but always he came to bathe expecting the very worst. Like me, Jack thought. Soon he was tempted to go by night and chisel out the center of the bath to drowning depth.

And when he left Mayhew Street those spring mornings, he began to go to work the way that thrasher eased into the water. Why should he trust the luck of that job? The only luck he really believed in was bad luck, yet the two best things in his life—that job and Bebe—fell in Jack's lap like fruit. That's why he knew there had to be a catch about George's beach: third time up and out. And still he went.

Jack had taken the Durham job in 1960, never meaning to stay. A gardener? What did he know about gardening? At State Technical College, all work on the grounds was supervised by college graduates with long titles, who called even crabgrass by its Latin name. Jack, who had quit school in the ninth grade, was only fit to clip hedges with a crew of colored workers. The pay was bad, worse than delivering milk or driving cabs. It was only a stopgap job.

But he had been dropped on that little campus like Brer Rabbit in his brier patch. It turned out plants would grow for Jack Sellars. Shrubs would leaf out to the invisible shape he set for them. He could remember instructions the college men gave though at first he learned them phonetically. In class the professors taught scientific farming but, deep down, they liked to joke about Jack's green thumb and quote him in faculty meetings on how to plant by the waxing and waning of the moon. For them he was like some Indian who buried dead fish in his hills of corn without knowing why. He kept the horticulturists from "losing touch," they said.

Not knowing how ignorant he was, they thought he had some kind of folk wisdom and were gullible about it. But on the campus, Jack saw his own ignorance for the first time, at the one point in his life he had every chance to teach it away. He could eavesdrop on classes while he pruned the holly. He could stare through a window at a chart of bird bones so delicate one good raindrop ought to fracture a sparrow's skull. He was glad to haul teachers' books back to the library and take home new ones for himself. What would his mother have thought? It was a long way from a river shack to a college campus.

He lived in that college like a seed in a sidewalk crack. He sprouted and put out a network of roots that ran under every building to feed on what the others knew. He was self-educated, but the books did not make him optimistic.

Nitrogen, anaerobic bacteria, mycelia, azotobacter, nemotodes, mycorrhiza—when he looked up from botany texts the world changed to Jack's eye; the very air swarmed with life. There was a roar of it under his boots. Seventy-six thousand harmless species of insects and ten thousand more of pests. Their wings beat everywhere. And in a few weeks one tiny chickadee could eat one hundred thousand cankerworm eggs, and still the cankerworm survived.

It scared him. Maybe you need to get an education young, Jack thought, when you don't have sense enough to be frightened by it.

He sat drinking coffee in the café where Bebe worked, and heard the students talking about astronauts and rocket ships while there he was, staring not up into space, but down. No end to it. On that scale, there were miles and miles stretching between the microbes and, beyond that, a solar system of atoms which would split. We were all hung between two forevers, and when Jack told one teacher that, he said, "Pascal," so Jack read him, too.

Those eight years in Durham, raking leaves, Jack went to college all the time. Matriculated twice. And scary knowledge tumbled about him the way rain must rush in the earth with its load of food and minerals. Roots growing toward water, the books said, were hydrotropic. Jack's were gnostropic. Toward knowledge. Him and the dictionary—no, nominative case—he and the dictionary made that up. There was so much to learn. With that, with the knowledge in one's head, plans could be made and events controlled.

I can live here, Jack thought, as long as a redwood. *Sequoia sempervirens.* Or better yet, *Sequoia gigantea.*

He was home reading one night in the house on Mayhew Street. It was raining outside, slow and even; good for my fescue, he thought. Good for the young camellias near the street.

The front screen rattled in its frame. Might be the wind. Jack leaned closer to his book about earthworms; Aristotle called them the intestines of the soil. He thought he might breed some in a culture box and feed them old coffee grounds.

"Somebody's knocking?" Bebe, bent double, brushed her blond hair toward the floor. It fell like yellow silk but her face was red and out of shape.

Jack went to the door. They had on khaki raincoats and stood so stiffly he felt AWOL. A new war and somebody had come for him. When the porch bulb lit up, the tall one staggered as if the overhead light fell heavy on his head. "Hey, Jack. Howsaboy?" He laughed.

Jack didn't recognize him, but the short man with rain running off his jaw was . . . what was his name? McCane. McCane said, with care, "The mountain has come to Mo . . ." and turned, and the tall one whispered, "Mohammed."

Bennett. That's who he was. Sergeant Bennett. Both men

reached for the screen, bumped each other getting it open, edged forward.

Bennett said, "New friends are silver, old friends are gold."

They pressed by Jack into the hall, smelling like dogs that fell in the beer vat, and Mickey McCane slapped him on both shoulders. He tried to wink but the muscles in his face were drunk, too.

"I'll be damned," breathed Jack. It was them he wanted damned. Then Bebe came to see what the noise was, wearing those red Chinese pajamas with her hair smoothed back and both cheeks still pink. "My wife. Bebe, this is Mickey McCane and Sergeant Bennett."

"George," said the tall one. He already had his raincoat off. As Bebe took it, he fished two bottles, rum and bourbon, from the pockets and swooped them in the air. Jack thought for a minute he planned to juggle. "No wonder you didn't come to the reunion. I'd have stayed home, too, if my wife looked this good!" And Bebe—she could be so simpleminded—let out a nervous giggle.

"He's surprised, all right," said Mickey McCane.

By the time Jack got the door closed and light off, they were in the kitchen helping with ice and glasses, and both raincoats were spread on his radiators. Mickey had stepped out of his shoes. He had run across Mickey a time or two in Durham. He hadn't seen George since Berlin nor missed him once in all those years.

"What's this?" said Mickey, padding in his smelly socks, bending over Jack's book. "Phylum . . . Phylum Ann-Nell-*Leeda*?"

"Worms," Jack said, and put the book away.

George handed him a drink. "So why didn't you come? You never seen so many fat old men in your life . . . do you good to see them. Every one a hero. Jack, you wouldn't even recognize the *war* they were in." He moved about the room and his hand seemed to fall on every flaw—the grease stain on Jack's chair, warts in the plaster, a tabletop warped near a steamy window.

Mickey still wore his black hair cropped. His face was rougher and redder and the sideburns grew lower down. He watched Bebe bounce into the room. She looked young and tickled.

George was going bald. ". . . sez, Yeah, I seen him in Durham a time or two and I said, Mickey, then that's where we'll go. See how old Jack's making out these days." He sat in Jack's chair. "How you been? I've got two boys, one of them strong as a bull, plays fullback on the high school team. You have kids, Jack?"

"No," he said, and moved a little closer to Bebe in case that would hurt.

"Turned into a dentist—can you feature it? Of course, I trade a little real estate on the side."

"I want you," said Bebe, "to tell me the truth about Jack and all those German girls."

Jack showed his teeth.

". . . play a little golf now and then," said George, patting his middle. From the men in their old outfit he gave Jack five or ten remembers. They were all working for TV stations, drilling wells, rewinding motors. One ran a tire company and owned a drag strip out of town. Another was in the bottled gas business. "The GI Bill got me to dental school. How about you, Jack? Did you use it?"

He would have needed to finish high school first. He said shortly, "I work at a college here," and Bebe blinked.

"I sent you a Christmas card one year to Winston-Salem but it came back. Had it printed on the envelope—George Bennett, DDS." He closed his eyes. "I won't tell your wife what some people think those letters stand for."

Jack walked slowly around the room. Why had George come? In his own way, George had always been superstitious, sure nothing happened without having inside it potential advantages to George, like raisins in a bun. Invite him to a card game and his eyes lit up; what's he supposed to win? He'd listen to every joke in the barracks so he could mail them to *Reader's Digest*—made five hundred dollars once. Mickey (Jack glanced at the man on the floor, leaning against the radiator)—Mickey was the fighter. On leave, even under fire, Mickey plowed out in front like George's private bodyguard. I've never been much use to George, he thought. Until now?

"Richmond," George was saying to Bebe. "Mickey, what's that place you live?"

"Angier. Little town in Harnett County. You heard what I told that lieutenant, didn't you? The one that sold securities?" Mickey pursed his mouth. "Said he was the 'son' in Brittain and Son. I told him: I'm the Self in Self-Service Laundromat." He turned his stiff fingers toward his heart. Bebe laughed.

Sitting the way she was on the Hide-a-Bed, her laughter threw her breasts out so Mickey had a good view from underneath. He pulled his knees together, hugged them, rocked on the linoleum. Jack wondered what his married life was like. Mickey used to be best with the girls he'd find unexpectedly, in a field, cutting hay, milking, sweeping out factories. If he could take a woman right then, while her husband had stepped into the barn and might be back any minute, Mickey would be O.K. One time he paid a whore to go in a city park and run from him and fall down a time or two—then he had her in some low bushes close to a public dock. They could see shoes and ankles walking by to the boats. Dogs would bark and try to reach them. He was quick and impatient, the girl said; afterward made her lie spraddled on top of him in the leaves right by the path. With my ass shining, she said, and people walking by. She wouldn't take his money the second time.

Mickey said, "You let a woman this pretty work in a café?"

"We'll have to do something about that," said George. He sat by Bebe on the brown couch and smiled into her eyes.

"I don't mind it," Bebe said.

A lie if Jack ever heard one. Every Friday night Bebe would come in, prop her check and his check on the television, and call on him to take a look. "Two sports coats," she'd say, pointing. "Enough to buy two fine sports coats with slippery lining. You know how many sports coats was in and out that café last night?" She minded it, all right. She wanted to eat at the Stork Club, the way Anne Baxter did.

George was saying, "Little vacation, maybe, as long as I've closed the office. Remember that beach property I won on a full house? I've been buying lots near there ever since, down near Brunswick and Southport. You ought to see the spread I've got." Slowly he rolled the ice cubes in his glass. "You'd like the beach, Jack. It's better than living by a river any day."

And Jack felt the ice swirl inside him, bumping lightly on his bones. One time in his whole life he got really drunk. One time he talked too much. George Bennett remembered. Jack shot a look at Mickey but he hadn't been there the whole time and, besides, he wouldn't have cared. His mother had given him a hard time, too. Jack unwound one of the radiator knobs. The room felt damp.

A couple of drinks later Bebe was saying, "Why not, Jack? Just for the weekend? I haven't been to the beach in twenty years."

"Must have been a little girl then," said Mickey, winking.

"Look it over, Jack, that's all I ask." George grinned. "What can it hurt?"

"I love the ocean," Bebe said. It was the first Jack had heard of it.

Around 2 A.M., Mickey went home. He wanted to come to Pickerel, too, but there was a new Bendix being delivered the next day. George spent the night on the couch and Saturday morning they drove east and south to Brunswick County, an oceanfront which had once been called Lockwood Folly Inlet, now filled in with sand, built up by storms, a finger-shaped afterthought of the Atlantic Ocean running north and south in a curve that pointed to South Carolina. Some hurricane season, Jack thought, the sea might change her mind and gouge it out again. A tidal creek entered at the tip and split the land into beach and marshes.

Before they left, Jack looked up in a flower book the aquatic plant which gave the beach its name. Pickerelweed. Sometimes called wampee, it grew in a soggy mass in the background marshes, the leaves like small green spades thrust three feet above the brackish water. Pickerel, said his book, produced tall spikes of purple bloom which give off an unpleasant smell. Each blossom lasted a single day, then the spike lengthened to permit further flowering, and for weeks the wet fields would be matted with stinking flowers.

He put that book, and Audubon's shore bird guide, into Bebe's suitcase. George should have asked advice before he chose that name, Jack thought. Any fool could've told him people would call it Pickle Beach. And when he saw it—rundown, shabby, the trailers empty and old beer cans on the dunes—he called it Pickle Beach himself.

At first he thought he might take the job to make Bebe happy. She ran through the surf with her red halter thudding on her chest. Her hair got stiff and stuck out like a crown. Married eighteen years—and what had Jack done for her, just for her, like a present? On the beach she built tunnels and houses and had sand stuck to her like brown sugar. After dark, she floated out alone on a rubber raft, came indoors dreamy, saying, "You could smother in those stars." In bed her skin had a tangy smell, like citrus rind.

He meant to decide for rational reasons. What was the pay? How to attract vacationers and would he get a percentage? Could George offer security?

But in the end, it was none of those things. Jack had just been in Durham too long, like *Toxostoma rufum,* getting free water in an artificial bowl; that good luck made him nervous. And the new good luck had a threat in it, almost audible under the ocean's roar. In April before George came, that brown thrasher hunched in his scuppernongs, doubting the crumbs, mistrusting the water, watching Jack stiff-necked with one urine-colored eye. He only came into the Sellars yard roundabout through the fallen leaves. Ambushed his breakfast. Rushed through a tense suspicious bath before winging just far enough away to give to the neighbors on Mayhew Street what little music was in him. Somebody shot at him once, perhaps, or set the cats on him. He knew there were guns and predators now.

The last day, Jack pulled up the whole birdbath and loaded it onto Mickey's truck. Next spring, he thought, when that thrasher comes by there won't be a drop nor a crumb put out for him here and maybe that will satisfy him at last.

Late the same afternoon they set the clay-streaked base in its new place at Pickle Beach and filled the bowl with water, though Mickey said, "They's not a thing but gulls." Only through the kitchen window would they be able to watch the birdbath, and there was no nearby tree where a robin might dry himself. Jack felt certain there would be no robins, either. Around the concrete bowl was a ring the color of dried blood. Algae. Dead.

Jack and Bebe, waving like fools, stood by the birdbath while Mickey McCane drove off in his pickup truck toward his laundromats. Jack said, "He might have spent the night anyway, if you'd asked a second time."

"He gets on my nerves," said Bebe, flapping her hand.

But he knew she had other plans, to make the house their own. Jack slid his arm around her and scratched her hard brassiere lightly with his fingernails.

"With Mickey gone," he said, "at least we can go to bed early and get a good rest."

"At least go to bed early." Bebe turned and worked her forehead into his neck and they leaned on each other behind George's ugly house. "Get some groceries?" she mumbled.

"Might as well." But they went on standing there, Jack looking over her yellow hair at the waves. And he got a funny double image, a flashed pair of snapshots twenty-five years apart. He looked at the beach from far out to sea, the way he had looked over the gulf at Salerno in 1943. And then looked seaward back at himself, the way the Sixteenth Panzer Division was watching their ships come in at dawn. He'd never liked beaches much since then. Then he had thought of the German troops as the only danger to him. Now the sea itself looked implacable and malevolent. "Groceries," he finally said. Bebe went inside for her pocketbook.

Buncombe's Supermart was three miles down the road and had a small frame house connected by a breezeway. They parked before the brick store building, which had freshly painted trim. A woman passing along the breezeway to the house waved and called, "He's *in* there!"

Bebe pushed open the rusted screen. Inside, the first thing Jack saw was one of those round mirrors set high to spot shoplifters. There must have been four such mirrors, glaring like suns, and not half a dozen shopping carts. Bebe pushed one to the vegetable counter.

"Afternoon," somebody said.

Jack looked down one aisle and then two without seeing him, and he wasn't visible in a single mirror. "You can't find something, let me know." It was a fast, squeaky voice. Jack found him leaning on a workbench in the back corner and stepped at last into the angle where his head lit up in three of the mirrors. The head was nearly bald but brown in color as if he had tinted the scalp, and later Jack learned he painted it with Tufskin, the liquid football players use, to tan the scalp like hard leather in the summer sun. He did not look up from under the gooseneck lamp. "You people passing through?"

"Moving in." Jack started past the bread loaves. "George Bennett said he'd leave some keys and papers with you. . . ."

The bald man jumped up and put out a hand. "Willis Buncombe, Mr. Sellars. Glad you're here." Quickly Jack moved his gaze overhead to the magnified mirror and in it watched his own arm reaching forward. There was only a thumb and little finger growing on Mr. Buncombe's right hand. Jack managed to shake without looking down. It felt like sliding his fingers into a toothless mouth. Buncombe was smiling, as if he enjoyed the sensation his missing fingers caused.

Then he lifted a black tin box off the floor and clicked its latches loose. He set it on his gray steel workbench and swept aside a clutter of wheels and flopping springs. A row of clocks, none ticking, was lined against the wall and the works of another sat in the center, so intricate Jack felt like a giant looking through the roof of a factory. Buncombe took out a heavy envelope.

"Do you fix watches, too? My wife wound hers too tight."

"It's only a hobby. I started after the accident to make my left hand more . . . precise." Buncombe tapped the clockworks with a thin screwdriver, naming parts. "Hammer, center wheel, main wheel, time escape wheel. If these look small, they're even smaller in a watch. You can't really do good repair work on both watches and clocks, switching back and forth. It's a matter of scale." He smiled. His teeth were worn very shallow. "Call me Willis."

He had to say, "Call me Jack." Inside George's envelope were keys to the three trailers at Pickle Beach, separate keys for the two shell houses, plus a map like the one he had sketched on the kitchen tablecloth, with the septic tanks marked X. Buried treasure. "Does Mr. Bennett spend much time at the beach?"

"Not much. Comes fishing with his boys sometimes. Here, have a seat." Buncombe nudged out a barrel with one shoe before scooting to the meat counter to see what interested Bebe behind the glass. Maybe he'd hurt his hand that way: slicing chops, grinding chuck. He looked too old to have lost it in the war.

Jack tried to see Bebe's face when she reached over the white cooler and counted how many fingers were waiting for her own. She chose sausage and wieners and a flounder Willis Buncombe said he'd caught himself.

"Last guy out at Pickle was a crook," said Buncombe, still talking to Jack even as he sealed up the flounder. "Never paid his bill here. Always drove Mr. Bennett crazy, one kind of trouble or another."

Without warning, at Jack's elbow, a clock spring broke loose from its clamp and flew singing into the air like a hornet. He jumped and dodged. It fell limp on the edge of the strongbox, slithered to the floor. Buncombe called, "One of those things hits you in the eye, it's no joke." The string of loose steel lay at Jack's feet with only its tail coiled.

Willis Buncombe took hold of Bebe's wrist and she tried not

to look at his finger stubs. "Sometimes a thunderstorm will break a spring in a brand-new watch. Then sometimes they just break for the hell of it." Bebe said she might leave hers with him and he said he'd be glad to fix it.

What is it about Bebe, Jack wondered, that makes people change their minds? "House paint? You carry house paint?" he asked.

"Nothing but white." He came back and fished color samples out of a steel drawer. "Get you anything you want out of Wilmington, though. Bennett said you'd be making repairs out there. Guess you'll want everything done before July."

"Why July?" Jack looked up from the folder. "I said, why then?"

Buncombe stood looking into the drawer, stirring tweezers, files, and pliers with his good hand. The knuckles and joints were swollen. "Just seemed as if you would," he said without looking up. "It gets busy in July."

"George said the trouble was it never got busy enough to make any money."

Buncombe seemed relieved when his wife came into the store. He called her back to be introduced. Seeing them together, Jack estimated Willis in his sixties, Pauline closer to his own age. She was a small tough woman, tanned, wrinkled, as if she had just lost twenty pounds on a diet of bran meal. Maybe the seashore dehydrated people.

Jack said, "Is that when George's sister comes to the beach? In July?"

"Oh, he mentioned it," said Willis. His wife put out a heavy oxford and stepped on his foot. "About then, I think." He called Bebe over and introduced the two women, who, right away, began to look for bruises on the early tomatoes in Bebe's cart. Mrs. Buncombe had grown them herself, she said, under plastic.

"George said she came down every summer, wouldn't be any trouble. You've met her, then."

"This is a fine piece of work," said Willis, turning the clock mechanism on his bench. The sound of birds calling *keer, keer* came through the store windows. "The cabinet's gone, of course. I found it in a junk shop. Every piece of the movement is brass." He held up the clock face, warped so the hands could not possibly turn.

Jack was uneasy. "How long does Miss Bennett usually stay?"

Before he spoke, carefully, Willis rubbed his tan scalp. "I don't think it's Miss. Do you, Polly?" He took a step toward the shopping cart. "Since she brings her son. How long were they here last summer? About a month?"

"At least," she said. "I never saw such people for applesauce. I ran into Wilmington twice a week to keep in stock." She smiled at Bebe. "They must have bad teeth." Then she started telling Bebe what church the Buncombes went to and how she hoped the Sellars family would come. "You have any children?"

"No," said Bebe.

"Well, it's hard to get the young people to go to church anyway," she said. The subject of church got Jack to moving, pulling his wallet out. People that pray and brag about it—he couldn't stand them. Why any Son of God should come down to preach to the ones on the top of the food chain, he'd never know. Bebe would listen all day and smile and nod. She might even promise to come to church, just to be polite. One time she had met a nun in the café and for months had talked about nothing else. The nun took her coffee black, just as it was, without cream or sugar; Bebe marveled at it. The nun worked at a mission in a black neighborhood in Durham. The nun said all men had only one question—whether the universe was friendly or unfriendly—and everything else followed from that. Jack got very tired of the nun, who seemed to come home with Bebe and sit on the kitchen shelves, whispering.

The Buncombes helped carry their boxes of groceries to the car. Jack lifted them, frowning, into the trunk and backseat. Bebe had bought strange things—dried beans and noodles, pecans, raisins, gelatin, powdered drinks—as if they were going on a long voyage.

Pauline wrote notes on the back of a charge pad. "Send out the telephone man to connect you up," Willis repeated, and she wrote that down. "And I'll deliver a trash burner and the paint. You got a flashlight and batteries? Sometimes the power just goes off." Even here, on the lee side of the store, the wind seemed to blow off the sea and find them.

Pauline stuck the pad in the pocket of her floppy sweater and leaned in the car window to tell Bebe, "You'll just love our preacher. And he's not long-winded. The sweetest prayers. There's not a sick or shut-in he doesn't visit and the children sit up front to hear a special sermonette."

Bebe said that was nice. When they drove off she thumped Jack's leg. "You could have been friendlier."

"This road would break axles," he said. The highway ran between the marsh and a row of low dunes holding back erosion on the ocean side. Now and then, there'd be on his left a strip of ocean between two shuttered houses, not an expanse but a dark blue fence. It was the most artificial thing he ever saw, the neatness of it, as if the world were—after all—some ordinary room and the sea a painted wainscoting partway up its wall. Standing in the water's edge was different. The motion of the waves pulled him sideways and where he stood the sand washed out from under his feet and rose over his ankles.

He was thinking about George's sister, who would visit in July. George had mentioned her, but hastily. Hurried over it.

"George's sister must be a bitch. He must send her to the beach to get rid of her."

"Pauline says there's something wrong with her health, or maybe the boy's. Anyway, they brought a nurse along."

A nurse? For a month? Maybe the sea air was healthy for them, thick with oxygen. Maybe that's why the trees here were so stunted; they needed people to breathe their wastes upon the leaves. The chlorophyll here was starving.

"The Buncombes seem nice."

Everybody seemed nice to Bebe. He wondered if the brown thrasher was sitting on a twig on Mayhew Street, trying to figure out what happened.

"You sure are quiet," Bebe said softly.

"Well, look at it!" They had turned slightly and there lay Pickerel Beach to the left of the road. A long, empty swatch of sand, some stubs of grass, three rusted trailers propped on concrete blocks, two unpainted shell houses made of raw wood which had not yet silvered in the spray, and the main house—two-story, older, moved out of some older town and dropped here slightly crooked on a foundation part piling and part pillar. The birdbath near the back steps looked like a monument. The wind had shifted and he could smell the rotting marsh.

Bebe nudged him with her knee. "Wait till you get things planted. I know you. You can make flowers grow anywhere."

Maybe with a few tons of peat moss. And fertilizer? My God, you'd need the bonemeal from a whole elephant graveyard! "You don't know the first thing about organic matter in the soil," he told Bebe, parking.

She opened the car door and let in the sound of the whole Atlantic. "Look at the ocean. It's so beautiful."

The surface did look flat and gray and safe as a tabletop.

"You're hungry," Bebe said. "You'll feel better after you eat."

It was like her to think the body could cure everything. She and the nun had talked about the soul but Bebe had shocked the nun. She thought, then, that everybody got to come back and live dozens of lives on earth, and the system worked so well that nobody really needed Heaven. It was all linked with genes and chromosomes, she told the nun, whose rosary must have trembled. The seed of yourself went into that tiny cell and it stayed there until some future conception when the time was right for you to be born again. The nun said stiffly that this was not what Jesus had meant about being born again. The reason you couldn't remember a past life, Bebe said, is because you were mixed each time with a half seed from somebody new, and you halfway remembered dreams of your own past and dreams of his. What, said the nun, became of those people who did not reproduce? Where did their genes and chromosomes go, and how did they get back into the cycle at the proper time? Bebe was embarrassed for the chaste nun and because she had no uterus herself. Forget it, she said. It was only a feeling.

Now Bebe held out her arms and Jack gave her boxes of dried fruits and cereals and soaps. "We'll eat that flounder," she said, "and after that we can walk on the beach in the moonlight." She gave him a look so arch the hairs in his groin rippled. Maybe she was right about the body. How else did love keep on?

Just after dark, they strolled up the hard-packed sand with their backs to the ugly buildings of Pickle Beach. The sea had spread out and seemed vaster and thicker, as if its bottom had fallen away from the earth while the sky fell outward. Jack could not make the blackening water look like a painted line again, even by will. It was hard to walk in the endless wind. By the water's edge, he began to lean off center as if some vacuum in that thick wet air were drawing on his arm and side, as if he might lose at least a rib to that wind.

Bebe picked up a mottled shell that looked like a shoehorn

and scratched in the sand: BEATRICE F. SELLARS. She drew a plus mark under her name, carved Jack's, and centered them in a fat, uneven heart. She said something happy which the wind blew out of her mouth. He made her shout. "*I like it!*" she shouted.

When they walked back to the house with an arm around each other's waist, it was easier to balance in the sucking sand, even though the wind was colder.

Undressing, Jack wondered how long it would take before both his ears got used to the sea wind and the pounding tide. Probably Willis Buncombe never heard the steady thunder anymore. Pulling down the window shades, he could imagine the wind was only soughing in the pines and the roar might be the same noise made by the Katsewa River winding its way below their old back porch. Stormy nights, his mother would cock her head and say to the children, "There goes the river," as if the river were a freight train . . . now coming, now passing, now gone.

He watched Bebe stretch, humming some song. He asked what it was.

Well, I'll go,
Rolling in my sweet baby's arms.
Rolling in my sweet baby's arms!
Yes, I'll hang around the shack
Till the mail train comes back
And I'll roll in my sweet baby's arms!

She sang it, laughed, turned down the fresh covers, and sat on the edge of the bed. Pulling off her blouse, she dropped it on the floor. Neat, Bebe was not. Slowly, watching Jack, she reached back to unhook the heavy brassiere. Her slacks were unbuttoned and drooped below her waist but did not uncover her scar. She never liked that to show. Who cared whether she was neat? In a soft, drowsy voice she said, "Expect you're tired, honey. Carrying heavy stuff all day."

Perhaps the ocean stopped. All he could hear was Bebe. "I'm not tired."

"We'll be happy here, Jack. Wait and see."

Jack turned off the light, touched himself. He was ready. Bebe would like it if he said, more often, right out loud, that he loved her. In the dimness, she shook loose from the white elastic and her breasts fell forth and downward. His mouth got wet. He crossed the room with his two hands out to that droop and that sweetness.

"Oh," said Bebe softly, "oh, come on in here where it's warm."

It was the first weekend after they moved to the beach. Jack worked, whistling, underneath the house.

Even the roar of the steady waves was softer. In another week, perhaps, he would forget the sea beat so near, the way he no longer saw the tip of his own nose or heard the thud in his arteries. Despite the steady repair work, this first week had seemed a long vacation. They ate when they were hungry. Bebe went swimming nude at night. He felt years younger, as if time had become as slow and unified for him as for the ocean.

He heard a motor, then a car horn.

"Thought I'd surprise you!"

Calling, Mickey drove right between the pillars and under the house and almost tore up the greenhouse Jack was building. Willis Buncombe had ordered wide rolls of heavy clear plastic, which Jack had nailed to piling and pillar, sealed, and anchored deep in the sand on three sides. With plywood framing he had made a lightweight door for the fourth side and it swung crazily on one hinge an inch from Mickey's front fender. Not the pickup this time. A little foreign car with the black finish waxed. Mickey swung out of it like a monkey. "What you building?" The squirrel tail mounted on his radiator cap sagged and left a feathery mark on the dusty hood. The chrome was blinding.

The anger Jack felt was like sunburn from inside. It almost scared him and he nearly said to himself, *Don't do it this time,* from a sudden shock of recognition. He laid the hammer gently on the sand between his shoes. "We weren't expecting you," he said, and managed to smile.

"Look on me as your first paying guest." Mickey grinned, pointed to fishing rods and baggage strapped to the roof of the car. "You're finally in business. How much is the weekend rent on a trailer?"

"I'll check on it."

Upstairs, Bebe was washing woodwork with a mixture of kerosene and water. The smell and her tuneless humming floated through the floorboards.

"Brought you some stuff," said Mickey. "Housewarming. A salt-cured ham—we got a little farm, you know. Raise pigs." The meat was actually swinging by a thong on the hook for coat hangers in the car's backseat. "I keep the farm for a tax loss, mostly. Last month the sow birthed more piglets than she had teats, so I had to kill two." He reached out and shoved the plywood door. "You getting settled?"

Jack had already planned the whole weekend. He was going to buy flower seeds, set a row of red cedar for a windbreak. He'd promised Bebe a trip to Wilmington to buy a dog. All these years, and no children, and he'd never thought of buying her a dog before.

He thanked Mickey for the ham, predicting gloomily they'd be eating it at breakfast together. Mickey said he'd drag it upstairs to Bebe. On the steps, with the hunk of meat slung on his shoulder, he said, "What you making out of all that plastic?"

"A place to grow seeds and cuttings."

"All you need is a few oak trees and some garbage for growing hogs." Mickey was wearing khaki shorts, which climbed out of sight, then hairy leg, hard knee, a pair of shoes with air vents at the arch. Jack heard him yell overhead, "Hey, Bebe? Guess who brought home the bacon?"

The weekend was shot. Jack reached out and slid the squirrel fur through his fingers. It felt cool as a Chinaman's pigtail. He squeezed; under the coarse hair the tube of dried flesh was tough and hard. He pulled it. World by the tail.

And suddenly, how insane everything was!

What was he doing there, next to this endless ocean, building a transparent room and holding a piece of dead animal in one fist? While all around him blew the fumes of kerosene? He knew every item had an explanation; there were causes and effects—yet everything seemed abruptly crazy, random, and accidental. His dusty face looked back at him off Mickey's car. Rubbed with a sleeve, it shone in the wax pictured there only because in the early forties somebody dealt George Bennett three jacks and a pair of sevens.

He felt a little sick, perhaps because it was too hot under the house and he had hammered too long. I'm not as young as I used to be, he thought. He started up the stairs after Mickey.

"Bebe?" he called.

3

Bebe Sellars

June 4, 1968

Bebe was not as silly about movies as Jack thought. Had she grown up in another time and place, other sources would have served. She might have known literature, or the lives of the saints, or myths, and mixed these into her life to ornament events.

But she had grown up in piedmont Greenway, North Carolina, during the hard thirties, and could hardly tell the Acts of the Apostles from *Ben-Hur.* On Saturday nights at the Greenway Playhouse, they gave away free dishes and called ticket numbers for the cash jackpot. "Be quiet, Bebe, it's an old-timey picture in just a minute." To Grace Fetner, her mother, old-timey meant the women on film wore long skirts. Queen Victoria was old-timey and so was Vivien Leigh. Bebe went to school and high school and even a little college at the Greenway Playhouse. Ashley Wilkes incarnated Georgia in Reconstruction. She knew how the Dead Sea rolled back over the Egyptians, having looked down on the closing waters. She and Jon Hall had seen volcanoes blow in Tahiti. Even for death of kin she might never cry again as hard as she did for the ending of *Kings Row.*

And Bebe even knew it was a lie, that world, and didn't mind. Nobody met Shakespeare at the A & P or, cutting pulpwood, stirred up the wood nymphs. What was the harm? If the wine at communion had really turned into Jesus' blood in the mouths of Baptists, wouldn't they all have spit? Every one? Nowadays every college kid on TV thought he could save the world. With that lie, he's in for harder times than me, Bebe thought.

The movies might not be much, but still, they lay behind her and gave the present *weight*.

Here's what she meant. Each day that came got heavier for Bebe—not worse, just heavier—because of all the days before. You couldn't eat a first ice cream cone but once, and after that all the other times pressed in upon this new one. The reason Grandma Fetner got forgetful near the end came from the great heaviness now borne late by the littlest events—something had to go in that overload. Otherwise, Bebe thought, you could hardly peel an apple without thinking back to Eve.

Even at forty, some things that happened would call up in Bebe fifty more and a dozen movies and songs besides, until even the air felt thick from pressure. Sometimes, then, she chose Sabu riding an elephant through the vines, and let him stand for everything. The choice seemed simpler, now and then, when she stared at the roaring ocean to think of no more than the MGM lion's mouth onscreen. Jack wouldn't let his own past weight come forward at all. Never mind; she couldn't blame him. But he didn't have Lon McCallister, either, and Eleanor Powell wouldn't tap-dance in spangles for him. Bebe had her dreams in daylight, that was all, and Jack at night.

In such a dream she lay with her head on the armrest of the

porch swing and let her blond hair fall between the chains. She was tall, and had to lie with her knees up as if for childbirth. There was a small gouge in the left kneecap, the spot Mickey's finger had touched.

Mickey brushed her shoulder as he walked by. "Sure you won't play some cards?"

"Not right now." Jack had promised to paint the wooden swing and hang it from new chains but she liked the rusty squawks it made when she went back and forth. *Here*-is, said the swing. *Here*-is Bebe. Across the porch, Jack and Mickey bent over their poker game. Bebe rested in the swing like June Haver, tapped both feet as if they wore saddle shoes and this were a sorority porch.

Even the lies the movies told were true sometimes, the way stopped clocks told the right time twice a day. Mickey and Jack and Bebe at Pickle Beach; she had seen that plot at a hundred matinees. Two men and one woman and the air electric. Earlier, the three had gone walking on the beach, arms hooked and Bebe in the middle like Maria Montez or Rita Hayworth. She called, "You all want a drink?"

"We'll wait for the others," Jack said before Mickey McCane could answer. They were using kitchen matches for poker chips. "Ante up," said Jack.

Here-is. From the start you knew John Payne and Dennis O'Keefe wouldn't get the girl. Those actors had, just like Mickey, losing faces, losing names on the marquee. It was nice to stand outside before the usher took down the velvet rope and know from the cast alone how the whole story would work out and who would get married and who would stay home in Cedar Falls and run the drugstore.

"You're mighty quiet." Mickey threw her a grin. John Payne had lines like that all the time.

"What time is it?" said Jack. He wished Mickey had not come. Had told Bebe ham gave him stomach gas, which was a lie.

She looked at the watch Jack gave her at Christmas. "Five o'clock. Pauline said they'd close up the store at five and come on down." He grunted. He'd only agreed to ask the Buncombes for a drink in hopes their presence might dilute Mickey. Besides, Willis wouldn't take anything for fixing her watch and Jack hated to feel beholden.

Jack was saying, "If you got down here that quick, you drove too fast."

Then Mickey talked awhile about how good he was at driving, told the one accident he ever had that was really his fault. *Here*-is. Bebe swung lazily, half listening.

". . . I was in Charlotte for the VFW. And I bumped into this new car at the parking lot at some big hotel; I mean I dented in the back door from the window right on down. So I smiled at all the people looking out of their car windows, and got out and wrote a note, looking very serious all the time, and I stuck that under the windshield wiper and took another look at the damage. Shaking my head all the time. Letting them see how bad I felt about it. Everybody nodded and drove on off." Mickey broke off to deal himself one card—he always bluffed high, thought Bebe; had no card sense—and laughed at Jack. "Only the number I wrote down for the guy was the Charlotte Dial-a-Prayer service, where right away some record is going to start off praying Our Fathers in the guy's ear." He laughed loudly and Jack vibrated a little in his seat to look like laughing.

Under the yellow light that was meant to keep gnats away, Jack's face looked strange. He watched Mickey. Thoughtful. Not glad he was here and yet, somehow, not surprised. People look at a snake that way, without moving.

Mickey was shaking his black head. No, he'd never met

George's sister, the one who came every summer in July. "I hear she's sickly."

"Sickly with what?"

Mickey didn't know. "George said once if it wasn't for Rosie's doctor bills, his taxes would go sky high; that's all I know."

Maybe Rosie was crippled. Bebe used to sit in a rocker, knees under a folded quilt, crippled in Technicolor till the crucial moment when she'd have to save the life of some child.

Frowning, Jack dealt the cards. "You don't think she's contagious, do you?"

"No, it's a condition of some kind," Mickey drawled. "More like sugar dye-bee-teez."

Again Jack watched him, glanced at Bebe. "You can't eat applesauce if you're diabetic, can you?" She didn't know. He looked across the ocean, was still looking at it when Mickey laid down a flush.

The trouble with the thundering noise of the tide was that it overrode everything else; people walked up on you, the way Willis and Pauline Buncombe did right through the house, coming out to join them.

Bebe jumped off the swing. Pauline is the oldest-looking thing. I've got to ask her what she uses on her face and then not use it. "Polly! There you are! Come on out in the breeze." They were already out. She was wearing a two-piece seersucker dress that hung on her. Willis took off his cap and almost bowed. Jack introduced Mickey McCane.

"And this is Willis." Bebe knew how Mickey bore down on a handshake and it did her good to watch him reach toward Willis, then hold back at the last minute.

"Not Crain. McCane." Willis got hold of him anyway and shook. "Sit down and I'll deal you in. O.K.?"

Bebe went inside for drinks, Pauline calling, "A soft one for me, Bebe. You've really got the house looking nice." She sounded out of breath. "I like your curtains."

Standing at the sink, Bebe could see Jack's birdbath down below, a dusty film over the water. Funny about these birds. They didn't seem to notice anyone lived at Pickle Beach. Jack put up a feeder on a pole and the seeds got damp and turned dark and clogged the tray. Not a single bird turned its head. When Bebe lay in the sun, she could see a gull's shadow coming up the sandy beach and it slid right over her. Now when she saw one coming, she put out her hand so the shadow for one instant could be laid against her palm.

Bebe put glasses and crackers on a tray and carried them outside. Pauline helped hand out the drinks, saying to Mickey, "Two boys, isn't that nice!" and to Bebe, "I told Willis you couldn't be old enough to have grown children."

She was, though. She could have had one old enough for college or Vietnam. Bebe shook her head. "How about you? You have any children?"

Pauline gave Willis his glass without looking at him. "I have a son. He lives in Kansas." Married before; Bebe knew that much. If Jack died, would I marry again? I might. The men decided to play stud instead of draw poker.

"You ought to start a VFW chapter down here," Mickey said. "I was just telling about this convention I went to in Charlotte." He told the story about denting the car and leaving the note about Dial-a-Prayer. This time Jack didn't laugh. "Jack and I were all over Europe together. Where were you?"

"The Pacific theater," said Willis quickly. Pauline cleared her throat.

"Is that where?"

He shook his bald head. "I lost three fingers in a sawmill accident."

That was funny. He'd told Jack it was the war. Shrapnel. She had pictured John Wayne holding the tourniquet.

Pauline Buncombe leaned back in the rocker, swung her brown oxfords up and propped them on the ledge. The skin of her tanned legs was prickly with dark stubble. "You don't know how glad I am to have a real neighbor. No, keep the swing. This is fine." She adjusted her skirt. "The beach is a lonesome place in the winters. This tastes good." Over her grape bottle she looked at the beating tide. "About November, all this daylight goes away and the ocean seems to get . . . bigger."

"Too big already," said Jack, dealing.

To Bebe she said, "The last man Mr. Bennett hired had women in and out but I sure couldn't talk to *them.*"

"Who was he?"

"I've forgot his name. He was hardly ever sober."

Here-is, said the swing.

"Queens bet." Willis bet his queens. He was keeping his half hand on the table, enjoying Mickey's effort not to stare.

"I knew," said Pauline, "he wouldn't be back after that trouble last July."

"What trouble?" asked Bebe.

"The boy got lost or something, wandered off; he didn't go far."

Bebe asked how old the boy was but Pauline didn't answer. "Now if there's a storm this fall," she said, "you two come to the store. These pillars might not hold if the water comes in. How's your tomatoes, Jack?"

He said he wished they were already bearing, so he could pay Willis off in produce. "I never saw such luck."

"I've never been on the coast in hurricane season." Bebe gave the swing a push in the cool wind. "I almost look forward to that."

"I never do." Her shoe soles rasped on the screen. "We listen on shortwave radio. Florida and WJO in Charleston. You can always get the coast guard stations. Sit up late with our candles ready and follow reports and listen how fast the wind is getting. Willis moves his thumbtacks up the map. And after a while," said Pauline dreamily, "it doesn't even sound like a storm, but like some great wicked thing is coming, with a woman's name. And she destroys on purpose."

"That's not so," said Willis from the table. "She'd feel better if they named it Tom or Chester, that's all."

"The trouble comes from naming it at *all*," Pauline said. "People still show you wreckage around here, and they'll say, 'Hazel did that.' After a while I get this real *picture* of Hazel. Some kind of giant witch."

Jack did not even turn over his cards. He watched the sea. Sometimes Bebe thought he really wanted a wreck or a fire or a storm. As if they would break the tension. Maybe they would, too. Reassure him the way she could not. She caught Mickey's eyes resting upon her and almost understood the fascination of something you don't want that might happen anyway.

"They're smart to give hurricanes a name," argued Willis. "Otherwise, what can you say on the air except *it,* how strong *it* is, which way *it's* coming next? That's worse."

Pauline held up her grape soda. "There's a chiffon pie you can make with this, Bebe, that's real good."

Jack asked the men what kind of a dog he should buy. Mickey said a beagle but Willis suggested some water dog—spaniel, or retriever. "Your watch all right now, Bebe?" She held it up. He raked in another pot of kitchen matches. "Now me, I like these quiet winters at the beach. I don't have to sell one thing I don't want to to one man I don't like."

"Listen to him," said Pauline. "I do all the work. From eight to five he gets arthritis."

"Let me tell you, Jack, when I met Pauline she could drink me under the table and go on to another party. One winter down here and she got religion. You want to watch it." He winked at Bebe over his fan of cards.

But Pauline rattled her shoulder blades under the loose dress and, smiling, lifted her grape soda. "I'm older. We're both older."

The Buncombes had lived between Pickle Beach and Southport since 1944. They met during the war when she was married to somebody else and his ship or his plane went down. She had told Bebe they started the store with her first husband's insurance.

Mickey said, "The thing is not to get old without having any fun."

"People that go to church can have fun," Pauline said, bristling.

He said, "If they're careful about it."

Irritably she turned away to talk to Bebe. "I was raised Catholic but it didn't take. I'm Methodist now."

"I'm Methodist myself," said Mickey, laughing, tilting back his chair.

Bebe pushed the swing, feeling childless and churchless. The chains squawked. Pauline's calf muscles were knotted, her eyebrows up; she looked perky and talkative. And Bebe almost wanted her to talk more about how the big winter sea had turned her Methodist. Religion interested Bebe. (It *would,* Jack often said.) Bebe would have stayed Catholic, though, like the nun she knew once, who didn't look a bit like Ingrid Bergman. It would be nice to pray in Latin, light fires, count beads. She couldn't speak the ocean's language, either.

"I could pick you up Sunday morning if you want to come."

"I might," said Bebe politely, and shot a guilty look to see if Jack had heard. Jack thought there wasn't any God or, if there was, He made the world and then lost interest right away. Gave it a turn like a top and went off to play something else.

Bebe couldn't decide for sure. There really might not be a God and that would be a shame. There ought to be. She remembered asking the nun what she thought about Jennifer Jones in *Song of Bernadette.* The nun said crisply, "Deny metaphysics and the trivial will triumph." She talked like a book sometimes. "Wasn't it a true miracle about Bernadette?" asked Bebe. "Isn't it a true miracle about you?" shot back the nun.

Suddenly Jack's voice was loud above the noisy surf. "*Crazy?* What do you mean, crazy?" He pushed back his chair. Bebe could see face cards drooping in his hand.

"What do you think I mean?" said Willis, reading them shamelessly.

And Mickey, "He don't mean really *crazy.*"

Jack looked above their heads at Bebe and wouldn't sit down. "Willis says the sister is crazy. George Bennett's sister."

"Not crazy exactly." Leaning sideways, Pauline tapped her husband's back with the mouth of her grape bottle. "Funny is more like it. Not all there."

"Feebleminded?" asked Mickey, laying down his own cards. "George has got feebleminded in his family?"

But Bebe could only think about Jack, and Jack's mother, and how that word must sound to him. Crazy. Another crazy woman. There was no way she could bend her face to send Jack any message. If she smiled, that was wrong; a frown wouldn't do. How could you make your face say: Don't you worry now?

Instead she blurted something she instantly regretted. "I don't care," she said. "I'm a little simpleminded myself."

Jack pointed the cards at Mickey McCane. "George never told me about that, not a word. She'd be no trouble, that's all he said. What I want to know is did you know about it?"

Mickey was insulted. "No, I did not. I'd have told him to keep her locked up."

Willis was tickled to draw such a big reaction. He raked in more matches with his two-fingered hand. Leaned back in the chair and looked from face to face. "I don't know what the rest of you call it. Dimwit? Dummy? I always say Pinhead myself."

Pauline's grape bottle nudged him again. "Say retarded."

Jack sat down again, still waiting for Bebe's face to reshape as it should. They eyed each other. She realized her anger at his told-you-so voice. Over them all he announced to her in a flat voice, "George's sister is a Pinhead." He may have meant: Look what you've done, Bebe, bringing us here.

Mickey wanted to know if now it was his deal. "Just tell George she can't come, that's all. Tell him she's not your problem."

"What about the boy?" asked Jack in the same flat tone, his blue eyes fixed on Bebe, getting brighter.

"I never saw him right good. Did you, Pauline?"

"The nurse never brought either one inside the store at all. Didn't you come right out one day and ask her?"

"She's never answered me yet. Listen, Jack, I thought you knew. I asked you the first day and you said you already knew."

Bebe thought of the boy who, last July, had wandered off and who seemed to have no name or age.

"Look out there!" Miles away from Pauline's finger, a light flickered in a dark patch of sea, under a streaky sky. "Bet it's raining out where they are."

"Sit down, Jack; might as well play cards. And pay attention."

Pinheads. There had flashed into Bebe's head a scene from that foreign movie where the dumb girl gets sold to a carnival man by her peasant mother, and rides around Italy in Anthony Quinn's ugly trailer, her face painted big-eyed like a clown's. And somewhere in the picture she meets this little Pinhead child in a farmhouse and she plays with him until two nuns run her off. Nuns shouldn't behave like that.

That was a sad story. Bebe didn't go to movies much anymore. The new ones kept her awake at night, worrying. It wasn't like watching Fred Astaire roll his top hat down one arm.

She looked out at the rainy piece of ocean. On its other side, in Italy, she thought, they see sad movies all the time.

When Bebe offered to freshen everybody's drink, Jack said he'd help. He jumped up and led the way to the kitchen with his finger stuck deep in Mickey's glass. He leaned on the stove, folding his arms.

"Well, Bebe, you heard it. Pinheads. I bet they're both Pinheads." He looked almost satisfied. "Didn't I tell you from the beginning? There's something wrong, I said."

Bebe couldn't see what difference it made. She counted each ice cube as it dropped, asked carefully, "Will it really bother us, Jack? One month out of twelve. They bring their own nurse along. All we do is collect rent on the first day. We don't have to be . . ." She couldn't think of the right word.

"Keepers? What else will we be but keepers?" He rattled the back doorknob just to see if it worked. "What burns me up is knowing George Bennett picked me the way he's always picked his suckers."

"How could he do that?"

"I talked too much, that time he got me falling-down drunk. I told him things. He thought it wouldn't bother me."

"Hand me the ginger ale. Well, if George thought you'd be more sympathetic than the average guy, he sure had you wrong." Her flat voice made Jack walk out of the kitchen without touching that ginger ale. Bebe decided to mix her own drink a little stronger. Maybe she did talk Jack into taking this job—easier work and higher pay. That's bad? Could she have read George Bennett's mind? Whose friend was he, anyway? She put the glasses in a circle on a tray, her drink the darkest one.

On the porch Jack had only one shoulder turned toward the card game and was looking out to sea where the smeared rainstorm was. The air seemed cooler.

Willis was saying, "You ought to get you one." He held his good hand toward Mickey, tapping one finger on a metal plate hooked to his watchband. "For convenience. Now see? Today's June the fourth. They sell the whole set at the first of the year and you just clip on a new calendar every month."

Bored, Mickey gave Bebe a look he copied from Victor Mature.

Willis looked at his small calendar again. "It'll soon be D day. I wasn't in that first landing at Normandy but a week afterward when we went in, I—"

"I thought you said you were in the Pacific."

"*Later* I was in the Pacific." Willis poked Jack so he'd raise the bet.

"Let me ask you," said Jack, turning. "These Pinheads. They don't just run around loose? The nurse stays with them all the time?" Willis nodded his glossy head. Then he asked Mickey, "You're sure George never told you? You're sure he didn't handpick me for this job?"

"Listen," said Mickey. "The worst I thought was they might both have asthma."

"Even that's more than you ever said."

Bebe crossed the porch to stand behind Jack, drinking her bourbon as if it were tea. "How bad can it be," she asked, "never to get past the age of children?"

He dropped his head back to look at her. "O.K.," he said softly.

"Children get careless," she said, "but not really mean."

"You're right." He was making an effort to calm down, for her sake.

"It takes somebody grown up to be mean."

Jack reached an arm behind his chair and his fingers wound up near her knee. "We probably won't even know they're here," he said, squeezing.

Mickey stared straight at her and ran his tongue across his lower lip. Bebe saw it excited him to flirt while Jack sat just across the table, that being married made her even fairer game. For an instant she believed that she *could* cure Mickey, take him into her bed and send him out a man, and it halfway tempted her. She knew how to put her hands on him, and where, and how hard, and that there were no places on the body where her mouth could not go. And he would be slightly cruel in return, she suspected, and maybe that could be exciting, too, and maybe she would not be teacher after all, but taught; and perhaps he would make her cry out in a different way from Jack. She saw all that in a flash, admitted it, and just for a minute wanted to lie back naked for him with her eyes closed. She said no.

Aloud she heard herself say, "Why don't we walk on the beach before it rains?" and she laid her hand on Jack's shoulder where Mickey could see it.

They strengthened their drinks, carried them down the steps and over the dune to go wading in the surf. Bebe still hoped to make the evening seem like a party instead of just before D day. P day. The day the Pinheads came.

Pauline stuck her leathery feet into the water first and giggled. Jack stood by Bebe but would not take off his shoes.

"It's cold." Pauline caught Willis by the sleeve and pulled him in beside her. He hadn't rolled his pants legs high enough. "One time," chortled Pauline, "Willis chased me in the water down the whole strand at Virginia Beach. It was after midnight and I had on a party dress and high heel shoes."

"You didn't run very fast," said Willis, and took a swipe at her rear with his partial hand. She nearly fell and Jack stepped aside with his hand out to her.

Bebe felt Mickey's hip bump hers. Copycat. Must have thrown it sideways, quick, like a hula dancer. Mickey knocked her another time. I could if I wanted to, Bebe thought, letting the idea linger. But I won't and maybe for a change he'll go home to Angier nice and horny for his wife. She threw her head back so the line of her throat would be nice in the dim light, then stepped away from him into the water. Foam caught on her legs. "You swim, Pauline?"

"Like a rock she swims," grunted Willis. Pauline gave him a push. And that was the first time they realized Willis was a little drunk, for he spun slowly around with his arms spread wide and then started to walk into the water up to the knee. It covered his rolled pants, came halfway up his thighs.

"What's he doing, Jack?"

"He was tanked when he got here and we both let him drink from ours, hoping he'd finally start to lose." Jack grinned.

Willis turned again in the water, his hands rising above his head. "Come on now, this water's cold," said Pauline, and while they watched he walked deeper.

About the time waves were breaking on Willis's belt, Jack hollered for him to come on out of the ocean.

Willis laughed. "I can't!" he shouted. "Because I am pissing in it! Out of sight!"

Pauline was laughing, too, and hollering what an old fool he was, but she said quietly to Jack and Mickey, "Get him out now. Make him come out."

Bebe called, "That's enough, Willis!" and he elbowed through a breaker and marched on chest deep. Maybe he coughed.

"This damned ocean," said Pauline to herself.

Jack started after him. "Why should we all get wet?" said Mickey, only calling Willis by name and making big swoops with his hand to motion him back to shore. The moon fell under a raincloud. Pauline began to scream.

And just at that moment, Mickey McCane crammed all five fingers into Bebe from behind and started rooting around. It was such a shock that without even thinking she shoved away with her whole back, just while a wave was rolling in. Mickey was off balance. He went down sideways in the surf, on his hands and knees in the water like somebody playing leapfrog. Maybe he swore. Bebe was busy watching the two men walking in the sea.

Jack reached Willis and caught hold of him. They looked so silly, standing in the quiet trough just beyond the breakers, talking like men at a bus stop. They were so far out now that when Jack wanted to point back to the beach he had to pull his whole arm out of the dark water.

Splashing, Pauline jumped around. They watched Willis bob away, parallel to the shoreline, Jack right behind. Through cupped hands Jack shouted something to the shore. "What?" called Bebe.

"He's what?" Pauline listened, said to Bebe, "He's walking home, Jack says."

"In the water?"

They got Willis between them and began to work him the way two farmers drive a bull. Pauline waded out a little deeper. Jack edged Willis gradually into the shallow water, then slowly the two of them closed ranks. Bebe brought up the rear, leaving Mickey, soaked, to sit in the ocean's edge. Soon they had hold of Willis by the elbows and walked him almost on tiptoe onto the wet sand.

Willis, of course, claimed to have been playing a big joke. "Heh, heh, you thought I meant it, didn't you?"

"I just hope that's a waterproof watch," was all Jack said.

There's something else about the ocean, Bebe thought, following them over the dune toward the lighted house. You build a new bridge and somebody's just waiting to jump off it. There's something out there in the water, and it pulls.

Since Pauline couldn't see to drive at night, it was up to Willis to get them home. They wrapped him in a blanket and shoved him under the steering wheel. He was still pretending to laugh, although his teeth were chattering. "Slow and careful, easy and slow," Jack told him.

Pauline said make it *fast* and careful. "I never smelled so much wet wool in my life."

Willis turned on the motor and revved it like a jet. "It isn't wool," he said. "You Methodist."

He must have been sober since he made the turn smoothly onto the highway, but he left the rear blinker on. Jack and Bebe watched them go down the road lighting on and off like a firefly.

They were inside locking doors before Jack even remembered Mickey McCane.

"He fell in," Bebe said. "I'll close up if you'll just quit walking around and dripping all over the floor."

Jack made a wet trail through the kitchen and living room. Soon she could hear him trickling water on the porch. The light went off and he slammed the swollen screen door to latch it, then called in a funny voice, "Come out here a minute, Bebe."

She collected ashtrays on the way. Jack stood by the swing, pointing over the dune. Finally she spotted Mickey, still sitting by himself in the shallow water where he had fallen, his head bent. While they watched he stood up, stepped out of his trousers and knotted the legs over his shoulders like a cape. It flapped in the night wind all the way down the beach to his rented trailer. They stood on the porch a little longer; but he must have gotten ready for bed in the absolute dark.

4

Jack Sellars

June 4–6

Maybe it was that fool Willis made Jack have the dream again. Walking out in the water that way. His bald head looked like something floating out to sea, a canteloupe, a coconut.

Or maybe it was the uneasy thought Jack carried inside his own head into sleep: The Pinheads are coming. It sounded like an advertising slogan for one of Bebe's bad movies.

Maybe the dream had just been waiting for any excuse. Once, by the Katsewa River, the militia shot off cannon on the bank to float dead vacationers and even the ears on drowned bodies came up through the water to hear that noise. Bebe said something to him, just before they fell asleep that night, which sounded loud as cannons.

Soon as they got in bed, he had reached for Bebe. He liked to sleep on one side curled around her back with her knees up and his under them as if he were her shadow, or she was his.

"Your feet are like ice chunks," she said as he folded around her. Jack got his arm located just right for sleeping. She said, "Now don't *lean*." I do lean, he thought. No wonder Mickey would like to. He heard her breathe; he heard the waves falling uphill on the sand. He wondered if the Pinheads could swim. Aloud he said, "I took things out on you."

Bebe said sleepily that it was O.K. "Big deal," she said.

"Hearing about it that way, over a poker game, I don't know." Another accident—and it seemed design. George had arranged this somehow.

"Urf," said Bebe into the pillowcase.

He rolled away. The Pinheads are coming. "They're both abnormal, I'm sure of that." He pictured the woman Rosie and her idiot son. Sharp unbrushed teeth and spittle. "I can't sleep."

Bebe muttered that she could if he'd let her.

Jack scratched his navel. "Something was wrong with the whole thing from the start. I had this feeling something bad might happen." The pillow was lumpy. He untwisted that. "I feel it worse now."

Sighing, Bebe sat up and stared at the blowing curtains.

"See? You don't like it either."

She took a deep breath, then said to him with slow care, "You know what your trouble is, Jack? You don't believe in God—O.K. But you do believe in the Devil."

Cannon words. What a stupid thing to say! Both were superstitions, empty names. It was a shame Bebe lacked the education that might have dealt with some of her ideas. Pauline Buncombe had started it this time. Jack was probably in for another of Bebe's Episodes. The nun in the café had been one such Episode. There had been another when she lost the baby. Wonder Episodes, he called them privately. I wonder if, Bebe would say. Wonder if babies started here got a chance to finish elsewhere. Wonder if we're like a big color movie someone on Mars or the moon could watch.

"Let's go to sleep," Jack grunted, but he reached out and rubbed her spine, low, until she lay down and let him curl around her again. She went to sleep like a child. Much later, he entered the dream.

He had not dreamed the dream since April, maybe March. Now it came back stronger than ever, colors sharper, every line distinct. Just as scary as if it were the first instead of the hundredth time.

. . . In the dream I am standing on the back porch looking downhill to the Katsewa River and my mother is on the bank, shading her eyes upstream. Her image is heavily outlined as if it were leaded and set in a stained glass window. She is a knotty little woman, a knob of graying hair low on her neck. Her oversize green dress, faded in streaks, blows in the wind as the leaves are blowing, and shows their blending colors. She jerks once, and I see that as usual it is floating toward her, downstream, on the water's surface. I turn my head to watch. It is large, irregular, blue black, of some soft texture; and it rides the river's current not like a stain but like some velvet inkblot. When I look back, I see that Serena Mae Sellars has grabbed a crooked limb and waded out nearly waist deep to wait for it. The wind grows colder. She begins to thrash at the thing when it nears, but it glides just barely beyond her reach and only the margins are struck. A few purplish drops spatter and rain down into her face. She draws back with a cry. . . .

"Jack? Jack! Wake up. You hear me?"

He could feel his own mouth moving and hear himself saying, "Don't do it this time. Don't do it this time."

Something beat on his shoulder. "Jack? Wake up!" Bebe leaned over him, her face huge in the dimness. He came awake with a single spasm, jerking himself hard from the dream to a bed in a familiar room. Don't do it this time. For a minute he could not remember what made the night roar so loud. "All right now?" said Bebe. "Did you dream it?"

"Yes. I think so."

She lay back, facing him. "Stay awake a minute so you won't go right back to the same dream." And watch her do it again.

Jack could hardly see her and the sea was noisy. Bebe, broad-cheeked and wide-mouthed, looked nothing like Serena Mae Sellars. He pulled her close, a long bag of marshmallows, put his face in her warm neck. She swallowed and her throat moved as if something thick as egg white had slid by.

She whispered, "Those Pinheads. You wait and see. They'll just be like two little children."

Jack asked her why she was whispering with nobody else in the house.

She put her arm around his neck. "What did you tell George Bennett about your mother? Everything?"

"I can't remember." But he didn't even know everything and didn't want to. It happened too long ago.

"You're not to worry." She touched his ear with her fingertip, then drew a light line to his shoulder. Jack pulled back slightly, knowing where her hands would move next. He could feel a smile stretch his face. One thing about being married eighteen years—he knew each move to come, the order of their sex. He could anticipate. That was half the pleasure. He always started with Bebe's nipples. The way they came alive to his touch was a marvel to him. I'll never know why she starts with my god-damn ear. The last bits of the dream broke up and scattered.

Then—yes—she drew a few circles on his chest, trailed her warm fingers down. At the last minute, slid them aside on his thigh. Then drifted lightly across to the other leg. At last, a flickering touch, a tickle in the hair at his groin. Then her hand closed. Jack shivered, heard her giggle. She said in his ear, "See if we can't give you better things to dream about."

He reached for her, thinking: I have screwed plenty of women in my day and Bebe is the best. Even now. Even yet.

When finally he rolled off her, sticky and cooling, she flopped on her stomach and hooked her toes over his heel. She kissed his hand once—a sign it was good, very good—and slid his fingers between the pillow and her face. He didn't even remember falling asleep but just was, deep, for a long time.

When he woke it was almost sunrise and he was turned sideways in bed with one hand hanging numb toward the floor. He rolled over to rub it. Bebe slept face up with an arm across her eyes. In the early light, the main thing he saw was her yellow hair. It had looked just that misty the first time he saw her, on a spring night in Greenway, when she sat looking out her upstairs window at whatever young girls look toward. Their futures, maybe. And Jack had been walking around next door at Aunt Tyna's house on Connor Street, trying to see through the dirty windows on the porch.

"Listen," a girl's voice called down to him softly from the dark. "Listen! They're all dead."

And Jack pushed through Aunt Tyna's overgrown bushes, his head thrown back. All he could see was a dim face in a pale ring of hair. The voice sounded young. He thought she might be a schoolkid. "You couldn't come down here and tell me what happened to Aunt Tyna, could you?" Of course, he wanted to know much more than that. He wanted to know about his mother. He wanted to know how Serena Mae Sellars got to be a murderess, and then a crazy murderess, and at last a crazy dead murderess.

"Yes, I could," the girl said, and swung a bare leg out the window, wiggled it until her foot was planted on the back-porch roof. Her white skirt flew out like a flag. Then she walked away into the chimney shadow.

"Hey! You all right?"

Right on the ground at Jack's elbow she said, "I keep a ladder on that roof. Bought it myself at the hardware store." Her face, nearly as pale as that fluffy hair, was turned up to his and her mouth looked dark and wet. He had traveled a long way back to that town, determined to accept everything, even embrace it, and the girl was the first thing to offer itself. Jack thought about raping her; she had come down to him so easily like that. What else but rape would Greenway expect from a Sellars?

She seemed unafraid, even cocky. Looking back now, Jack would call this her simpleminded trust in strangers, but at the time it seemed arrogant.

"I'm Beatrice Fetner," she said, "and if Tyna was your aunt, you've got to be a Sellars." That spoiled everything, having her know his name, so he hooked both hands in his back pockets instead of grabbing her. "Which Sellars?" she asked. So he told her. The runaway one. Serena Mae's oldest boy. The one with the best memory.

"The one that saw it?" she whispered, amazed, and then went on talking without letting Jack say, Yes, the one that saw it.

She said if he borrowed her ladder he could probably get inside the house through an upstairs window. "What do you want in there?"

"What have they got?"

Tyna's furniture was still there, she said, and people weren't as careful about second-story locks. "You wouldn't steal anything," she said firmly. "I just know that." They fooled with the ladder, first trying the windows that faced the dark backyards. Bebe braced and Jack climbed. "They had your mother's funeral right in this house," she called up to him once, but he didn't answer.

He rattled one window and then the next. They kept dragging the ladder along the wall and it squawked against the paint until he expected every Fetner in her house to run out and ask what was going on. "We're eloping," he planned to say if her father came. Not knowing, then, that in an early stage they were. The ladder made so much noise, threatening to tip aside and fall through clotheslines, that in spite of himself he started laughing. There had been nothing else in Greenway to laugh about on his first trip home in . . . fourteen years, it was. Half his life at that time.

At last one of the windows shook loose; he crawled in and the girl climbed in behind him and helped pull the ladder after them. They were in a musty bedroom. The smell of mothballs and camphor seeped out of Aunt Tyna's big clothespress. It was dark as a closet. He didn't know, then, about Serena Mae's closet, and the word was ordinary and came to his mind without pain.

"Now we can talk," Bebe said, and for the first time her voice in the big room sounded hollow, maybe frightened. In the black air, all he could see was a hint of her yellow hair. He didn't have to rape her after all.

Remembering, Jack must have gone back to sleep, because broad daylight was bearing down on his eyelids and there was a new noise in the ocean's roar, perhaps Bebe crying somewhere. He sat up before both eyes were open. Maybe several women were crying. Bebe stood by the bedroom window, holding the curtain, saying, "Somebody shot him in the head."

Another nightmare. He tried to wake up from this one, too. She said louder, "They shot Bobby Kennedy just like the president. Some drunk man shot him out in California."

Jack got both feet on the grainy floor and sat there, trying to figure out what she meant. She looked short of air, like a marathon runner. "It's on the TV."

That's where the women were crying, on television. Now he heard snatches of talk from the living room. The Ambassador

Hotel. Robert Kennedy's victory speech to campaign workers. Something about bullets, bone fragments, the brain stem.

He felt numb. "Is he dead? Did they catch the man?"

"He's still alive. It was just a boy that shot him, with curly hair, no older than a boy."

Jack didn't feel like standing up. My mother wasn't any crazier than the rest of them. This country's crazy. The stars come out by accident. Maybe I do believe in the Devil or, if I don't, he gets along even better without that interference.

Jack put on his underwear and followed Bebe to watch a video bulletin from Good Samaritan Hospital. The man talking about life signs wore Bebe's numb, sleepwalker look. Then came a film of Robert Kennedy, alive, confident, saying, "I think we can end the divisions within the United States. The violence." He walked away, smiling, down a corridor into a series of mild popping noises as if from flashbulbs, or maybe some startled hotel cook dropping eggs. People cried out. The screen filled up with heads and shoulders.

Bebe closed her eyes. Jack went to the kitchen and poured a cup of coffee he didn't want to drink. Bacon was still frying on the stove, brown and brittle. He set the sizzling pan in the sink. "Who did it? Have they said?"

"I haven't heard the boy's name. I saw them push him into a police car," Bebe called back.

Saw. Wasn't that half the trouble? Jack despised television, had only bought a set so Bebe could watch Errol Flynn at home. The big eye of television looked on the wrong things and made the whole country see. Over sandwiches, like games at a picnic, they stared at the war in Vietnam. Reading about evolution, Jack had glanced up from his book and seen a president's brain spilled in his wife's lap. Only last month, back home in Durham, they had a bird's-eye view of Martin Luther King, hunted and shot like quail.

The coffee had perked too long but he carried it to the living room and sat on the hearth under Bebe's cups and saucers. He had seen, up close, the teeth on Alabama police dogs. Had felt his own excitement when films of a riot came on. The Romans in the Colosseum felt that way; he was sure of it.

"I feel like the world's gone crazy," he said. Worse, he felt it had never been anything but that.

Wouldn't it look crazy to a TV cameraman? The way doctors saw illness all the time, and cops were alert to crime? "This stuff is coffee *jam,*" he said irritably to Bebe.

"I wonder where Jackie is," said Bebe.

They sat in silence while the cameras rolled around trying to find something terrible enough to show them. Preachers used to say you couldn't hide anything from a watchful God; now the camera was the watchful one. The camera rolled up and down American streets in search of the worst possible picture, the biggest fire, meanest riot, reddest blood. Jack shifted on the brick hearth. How that camera would have loved the picture of his mother, standing in the river, getting ready! Television was like having bad dreams all the time, everybody, in daylight.

"To think," said Bebe softly, "a big man like Bobby Kennedy would be shot down in a place like that. With food warmers and ice machines. Stinking of grease. Can you imagine it?"

Like the café where she worked. There was no point in trying to make sense of things. Jack thought someday they might make a camera that turned a man's thoughts into pictures, and they'd hook wires into his scalp, and every time he imagined something really awful the director would yell: There! Print that!

He carried back his coffee cup and set it by the floating bacon in its oily puddle. Bebe followed. "And Ethel Kennedy with another baby coming. I doubt he lives to see it."

Jack noticed the trailer key and tag had been returned to its hook. "Has Mickey already left?"

"It was there when I got up. He must have gone before daylight. Want me to fry some more bacon?"

Neither one was hungry. That's why Jack suggested they drive up to Wilmington and buy a dog. He thought it would take Bebe's mind off the shooting and Kennedy's unborn baby. She had wanted babies so bad herself.

"What's the hurry about a dog?" she said. "It's not because of the Pinheads, is it?"

He'd half forgotten them. Besides, there might be an earthquake, or buffalo might stampede through the house before then. "Willis gave me the name of a kennel. I'd have gone Saturday if McCane hadn't come." He guessed Mickey was riding home by now, listening to the assassination news on his radio. Since he liked Wallace, this would probably suit him fine.

While Jack shaved, Bebe put on a dress. "First time you've worn a skirt since we moved here," he said. The memory of the night came back.

"The damn thing flaps," she said. On television they were talking about neurosurgery and the stem on which a brain grew like some gray mushroom on a stalk.

"A dog will be a lot of company," said Jack, passing through the living room. He didn't look at the screen.

Outside, the hot bare sand seemed to slap him in the eye. What he would have given for a little green shade, moss, a patch of blue violets on a slope!

From a window Bebe called, "Is my pocketbook out there?"

On the floor of the car, as usual. Bebe was careless with everything she owned. He waited in the hot unfriendly landscape of Pickle Beach, smoking too much. He guessed the Pinheads would live to be a hundred and never even know who Kennedy was.

The summer Jack was ten, his dad bought himself a spotted hunting dog. Hardly had he handed over the cash when it tried to bite him on his money hand, so he fetched it home with clothesline knotted around the jaws and turned it loose in the chicken lot, since Serena Mae by then had boiled the last and the oldest hen. She was too mad to talk to him for wasting money on a hound, and the dog was too mad to settle down. Around the line of fence he marched, wearing a slick path in the dirt. He would not eat. He threw himself snarling on the wire as soon as the children came near. He rarely slept, and at night he managed to jump or climb into the deserted hen nests and throw straw and pine needles on the ground. When he was given a dish of water he would urinate in it before nosing the whole thing over. Jack's father said only, "He sure must of liked it someplace else."

Bebe slid into the hot car.

"This place is a desert," Jack said, pulling around potholes in the asphalt road that ran behind their house. "Want to go see the azalea gardens while we're in Wilmington?"

"They're past their prime." Bebe had put on a pair of sunglasses that made her look like an owl. What Jack really wanted to see was the topel tree somebody got by grafting yaupon onto holly, but he could tell this wasn't the day.

She said in a sad voice, "I planned to vote for Kennedy for president."

"You've never cared about politics."

They drove past Buncombe's Supermart. She gave the building a hard look, saying, "They still haven't even caught the man that shot King."

It took Jack some time to connect that look with the time Willis told Bebe she was softhearted and didn't know niggers like he did. "The FBI can catch anybody."

They drove through Long Beach, Yaupon Beach, past the live oaks and galleried houses of Southport. Compared to these, Jack thought, we're running a slum beach. Bebe turned on the radio to hear that the Kennedy family was with him in the intensive care unit and crowds of people were standing outside on Lucas Street, praying.

Jack said, "People gather to blood like flies." There had been more people standing by the Katsewa River when the deputies dragged his mother ashore than ever waited by the Sea of Galilee.

"They only want to help."

"How does it help to make a traffic jam?" They only wanted to see, to see even closer than the camera could. Maybe all of them were Catholics like the Kennedys. Maybe Bebe's nun had been transferred out there. Maybe they thought God lets certain things happen to see if men care and then—if they care—He takes it back. Like that kids' cartoon Bebe made Jack take her to see: Clap your hands for Tinker Bell. Jack would swear that Bebe clapped. She had always denied it.

They were driving between walls of woodland along the Old River Road. Alligators were supposed to live in these canals, deer and wild turkey in the thickets. The odor of black decay on the air was almost sweet. "You got a headache this morning?" Bebe asked.

"Little one. Why?"

"That dream always gives you a headache. You must go back to sleep with your teeth set."

He wouldn't think about that dream. Beyond the Brunswick County line they passed the moored USS *North Carolina*. On summer nights there were tourist shows on the battleship's decks, with flashing lights and a soundtrack of naval bombardment. The state's war souvenir. Bebe took out the envelope on which Willis had drawn a map to the kennel and complained she couldn't read his writing. "Left at the fifth stoplight? Does that sound right?"

Jack turned left. Soon they were into farm country on unpaved roads. Willis had said to look for chicken houses since the owner also raised fryers. There were four of those, then a last low building with a fenced yard which ran along the bank of a black coastal creek. Jack parked by the road. He would never get used to the rivers here, after the rushing Katsewa, a muddy red artery in the foothills. Down east the streams ran through flat land as dark as veins, and the water looked too thick to stir. They got out. They saw no dogs but a dusty car was parked by the fence, its radio playing.

"Smells like a stable," Bebe said. She left her pocketbook on the floorboards for any passing thief.

The barking started. Black dogs scrambled into the runs and propped their feet high on the chicken wire as Jack and Bebe walked toward them through the stubby field. Standing up that way, every one looked twice as big as what Jack had in mind.

Somebody turned down the radio. A farmer swung open his car door and put his boots on the ground. "Morning," he called when they were still downhill, but he didn't stand up. Jack read off the envelope that his name was Farley Puckett. Willis said every dog was registered and he shipped by plane all over the country.

"Oh, look!" Bebe ran straight to the fence where a dog as tall as she was had every tooth showing, and stuck her fingers through the wire to feel his black ear. That's what Jack meant by simpleminded.

"Be careful, Bebe!" The dog got down, wagging his tail, and tried to press through the fence to her.

The farmer reached behind him to change radio stations,

saying, "That is too bad. That is just too bad." That Robert Kennedy got shot, he meant. They introduced themselves and Jack shook his hand—felt like tree bark. "I have been running my battery down," Puckett said, and spat near his shoe. "The way it tore up his brain it might be a blessing if he died."

Jack got a quick, awful picture of Bobby Kennedy as another Pinhead. His jaw hanging down. Both eyeballs showing white. There, said some director. Print that!

"Mr. Puckett, this is my wife. We understand you have Labrador puppies for sale."

"Pups," he corrected. "Yes." He looked Bebe over. "Like dogs, do you, Mrs. Sellars?" Bebe squatted by the fence so the dog could slobber on her wrist. "That's King Ahab, about three years old, weighs about a hundred pounds. Good stock."

Bebe said he needed a bath.

"All Labradors smell a little high. They got an oily coat, good for swimming in cold weather. This next one is called Pharaoh. They're both the sires of the two litters I've got for sale. The pups will take after them. Ahab's come a little cheaper."

Pharaoh's skull was wider. Not a white hair on either dog, and both had the same brown eyes. Jack asked if all the male dogs were named after kings.

"I just name them all out of the Bible. That's a trademark of my kennel. I bred Pharaoh to Naomi—got four of those pups left. The new owners pick names for the pups, of course."

Jack grinned. "How about Matthew, Mark, Luke and John?"

But Puckett didn't grin back. "The Old Testament has the best names," he said. "Plus two are females. You hunt duck?" He was about a foot taller than Jack and weighed forty pounds less.

"We just want a pet." Jack said he had heard Labs were gentle and good-natured.

"That one, Samson." Puckett pointed. "He's mean and all his pups has been mean." The dog looked calm enough, not barking, his feet planted wide apart, his thick tail held out stiffly. Bebe had Pharaoh upright on the fence so she could stroke his chest. She was crooning.

Puckett swung open a gate to fetch Ahab's two male pups. "If we bred people as careful as dogs," he said, glancing at his car where the radio still played, "we might could cut down on meanness."

Jack lounged by the fence and listened to Samson growl. Not to let Lee Harvey Oswald get born, or John Wilkes Booth or Al Capone or Hitler or Jack the Ripper or Richard Speck or whoever the boy was that shot Robert Kennedy? Or Serena Mae Sellars.

Puckett carried out two fat black pups and set them down on their short legs. They tumbled onto Bebe's sandals right away and gnawed at her painted toenails. One at a time she lifted them and rubbed their heads underneath her chin. "Oh," she said breathlessly. "Oh, Jack! Look at them!" But he was looking at her. If he could see her face at night, making love, would it look like that?

"Seventy-five dollars apiece." Pharaoh's litter cost a hundred. "If you hunted ducks, Mr. Sellars, I'd say take one of Pharaoh's; the bloodline's stronger. You just want a pet, though, these dogs will do fine."

The dogs seemed identical and Bebe had a hard time choosing just between two. At last she picked on some quality of disposition she claimed to see in one puppy's eye. Jack wrote Puckett's check, got papers about shots and registration, and put a cardboard box inside the car for the dog, although he knew the son of Ahab and Hannah would ride home in Bebe's lap.

She was happy driving home, and seemed to have forgotten

Kennedy's wounds. She examined the sleeping dog and reported every detail: he really *did* have webbing between his toes, as Puckett said. His ears were scraps of velvet and inside the skin was mottled. His nose was not only wet but maybe too wet. Was he catching cold?

Jack asked, "What do you want to name him? You need a fancy name to register, even if you call him something else." He, too, was smiling. Maybe they'd call the dog Devil. He could say sure he believed in Devil—paid seventy-five bucks for that reality.

But Bebe would not have him called Satan, Devil, Lucifer, Sinbad, Pluto. Jack had to explain who Othello was. Her own first suggestion was Gunga Din and then she thought of Zorro.

Who? Somebody in the movies, of course. Didn't Jack remember? Zorro was masked and wore a black suit and fought for justice. "Out in California," she said, but stopped before she finished the name of the state.

"Why wouldn't Tonto do just as well?"

No. She considered and turned down Tarbaby, Snoopy, Tarzan, Inky, Phantom, Charcoal, Captain, Duke, and King. No. They now owned a seventy-five-dollar Zorro. Jack was pretty sure that would be a first-timer at the American Kennel Club.

When they stopped for hamburgers, she bought one for Zorro, too, and scraped off all the slaw into the palm of one hand before breaking the meat into tiny bites. Jack was glad the new pup had taken her mind off Kennedy and his off the dream and the Pinheads coming. They had to wipe urine off the car seat and—back home—worse off the kitchen floor. Zorro, running, hit a shag rug and rode it all the way under the couch while Bebe sat on the hearth and laughed out loud.

At dusk, Bebe was pouring milk over a special brand of puppy food when their telephone rang. Jack answered and mouthed silently toward her eyebrows that it was Pauline Buncombe. "Bebe can't come to the phone right now."

Polly said Willis had just bought a color TV set that very day, after all these years. "You two want to come up and watch? Mayor Yorty's been on. President Johnson is coming on tonight. The sweetest scenes of the Kennedy children at Hickory Hill."

"No," Jack said quickly. "Not tonight." He explained about the trip and the new dog. He explained they were tired.

Next Willis got on the telephone. Not a word about walking through the Atlantic Ocean, fully dressed. "I got a good discount on this television." Probably he had run his mutilated hand over the walnut finish and allowed the salesman to mistake him for a Korean veteran.

Zorro, his face deep in the feeding bowl, snuffled. Jack watched Bebe turn on their TV set to light up Robert Kennedy and Jimmy Hoffa in a heated exchange. It looked heated. There was no audio. In Jack's ear, Willis went on bragging about his bargain. Then the sound swelled up as an announcer came onscreen to read from a list of disasters which had befallen that well-known Massachusetts family. Four of nine Kennedy children dead. One retarded and living in an institution. That made Jack hurry Willis off the telephone. There seemed to be Pinheads everywhere. He wondered if the Kennedys believed in the Devil.

"There's ham in the oven," Bebe said when he hung up. She rearranged her cups on the mantelpiece, listening to the telecast. The catalogue of announced griefs went on and got longer, spread out in ripples to touch those who had merely married Kennedys: plane crashes, stillbirths, an in-law who strangled from food caught in his windpipe. Accidents, Jack thought. All accidents.

Bebe wiped out a cup on her skirt and looked inside for a

while, then set it back. "It doesn't help much to be rich, I guess," she said.

Jack guessed not. "Look at your dog," he said hastily. She mopped up the new yellow puddle. Then she sat back on the living room floor while Zorro pawed under her blue skirt, trying to sniff at her fragrant crotch. Her face looked tired.

"Jack?" She looked at the dog, scratching his back. "Jack, you must have thought about things like this more than most people ever need to. Why do you think they happen?" With perfect trust, then, she turned to him as if he would give her the final answer.

Jack felt uneasy. "There's a chain of events, but not a why," he said. That's what he had learned in the eight years he went surreptitiously to State Technical College. That all life, from butterfly to comet, was interlocked and had happened the way dice could turn up showing twelve black dots. He said, "Where have you put the aspirin?"

"You mean there's no reason to it we can see?"

"There just isn't one. You going to let that dog wallow all over you, fleas and everything?" He went into the bathroom and swallowed two aspirin. Why Bebe asked questions in search of order baffled him. She was not orderly. Her mind, he was convinced, was a hodgepodge. She was ruled by feeling. And she certainly wasn't fastidious—he'd told her that once. Jack stood in the bathroom, grinning. *Fastidious* had been a new word to him then, and he wanted to use it three times as part of his self-education. He could have used it a thousand times. Bebe hardly ever flushed toilets, for instance. That was one of the first things they had fussed about after she ran away from Greenway to marry him. Jack was flushing the toilet every single time he went into the bathroom. Finally he mentioned it. Bebe turned dark red. Threw back her head and shook her yellow hair. Said in a snooty voice, "Well, I always flush *number two!*" Jack nearly fell laughing into the tub and drowned.

Thinking of that, he came back grinning into the living room.

She made a face at the sight of his good humor. "Don't you get tickled at me! I asked you a serious question!" She was still sitting on the floor, patting the dog. "Do you think television's right, and America is just sick in its mind in some way?"

"America doesn't have a mind."

"You think things happen with no meaning at all and people won't admit it. That's it, isn't it?" She leaned forward and wiped again where the linoleum was already dry. "Troy used to sing that song, 'We'll Understand It Better By and By.' You think that's a big joke, I guess."

"I don't think it's funny, no. I think it's too damn bad."

"Hah!" she said to the dog. "You like it that way." She yanked Zorro out from under her skirt and, for a change, he ran at Jack's shoelaces and let him rub his head, which felt very soft. He wondered if dogs, like babies, had an open place in the middle of their skulls.

"I think it's too bad we waste so much time trying to figure things out," Jack said. "Look at Zorro. He's luckier. A dog doesn't know in advance he's going to die so when the time comes he just, well, lays there and lets himself die."

"I'm not talking about *dying,*" said Bebe. "I mean *everything.*"

"You better leave *everything* alone." He was ashamed when she looked hurt. "Dying is what makes us wonder. We see people die, and we remember. We read what dead people wrote down in books." ("I don't," Bebe said, softly.)

She got up off the floor, shaking her head, and went to the oven to check the ham.

Jack said, louder, "If I'd run over one of Puckett's dogs,

Pharaoh or Ahab wouldn't have noticed. That's what does it, Bebe. If dogs had the kind of memory we have, they'd ask why, too; but it wouldn't change anything. They'd think some deaths were better than others, but it wouldn't be true."

"Some *are* better," she said from inside the oven, basting the meat. The way she was bent over, Jack might have pinched her lightly if the dog hadn't been in the way. He was tempted to go on with the discussion, to say it was his belief in Death, not in the Devil, that had stained the world for him. There was a force which kept people from being as happy as dogs, that's all there was to it. So all a man could do was develop the one thing that made him different from other animals, his brain, and try to think his way through.

"We think we're not like dogs but we all die the same way the animals die," he decided to say.

Bebe looked personally insulted. "Dogs can't . . ." she began, and stopped by the sink with her ladle held high as a torch. "They don't know how . . . They can't make promises."

He didn't see what that had to do with anything.

After supper, Jack tried to read a magazine article about budding and cleft-grafting roses. Bebe listened to Lyndon Johnson explain on camera that two hundred million Americans had *not* shot Robert Kennedy. Zorro slept peacefully in her lap. Senator Kennedy was still alive but, if he survived, said newsmen, there would probably be brain damage. Maybe he'd have to be kept in the same place as his Pinhead sister. Jack wondered if families with two got cut rates. He was ashamed of wondering that.

He said suddenly, "Why did you ask me all that stuff in the first place?"

His question suddenly cutting across the sound of television made Bebe jump. She said sharply, "I thought maybe once I could make you say something, that's all."

"What does that mean?"

"Things go on inside your mind I never know about." She set the puppy on the floor. "Things I know you think about."

"Because of my mother, you mean."

"Maybe."

Jack knew she was thinking of his dream. Even his father's bitter hound had dreamed, sleeping on one side in a corner of his hated pen, whimpering, making running movements with his paws. Awake, he only bared his fangs and charged the fence wire. Watching him shiver in his sleep, none of the children could tell if he chased or was being chased. Two months it took to quiet the bluetick's rage, near starvation before he would eat, a length of chain to beat off his attack. Finally they hunted rabbits and squirrels together. But the first night they went out after coon the dog struck out ahead of them, bawled once, and kept on running. He never did come back.

Bebe picked up the dog and rubbed her chin against his fur. "I heard once you ought to wrap up a loud clock in a towel and put it where a new puppy sleeps. He'll think it's his mother's heart beating and won't whine."

Jack dropped his book to stare at her, but she didn't seem to mean anything special by what she said.

At bedtime Bebe set Zorro's box right by their bed, and any time the pup whimpered she dropped her hand onto him and let her pulse tick in his ear.

The next morning, June 6, 1968, they heard Senator Kennedy had died, and there was a statement in Sirhan Sirhan's notebook: Kennedy must die by June 5. Jordan and Israel were the cause of it, whatever that meant.

Jack couldn't feel even as sad as when JFK was shot, merely confirmed in his view of the world. That confirmation alone kept him watching the TV screen while Bebe took Zorro outside and tried to teach him to shit on sand instead of rugs. Now that there was no more hope for Kennedy's life, she seemed to be neutral toward the rest. Jack was the one wanting her kept up to date. He'd call out the window, "They plan to bury him in Arlington close to his brother."

"Big deal," said Bebe, and pivoted on one bare heel while the hose was running into the birdbath. Zorro squatted nearby and let loose a puddle as round as a silver dollar.

If Kennedy had only left the ballroom a different way, thought Jack. There must be things people could do to prevent such acts. He was pacing up and down by the hearth when Bebe carried the dog inside. "Bebe, I ought to just pick up that telephone and ask George Bennett why he lied about his goddamn sister."

"Did he lie? What good would it do?"

He followed her to the kitchen, where she shifted clean glasses from the drainer to a shelf. "We could move straight back to Durham. I don't owe George anything. I don't owe a thing to his Pinhead sister." Bebe stacked plates. "I could get my job back at the college."

Out of their living room Cardinal Cushing suddenly spoke in a resonant voice. He quoted Rose Kennedy. No matter what happened, Rose had told him, she knew God was all-wise, all-powerful, and all-loving. Though it was a repeat telecast, Bebe hurried away to see the old Cardinal again, his lined face astonished that he could ever have taught faith that well, and someone have taken it that seriously. Zorro raced after her.

Jack had to talk louder. "I could call George right now. Let him leave his patient in the chair. I owe him a piece of my mind. Maybe he'll keep the Pinheads home."

"He might." She stood wiping dust off the screen with her petticoat. "He's not pulling teeth today. He's home watching television." Somebody on camera read a memorial tribute into her skirt. She lifted the dog. "Why don't you come swimming with us?" Jack shook his head.

Alone again, he tried to read, but network announcers kept interrupting. A panel questioned the nature of Sirhan Sirhan's mind, what had boiled up in him that led to murder. Soon doctors would run every test in the book till they knew—better than he did—his childhood, sex life, nightmares. They'd known, Jack guessed, all about Serena Mae Sellars after a while. All about the fishhook in her eye, and the stillbirths, the river, her husband drinking. He wondered what they knew after they knew all that.

He walked to the screen porch. In her red bathing suit Bebe wandered down the beach, head bent. She stood motionless a long time staring over the waves, like somebody marooned here, and homesick. Sometimes Jack saw her stoop to put in her pail the ark shells and angel wings and chambered nautiluses. Nautilusi? Nautilusae? He needed a book on seashells.

She raced Zorro up and down the beach, made him swim toward her in the surf, then lay down in the foam and let him crawl on her body and chew her hair. Her knees were flexed and the sea washed between them. The glare hurt Jack's eyes and when he looked away her fiery image shone on the walls and furniture. Even though he closed off that scene with the heels of both hands, Bebe's body lay burning in his head and he wanted her, then, just like that first night in Greenway when she came to him down the ladder. After eighteen years he could still want her that suddenly, that sharply, could still get a hard-on just like that, for nothing really but the picture of her.

He sat in the swing he had meant to oil and listened to the chains rasp. Willis Buncombe had told Mickey only one thing kept him married. After so many years, he knew Pauline inside and out, knew exactly what she'd do and say—she had turned into the one thing he could always predict.

That wasn't what kept Jack married. He'd never known Bebe inside and out, simpleminded or not. But he still wanted to.

Mickey McCane

June 6, 1968

They did not know it then, but at that moment Mickey McCane sat drinking with friends at the Cotton Club outside Angier, telling them what he had found at his laundromat when he got home from Pickle Beach. He was more shocked by this than by national events.

Three of his washing machines had human shit in them. That's right. Shit. Down in those porcelain tubs. Perhaps, from the smell, it had been left there Saturday night, behind plate glass windows with every fluorescent light ablaze and some fool (or fools, from the amount) using his equipment practically in public like a three-holer outhouse. Sat right down and let fly.

Mickey couldn't get over it. No white man would do such a thing. The other club members agreed. For a long time he had not wanted blacks to use the laundromat and one woman with bristly hair had cursed him and thrown her whole basket of filthy clothes at his legs.

"And they sure will stick together," said one of the men.

"A thing like that—it wasn't a joke." Mickey nursed his drink. He sat on a leatherette couch at the end of a long barn-like room. The walls were unfinished and there was fiber matting on the floor. At benches and narrow wood tables a few other men were finishing barbecue plates, but five or six stood around Mickey, muttering.

"And the cops didn't even care." Mickey reached up and caught his nose between thumb and finger. "They did like this and just couldn't wait to get out in the air."

"Well, it did wash out, didn't it?" asked somebody in the group. "After a few cycles?"

It washed out, hell! The turds had hardened and had to be lifted out with newspaper and flushed away one by one through the sewer pipes. And scrubbing powder and steel wool used on the bottoms of the tubs. Even after Clorox in each machine and ammonia on the floor, he could smell it. The stink alone was enough to give him some disease. You could tell it had never come from a clean healthy person.

"See you made the papers, too."

Mickey snatched at the *Angier Daily News.* The front page was nothing but Kennedy, of course, and there was his own piece on the bottom of page five. VANDALISM AT THE SELF-SERVICE LAUNDROMAT. Vandalism! Mickey shook the paper in midair. "This goes way beyond vandalism!" What was the world coming to when people did things like that? They weren't even people.

"You think it was done by colored, and I do, too," said Vetch. Vetch was in the VFW with him and was all *right.*

Most likely boys and girls together had done it. Some of that prancing high school crowd with the Afro combs stuck in hip pockets like blackjack handles. Maybe some college kids on dope.

Mickey thought about Bebe Sellars. He wouldn't want Bebe to know a thing like this, and that anybody could do Mickey McCane like that and get away with it. Leaning back on the couch, Mickey thought of how she had looked standing in the surf while Willis was in both the water and his second childhood. He'd been too quick to grab hold of her (he knew that now) and no wonder she had been surprised and had acted by reflex. But she would come around, and when she did, she would be the best he ever had, and he'd be the best with her, too. What could she see in a man like Jack?

Maybe if Bebe once met his wife, Eunice, she'd also be amazed. Would wonder what he had seen in a woman like that! "Why didn't you wait for me?" she'd ask. They might even go off together to a foreign country.

Smoothly, Mickey came out of his thoughts and dropped into the middle of law-and-order conversation.

That night about 1 A.M., two carloads of white men rode through Redfield, a hollow south of town where only Negroes lived, and where there were rumored petitions under way to hook up to Angier's water lines. Three or four outdoor toilets were overturned and somebody's barking dog had his jaw kicked and broken, but nobody came outside to see what was going on.

"They were all indoors," Mickey told Eunice in his bedroom later, "looking at Bobby on their welfare TV sets."

5

Bebe Sellars

June 6–8

In spite of what Bebe said, Jack placed a call to Richmond about the Pinheads who would be coming to the beach next month. George Bennett tried to calm him down by vowing to make things right, which—knowing George—probably meant he'd raise the pay. At first he wouldn't admit that hiring Jack Sellars was anything but his own good luck and Jack's as well. Then he said it was a long story and maybe he'd better come to Pickerel and explain it in person to them both.

"Explain it now," said Jack. George said he had Richmond friends who'd be there for the weekend to fish; he could just ride down with them. He said heartily, "We'll have a long and honest talk." Jack said that would be a novelty. George hung up the telephone.

He walked down the beach to tell Bebe, who was standing in the ocean's edge, letting sand slide loose from her arches, float over and bury both feet, rise like a gray cloud to tickle her ankle bones. Her mind was on James Mason, who in some film walked off from Judy Garland into the Pacific Ocean forever. Some deaths *are* better than others, Bebe thought, barely listening to what George had said and Jack had answered. Should she stand in this same spot until dark, high tide might find her in quicksand to the waist, watching the beautiful death roll in to carry her away.

"So George will be down tomorrow," said Jack. She shrugged. Big deal.

George, plus some fishermen, plus any tourists who happened by, he added. And he wouldn't be surprised if Mickey showed up Saturday as well. Jack picked up a seashell and hurled it over the waves. Zorro ran after it till the saltwater filled his nose.

Bebe said suddenly, "I might take a trip to Greenway."

"What brought that on?"

She wasn't sure. The beach was ready, trailers clean, both houses repaired. Jack's marigolds were already blooming. Now they would sit all summer long while the sea washed in and strangers poured down to the coast and stopped off and then left again and went someplace else. Given three months of that, Bebe thought, she might feel like an invalid with visiting hours.

She said, "I haven't been home in a long time to see my family." Not since her father died, in fact, except one day when Grace Fetner broke her hip. You ought to go home for more than the rare catastrophe.

"This is your home," said Jack.

"If I was to go at all, it ought to be in June."

Before *they* came. "Let's wait and see what George has to say. Maybe we'll both go to Greenway. Permanently. Come here, Zorro." He put a leash on the pup's collar to walk him along the beach and show the Buncombes.

Bebe watched their moving shapes shrink, turning in her fingers the best shell she had found, the perfect ear of a very fat baby with a blue center where the wax should have been. She felt morbid, perhaps because Kennedy had died and she had been waiting for it. In Greenway she had been the surviving daughter who waited by Walt Fetner's bed, and had watched him go in some kind of melting; his heart beat, then it didn't. Maybe he had time to know he'd heard its final thump, to think: Here it comes. And then to let it come easy.

Alone in their bedroom, Bebe squirmed out of the wet suit and dropped it over the back of a chair, trying not to hear the TV announce that Kennedy's body had been transferred to a Boeing 707, nor how it would lie in state at Saint Patrick's Cathedral in New York City. The baby's ear shell fell without breaking on the rug. She laid it on a windowsill. Its blue center shone like a single eye. Bebe pulled the shade down over its steady gaze. Across one shoulder she examined her nude body in the mirror, shifted weight to watch first one buttock sag, then the other. Artists liked to draw that droop. Big deal. She grinned.

"Teddy Kennedy," the TV said to the empty living room.

Instead of going home, perhaps, she could invite her two brothers to come to Pickle Beach on their vacations. Troy and Earl Fetner, bring your families to the fun spot of the Carolina coast! No, she ought to go home to see them, in Greenway. When you lived at a beach, you waited for things. For people to come and then leave. For the season, the tides, the storms. You weren't in charge of much. No wonder Pauline got religion, gazing down that empty road for customers.

She faced the mirror. Hands on pelvic bones. The white scar almost glistened, but she'd been kissed on it, which was more than most women could say. Her breasts were looser than they used to be, the tips browner. Often she grew a few pale hairs between them. Now she yanked out the latest crop.

A horn blew and she threw on a dress that zipped. A fat man wearing a straw hat wanted to rent a trailer overnight. His wife was picking one of Jack's marigolds while a girl with brown pigtails stirred the birdbath with a plastic shovel. They paid and took the key, complaining because Bebe didn't sell beer. The child wanted to wee-wee *here.* Her sunburned mother, angry, smacked her thigh and hissed, "Hush!"

When next Bebe glanced through the porch screening, she saw the fat man spread on a towel by himself, getting hotter and sleepier, while his daughter dug a long trench to guide ocean water into a moat around her sand igloo. They made a lonely-looking sight.

The Fetners had never been able to take Bebe, or Earl, or Troy to the beach. They couldn't afford it even when Greenway Cotton Mill closed down the first week in July. She'd grown up believing every beach had palm trees and people would sit around underneath and sing in Hawaiian.

On television, a man said the Kennedy plane would land at nine o'clock and already people were lined up along Fifth Avenue outside the church. There were three widows riding on the plane—the Kennedy women and Mrs. Coretta King.

"They'll integrate anything," Willis would say.

Friday morning the fishermen arrived from Richmond, without George. Had a chance to come early, they said. Old George would join them Saturday. They moved into the nearest shell house. In an hour they used up their ice and half of Bebe's, drinking, and had to go stand in the surf and struggle with their ten-foot rods.

The pigtailed girl from the trailer next door kept getting in their way and scaring the fish. She did it on purpose. Mrs. Morris told Jack one of those men swore right out loud at Sheila; what was he going to do about that? All day Zorro barked. And, for background, the Kennedy train was rolling from New York toward Washington for the burial.

By now Bebe was worn out with it. They could shovel him under anyplace by now—she'd be relieved. Oswald and Sirhan had begun to look alike.

She drove to Buncombe's for weekend supplies and had to step down the breezeway to the house and admire Willis's new TV set.

"Now, Bebe, look at this!" Across the room he propped his feet on a hassock, changing channels by remote control. On one station, the train roared from right to left. "Mine eyes have seen the glory," people were singing in dry weeds beside the tracks. Willis clicked his box. The train ran rapidly in the opposite direction. Other crowds sang, off key, "His terrible swift sword!" Old men swept off their hats when Peter Lawford waved from the caboose.

"Look how clear the picture is," said Willis. "You ever want to trade, ought to get you one like this." He was indoors for the day, bothered by arthritis. Said it would rain. Bebe didn't even believe he had arthritis. It wouldn't have surprised her much to learn he kept a set of three spare fingers in a drawer and wore them whenever it suited his latest story.

"While you're here, look at this." Willis handed her a color postcard, postmarked Angier, which showed four men sitting around a gambling table. He grinned. "Came from Mickey. Look what it says." The caption under the long-faced card-players read: POKER: WAITING FOR THE CHIP THAT NEVER COMES IN. On the other side was a scrawl about how Mickey hoped to win back his losses this Saturday night.

"Look close at the front picture, Bebe." She missed it. Willis had to touch with a yellow fingernail the place where Mickey had inked out three fingers on the hand raking chips home across the tabletop. Willis got so tickled he pressed the remote control by mistake and Bebe heard again the rumbling train. "I've got to get back at him for that," Willis said, laughing.

Halfway along the breezeway came his call: "Don't let Pauline forget to give you the box."

What box? Bebe pushed open the rusted screen and walked by the workbench, calling. Polly had been getting up her list. At the checkout counter, waiting, she cracked a purple smile—must have been wetting the indelible pencil on her tongue again. "Everything's ready, Bebe." The groceries were neatly stacked in a crate beside a hatbox with the lid left off. "Did Willis tell you? He can't keep anybody's secrets but his own."

"Something about a box."

"It's a present. Welcome to the beach even if it *is* a few weeks late." With two hands she lifted out an old mantel clock with gilt garlands painted in harsh colors on its glass door and a stairstep base of wood that was nearly black. "Oh, my." Bebe touched the Roman numerals. They were metal and had sharp edges. The pendulum shivered. Something about the face of the clock looked fierce.

"The key's inside the glass. Willis had to make a new one before it would wind."

"It must be antique," said Bebe. "It's just . . . just beautiful." The clock was not really beautiful so much as complicated.

Pauline brushed a Kleenex over its fluted frame, her face so tense Bebe thought she had probably wanted the clock herself. "It used to strike hours only but Willis fixed it to strike quarters on a different chime—very quick and high. Now you can tell time in the dark."

Imagine the noise it would make every fifteen minutes, all night long. "Polly, I can't thank you both enough. What a surprise," she added weakly. Baby Ben windups from the corner drugstore had always been enough for Bebe.

"Let me carry it to the car." Pauline backed out of the screen door with one thump of her bony rear. Bebe dragged the crate of food onto a shopping cart and rolled that outdoors behind her. "Over your fireplace, I think," Pauline said, bracing the hatbox on the front seat of the car.

It'll crowd my cups and saucers. "This is real sweet of you both."

"We want you and Jack to enjoy it."

And that night, when they buried Bobby Kennedy in the pitch dark at Arlington Cemetery, the clock chimed deep on the hours, then tapped a treble bell once, twice, three times, and four, every fifteen minutes in between. The night seemed very long and the distance between birthdays very great.

In bed Bebe wound both legs around Jack's and pressed her face on his sweaty back. He reached back, dropped a sleepy pat on her hip. "All right?"

She said, "Yes." Hanging on him. Hanging as if she were in the sea and he were a log. Holding him. Listening to the goddamn clock.

Saturday morning. Jack lay in bed, half asleep, and watched through slit eyelids as Bebe moved naked in the room. She knew he was watching and would sometimes turn to one side, suck in her belly and throw both shoulders back, because she knew a man wanted a woman most at a distance. She felt like an actress. Elizabeth Taylor in her plumper years, wearing short bleached hair.

More than anything else, thought Bebe, smiling, Jack likes to think he has caught me off guard with my True Self showing, at times I don't know I'm being watched.

She had learned about this in the backseats of cars driven by milltown boys. They'd take her thirty miles away to a picture show and behave in the theater rows so roughly they must have known she would pop their busy hands, all so she could drowse in their arms on the way home. And what really excited them, she decided, were not the times a girl said yes, not the times a girl moved toward them or opened to them, but when they thought she lay helpless alongside, trusting and asleep. How slowly they'd ease their fingers, then, inside the sweater and up, along a breast, and at last so lightly touch the nipple.

And Bebe and the others would stir in their sleep, shift, settle into that grip, sometimes even snore. At any movement, the searching hand would freeze, the veins on its back stand out like wires. An eternity would pass while the hand became still and as neutral as cloth, till the girls would drift back into false, deep sleep; and another year might end before that second hand would move up the leg like a fly on the rim of a sugar bowl, tasting as it went.

Did they really believe I was sleeping all that time? And my girlfriends? Sleeping? Their sisters, sleeping?

Sometimes Bebe believed it herself, that she was home in bed and this was a dream which would last until morning, so slowly did it unfold. Surely she was never to blame. She had not given this boy, or that, permission to touch those secret places. Let him have all guilt for taking advantage! And he wanted that guilt. That was half what his cautious hands were looking for.

Bebe spun on her heel now and watched Jack jam his eyelids tight. You give a man not what he says he wants but what he really needs, and he gives you—oh, I don't know. Whatever he can spare.

Slowly she put on a blouse and shorts with no button at the waistband, scratched in a drawer till her fingers scraped loose a safety pin coated with face powder. In the kitchen she propped one hand against the kitchen wall, staring at the coffeepot. Water takes forever to boil at sea level. The clock had kept her awake all night.

The toilet flushed, refilled, and whistled. "Jack? I hear a car coming."

"If it's George, tell him I quit."

"Tell him yourself." She picked up the barking puppy and unlatched the back door. "Come on now. You can shave later." She turned down the flame under the thumping coffee. George Bennett came carrying his paunch up the high back stairs, setting his face with each step in a wider and wider smile. From the landing he called out, "Morning, Bebe!" She pushed open the screen and he shook the hand holding Zorro and got his fingers licked. "Well, listen! How've you been? And where did you get the dog? I'm telling you it's hot to be this early in the day."

She could hear the bathroom faucet running. "We're all right."

"Tell Jack no hurry, let him sleep, do him good. I can see all the work he's been doing around this place."

"He's already up, George."

Like a nervous embezzler he wandered through the kitchen, talking fast. He was glad to hear the men from Richmond got here all right. "And a trailer rented, too? That's great. It sure looks better from the road with those bushes on the side. What are they? Cedars?" He blew into the coffee cup Bebe handed him. A very full lower lip, too full, with too much spongy underside sagging into view. "I guess Jack can see how things are looking up." The puffy lip attached itself to the cup by suction. "When Jack called me the other day he was right upset."

Bebe sat across from him with her orange juice, saying nothing. Both lifted their heads at the sound of a slamming door.

"I know he's had time to think it over since." George bent to Zorro, who was slobbering on one shoe. "This is a nice breed, a Labrador, and it grows to be some size. Real protection for you, Bebe."

From the doorway Jack said in a cold voice, "Is she going to need protection?"

George jumped up to shake his hand. He began asking rapid questions. Would property tax go up in Brunswick County this year; what did Jack think? How many reservations from those ads in the *Raleigh News & Observer*? Wasn't this hot for June! The Kennedy shooting, well. What was there to say?

Bebe started link sausages and stirred the waffle batter while Jack led him outdoors to look at rotted windowsills and a sagging gutter. She could hear George promising everything, even her double clothesline, which would have poles sunk in concrete. Steam rose from the waffle iron. "And what are these?" George boomed from outside. "Beautiful! What a green thumb you've got, Jack." The better to mash you with, Bebe thought.

"Marigolds," answered Jack.

"I can't get over how much you've done so fast. The guy I used to have—a drunk, did I tell you?"

"Yes."

"Couldn't do nothing right." They moved around the house discussing spar varnish for the steps.

At last she called them to breakfast and George had less to say, except how good the waffles were. He chewed them a long time, smiling. Soon the three ate in silence. Bebe could hear her own teeth grind. Every spoon clanked in its saucer. George blotted his full mouth on a napkin, wiped repeatedly as if the skin might be oozing. He's afraid, she thought suddenly.

Then Jack tilted the wooden chair back on two legs and said, "Just any time you're ready, George." They waited. Bebe stacked plates and set them in the sink while George pulled a small notepad from his shirt pocket and laid it on the table. He pulled out his wallet, too. At that Jack winked at Bebe and lit her cigarette.

"I hardly know where to start."

They kept waiting. Blowing smoke.

"How far back, I mean. I want to give you the whole picture. The older I get the more I tend to start a story with the day I was born. You know?"

Impassive, they stared at him, determined not to know.

"Maybe it starts way back in Germany at least, that time Jack told me what had happened with his mother and daddy. We'd been drinking, Bebe, and he got to talking about what he could remember of it. Mickey was with us. It was the night . . ."

Jack interrupted to say Bebe knew all that.

George nodded, gave his embezzler's smile. "I wasn't married then. I forgot all about it until the time your problem and mine seemed to run together. They'll do that sometimes. You know?" He tried to guess what Jack might be thinking, cleared his throat, started tracing the wallet's edge with one finger. "After I got out of the service I married LaVerne Baker. Met her while I was at dental school. She's my age, forty-six now. We can't all be young as Bebe." The smile again. He gave up on it. "LaVerne had this sister."

With an *ah* sound Bebe's breath slid out. "I thought she was *your* sister."

He looked quite shocked. "Certainly not."

"Go on," said Jack.

"This sister, born when LaVerne was six. One of those change-of-life babies." George strangled out a laugh. "Everybody in LaVerne's family seemed to get married late. They named her Rosemary. Rosie. And she wasn't quite right. You could even tell by how she looked. Big-headed. Had a face like a Chinese."

Bebe bent down to lift Zorro into her lap. He went to sleep there.

"LaVerne's mama was so broke up that any little thing could

have carried her off and appendicitis did—she was one of those people that had it on the left instead of the right so it ruptured before anybody knew what was wrong. Some families have the worst luck."

That's all right; that's the rule Jack lives by, Bebe thought.

George turned the notebook over. His voice was dull, as if he were reading aloud from it. "LaVerne's daddy was a preacher. Well. Believing in the will of God like he did? The two things got to him. He did his best but the feeling wasn't there for Rosie. LaVerne was seven, eight years old. She's seen him rock Rosie to sleep and then go wash his hands—he couldn't help it. He never even noticed it."

Jack and Bebe had stopped watching his face and looked, instead, at his nervous hands, wiping each other with the empty air.

"Everything fell on LaVerne. It was still on her when we met. She wasn't in college, just living in that town, since she had to look after Rosie all the time. No boyfriends, no social life at all, and by then Rosie was twenty-four and the preacher was dead and Rosie's brain was nobody knows how few years old. She understood more than she said, but how old was that? Five? Seven? And happy all the time. After we got married and she lived with us that nearly drove me crazy, how happy she always was. It's not normal."

Abruptly Jack got up to pour more coffee. Bebe said, "I'm sorry, George." George was sliding a plastic photo folder out of the wallet. He pushed the top picture across the table toward them, upside down.

"That's Rosie about that time. She lived with us a year."

All Bebe could see was a side view of a stocky woman with bobbed hair wearing a man's sweater. The telephone rang. She answered while the men kept talking softly. She told some stranger, yes, they had places to rent. The new clock was pinging. On the loud hour chimes, some of her fragile cups would tremble.

When she sat again at the table George was saying, ". . . a nice place where they know how to treat them, or that's what I thought then. It was like a honeymoon for LaVerne and me. The whole house ours. Dinner parties. You should have been there. We could have people in for bridge."

Bebe saw Zorro was climbing into the trash can and had to go pour food in his dish. If I'd had a slant-eyed baby, she thought, I'd just as soon run after it as some puppy dog.

Jack said, "So that's where she lives. Then who is the boy that's been coming to the beach with her?"

George offered him a cigar but Jack said no. Then he bit off the tip of one, stared at it, and almost laughed. He put it away unlit. "One day they had some kind of picnic and Rosie just walked off. They called us up. And the way LaVerne carried on? She was pregnant then. When a week and two weeks went by without a sign, we all thought Rosie must be dead out in the world like that no better than a baby. This was in nineteen fifty-three and the weather turned cold all of a sudden."

Nineteen fifty-three. That winter they were in Winston-Salem and Jack delivered milk in the snow. Bebe was tempted to reach under the table and squeeze his hand. He was sitting so still, under such stiff control. He had a fear of his own temper; Bebe knew that.

"The police found Rosie in Maryland, sitting by herself on some railroad trestle, wearing a navy overcoat. She was eating sardines out of a can somebody else had opened since Rosie couldn't even remember which way to turn the spigot to make it go on and off. There she was with her fish and the oil running down her arms." George tapped the photo folder and for a minute Bebe feared he had a picture of that, too, but he kept on. "She came home while I looked for a new place, better supervised. She was different. She got quieter. For the first time she was scared of me. If I walked in the room, Rosie would shake. Then we found a new place to take care of her that didn't have picnics."

He finished the coffee and looked for a long time into the empty cup. Silence. Bebe jumped when something pressed her hand. Jack was touching her out of sight until she said, "Wouldn't it be cooler on the porch?" The two men nodded, George gathering up his notebook, billfold, and pictures while she shut Zorro into the bedroom and tried not to care when he whimpered. She heard herself babbling now, worse than George. "This clock is a present from Willis Buncombe at the store; we just got it."

Leaning on the hearth, George said something favorable about old-fashioned craftsmanship. "And this is a pretty thing." He lifted her least favorite cup. She nearly ran over and grabbed the right one, trimmed with stars, and pressed it into his hand. But he said grimly, touching the clock, "They don't let you visit in a new place right at first but La Verne couldn't travel much anyway; she was sick a lot. For a long time I didn't even tell her about getting the doctor's letter that Rosie was pregnant, too. It just about killed her when I did."

Another silence. "Out this way," Jack said suddenly, directing the man through his own house.

Without a word they followed him onto the porch, where the wind struck them like a tide. Bebe was surprised to see how beautiful the morning still was, how the seawater shone. What a relief to get out of that room and to have so much to look at. Her throat swelled suddenly: to be looking out at the ocean now, with Kennedy never to go to Hyannis Port again! I really *am* simpleminded, she thought, forcing the thought away.

Jack pointed out a line of flying pelicans. He sounded almost dreamy. "I guess you never found out who?"

George dropped into a recently painted chair. "Rosie sure couldn't tell. What kind of man would take advantage of a poor ugly thing like that? Somebody sick himself. I was relieved Rosie's baby was even white. It was a boy—you know that now—and nearly as bad off as Rosie ever was. Oh, he could learn a few things. He can make baskets and stuff." George lit the fat cigar at last. "Do try one of these, Jack," and Jack did although he hated cigars. Just to have something to do, Bebe guessed. They sat puffing in the green rockers and she hung motionless in the swing, not wanting the chains to squawk.

"That's about it," said George. With relief he spotted one of the Richmond fishermen hanging out towels next door. "I've got to go speak to Harold. Be right back." He set off almost running through the sand and not only spoke to Harold but hung up a towel or two.

As soon as he'd gone, Jack ground his cigar into an ashtray. "That's about it, hell."

"It's a terrible story."

"And you're feeling sorry, just the way George Bennett wants you to feel."

"I do feel sorry; why not?"

He paced between the swing and the door. Maybe it's that Jack never asked Bebe to feel sorry for him—could she help it if she did? Nobody should ever have to see, at fourteen, what Jack Sellars sat in a tree and saw happen in the Katsewa River. And then, years later, to travel home to Greenway and have to hear from a girl he didn't know how his mother had finally hanged herself by a light cord, inside a linen closet, and clawed off the plaster down one wall while she died. Sure she felt sorry, and numb besides. Big deal.

Jack marched. "And what if George had told us all this the first night? Right there in Durham. What if he'd asked me to look after his Pinhead kinfolks in the summers? I'd never have come to his damn beach, Bebe. He got us to burn our bridges first. *Then* he told us, when he finally had to."

But bridges didn't burn. Never burn. Everything stayed hooked together, yesterday to today to tomorrow, in a long chain. George's past and present, or hers. Jack's. Even Sirhan's. If you went far enough back in everybody's story, it would be full of murders and madness and grief, all leaning into *this* moment, *this* day. To make it sweeter, somehow.

Again she felt a sharp need to go home to Greenway to see her mama and her brothers. See how her own childhood was doing far down that chain. "Yonder he comes," said Bebe. "Want me to leave?"

Jack bent over the drifting swing, fixed her with those wide blue eyes. "Not ever."

He's right, she thought. I *am* home.

George could tell their sympathy had changed, they had recovered from his story. He said nervously, "I see how you fixed up that house inside. Harold says he'll come here to do his fishing from now on."

Trying to sound impatient, Bebe said, "You got as far as Rosie's baby."

He dragged the rocker closer to the swing, concentrated on her. "Bebe, you can surely see how LaVerne felt about both our own boys. She was so scared of passing something on to them. I had to consider LaVerne's peace of mind. She wanted to think Rosie had never even happened."

The notebook came out again and George unfolded a sheet showing an old-fashioned hotel in a mountain valley. "You don't know what it's like in a place like that where grown men can't go to the toilet, and thank God you don't know what it costs to keep somebody there. They close down a month in the summers to give the staff a rest. The worst patients go into hospitals and other homes. Some go to their families." He made a bitter face. "That's the modern way. They claim it makes for better adjustment. Jesus Christ! You're going on with your life trying to forget Rosie exists, and now they want to send her for a visit!" Bebe shot a look at Jack. "Rosie's boy is the age of our oldest son. Our kids don't know. We can't. We just can't."

So he sent them here, with a nurse, in July. The boy must be nearly fifteen by now. Bebe's hand rested on her stomach just above the scar. She looked up as Sheila Morris and her parents, all three in short terrycloth robes, filed out of the trailer and took snapshots on Pickle Beach against the backdrop of the ocean, blazing now with light. The fluffy clouds overhead would look artificial on their film. Holding hands, they waded out to stand in a row beyond the breakers and bob above the crests, their backs too stiff to ride on the ocean's rhythm. Soon the Morris family was back on the beach, laid out on matching towels in the sunshine.

Watching, George said, "That's what I'd like this place to be, a family beach," and Jack snorted. Inside, Willis's clock tuned up and gave them all four quarters, then ten loud bongs. It seemed much later in the day than that.

"All right, Jack, here comes the hardest part." He dragged the rocker away from Bebe this time. "I had a drunk running this place and was that a mess! He ran up debts, he had women living out here, and one husband would ride by Sundays and shoot the windows out. And he cheated me. I've had others."

"A lot of them left in July, I bet," Jack said. He sat very still.

"Two years ago they started planning that reunion at Fort Bragg, getting the letters out. Patriotism has gone to pot in this country, Jack, you know that? And when I got mine I . . . I remembered you."

Remembered. Bebe looked quickly at Jack. The air felt thick as it does before a storm, but she knew it was only the past, bearing down, and she couldn't think of a single movie which would ease the tension.

"Move your feet, Bebe." Jack joined her in the swing and gave it a hard shove. *Here*-is. *Here*-is. Bebe looked past him at the foaming surf. Jane Wyman got raped in a haymow once, but she was just deaf and dumb. As far as she knew, Helen Keller stayed a virgin. You'd have to go all the way to Italy to see a film like the one George Bennett told.

George kept on in a tone of sincere goodwill. "Nobody in the outfit had your address and there were plenty of other guys nobody could locate. I helped them find a few. And when I started off looking for you I thought—honest, Jack—that maybe you'd just buy the place and rent me a house in July. You could have been filthy rich for all I knew. The VA said they'd lost track of you after you had that hernia fixed in Columbia. I called the last address they had, but you and your wife had moved."

That would be Winston-Salem, that stack of brick apartments in a flat field, before they moved to Durham and Jack started reading books. The swing was moving faster and louder. Around the rusty chain Jack's fingers looked white as bone.

"Then I remembered that river you talked about, the Katsewa River. *Cat*-see-waw, you used to say. Must be Indian. I found it and Stone County on the map, close to the Blue Ridge. I found the two towns, Stoneville and Greenway. I made some calls to the courthouse. Nobody knew Jack, but in Greenway they sure did know the Sellars name."

"Don't push so fast, Jack," Bebe whispered, but he kept pumping as if they were traveling away at speed. They swung back and forth so quickly George seemed to blur to her eye and his cigar stuck out like a second nose.

"They told me about the nine Sellars kids and the orphanage

and how you ran off, but I knew all that from Germany. I didn't know till then your mama was dead and none of the kids came back for her funeral, not even you." He paused, shot a quick uneasy look at Jack. "I hope I'm not the bearer of bad news—I mean, I guess you know that by now?"

Dead in that linen closet in Morganton, Bebe thought, in 1949 and Jack knows because I told him. They buried her right beside her husband—wasn't that strange?

Bebe planted both feet and stopped the swing, getting angry for the first time. "You've got some goddamn nerve, George Bennett."

"This is in strictest confidence. It's always been in strictest confidence, Bebe. I'm telling you all my family secrets, too."

Jack didn't move.

George said again, "Strictest confidence. I kept looking for you now and then out of curiosity, sure. When I'd think about it. I felt a little like a detective—you people read that stuff? Mickey Spillane? Travis McGee?" He saw neither one was going to answer. "People said you'd never set foot in Greenway in all those years that anybody knew about. It seemed like a dead end so I quit it, and another summer came and Rosie came down to Pickerel and then last fall I fired the drunk. I got tired of putting in window glass. Ha ha."

Bebe's bare feet, still pressed flat on the porch floor, kept the swing from moving. Jack's heavier side leaned forward.

George laid his dead cigar on the framing of the porch. "The reunion people found Mickey McCane O.K., and when I met him again at Bragg it called the whole thing to mind again, that's all. Damned if he hadn't seen you someplace in Durham but he didn't know where you lived. I checked with the Durham operator. Nothing. So I thought: Forget it, George. If Jack had showed up down at Bragg, you might have made him some proposition. . . . But Mickey had told you about the reunion. He said you weren't a bit interested."

Bebe stood up, walked across the porch. Remembering all Jack had said: There's a catch in it somewhere. Something wrong with it. . . . The clock pinged ten-fifteen.

"How did you find me then?" If George had only understood that quiet voice he'd have run for his car and driven back to Richmond.

"Just lucky." George smiled. "They had your wife's name on those hospital records, of course. Beatrice Fetner Sellars. I'd written that down." He nodded to her. "It's a pretty name."

Again Jack said softly, "So how did you find me?" Bebe leaned on the screen to watch the Morris family tiptoe into the trailer off the beach, dizzy from the sun.

Rearing back in his chair, George looked proud of this part. "Tell you what I did, Jack. I was in Fayetteville for the reunion and it seemed too close just to *quit,* you know. How far is Durham from Fayetteville—eighty miles or so? I sat in the motel and thought about it. Then I called up the telephone operator back in Greenway, North Carolina, and said I wanted to speak to every Fetner she had listed in the book. And one at a time I asked them all if they had any daughter named Beatrice that might live in Durham. And the fourth one said yes."

There wasn't time for Bebe to stop it. Jack leaped off the swing. He grabbed a handful of George's shirt front and jerked him half out of the rocking chair; he landed a good one midway down his chin. The lower lip split and bled. Bebe never saw so much blood, so quick and red. It trickled under George's hanging jaw, thick as jam, and George threw an arm across his face and bloodied that, too. Jack drew back to hit him again, stared at his own fist, then dropped George into the chair so hard it rocked way back and nearly turned over.

Nobody made a sound and for the first time she knew what slow motion was really like. She moved then but Jack pushed her aside and flung open the screen door and the spring came unscrewed from the wood so the whole door flapped there in the seabreeze. Down the steps two at a time, then he was striding in slow motion over the gray sand, passing the fishermen up the beach. One of them waved.

Then George said, "Oh, my God."

"I'll bring you a wet towel."

He worked two fingers over his dripping chin.

"Don't move," snapped Bebe. "I might hit you myself."

She wrapped ice in a cloth and carried that to the porch and tossed it to him. Pink teeth were balanced on George's knee. "It's a bwidge," he mumbled. "Not weal teeth. Don't wowwy."

"I'm not worried." Not about him. She peered up the beach.

Jack was already out of sight. Somebody—Harold?—had hooked a big fish and was backing out of the surf to reel it in.

Carrying the false lower teeth, George leaned out over the steps to spit. "I told him on the phone I'd make it all up to him. I don't see what he's so goddamn mad about." He yanked but the screen door wouldn't close.

"You had no right," Bebe said.

"Some men," said George, pressing the cold towel to his jaw, "would be flattered. It was like trying to find Judge Crater." Carefully he slid the four false teeth onto his tender gum. The long blood clot on his cracked and swollen lip looked like the black mark of a crayon. "I feel like a patient with Novocain. My whole jaw's numb. Say something, Bebe."

"I'm glad Jack hit you."

At that George wrapped ice over his mouth and closed his eyes. The ice pack muffled something he said about the door. He repeated it. "Can you hear me telling LaVerne I ran into a door?"

Maybe she ought to go after Jack. Bebe could hardly see him down the beach, a small speck moving toward South Carolina. Or could he be headed back this way?

"What was the harm in it?" asked George through the ice cubes. "I needed a manager for some beach property and thought of this guy I knew in the army. The only reason I told him how much trouble I went to was to please him. You tell me, Bebe—what was the harm in that?"

"You could have hired a man from Richmond." George didn't comment. They all knew about Rosie in Richmond.

She sat back in the swing. "You used him, something you knew about him. You even used me." She pictured Grace Fetner picking up her telephone, crying out, "You know my Bebe?" She would have told George everything: Bebe's weight, old smallpox shots, how she won the Greenway spelling bee for eighth graders, where Jack and Bebe lived in Durham and who they both worked for. She would have told him what they bought her last Christmas and which year Bebe wired her a live Easter lily. All about Serena Mae and Walt Fetner besides.

Yes, that might be Jack way down the beach, turning now, headed back to Pickerel. Grace Fetner must be dying to hear if their old friend had ever got in touch with them. Bebe pushed the swing with bare toes and the chains scraped overhead.

"This damn thing hurts."

"There's aspirin in the bathroom, bottom shelf." She wouldn't even look at George. He opened a few wrong doors and turned Zorro loose, tracing them to the porch and letting fall all the urine he had saved up. The hell with it, Bebe thought. Let the wind dry the stain. It's George's floor, not mine.

Sure enough Jack was marching back, getting larger and walking fast, passing the trailers and shell houses at a good clip, stepping where the damp sand gave his bare feet easy grip. He'd hung his shoes around his neck and tied them by the laces. Bebe stopped the swing and opened her mouth to call but he walked right past the house without turning his head, and climbed quickly over a groin going inland from Pickle Beach.

George stepped over the drying puddle on the floor. "I thought that was Jack."

"It was." Maybe Willis and Polly could talk to him.

"It's only one month out of the year and the nurse does everything," George nearly whined. "You'll never know they're here."

One time a preacher called on Walt Fetner about pledging a tithe to the Holiness church, when to make up ten percent her daddy would have needed to give up whiskey. He truly thought the man was mad.

"I'll give you a lifetime deed on this house, Bebe. I'll pay you even if the beach never makes a dime. I'd do more if I didn't have kids of my own."

Big deal. He'd made plenty of money. She knew that.

"George, I've got housework to do. You're welcome to wait but I can tell you Jack won't be home anytime soon. You want to move in one of the trailers?"

"Never thought he'd take this so goddamn hard." George went off with the dripping ice tucked under his chin, stopping to tell Harold and the other fishermen some tale about falling on the steps.

Bebe went straight to the telephone and dialed Greenway direct and got hold of Troy, because he was her favorite. Troy didn't know a thing about it. "Now what was it Mama did? Was this some bill collector?"

"In a way. He could have been some crazy man, some killer, and Mama just pouring out everything. . . . Troy, is she getting childish?"

"We'll neither one live long enough to see Mama get childish." Troy wasn't too clear what Bebe wanted him to do. "Just tell her?"

"Tell her not to do it anymore."

Everybody at home was fine, Troy said, relieved. She began to enjoy the sound of his voice, the twang of it. Earl was getting rich in the used car market. They talked family news—who was sick, in the army, having babies, due in court. In the end she told him she might come home for a few days. "Believe it when I see it," said Troy.

Later, feeding Zorro cold waffles and washing plates, Bebe watched her two hands move in front of her as if somebody else were in charge of them. She didn't feel located in this kitchen at all but scattered loose like pollen on the wind, blowing by Mama and Troy, LaVerne Bennett, floating high over Rosie's railroad bridge where she ate sardines. She thought about Walt Fetner falling in the dark front yard on Connor Street and finally leaning back in the crooked wisteria and hollering for somebody to hold the house still while he came inside. She thought about the cotton mill Allens in Greenway, too rich to speak to the Fetners, though Toby wanted to date her once. And that hot August day they unloaded Serena Mae Sellars's coffin on the porch next door and left it sitting there for hours with Tyna's potted ferns. "Will she spoil?" Troy wanted to know. "How soon does a corpse rot?"

One time Bebe went swimming with her brothers; they were growing hair down there. For all she knew it might grow long as the hair on a head and cover up everything. She'd had great curiosity about bald-headed men for a while. She wondered what a Pinhead like Rosie thought when she got fat and then got skinny and they laid down a baby in her lap. Bebe had wanted five babies, all of them boys. When she got married, Grace Fetner said one thing about babies: if you don't want them, sleep with your feet in a bucket.

So, dreaming and remembering, she cleaned up the house, or at least her hands did. Another part worried about Jack. She made beds, swept sand out the door, dropped dirty clothes in the washing machine. Grinned. Once she had wet her pants and didn't want a whipping so she hung them in the sun where Earl was staking tomato vines. He called her scarecrow-britches for a while.

Used to pull up turnips and eat them raw in the woods. Bums did that, too. They'd drop off the train and be right at the edge of our garden. . . . Depression days then. Daddy could see them picking and digging from his upstairs window. "Let the man be," he'd say. "I been hungry." The garden had gone to weeds long before he died. It was mostly weeds when Jack came home in his uniform and called up in the dusk to ask me if I was dead. I could have been. Came down the ladder and wasn't.

One day, she thought, I hung with my fingernails on a boxcar four miles and had to walk back. I might have gone to Hollywood if people in the sawmills hadn't seen me and yelled and pointed.

To be in this mood, this drifting absent mood . . . Well. That's where she was and the hours went by without Jack coming home. Maybe she took refuge in remembering. Soon it was 2 P.M. by that noisy clock, and still not a word from Jack, and Bebe was passing through the rooms like thistledown.

So Mickey McCane arrived.

And he walked up behind Bebe while the wind was blowing over the sea and through the porch screen onto her face and hair. She simply turned and he stood there, looking at her like a hungry man, starved perhaps, so his look alone changed her and made her more beautiful than Carole Lombard had ever been. Not another thought stirred in Bebe's head. She wrapped her arms around his neck, just by reflex, the way an iron filing is pulled against a magnet. Quickly she was grabbed hard against him. She hardly noticed who he was—just a warm body, male, to rest on. Lord! He seemed to be her daddy and Troy and part Jack. He was like a stranger dropped off some passing train. Under her ear there was the beat of his heart, any heart, maybe every heart. Just for a minute it felt so good standing there, holding tight, waiting for the cameras to dolly into position and the violins to rise; but she couldn't keep her eyes shut forever, and he began to speak his lines. She began to guess who he really was. She tried to get loose. He pulled harder, talking, saying the wrong things. She put her hand over the heart that was Mickey's, now, and pushed it back from her, hard. Now he was staring at her, surprised, his mouth ugly. "What the hell?" he said, or something like that.

She screamed at him, "*You get out of my house!*" He reached again. "*Get out and stay out!*"

Without another word, Mickey left the way he had come. He didn't understand what had happened and, hell, Bebe didn't understand it either. Her chest began to hurt. Not a dream, and yet at the time it felt so much like dreaming.

6

Jack Sellars

June 8–11

Jack almost ran up the beach, pursued, shocked at his own black rage. He had not decided to hit George Bennett. The socket in his shoulder decided that. Jack watched his fist float toward that mouth like a balloon rising on a string. When it hit, the blow ran up Jack's arm and fell down the right side of his body like a lightning bolt that might strike him twice, or three times, or more, until he was nothing but ashes. Maybe Serena Mae felt struck like that when she stood waist deep in the river, uncertain who was victim and who was not. Maybe she couldn't even tell whose blood it was.

He walked faster, leaving Pickle Beach behind. Was it the part about Bebe he couldn't take so the blow was a loyal one struck in her behalf? Or did Serena Mae's nature come to life in him then? Why had George run him down the way dogs run a fox? Why were some brains created with no room to grow and left lying around like clues to an eternal senselessness? Not even sure what his own thoughts were, Jack rushed on.

Pickle Beach angled north and south so the morning was on his left hand and the evening on his right, and the matter of striking George took on that scale to him. What Bebe tried to do with movies, Jack had long tried to do with books; but he had been studying plant cells, photosynthesis, birds and their habits, minerals in the soil, and insects. He had read nothing on the nature of evil, which did not enter into biology anywhere. He did not even know which writers had systematically proved that evil did not exist, and most of his views on environment, heredity, and human progress had been formed by *Life* magazine and were no help to him. Before these questions, he was no better off than the boy who had clung to an overhanging tree limb and watched his mother carry her sharpened ax into the rushing river. Only one difference. In the tree he had not been able to believe that the worst could happen, that she could do it; but she did. Now he was certain the worst could always happen.

But not through me, he thought. Don't let it be through me.

Trailers and houses dipped nearly out of sight when—still hurrying—he reached the southern tip of Pickle and stood by the tidal creek which cut in at an angle and made the highway wheel inland to cross on a causeway. The brackish creek was good for fishing, crabbing, raking up clams. He dropped to the sand beside it and pulled off his shoes. Blood and seawater boomed in his ears. Our protoplasm is like seawater—he'd told Bebe that and she had smiled. Jack didn't smile. Life maybe did start in the ocean, and look how desolate the edges were! Had there ever been landscape so indifferent as the meeting of land and sea? Would he ever have looked at this shore and then crawled out on the hot sand and tried to breathe in the scalding air?

For that you'd have to be more like Bebe, and love life however it could be claimed, without ever needing to love the meaning of life. You'd need to be simpleminded and not give a damn for making sense of things.

Calmer now, and panting less, Jack rubbed the knuckle that had a toothmark in it. That son of a bitch, using Bebe to find me. He was immediately ashamed. If George made use of Bebe, what else had Jack always done?

In the army George and Mickey and he worked their way with the others up the Italian peninsula, in the rain mostly. Mickey would shoot at twigs and shadows. Sometimes he fired that BAR till the steel of its barrel turned reddish purple and warped from the heat and then he'd swap off for a dead man's and shoot some more. In Naples a girl put flowers in Jack's helmet and he carried them around until they had wilted down to weeds. (Now he knew Latin names for the blooms he picked, and still they wilted.) The Germans, before they pulled out, had set time bombs all over Naples, especially inside post offices and telephone exchanges. *Hello? Boom.* The whole city seemed to be ticking. You never knew when a blast would go off. Jack kept moving. George could catnap on top of a minefield, confident, not knowing yet that Rosie and Rosie's son were in his future. He could run black markets under fire. Mickey led the way, pouring out bullets like a machine, proving how brave he was. To one side Jack dodged and listened; his own pulse sounded dangerous. In the center of war, as if in a hurricane's eye, George shook dice for suckers.

Somehow Jack kept expecting to turn into Mickey. Perhaps he had inherited something. Would he not, any minute, turn on the enemy and lash out? He came through the war without discovering that he had any special taste for killing. Only this morning, hitting George, did he feel at last the feeling he expected.

More slowly now, Jack headed north along the beach, again passed the trailers. George's friends from Richmond were casting in the surf. He wondered which house the Pinheads would live in, in July. One of the fishermen spoke to him when he got close, but Jack kept his head down. Any friend of George's is no friend of mine.

Maybe he meant to stop and see if George's jaw was broken but when the house came near he speeded up past whoever might be watching from the porch, climbed over a groin, and walked on. Zorro barked.

Over Willis's store the sun was high and hot. He went in the back door. He was thirsty and his mouth tasted like brass.

Looking up from his clock repairs, Willis lifted his two-digit hand. "I knew you'd have to come see that television set." Jack took a Coke out of the drink box while Willis eased a set of clockworks into a bowl of cleaning solution and removed the verge. "Soon as I get this caked oil out, we'll try it. They're still running special stuff on Kennedy and some of that's in color."

"He's buried, let him stay buried," said Jack.

With a small stiff brush, Willis went over the clock's movement. "Somebody must have used lard in this thing," he grumbled. "The best watch oil, you know, is made from porpoise jaw. Maybe we ought to set up a business at Pickle Beach."

"Willis, how about lending me your truck?"

"Need it for deliveries." Clearly he was irritated because Jack showed no interest in the new television. "What's wrong with your car?"

"I don't want to walk back for it. I might drive up to Wilmington. It's crowded at home."

At that Willis hollered to the cash register that he really *did* see Mickey McCane drive by with that squirrel tail flapping, and tried to tell Jack about Mickey's postcard. "You could borrow the jeep. Have to buy gas." Something was wrong, he saw.

Jack bought the gas. He had not driven a jeep in years, not since they roared through Rome and got lost in old lumpy streets no wider than cowpaths.

In Wilmington's Airlie Gardens, he walked between low

walls of azaleas till he found the topel tree, a hybrid of yaupon and holly. On its limbs grew young berries which would mature three times the size of holly among dark leaves without sharp prickles. He broke off a green berry and let it roll downhill to his palm. At Pickerel he'd planned to develop new plant varieties himself, cross-pollinate, graft strange rootstocks and scions. The untutored Burbank of the Carolina coast!

He wandered along the paths. Plants were so clearly fulfilling their functions at every moment as they grew and flowered and set seed. That some were beautiful or fragrant while some—like poison ivy—raised a rash was all irrelevant. Of course, they fed other creatures and, by their own rhythms, breathed out new oxygen into the air. And rooted the earth so it stayed in place and then died and turned into earth themselves. . . . Jack paused, no longer certain he could distinguish their real functions from those he imposed by wishing. Maybe the holly fruit which the catbirds ate was as random in its way as the sequence of events which had brought him and the others to Pickle Beach.

He almost felt he was doing something at war with this randomness, exercising his own free will, by simply not going home and facing George.

From Airlie he drove to Clarendon plantation, where a fifty-foot-wide canal ran from the steps of the house to the Cape Fear River. He stopped at the cemetery in Wilmington and raked up an armload of Spanish moss and dropped it in the jeep. Maybe he could make it live on that row of cedars. There was a woman buried in that cemetery who died at sea, was propped in a seat and pickled—chair and all—in a cask of rum. All it said over her grave was "Nance."

Mostly he rode around to burn up the gas he'd bought and burn out his anger at George Bennett. In late afternoon he trusted himself to go home again. At Buncombe's, he threw Pauline the jeep's keychain but she caught it one-handed and pitched it, jingling, right back. "Willis?" she called. "He wants to ride home with you. Something about a postcard Mickey sent."

Willis bustled out wearing a contraption laced up around his neck which he'd made by cutting up a tire. He claimed it was a brace to take pressure off his spine and shoulder on rheumatic days. He smelled of hot rubber and menthol. Some days Willis claimed that when he caught his hand in that threshing machine it mangled the nerves and that's what caused the ache in assorted joints. He was the biggest liar Jack had ever met.

Climbing into the jeep, Willis poked at the Spanish moss. "You hang that stuff up, it'll kill your trees."

"No it won't. It's an air plant."

"That's right. Smothers out air and sucks out tree sap."

"It's a bromeliad and doesn't even have any roots, Willis. It lives off air and rainwater."

"Nothing can do that," Willis said flatly.

They parked the jeep by the birdbath at Pickle Beach and a real bird flew off, a black bird with wing patches as red and yellow as Jack's marigolds, crying *konk-a-lee!* It lit on a crooked yaupon tree. Jack leaned forward. "That is the first bird. . . ."

Willis was leaning forward, too, but he asked sharply, "Is that gunfire?"

The redwing flew and, underneath, looked like any other crow. Now Jack heard shots coming from the beach. He ran ahead up the shell-strewn path until he saw a crowd at the water's edge, Bebe off by herself, thank God. Somebody had a gun lined up at his shoulder. He stepped forward out of the fishermen and aimed upward at a bird—not black, some kind of gull—and fired. Shotgun. The bird gave off bits of tissue paper falling into the ocean. The fishermen laughed, George

Bennett with them. Sheila Morris ran back and forth pointing out other things to be shot. Then Mickey bent to lay his shotgun down and took up a pistol and sent George aside to toss up a beer can for him. The first two times he missed, but then the can jerked loose from gravity, sprang higher, followed the gull into the waves.

Behind him Willis said, "Mickey can handle that thing," and passed Jack going down the dune.

"Always could," said Jack.

Bebe had seen them. She lifted one hand over her head. When Jack did nothing she just went on standing there with one arm straight up like the Statue of Liberty, and waited. Finally Jack raised his own. She walked away from the others uphill through the beach poppies and sea oats. She was wearing one of his shirts and looked like a barefoot child in a smock. Closer, he could see her wide smile.

"You busted his lip good," she chortled. "And one of his false teeth bent." She laid two fingertips against his throat. She said softly, "I hate that George found you through me."

"Let's go out to supper," said Jack. "I'm tired of all these people."

Bebe nodded. They left the crowd still shooting on the beach, tearing up beer cans and sheets of cardboard. By the time both were dressed and ready to leave, Mickey had Sheila Morris trying a rifle, helping her hold it up and absorb the recoil while Mr. Morris made a photograph for their memory book. They seemed, together, to be aiming the rifle southwest past the creek where the sun was sliding down, as if it were a light bulb anyone could pop. On the side, Mickey flirted a little with Mrs. Morris. Next to whores, Jack thought, he's always liked mothers. Raved all over Italy about young women who nursed their babies in public. He claimed once to have screwed a *mamma mia* with her baby in the same bed, and said that while he pumped up and down the kid lay on a pillow and stared at his face. Never blinked a time.

"What about Willis?" Bebe said.

Jack laid the keys to the jeep on the porch table. "Mickey and he can find them and see he gets home," he said shortly. "I don't know which one lies the worst."

Sunday, before George left, he handed Jack a lifetime deed to the beach house and promised to raise his monthly check. George's mouth was blue and hung out like a tree gall on his chin. He stood by the station wagon and waited for Jack to say he was sorry about hitting him; but Jack wasn't sorry.

Jack carried the papers into the house, sat on the raised brick hearth to unlock his strongbox and put the deed inside. There were snapshots in the box. Bebe on an Easter Sunday, wearing a rose corsage. High heels with platform soles and her big toe showing. One of Jack in his corporal's uniform, taken in a do-it-yourself booth at some county fair. His head was nearly shaved and there was something stripped and gullible about the face, too—the country boy who doesn't know yet that corporal is as high as he'll ever go.

Under these, wrapped in waxed paper, the dim face of Serena Mae Sellars when she was twenty years younger than Jack was now. Such a high brow and pointed chin, the mouth so small it did not match the curve of his fingernail. Only small, harmless words should have ever been in that mouth. And maybe they would have, had she not married and gone to that river shack, each year harder and poorer, each year one more baby, some years a dead one.

Jack could not remember this pictured gentle woman with

her slender not-quite-smiling face. She was knit of strings and thongs and calluses when he knew her, and one of those dreamy eyes had twitched day and night. She could not sleep, she said, since the Lord had his fishhook in her eye and jerked eternally on his long, immortal line. He put the box away.

A few days later Bebe handed him a postcard addressed to her, unsigned, mailed from Greenway. One handwritten sentence on the back. "I didn't know you was hiding."

"It's from Mama," Bebe said. She tried to sound angry but her mouth smiled. "I told Troy how mad I was." She rolled it into a tube and stuck it behind the clock. "I ought to go see her, no kidding."

The beach was full of vacationers by then, mostly middle-aged couples who fished all day with cigarettes in their mouths and never talked to each other. At supper Bebe said, "Mama must have laid awake half the night thinking that through. She stuck it in the corner mailbox—I can just see her—and banged the handle shut and started home and then had to go back and look in to make sure her card really fell out of sight."

He saw she was determined to go. "Have you answered it yet?"

She shook her head. A loose yellow hair drifted to the rim of her plate. "Mama thinks it's possible for a letter to get stuck in that flip-handle and stay there till the year two thousand." She smiled at her fork, turned it over in her hand and smiled at that side, too.

Jack didn't want her to go. Her last trip home was to the Stone County Hospital, where her daddy died with Bebe sitting by his bed. That, and one quick day when Grace Fetner broke her hip. Both times she came back white and tired, drained, almost translucent, and it was weeks before she felt like his again. He'd ask her what she was thinking and she'd spread wide her arms. "There is this big . . ." she'd say and stop, shaking her head. Or she'd slide her fingers between each other and hook them the way kids play church-and-steeple, look at her interlocked knuckles, try again. "Things go together more than . . ." and then give up that sentence, too.

But he reached across the table and tapped her hand. "Well, if you're going to go, now's the best time, before the Pinheads come."

"I think I will," Bebe said. A rising wind suddenly blew through the house and slammed doors open, scaring the dog, and while they were pulling down windows the rain began.

Mickey McCane

June 11

The more he thought about it, the more Mickey viewed that moment when Bebe came into his arms as a foretaste of things to come. He was even relieved that she had resisted him. This proved how strong the attraction was and that unfaithfulness was no everyday thing with her.

He drove home to Angier, whistling. She had avoided him ever since at the beach, except in groups, and he understood that. Wouldn't shoot targets with him. He had placed every bullet clean and true in her honor, certain she understood. In his presence Bebe seemed tense and would not even let her gaze touch his. To Mickey, guilt and desire were twins and she seemed half won by her very stiffness and avoidance.

He had seen prettier women, even bought a few. Joining the army underage, he had come to manhood with his wallet and, even now, preferred the clean air of businesslike sex. No, Bebe was not the most beautiful. Even Eunice, at twenty, had been delicate and ladylike, with body hair unbelievably fine, and low-slung heavy hips almost out of place on such a small woman. Now she had grown dumpy with a patchy scalp, was shaped like a pear, and spoiled his sons. One of them even played the flute at school. At least she stayed home and ran the house—more than his own mother ever did. Eunice boiled her own jellies, canned, cooked homemade soups. She went to the PTA as she was supposed to. Migraine and hay fever bothered her, skin rashes, monthly cramps, palpitations—harmless and chronic, the small ailments women expected to have when their lives ran so smoothly they were protected from serious matters like money or war.

For sex, Eunice was boring. Naturally. He went in full and came out empty and that was about it. Eunice felt no more from him than from her greasy diaphragm—another foreign body she would, after a while, dislodge. He had expected no more from a wife than this and left her alone for long stretches of time. Some days he sat in the laundromat reading paperbacks from the Angier newsstands, mostly about queers and lesbians and foursomes, none of which he could stand, and later might couple with Eunice with some sense of setting the world a normal example. Mickey was especially alert to queers. Any man wearing cufflinks in his shirt made Mickey sneer. He'd heard the navy and the North Carolina prison camps were full of queers and he followed the Harnett County courts, watching for young men who would be sentenced and confined and punished for auto theft in ways they never dreamed. There was a justice at work that evened all things out. He was sure of that.

Bebe was part of the justice due him. Some loose generosity in the way she walked went straight to his loins. He saw she was slowly coming to him the way apples come to their own ripeness and let go of the tree for no more reason than the one extra minute of sunshine which breaks the stem.

Probably, although she didn't know it yet, she would set out for Greenway and come to him. Would walk right into the laundromat in Angier, surprised at herself. Would follow him silently to the car. Maybe he wouldn't even drive out of the alley but would watch her while she turned around in the backseat and let him get both hands under her and take her from behind so her face would be hidden but all the sounds she made familiar; and the wild rolling of her head exactly as he had thought, years ago, it would be bound to feel, grinding against his shoulder.

He would go back to the beach once more before she left and remind her how easy he was to find. Two blocks from the Angier bus station; she could walk it. They would go out to the alley without a word.

After that Mickey did not know what would happen, except that his life would change.

7

Bebe Sellars

June 12–16

Now that she planned to go home to Greenway, the week was boring and passed slowly. Her mind was on that, and Jack's on the Pinheads coming. She pictured the Pinheads in their institution, the boy weaving baskets, neither of them able to predict which month they would travel to the coast. Perhaps they had both forgotten the Atlantic altogether.

At Pickle Beach the houses and trailers were full of retired clerks and their gray-haired wives. The wives wore pink playsuits from Belk's, size sixteen, and the men looked like schoolboys playing hooky and trying to figure out when the fun of it would start. Afternoons they wandered over to visit Jack and Bebe, talking of those parts of the past which were harmless and, therefore, uninteresting. Something had gone out of life for them, Bebe thought, when the fears went out. Now their checks arrived on the right dates in the mail, and the children had outlived childhood and gone on. They talked about chiropractors and tonics. Sunshine, they said, was full of vitamin D and fresh fish were low in cholesterol. Only one fear remained to them and spiced up their quiet lives. The merriest of the lot was a man who had once had cancer and had it cut out and now, he said, lived one day at a time. That reminded Bebe of a string of beads with only one bead on it.

Wednesday she was viewing the morning TV movie, *Picnic,* and waiting for the moment Kim Novak and William Holden would dance while the orchestra played "Moonglow." In the kitchen Jack rattled the trailer keys. One was emptying that day. His voice sounded funny. "Guess who's out here?"

She was almost into the movie herself, almost dancing. "Richard Burton," she snapped.

"It's Mickey and some other man from Angier."

In the middle of the week? Why didn't he just move in? Through her teeth Bebe said, "Jesus Christ."

"His cash is as good as anybody's."

"Doesn't he have anything else to do with his time or anyplace else to go? Couldn't he bring his wife once? Or does she have to run the laundromat?" She watched Rosalind Russell on the little screen. Her stomach felt funny.

Jack said quietly, "I guess a laundromat pretty well runs itself by staying open twenty-four hours a day. The customers do the rest."

"Aren't you beginning to feel like a laundromat?"

He came to the door and stared at her. "What's the matter, Bebe?"

"Nothing. Instead of Saturday I might leave Friday. Is that O.K.?"

"He's not getting to you, is he?"

"He stinks."

Once Mickey had told Jack about this job he used to have filling up gum and peanut machines. . . . He'd watch the newspaper for obituaries of men under forty-five along his route, in a month or so call on their widows and claim to have known Phil or Ralph or Lincoln in the Elks, the Legion, the Moose. In time, some of these women lay cooling and drying in his arms, half convinced that by screwing Jonathan they had done something fine in King David's memory.

Big deal, thought Bebe.

Jack said, "How long will you stay in Greenway?"

"Four or five days." By the time Bill Holden and Kim began to gaze at each other and move at arm's length under the Japanese lanterns, she wasn't in the mood, but felt tense as the schoolteacher who would rip his shirt in the next scene.

The day dragged by. She'd see Mickey at a distance, aiming his gun, shooting down pyramids of soft-drink bottles. She complained to Jack about broken glass left scattered on the sand.

And she couldn't relax. It might not matter whether a woman chases or runs from a man, whether she's drawn to him or repelled. Any strong feeling could have the same effect. Either way, the thought of him was stuck in Bebe's brain like a splinter. Outdoors, she looked carefully away from the trailer where Mickey was staying. If he stood in the yard, she hurried back upstairs with her full bag of garbage, not even wanting him to wave. She no longer spoke his name, and it did in her head what her brother Earl's TB had done in his lungs—got sealed off alive and churning with a shell around it.

Later, as she sunbathed behind the cedars, his voice caught up with her. "Hello, beautiful." Eyes closed, she lay spread on her stomach and barely grunted an answer.

"You hiding from me?"

Not even a grunt. Mickey lowered himself alongside. She could see the black hairs above his ankle. He slid a burnt match into the sand, blew cigarette smoke at her head. "I hear George got hit, heh heh, by a guided muscle."

Bebe lay very stiff. She was not sure why she had caught hold of him that day on the porch. Maybe it was accidental, the act of a dream as she thought. But maybe worse. Maybe she was even sunbathing in this spot so he would find her. Once Jack had scared Bebe by saying nobody could ever be sure why he did things; Froyd—(Froid?)—had proved that. She'd laughed. Now she wished she had listened more closely.

Mickey looked around to make sure Jack wasn't in sight. Then he wrapped his dry hand around her wrist. "How you been, honey?"

"You want to get hit your own self?"

"Nobody here but us chickens."

Chicken hawks. She moved away, more distrustful of her own natural reactions than she had ever been in her life. Mickey seemed, in some ways, a paler Jack, washed out like those light blue eyes. His want made her see her own body as it must look to him, and it looked younger. What if I couldn't help myself? The idea was almost sweet, like being carried away by the current. She rolled farther away and sat up on the towel. "Mickey, let me alone."

"You don't want me to let you alone."

And maybe she didn't. Temptation, all by itself, was exciting no matter who tempted or what he was like. He's cruel, she thought, and shivered.

She said firmly, "I said let me alone." She would try to explain it to him. "The other day, Mickey, had nothing to do with you. It didn't mean a thing. You could have been a doorpost for all I cared."

"That's a damn lie." He scooted across the sand to face her. He wore a pistol strapped to his belt like a deputy. Bebe was afraid of guns. "Why do you think I hotfooted it back down here, Bebe? I read you loud and clear." There unreeled in her head long celluloid strips of girls kissed against their will and weakening, reprobates courting heiresses, evil hypnotists and magicians. She saw Paulette Goddard carried screaming (with delight?) through the jungle by savages.

Mickey pushed his face forward. "I read you, all right. Too much woman for old Jack, that's all. And just enough woman for Mickey McCane." He tried for a burning look under his black eyebrows—the second childhood of Elvis Presley. Suddenly it was laughable. He was stupid. Not Svengali but the gambler in a lace shirt from a hundred westerns. A loser. Bebe smiled.

"Jack would make ten of you," she said, "in bed or out."

"Don't knock it till you've tried it." Mickey laughed.

She was tempted to tell him what a bluff he was and that she knew it. Still, she thought to stand him off without hurting his feelings, since it was her own fault he was making this try; so she took a deep breath and said, in just the kind way Loretta Young would have said it, "Let's just say I'm happy at home, O.K.? If I gave you the wrong impression, Mickey . . ."

"You don't know yet what happy is."

She jumped up and started shaking sand out of the towel. His look ran over her like hot water. She didn't even like him. If some hunchback had looked at her with desire she might, even briefly, desire that desire the way any doctor thumping her knee with his red rubber hammer could make her whole leg fly up. But Mickey seemed so confident that it shook her, as if he knew weaknesses in her she had not spotted yet.

"Get one thing straight," she said, and heard the rising anger in her voice. "I don't sleep around. I know plenty do. For all I know even Jack Sellars has—but I don't care about that. I don't even care that it's stylish now. I'm not in charge of anybody but me."

He looked, at first, astonished. He looked like a comic skating on ice which suddenly cracks in a zigzag between his feet and again she almost laughed. But quickly his sideburns sprang low on his jaws when he frowned. "Don't give me that sweet sixteen stuff, not at your age. You know the score, all right." He tensed his muscles and slid the hand with its Moose club ring around his leather belt. "A middle-aged prick tease—that's the limit."

Bebe threw the towel out like a sail and flapped sand grains all over him. "The limit," she screeched back, "is a guy with a powder puff in his britches bragging himself to death!" Her hands were quivering.

Mickey's face flamed suddenly red. He lit up with sunstroke. Nothing moved but his right hand over the gun butt. She thought he might jerk it out and hit her in the throat. Bebe dropped the towel and stumbled up the back steps into the kitchen, locking the door behind her. Shaking all over.

I've got to get out of here, away from him, go home. He's not just a flirt—I could understand that—but the way his face looked! I thought his whole head might explode. He's more like a rapist that can't do the rape and blames me for it.

Bebe jerked Zorro off the kitchen floor and carried him back and forth through the house while he gnawed at her hand.

I'll tell Jack what happened, of course. I can't do that.

She peeped out the edge of the window shade. Mickey had walked over the dune and met Jack. They stopped to talk. Maybe Mickey was telling his version, even now: That broad you married threw herself all over me and now she thinks she's Queen Victoria. Standing in the sunlight they looked the same size, Mickey a little leaner. Bebe knew every part of Jack's body, could walk up to him now and touch through his clothes the place where that wart grew low on his spine.

In the pastures around Greenway there used to be a plant in a little brown ball against the ground. If you walked on it a rusty powder flew out and spattered your bare foot. Satan's snuffbox. That dark bulb low in the grass, ripening its dust for the first foot that came its way. She felt she had walked on the thought of Mickey, and it had burst and dirtied her.

She worked her way through the rest of Wednesday, doing penance. She baked cakes, froze spaghetti sauce, sewed buttons on Jack's shirts, ran new elastic through the waistband of his boxer shorts. She cleaned out drawers and used her ruined nylons to stuff porch cushions. Polished his shoes, cleaned doorknobs with steel wool. Cut a bleach bottle into an imitation birdhouse for Jack to hang from the yaupon tree. By nightfall Bebe almost ached.

After supper she popped corn for Jack, laced with real butter instead of margarine, and heaped it in a salad bowl so they could eat together on the dark porch. She arranged herself in the swing, Jack opposite in a chair against a new lumpy cushion.

"Let's talk," said Bebe, biting down on a fluff of popcorn which quickly turned back into the hard kernel it used to be. I'll explain that it's up to him to get rid of Mickey McCane.

"You think poinciana would live through the winter here?"

Poinciana! Big deal.

"I can take a bus out of Wilmington and leave you the car. Mama must be lonesome."

"Your brothers live in Greenway and their wives." He did not add, "and their children," closing his mouth slowly to trap those words before they could get out. This made Bebe tender toward him and she slipped her own hand under the loose shirt around her left breast, as if Jack had pressed her on the heart and said: There now. It even felt like his hand. She couldn't mention Mickey then.

"You wouldn't like to come with me? You've never been home one time since we got married."

"That place stopped being home when I was fourteen. Besides, I've got the beach to run."

And he's got me. Take that, Mickey! She smiled in the dark. Her own flesh was a damp weight in her hand as if her heart might fall.

It was too dark for Jack to see her smile and besides, he was rustling his fingers in the popcorn bowl. "Saturday, then. I'll drive you."

Why couldn't he say: I'll miss you? She knew it was true.

She squirmed in the swing, restless. The beach lay around them so still it seemed like a foreign place, nothing at all the way it looked in daylight. Take away that harsh glare of sun and there was nothing left but this enormous beauty in a few colors, by itself, with no purpose to it. The moon cast black shadows like noontime and the stars seemed so thick they almost showered down. The ocean looked solid. I could walk on top of it, Bebe thought, or lie down and roll on its cool silver waves and be silver myself. Lights burned in the trailer windows as if to decorate the dunes. She sucked in the salty air and felt light-headed, swollen, stuffed with air. Maybe a conch in its shell, rolling on the ocean floor, felt stuffed with water.

In a place looking like this, in her mood, they should be talking of life or death or God or time or even Froyd—she couldn't imagine such a thing nor how other people got started at it. That nun could eat hot dogs and onions and talk about Jesus anytime, she thought; and let the chains on the porch swing groan as she moved. That nun had practiced. She and Jack didn't know how. But I'd like to, she thought—and the chains groaned—I'd like to know: Does the world breathe? Am I part of what it blows lightly into space?

Nobody but nuns could say things like that out loud. Maybe if she talked first about the reality both could see, they'd get promoted up as the conversation went along. She scanned the beach: sand, the wide water on which stars rained down like light through a colander. It seemed worth a try when she was leaving soon and, for all Jack knew, might be in a bus wreck on the way.

So Bebe pointed out to sea and said nervously, "No sky was

ever like this in Durham." Jack ate popcorn by the double handfuls. Bebe tried pointing upward. "How clear it is!" He was chewing, chewing, like a rat in the walls.

She cried out, "Jack, if I died would you remember me?"

He almost dropped the bowl. "What brought that on? Don't say that, Bebe!"

She guessed there was no *way* to say it. They tried to make out each other's faces in the dark. There were hardly ever long silences in movies. Even when people failed to talk, the music rose and seemed to be talking for them.

Suddenly Jack said, "There's Mickey."

"Where?" Bebe jumped, trying to see all directions at once. At the first gunshot she jumped again. "I wish he'd quit that."

"He's a good shot. He keeps in practice on a shooting range at home and goes hunting all the time. Got two buck up in Linville Gorge last fall."

"When are they going home?"

"He hasn't said. They've got a charter picking them up tomorrow for deep sea fishing." Jack leaned back in his chair. The shots didn't bother him.

Bebe asked, "Has Mickey ever been in trouble with the law?" Wasn't life crazy? She was in the mood to talk about the universe and had to talk about *him*.

"Not that I know of. Why?"

"He seems like the kind of man that might lose his temper and beat a guy to death. I get that feeling."

"I don't think he'd beat a man to death. Maybe a woman."

Goosebumps along her skin. "Why a woman?"

"Things he's said. Maybe a nigger, too. I think he's in the Klan, myself. He talks about that Cotton Club back home and it smells like Klan to me."

"A real peach," Bebe said. "Have you ever met his wife?"

"George has. Says Eunice had money and Mickey married

her for it, but you know how George is. That would make sense to him."

A tin can leaped, caught the light, and winked out. Bebe couldn't tell whether Mickey was using his rifle or a pistol. Jack said he'd brought a shotgun, too. "And he's really no good in the sex department?"

"Well, he's weak, more or less. Undependable. That's what he's got against blacks. The size."

"He never admitted to you about being impotent?"

"No, a hooker told me. Said nothing much happened, but Mickey had already bragged about how she returned his money because he made her moan so good and all." Jack yawned. "Mickey's supposed to have told her he always wanted a woman who would lick him between the toes."

Bebe laughed aloud. Did he think I ever would? She dismissed him. He and the others at Pickle Beach had come out of nowhere and would go back again. So everybody here was a bit peculiar, but living awhile did that, served up surprises. Cut off fingers and dealt face cards. Little jokes. All Rosie did was run off from a picnic and next thing you know there was a new pinheaded baby in the world. She remembered the nun saying, "Even to be an error and to be cast out is part of God's design." Bebe liked that and copied it out on a charge slip although the nun said it wasn't original. If I could see Mickey from up where the moon is, I know I'd laugh. The laughter swelled in her on general principles, and she began pushing the swing at a great rate until it said *hee-haw* almost as loud as Mickey's gun could shoot.

Jack leaned forward and caught one of her ankles with his buttered hand. "What's funny?"

"Everything," Bebe said.

"Let's take a shower." She knew he was smiling now, dark or not. In their early marriage, they soaped each other in the spray and the smaller the shower stall was, the better they liked it. So tonight it seemed the right end to a day Bebe had spent sewing and cooking for him. Their bodies were heavier now, the narrow stall crowded. If Bebe looked down her wet stomach bulged and she had to suck in a hard breath to see her own pubic hair. High on her right thigh was a varicose web . . . she called them webs. It made her think of hidden spiders and tonight she could smile about them, too. Jack had a growing swayback and his chest sloped down to his stomach. He rubbed his wet palms down her sides and the clean skin squeaked. Jack was already horny but when his mouth first opened hers, Bebe felt more like a child, limp with trust. His tongue tasted of her own wet hair and she closed her eyes thinking of oatmeal and safety.

Against her chin Jack said, "Turn off the water."

Blindly she reached behind him to close the taps. Cool, still dripping, her nipples shriveled. They stepped together onto the mat, leaving the lights off, scrubbing each other with the nubby towels. Slowly she began to feel what he felt as her spine grew hot under the moving cloth, so she leaned on him, walking unevenly to the bed, falling facedown so he could coax her slowly over.

"I love you, Jack."

He did not seem to hear. They were not talkers at such times. When Bebe rolled to her back his face was dark but the air in the room was light around him, almost vaporous. She touched, unerringly, the place where the wart grew near his vertebrae. The small of his back was downy. Outside, in the wrong rhythm, the gunshots sounded.

Saturday morning they arrived in Wilmington too early for the bus. She had kept away from Mickey all that week, and hurried them away to the bus before anyone stirred in the trailers.

Mickey worked hard to see her alone and once slipped her a note which had the address of his laundromat and the sentence, "I don't know who told you that lie." She wrote back, "Willis, who else?" and passed it back in plain view of everybody, winking at Jack and telling Pauline it was ticktacktoe.

So they were in Wilmington long before the bus was ready. Jack insisted on waiting with her. He had stayed with her in the hospital, too, even after the sedatives, although Bebe had begged him to go home because he made her nervous. When the doctor said they were taking Mrs. Sellars now, Jack nearly broke his neck getting out into the air. The last injection made Bebe silly. She had meant to be Jennifer Jones. Instead they rolled Betty Hutton down the hall and she kept sitting up on the cart and telling the orderly her womb was doomed.

At last the bus arrived, blowing air from its brakes, and Jack gave her hairline a quick rub with his chin before she boarded. He never kissed her in a public place. Bebe waved through the dusty window. He nodded. As they backed from the curb she thought of dragging down the window and letting the whole crowd hear that she loved Jack Sellars and making him, for once, say the same words right out loud. She had been made to recite, every night before sleeping, "If I die before I wake, I pray the Lord my soul to take," on the theory nobody ever knew which words were his last ones. The last thing her uncle said to his wife was, "Oh, hell, I'm out of razor blades." What was *that* to remember? She put a kiss on her fingers and pressed it toward Jack through the window glass.

The bus was half empty and after the seabreeze its cool air tasted artificial. The wet land they passed was deep green and black, a rich home for the cottonmouth moccasin, its oaks and pines strung with moss which hung and blew like dirty cheesecloth. In seats ahead of Bebe, necks relaxed, heads began to loll against mats already stained with sweat and hair grease.

She could only see into two faces directly across the aisle—a young girl and her baby. The girl couldn't be much over sixteen. Both looked hypnotized. The baby lay crosswise in her lap as if he had fallen there from a height and been too dazed to struggle. One bare foot flexed from time to time. The mother stared straight ahead, her hand dropped on the child's navel as it might lie on the snap of a pocketbook.

The bus passed through the town of Maco, recently featured in newspapers again because of its ghost light which appeared along the railroad on moonless nights and was thought to be a lantern carried by a headless flagman run down by a train long ago. Still the ghost searched for his head beside the tracks. Some townsmen said nothing but swamp gas made that light. Bebe wished she could see it once.

The girl shifted her baby onto the seat beside her, found a bottle of red medicine in the diaper bag, and took a swallow. She gave Bebe an angry look. "I've got this headache."

Paregoric, maybe. Or phenobarbital? Bebe used to read Dr. Spock learning symptoms and remedies when she still thought there might be babies. She wanted to know in advance whether a child should drink ipecac or milk when he swallowed a certain poison, and which bumps were roseola and which were scarlet fever.

She watched the mother replace the medicine. And the child had such a stunned exhausted face that maybe he was being treated for headache, too? "Little boy?"

"Yes." Eyes closed, she leaned back so Bebe could go on looking at her pinched face—an adolescent squirrel's face, an immature weasel's. Acne had left pits on her sharp chin. Even so, she was very young with eyelids as smooth as eggs. Her discarded baby flipped his foot and watched the light and shade flow by.

She did not leave the bus for lunch in Lumberton and from a stool in the station café Bebe could see her bent head framed in the window. She bolted her own sandwich so she could offer to watch the baby and let the mother eat.

"You mean it?" Despite her suspicious stare, both hands were scrambling on the seat for cigarettes and money. "He's got a bottle in the bag if he starts crying. I sure do thank . . ." She was gone, half skipping among the baggage carts, biting an unlit filter cigarette with her grin. Bebe heard her laugh at the driver and warn him not to leave without her. She eased the baby to her right shoulder, where he attached himself by suction like a caterpillar. His scalp was damp, almost sour. How soft the skin on his temple where the blood beat! She traced his balled fist. A thread of spit and curdled milk hung from his mouth.

"Yes," she cooed to him, rocking them both in the stiff seat. "Yes, it's fine, it's just fine, yes." His eyes were the color of ink. "Yes, it's all right, laddy, yes." When his hair brushed her face it felt nothing like hair. More like the edge of the wind.

What if the driver should really forget her? The idea knifed through Bebe. Would it be so strange if, even by accident, she earned a child at last?

Under the plastic pants his diaper was a twisted wad of wet cloth. Bebe laid him carefully on his back, pulled off the pants, and stuck the pins in the fat upholstery. His skin was raw. With the air-conditioning turned off while the bus was parked, the smell of ammonia seemed very strong. She found clean diapers in the bag, even dusting powder, and the baby did not make a sound even when lifted by both ankles and repinned. His navel stuck out like a tiny mushroom.

One by one the passengers drifted back from lunch. Bebe could see the girl chewing her second hot dog at the counter.

Likely she'd never wanted a baby at all, no more than Rosie did, and some half-forgotten boy had left one growing in her by mistake.

The baby's bottle lay deep in the bag against another soiled diaper but well sealed. Bebe rested him in the cradle her left arm made and he drew the rubber nipple between his gums and sent long strands of bubbles through the milk. The driver, stepping into the bus, ran his eye over the seats. Bebe kept her head down, watching the baby drink.

But almost immediately the girl's voice was heard at the door. "Trying to get rid of me?" The driver laughed and answered something. Giggling she came down the aisle and put out both hands.

"I'll be glad to keep him awhile longer for you."

She said no, she'd do it. "Thank you."

Bebe stood, holding him so he fit against her as well as a peach pit in a peach. "I love children." (It's ugly to beg, she thought.)

"I'll be glad when this one finally sleeps the whole night. Maybe I can settle down to loving him when I get one decent night's sleep."

The baby, snatched away, was laid on his back on the prickly seat by the window. Hardly did he get his mouth open to cry before the nipple went in again. She propped the bottle on her hip and resettled herself with a magazine. "Your kids grown up and gone by now?"

Bebe turned away. "All gone, yes."

When the bus finally ground out of the station she could no longer hear him smack and bubble, and rode with both eyes tightly shut. They said when you had a newborn and he drew at your breast that your womb would throb in tune to his suck. Bebe had heard that in the hospital, just before surgery. It seemed to her that would be like having orgasm go on and on and that afterward you would fall down into sleep the way a star falls.

Later she heard the girl shuffling into loafers, scraping her bag off the rack. Bebe kept her eyelids down. The bus stopped and, one second later, her stomach stopped with a jerk against the skin. She could feel the girl's face coming warmly toward her closed one; the onions and mustard came, spearmint, sour milk, then the whisper, "Thank you." Bebe pretended to be asleep. Not until they were out the bus door did Bebe look, and she was stepping over the soft asphalt and spilled soda toward a taxi stand, the baby's head barely showing above her blue shoulder. Something moved in Bebe like an ache, maybe her womb trying to throb the way an amputee's foot will itch. For a minute it seemed the young mother, crawling into a cab, would not bend low enough to spare the baby's head. The bus drove away before the taxi did, and Bebe could not even tell whether she had carried him north or south in whatever town it was.

By dark she was nearly to Greenway. She staggered down the aisle to the boxed toilet, determined to arrive with clean hands and an empty bladder. She had not asked anyone to meet her. She was headed back down the aisle when they swerved off the highway onto the darker roads. From memory Bebe knew when they would pass the junked cars and Cooley's Body Shop, and after that a blackened lot where the Chat 'n' Nibble used to stand before its french fryer caught fire. Then came the big quiet houses with their balconies and oval doorpanes. When she was twelve her biggest goal had been to live on this side of town. Still lighting the business district were the old-fashioned streetlights which looked like giant tulips on green metal stems.

The bus wheezed into the ugly terminal behind Home Finance and the driver climbed down, disgusted because at this late hour he must lift the side flap of the bus to find Bebe's suitcase while she waited behind him testing one tickly foot and then the other. The pavement smelled. Oil, syrup, bird droppings, ketchup, spit—all were rotting in its pores.

She waved down the first taxi. "Connor Street—217 Connor."

Streets near the Allen Cotton Mill had names like that: Hill and Newton, Rickert, Armfield, Stimpson—easy streets to live on, not asking much of people, streets that were among the last in town to be paved, in a neighborhood where the last surviving icemen staggered across bare yards with cold blocks on their shoulders and turned over the yellow pasteboard octagons nailed on the front porch post when delivery was complete. Bebe was forty years old and for half her life had used an icebox. She could still remember the stables below the icehouse where retired horses, replaced in the end by trucks, lived out their days.

She leaned forward to see the broad street, Buena Vista (pronounced here Byoona Vesty), then the cab turned onto Connor, where the first downhill block of houses tried to have two stories and good chimneys and a brick retaining wall for the front yard. The second block—the Fetners'—was already falling toward the railroad tracks. Its few remaining big houses sold off their side yards in the thirties and grew tin-roofed boxes for neighbors, some of them fronted with false maroon sheets of asphalt brick.

Jack's Aunt Tyna had lived in the last tall one before the tracks, at 215. The Fetners lived in the box in the yard she sold, where once she grew roses and sweet corn, right by the railroad. Every dish in their cabinets got shaken by passing trains. Along the street downhill from the Fetners there had never been any big houses, just pastures turned into milltown, low tin roofs and chinaberry trees, one plywood plant, the line where a steel mesh fence ran around the Allen mill.

Bebe paid the cabdriver under a new blue streetlight drooping from an aluminum pole, harsh on the flaked paint and the porch Mama's old wisteria had pulled slightly to one side. The house looked dark.

Next door, Aunt Tyna's had been painted charcoal gray and bore, like a cancerous growth, six mailboxes on one side of the front door and six electric meters on the other. Hers was noisy and well lighted, all the shades pulled to different levels, one air-conditioner rusting in the attic window. Bebe's yard grew nothing but gray crabgrass and dusty thistle and plantain.

She dragged her suitcase to the low chunk of cement which served as a stoop. Walt Fetner brought that home in a pickup, drunk, one night after strikers dynamited the depot bridge. He always claimed to have set off the charge. He spent the rest of his life falling on it or off it in the dark.

She hoisted the suitcase onto the porch. She could choke on this sooty, dusty air after the wet tang of the beach. The scrolled elaborate door had been rescreened but its handle was still a large wooden spool.

"Mama?" she called, and was choking sure enough. The goddamn thing was latched; she rattled it on its hooks and called, "Mama?" After all that getting wet in her eye, Grace Fetner wasn't home. Some scrawny dog chained to a clothes-line barked from Aunt Tyna's yard. Should have written. What if Mama's staying with kinfolks this week, if somebody's sick, maybe even out in the country? Bebe kicked the old door half a dozen times.

"Mama, if you're in there, *wake up!*" Something fell inside the house; some tin thing passing trains had been inching for days toward the edge of a shelf or a table leaped off in a dark room and rattled on the hard floor. Too hard for linoleum. The hall, Bebe thought, or maybe the pantry.

She put one eye to the screen but the doorpane beyond was black. That gauze curtain on each side might be wavering only from memory. The old porch swing had been taken off its chains and turned backward to the wall and, in the blue light, shone with webs. Bebe sat on her daddy's cement chunk with the river pebbles embedded in it to slide off her shoes and unhook her stockings and pull them off. She put her bare feet flat on the orange ground she had so often swept. The clay was stony hard but the top quarter inch was as fine as ash. Fine as baby powder.

Must be a telephone next door, she thought. She rubbed her soles back and forth in the dust, remembering how when Jack's mother died in the asylum her coffin sat half a day on that front porch. Aunt Tyna's husband wouldn't have it inside his house. "All right," said she, and carried her lunch out—beans and buttermilk—and set it up right on the casket and dragged a chair over and ate off Serena Mae Sellars as if she were a banquet table.

Bebe's mama had to drink a Coke with ammonia just to bear up under watching the whole thing through her window. "Lord," Mama said. "She'll be getting wet rings on that coffin. From buttermilk! That is the ugliest thing I ever heard!"

Lester came once to the front door and swore at Tyna and later he hung out the attic window and yelled down to his wife that she was the craziest one *in* that family. With her mouth full of beans she screamed at him, "You just keep on, heah?" After lunch she made Bebe's brothers Earl and Troy carry her plush sofa onto that porch and she flapped around like a clipper ship spreading it with sheets and sprigged coverlets so she could spend the night with her poor sister's corpse. That did it for Lester and they rolled the coffin into the musty parlor where it belonged.

Bebe wriggled her toes, smiling. Even Jack laughed when I told him that.

Then Tyna got on her telephone to a few well-chosen people

and announced a morning funeral in her home on Connor Street with a viewing of the body by friends and neighbors. People came from way out in the country next day and stood in the yards whispering, and their kids borrowed the use of every toilet on the street. The preacher gave a very short speech on the need of the living to repent while there was still time and that coffin lid was never so much as cracked. They carried Serena Mae Sellars out through more mourners than came to bury Judge Templeton (the man who heard her case), and nobody in the crowd had the gall to say they had chiefly come for a look at the woman who killed her husband with an ax and herself with a plaited electric cord.

All this was running through Bebe's head as she crossed Aunt Tyna's porch past the place where the coffin had stood. She twisted the brass plug on the doorbell. A little girl who should have been asleep by now said she could use the telephone under the stairs, and since Troy had moved out on a rural route, she called up Earl, quickly, trying not to notice the dirt and wear that had happened to Lester Sherrill's house. Overhead, somebody's feet were pacing in the bedroom where she had climbed with Jack the first night they met.

"Earl? It's Bebe and I just got in town. Is Mama over there?"

Earl went on for a long time about his surprise and why she didn't let them know. Then he said yes, and she was asleep. Everybody in the house was asleep but him, and he'd come get her.

"Earl, if you'll tell me where Mama's putting the key these days, I'll spend the night over here." She had looked in the mailbox and over the right windowsill, and it was nearly midnight.

But Earl wouldn't allow that. And Tweet would never forgive either one of them—that was his wife, Treva, whose name got lisped so long by seven brothers and sisters she finally gave in to the nickname. It always embarrassed Bebe to have both of them in the same room and to listen to the sound of "Tweet and Bebe," like a pair of dimwits, not much better-sounding than Pinheads, glad to be known by any name at all. Which reminded her she never did hear what Rosie named her baby and what they called him now.

Earl was tall, lean, with snuff-brown skin and hair, and looked the way Gary Cooper would with some Cherokee blood. His hair, now graying, was still long on top and fell toward his snuff-brown eyes. As an old man he would resemble Walt, with whom he had little in common. His shirttail was out, one pants cuff unfolded. Troy always called him a cornstalk in October, rooted up by the hogs. Troy loved to talk hillbilly but Troy was smart, and mostly Earl wasn't.

"How you like this?" said Earl, leading Bebe between juniper and Chinese holly to the dark blue door of his new house. He turned on the hall lights with a rotating dimmer knob and banged one heel into the foyer tile, which was meant to look like marble. "How you like this?" Bebe carried her own suitcase while he ran an assortment of light fixtures from medium to blinding. The den had a brick fireplace with a built-in barbecue and a plasterboard eagle flying toward it from one wall. "So how you like it?"

"It's wonderful, Earl. I didn't even know you'd moved."

"It's a Gold Medallion home; you like it?" He thumped the den wall, which had vertical wood paneling with neat knotholes eighteen inches apart. Bebe dumped her luggage on the hearth. "Roman brick," he said. The eagle had a yellow plastic eye.

She sat in an orange chair, leatherette, which squirted air between her thighs.

"You like that?"

"Very comfortable."

"Just turn around, Bebe, now. Halfway." Earl leaned across a Formica bar, grabbed hold of a wagonwheel of light bulbs, and showed her how it ran up and down on its own cord. "Now watch!" he warned, reaching under the counter, and three plastic logs in the fireplace turned red and gold.

"That's nice," said Bebe. "Why is Mama—"

"Keep watching." Earl stuck his finger in the air to shush her and, sure enough, the red light rolled out of sight and a pale blue bubbled under the smooth bark. Red faded in again from the bottom, then passed away like a cloud in a box.

"Well," said Bebe, leaning back in the sighing chair, "you never did like to haul out ashes."

"Damn right." Earl yanked out a whole cabinet from the room divider and growled it over the tile floor on steel balls. "I got bourbon and gin. I got ginger ale and soda and tonic."

"Gin, I think. It's so hot. And ton—"

"You're hot?" He lifted up a painting of a bowl of zinnias, found some panel of switches, and flipped the room down thirty degrees. "Why didn't you say so right away?"

Bebe took off her shoes and threw them toward Earl's rainbow logs. She hoped there was no button that vibrated the damn chair. He mixed her a drink in a glass as wide as a quart jar.

"I didn't know what to think I heard you on the phone," he said, putting ice in his own glass.

"I told Troy I might come."

"Troy!" he groaned, and flipped the hair out of his eyes. "Anyway, whatever it is, you're right to come on home and Tweet's going to say the same. We got a bed in the playroom—that's downstairs—with your own toilet right there." He held up his glass in a toast. Bebe lifted hers and drank. She couldn't taste any tonic.

Earl broke into a big smile. The front tooth was still broken. "In the morning, you go upstairs to Mama with a pot of coffee—I can just picture her when she spots you walking in! Now, Bebe, she's gone downhill some; you've got to expect that. We bring her over here every chance we get, but no, she's got to strike off home in a few days. Sits over there by herself eating nothing but boiled eggs and watching the doctor shows on television."

Bebe managed to say, "Boiled eggs?"

"She read someplace Marlene Dietrich eats boiled eggs."

Bebe got tickled. She had learned to love movies with Mama. Together they had heard Marlene growl "Falling in Love Again," her black stocking supporters in plain view.

Earl took the matching chair under the spread eagle and looked moodily at his colored logs. "Christmas I got Mama this *apart*ment." The way he said it, Bebe seemed to hear the word for the first time: Apart, apart. "Right uptown, had an elevator straight to her door. Had grips in the shower walls so you wouldn't fall, even a little stool for old people to sit down and soap their feet. Acoustic tile everywhere. No, sir, she'd rather go home to the train whistle and that old bathtub with the animal paws." He grinned. "You remember that tub?"

"I remember." She always said they were lion feet and Troy said they were camel. One time Troy hid in the wicker hamper to see Bebe naked and got stuck and couldn't get out. She and Earl had to cut a slit in the back with the pruning shears and try to reclose it again with adhesive tape. Earl let the tub overflow one time and over the dining room table the light bulb started leaking.

What if I break out crying? Bebe thought. Earl slumped there, a long bone under a loose shirt. He coughed, so it seemed natural to ask, "How's your lung?"

"That old thing? I bet you're worn to a frazzle and ready to get some sleep. It's a Beautyrest mattress, by the way."

That would be nice, Bebe said.

He got the last remaining strength out of the glass and set it on the bar. "Now tell me first what's the trouble, Bebe, and what me and Troy can do. You want me to call up Troy?"

She saw from his frown he believed she had come back home for haven, that there was trouble; and maybe Mickey *was* in her brain like a brier that needed to be picked out. But Earl only wondered if Jack had turned out to be a Sellars after all, and had laid hands on her in some way.

"Lord no!" Bebe cried. "Let's get it straight now. I just took it in my head to come home to see Mama, maybe a week. I got this card from her and it made me think how long it's been—three years?" She let him see how easy and natural her smile could be. "You sure have bettered yourself in three short years." The gin was good and cold now, and she felt it running into her secret places. She might sit all night in Earl's magnificent air-conditioning and freeze inside and out. "Earl, you must be doing real well with those cars. And you're looking good."

Almost reassured, he threw back his hair in the old way. "Jack's not?"

"Jack is just fine. Everything's fine. I swear, with all your money, you'd think you could get that tooth capped." In Earl's face time melted and ran off. She saw him the night he won a trophy for eighth grade basketball; he was sweating and, for the first time, had a smell to his sweat. She saw him the day he charged into the hardware store and tried to take after Mr. Sloan with a ball-peen hammer, not looking at Bebe, not asking her if it was true she let Mr. Sloan do it from behind like Jesse said, just ready to murder the man and go on home. She saw Earl leaving from the Greenway depot, headed west to the sanitarium to close up the bloom an X ray had seen on his lung. She didn't know what love was if it wasn't that, things added up over years in a pile like a haymow, without much connection to them.

Softly Earl said, "Jesus, you scared us. I thought the very worst." He meant since Jack was a Sellars and blood would tell.

"There wasn't any need, Earl. I've been happy."

"Still happy, huh. Well, I'll be damned," he said, and suddenly yelled, "Come on out, Tweet, it's just a *plain* visit," and his wife ran in wearing an old flannel robe and gave her the hug Earl didn't know how to give.

"Hiding in the closet in my own house—it's a scream!" she cried. Earl looked sheepish and was making the hearth fire burn high and low and high again with electrical switches.

Over her shoulder, Bebe winked at Earl, who said he would have a *real* drink now. Pouring a heavy one, he said, with a smile that exposed his broken tooth, "I want you to notice the walls in your room will be pecan wood, *Pee*can; you can buy it in big sheets now, and a pecan bedstead to match, I guess." Bebe was laughing. "I'll show you," he said. "I want to see how you like it."

Next morning, when she tiptoed in carrying Tweet's percolator with two coffee mugs hooked on her fingers, Mama was still asleep and Bebe stopped at the door to take a good look. Grace Fetner looked fat as ever under the sheet but her head seemed smaller. Both cheeks used to swell out and spill over her neck; now there couldn't be more than one thin layer of skin over the bones in her face and the flesh hanging from her jawbone was flimsy, like the hem of a slip. The sight of what three years had done made Bebe ease the pot onto Tweet's bureau—solid walnut, as Earl had already explained.

Mama said suddenly, without raising her bruised eyelids, "Who's that came in?" The voice was still small and sweet. Walt Fetner used to say it was too little for the rest of her.

"Don't open your eyes yet. Guess."

That's my face after a while, Bebe thought, waiting.

"I looked for you all yesterday, Bebe," she said matter-of-factly, and her eyes flew open. She held up both broad freckled arms and Bebe laid her face gently against the bones of hers. "Ah, Bebe! How you been?" Her mouth smelled of yesterday's medicines: laxative pills and iron tonic, Nervine to help her sleep, cod liver oil to grease the joints, Geritol to pep her up, one waning soda belch. Mama laughed in the upper octaves. "I knew that card would bring you!" she crowed, then patted Bebe away so she could swing her feet to the floor and stare down. If they swelled much, she'd take a kidney stimulant, and if the skin stayed pale, more iron to darken her blood and move it around better. They watched her insteps pinken.

"How did you know? I meant to surprise you!"

"Naw, I knew it." She watched her toes fight. "That toenail's going to break again. Tweet never keeps gelatin in this house for me when I've told her and told her." She waggled the toe, pinched back the skin and looked inside the corner in case it should have the nerve to become ingrown. "I have got toenails like the cow has horns," she sighed.

Mama had never had any real health problems except for the one car wreck and the broken hip, which she'd rather not talk about. To have something go wrong without reason, just by chance, struck her as unfair, even insulting. Everything else she had warded off by daily dosage. Much as she worried at Walt's first heart attack, she couldn't help saying with some satisfaction, "He never looked after it." She stood up now and stamped the foot with the disobedient nail. "Jack come with you, Bebe?"

"He's got too much to do at the beach."

That was all Mama needed to open the subject of Jack's mental health, which had long concerned all the Fetners. "Now that he's living right *by* them, you see Jack eats more fish. I've always heard fish is good brain food and might stave off anything come down to him from his mama's side." She would not look at Bebe now, for fear she had offended. "You be pouring my coffee, hon." Very fat in her loose gown, she set off to the bathroom, limping on that right leg, her head looking dried as the stem on a tomato. The yellow hem hung crooked. Maybe the silver pin holding one leg in place drew it up shorter than its twin. At the door she said to Bebe grimly, "Now we'll see what's what."

Bebe started drinking her own coffee. Mama would be in the bathroom a long time. First she had to drink lemon juice in a glass of hot tap water. Then she would pee with great force—exerting force was one way to exercise what's on the inside, Mama said. She could lend her bladder to the Baltimore Colts, and Bebe hated to think what muscular strength was stored in her rectum and nostrils. She would bend low over the toilet, making certain her urine was the same color it was yesterday before she gave it up to the Greenway sewerage system, then sit again and allow her bowels to move with more force.

Bebe straightened the pillowcase and made up the bed. It was hardly mussed at all, as if Mama never turned over in the night. In high school once, she had been reading the dirty parts of the Song of Solomon and came to the part about the beloved putting in his hand by the hole of the door, "and my bowels were moved for him." Bebe got such a clear picture of Mama as the Queen of Sheba, taker of Ex-Lax and epsom salts, that she laughed herself sick. Really sick, and furious because it was Mama's fault the poem was forever spoiled for her.

For the second time, the toilet flushed. The sound of gargling bounced off Earl's neat ceramic walls. Mama came out smiling, pleased with herself, so naturally the first thing she talked about over her cup was how ugly she had become with age in spite of the vitamins and hard-boiled eggs.

"This head—you see this head?" She made it pivot almost like an owl's. "One night, I think, somebody unscrewed the thing and poured out all the juice and stuck it back on. Dry skin? I mean, when I spread one wrinkle to look there's two little wrinkles inside. It wouldn't help if I soaked in the Wesson oil. Now you, Bebe." She leaned back in her chair and propped both feet on the mattress because it helped her heart pump and she had told Walt that a hundred times. "Bebe, you do look good. Been out in the sun. You look looser in yourself than you did last time. You like it there? At the beach?" Bebe nodded.

Mama set down her cup and turned her mouth into a prune. "And exactly what difference did it make that I told this man you'd married Jack Sellars? This man on the telephone?"

"George Bennett. As it turned out, Mama, no difference."

She made a short jerky nod. Confirmed. "I knew it."

"I just wanted Troy to keep you from telling anybody whatever he wanted to know."

"The way he put it, I thought maybe the law was after Jack." Mama's yellow hair had grayed so that now it looked white but in need of a good shampoo. Streaky, she sometimes said. She sometimes recalled to Bebe the days you bought Nucoa margarine the color of lard and had to mix yellow powder in to make it resemble butter and the color turned out uneven. Me and my Nucoa hair! She took both hands and began to slap the strands this way and that, pinning it down at random. "I thought maybe you took out a warrant against him and then changed your mind." She had done that herself a few times, with Bebe's daddy.

Bebe shook her head. For eighteen years Jack had been to the Fetners like an unexploded shell that might go off someday because his mama did. They meant nothing ugly by asking, sure as they were it was nothing Jack could help. And if he led a good life all the way to the grave, they'd give him no credit for taming his own blood. "Damned if it didn't miss him after all!" That's what Earl would say.

Mama's hair was now pinned in an assortment of wads and bundles. "Well, the law got after Troy in April for turning in a false fire alarm and then driving into a parked car in his rush to get away. At his age! Did you ever hear the beat!" Her face glistened with pride. "Earl told Troy not to let on and worry me, but I wormed it out of him."

"Was he drinking?"

"He says not." Mama threw back her head so Heaven could see she was charitable even though Troy never fooled her for a minute, nor any other Fetner, either.

Bebe said, "Troy better grow up."

"Fish better give milk." She used her last swallow of coffee to wash down an orange pill. "He'll be lucky if Mary Ruth don't leave him."

"He's good to her." It looked like a prescription bottle. "What kind of a pill is that?"

"The doctor's," Mama said, dismissing that. "Sure, Troy's sweet-talking good to her, but hers is the paycheck that holds everything together and that just don't work. Lately he's almost as bad as his daddy."

A look of satisfaction came over her face that she, Grace Fetner, had coped with the champion devil of the family and finally outlived him. Undressed him and prayed him into a hundred drunken beds, fed him and screamed him off five thousand mornings to the mill. When Walt got older and had heart pangs and wanted to stay home nights with the radio turned up high, she'd say, "Why didn't you stay home when I needed you? When all three kids was little?" Bebe could hear him yet. "Ah, Grace. Don't hold it against me." "Go on out and have a drink," she'd bawl. "I have got used to it!" He wanted to hear the "Hit Parade." They passed the last years peacefully and even got the reputation of a devoted couple. Mama would interrupt "Mr. Keen, Tracer of Lost Persons" to tell him all the outrages he had committed over the years when he was too drunk to remember, when he was a missing person as far as she was concerned. "You still hold that against me?" he'd say. She talked so loud he could not hear what clue the police had found. "Remember when I went your bail that time and had to sell the only piece of Morrison land that ever came down to me?" He'd never meant Grace to go that far and sell *land,* he'd groan, only to borrow a little, that was all. She continued to list for him one horror after another, like a boring old general who relished his combat record. Sometimes she even made things up and said he'd forgotten he did them.

Bebe reached over now, the way he used to, and caught the fleshy part of her arm and shook it. "Mama, why don't you go back with me? Get some sunshine? Eat some of that fish yourself?"

"Pickle Beach!" She laughed, but pretended to think about it. She never did come to Durham or Winston-Salem. Hadn't lost anything there, she said.

"Marlene Dietrich takes a sunbath every day."

"Is that a fact? Well, I might, I just might." Both of them knew she never would. She stood up and took in several big drafts of oxygen, held her chest blown out full. It kept her lung fibers elastic. "But now I'll get my things together and we'll go right home to my house. Troy can take us. How you like Earl's fine new place?"

"He's the proudest thing."

"Listen, he would sit over on my porch with these big books of wallpaper till I nearly went crazy. I'd say I liked the ivy.

Right away he'd want to know what was wrong with the bell-and-fern. I'd change my mind to suit him and he'd be holding a page of ivy to the light. He carried around this board with paint colors on it so he could see it on bright and cloudy days. Whew."

"The car business must be pretty good."

Mama spat on her forefinger and wiped the backside of the walnut bureau. Not a speck. "Tweet is so careful she keeps this place nearly—I don't know—stinky clean." Mama leaned into the closet pulling on a flowered dress. "At my house you can't take off your shoes anyplace without getting your feet dirty. Here, if I'm in my stocking feet, I worry about tracking Tweet's floor."

"She's a good wife to Earl."

"Bebe, did I say different? And three fine chil . . . children." She pretended it was the stubborn side zipper which made her spread that word but Bebe knew different. Mama did leave Greenway once. She came to sit with Bebe in the hospital and help her get over it. Bebe was lying in the high bed with both ovaries gone, knowing there'd be no more monthly ticking in her left one and then the right, and she felt like a stopped clock. Mama kept looking at the picture the doctor had sketched for Bebe—womb, tubes, two ovaries—to let her know how much would be coming out. "It's funny how men and women are really made just alike," Mama had said, studying the sketch. "One thing in the middle, hanging down, and two balls up above." Bebe was trying not to blubber. "It just looks to me," Mama said, "like they could of give you a pill for it," and started to cry herself. Bebe told Jack to send her back home. Any more comfort like that would have killed her.

"These new zippers," Mama complained. "Iron them once and they melt down to nothing." She found an odd-looking plaid weskit which would drape over the waistline hole. If

Bebe told her about the dark stain on its shoulder, she'd throw a sweater atop that, although it was ninety degrees outside. Sometimes Mama went out in the streets, layer on layer, looking like one of those thick beds in a poor man's hall on which every blanket in the house has been spread for summer storage. "Bebe, you want to eat breakfast before we go?"

Bebe sure did. She could smell Tweet's biscuits and sausage.

But Mama said, "Me neither. There's a good cantaloupe at home and plenty of eggs."

Next thing Bebe knew she was sitting in Troy's front seat and they were both eating sausage-in-biscuit while he drove. Mama wouldn't touch it. All that sage and pepper, she declared, would eat your linings up.

From the backseat Mama said, "Troy? What fool thing you been up to now?"

Troy had changed, too. The family jester, he barely joked, in fits and starts, as if he were trying to remember how for Bebe's sake. When he first came to Earl's that morning, he had picked her up and whirled her like an ice skater. Now he acted as if that had wrenched his back.

"You notice the fatter Mama gets the higher up her voice goes?" He grinned and the freckles leaped. "Some days I can't tell if she's talking or not except when the dogs start howling."

Mama said, "Go ahead, eat that hot sausage, fill up with gas, see if I care!"

Troy was still handsome, blond, still cutting the fool, Bebe guessed. Still tall and hadn't gained a pound. Laugh lines around his eyes. Still squabbling with Earl over this and that, she thought.

Every word neat, Mama said, "I've already told Bebe how you had your wreck."

He stuffed his mouth with biscuit. "I was just helping them out. These volunteer fire departments go to seed without practice. Bebe, you like Earl's new house?" Bebe said she did. "He is so proud. And Tweet got so excited when they finally moved in, I thought she'd hang curtains over that window in the washing machine."

"You watch out now," said Mama, giggling.

Bebe asked where Mary Ruth was and he said she took Randy to Sunday school every week.

"I used to take you," said Mama, "and you see how much good it did." She'd always been crazy about Troy. Earl was the son who got ahead, remembered her birthday, visited her every day. Troy had been known to drink a pint of booze, then swallow liquid detergent and go ring doorbells and blow bubbles at whoever came. Troy once borrowed a motorcycle and rode it on Greenway's uptown sidewalks with a hubcap on his head.

"Slow down," cried Mama now, loving every minute of his recklessness. "You drive like you're going to be late for the accident."

"She got that one off the TV," muttered Troy. Troy's second wife, Mary Ruth, was a schoolteacher and he explained to Bebe that she had a summer job, "doing desk work at the Beauty Worsted. That's a new mill, came in last year from New York."

"They're all Jews," Mama said. "You sure are driving home the long way."

"Want to show Bebe how our brother paid for that house."

Bebe asked Troy what work *he* was doing now and he snapped with no smile, "I help Earl," and turned down Loray Avenue on two wheels. Most of the big houses where widows had lived were now funeral homes, antique or gift shops, florists. These were the tall ones with balconies and oval windows where Bebe had wanted to live someday, and serve Russian tea and cheese straws to her bridge club. One entire block of the gingerbread verandas and shingled towers had been torn down, the space parked thickly in new and used cars, the huge lot ringed by whirling red propellers on a high cable.

It seemed like a sacrilege to Bebe that one of the Fetners had made it to this side of town after all, in just this way. "That sign," said Troy crisply, "that sign flashes night and day."

In fuchsia neon letters, three feet high, it blinked at them: EARL'S PEARLS. Earl's Pearls. EARL'S PEARLS. Underneath, smaller and still neon but unflashing, read the motto in script: *A Gem of a Used Car—Priceless Value—Where Your Credit Is Good as Diamonds.*

Sourly, in what sounded like an imitation, Troy said, "How you like it?" Slowly he circled the huge lot. "Earl serves three counties now." The cars were parked by color instead of make, in sections marked *Earl's Emeralds,* and *Earl's Rubies,* and *Earl's Sapphires.*

"I never saw anything like it."

Trucks were sectioned off, too, as *Diamonds in the Rough.* Bebe squinted to read the smaller signs scattered here and there: *Become a Rich Pedestrian! Sell Us Your Car!* On one nicked and scratched coupé blew the placard: *Buy in Haste, Repaint at Leisure.* And the tag on a red Corvette said: *Owned by High School Boy—Used Mostly for Parking.*

Mama let out a sigh in the backseat. "This was all Troy's idea."

"Troy's?"

He was not even looking at the car lot, which he circumnavigated one more time. "Earl hasn't decided yet on calling the real old buggies 'Heirloom Jewels.' That's being thought through. There'd be a subline: 'It's the stone, not the setting, that counts.' " Troy floorboarded his own Nash—an heirloom jewel, Bebe guessed—back down Loray Avenue and braked hard at the stoplight. "Earl pays me a kind of consultant fee. For thinking up his signs and ads and radio jingles."

"And you're on the books as a vice president," Mama said.

"Yeah," said Troy wearily. "I'm on the books."

"The way it all got started, Troy was just teasing and cutting up, but Earl saw the possibilities." Mama leaned forward and with her knuckles knocked on the back of his head as if it were a door. "I been in one wreck already, Troy Fetner." He slowed down slightly. That was how Mama broke her hip. She was driving Walt Fetner's old car too fast and hit an ice slick, rode off the road and went sideways down a deep clay bank, and fell on top of somebody's tractor. Nobody knew why she wasn't killed. She claimed it was because she prayed, all the way down, "Lord, I got things to *do* tomorrow."

"What are you down to now, seventy?" she said, trying to see the speedometer over Troy's shoulder.

"Sorry, Mama."

"Earl would pay him a little more if he'd just sell for him, on the lot."

"I know that, Mama." Troy grinned at Bebe. "Last time you got home, Earl was selling used cars out of a cornfield by his house. Some difference, yeah? Now the banks send a v.p. out to *offer* him loans. If Earl lived within his income now, he wouldn't even think that was living."

"Does he pay you a fair price?" The truth was, Earl had always been stingy.

"I guess so. You tell me what stuff like that is really worth." He whipped them onto Buena Vista.

Bebe asked, "When did you and Mary Ruth move out from town? The operator had a hard time getting you on that party line, she said."

"Sixty-six, was it, Mama?"

She said, "It was the year they opened that skating rink on Hefner Street where you used to live."

"Sixty-six. Opened it right next door. People riding around

and around on little wheels till midnight every night? The noise drove me crazy."

Mama sighed. "You didn't have to go messing with the man's sign like that. 'Skating stinks.' Was that anything to paint up there?"

Bebe was laughing and spraying biscuit crumbs.

"Maybe it was sixty-seven. So we bought some land that wasn't worth farming and built a little house back in the woods. You remember where Cold Springs school was? They closed it down. Integration. All the land got cheap in that part of Stone County. We're about eight miles west of the school. You've got to come see us while you're here, Bebe." It seemed to her something was worrying Troy, the used cars or the house or something. Even when he laughed, his jaw seemed set and rigid. "It's not like Earl's, now; just a little place with a little mortgage."

"Earl thinks if he paid cash for anything," said Mama, "people would think his credit was no good. It makes some sense." She tapped Bebe's shoulder. "Listen, Troy's such an old hermit he hardly asks anybody to visit anymore. You better go when you can. Troy better paint you a raft of signs so you can find the place." She winked at Bebe. The Fetners used to look for Troy's handiwork all over town the way soldiers looked for evidence of Kilroy. He put up his own Burma-Shave signs, mostly dirty. Bebe would never forget when the owner of the gas station painted his name out front, Grant Tucker, and the words Troy turned that into one dark night.

Now they were riding downhill on Connor. Even half asleep, Bebe had been able to tell, once, when Daddy's old Plymouth made the last turn to home, by the way her shoe soles drove down against the car's floor. In the morning light, she could see that the first block of taller houses was changed, had cracked boards, gaps in banisters, and ragged yards. She spotted new outside doors and stair flights, extra oil drums, and how the roofs held up almost as many TV antennae as they once held silver lightning rods.

Troy drove straight into Mama's dirt yard, threatening to graze the porch just to hear her squeal. "You need your cane, old lady?"

"Not except to thrash *you.* If you'll let me lean on the step-up?" She held him while he hung her walking stick on his shoulder, set Bebe's suitcase by the door, heaved Mama's weight up the cement chunk, paused, onto the splintered boards.

"We've got a good ripe cantaloupe, so you come on in," she said, patting him in what sounded like a slap. She took a crochet hook out of her purse, stuck it through the copper mesh to undo the latches, then lifted the key off a high nail.

Then they were standing in that dim hall which was lined with all the things too good to throw away. A table with a dusty embroidered spread Grandma Fetner had made and, in its center, Grandma Morrison's kerosene lamp. They had borrowed it because when Grandma Fetner lived with them she wouldn't turn on electric lights in her room because they hurt her eyes.

There stood the milk crock with the same split umbrella in it. A doorstop made of a Sears catalogue, its pages rolled inward one at a time to the binding and spray-painted gold. A stiff chair with adhesive tape holding on a back leg, a wooden quilt chest, a rocker with a square of oilcloth laid over the frayed seat. Three large varnished conch shells in a corner, souvenirs of ocean trips the Fetners never took. Bebe stooped and pressed one against her ear and listened to Pickle Beach. "Watch out," called Mama over her shoulder. "Spiders get in them things." Mama's whatnot stand full of old pepper shakers, remains of children's toy dishes, cracked china cherubs, a castle that once went in a goldfish bowl, a solid glass bulldog with a broken ear. Troy threw that at Bebe once; she guessed the dent in the wall was still there.

And over all this a smell that had in it food and rust and resin and mildew, soot and sweat and Octagon soap—but was mixed into something new and indistinct. The odor of a year-old bird nest, maybe, wet down with dishwater.

Mama limped ahead down the hall, turning on every light in every room, some with their pull-chains tied to twine leaders down to nails or bedposts, some whose crinkled wall buttons twisted a long time before they would click.

"Coffee first," Mama said. "If you'll be peeling the melon, Bebe, and don't throw out the seeds. The redbirds like the seeds."

Nobody had made a single improvement in her kitchen. Every pipe showed under the sink. The refrigerator was freckled from chipped enamel. Over the gas stove, pots and spatulas hung on greasy nails and a cheese box she had hammered into the wall contained her kitchen matches.

"Troy's gone back to the car for something." Bebe reached for the drawer handle her fingers could find in the dark, then the big knife on the left where it belonged, right by the toothpicks in a Shirley Temple glass Mama got once by feeding them ten boxes of bad cereal. She peeled and sliced the cantaloupe onto Mama's platter with the blue waterwheel at the base of a blue mountain.

"Oh, Lord!" cried Mama. "He's brought that thing."

Her hall became an echo chamber for tremolo music. What was the song? "Hand Me Down My Walking Cane." Troy came into the kitchen singing every third or fourth word, a mandolin balanced on his middle, the flat pick leaping in his right hand. "Down," he sang. "Cane. Down . . . cane. Down . . . cane . . . leave . . . midnight train . . . taken away." He looked so foolish and at the same time so hopeful, Bebe could not help laughing.

"Where did you learn to play that?"

"Told you I did jingles. Now listen to this." Chewing his tongue, he twanged out the "Blue Danube" waltz, until they both launched into the lines and echo lines they sang to it in grade school. "Beautiful stream (so clear, and blue)/A radiant dream (we sing, to you)." Troy's left hand arched away from the frets as though it might leap off altogether, and his gaze was fixed on the tobacco-stained fingers which moved the plectrum up and down on the double strings like a beating wing.

Mama lowered the gas as the percolator made a rhythm of its own. "I hope for Mary Ruth's sake she don't have to listen to that thing too much," she said. "Bebe, you want a boiled egg?"

"Bought a book and taught myself," said Troy.

"There's Marlene Dietrich; she could afford anything, and still she eats eggs."

While Bebe was turning down the egg, Mama said he had plenty of time to learn music, working no more than he did. Troy watched his fingers fly. "It's not so hard. They're double strings so you've really got two less to worry about than the guitar and you remember when I had one of those. A Stella guitar? Tore up my fingers so bad?" He stopped the song to show Bebe how the strings were paired and to pluck off the notes in order. "G, D, A, E. I used to make up sentences to help me remember, when I first started. God Damned Adam and Eve." Mama and the grandmothers had sung from hymnals where you could tell the notes by the shape. Grandma Fetner had brought her pump organ when she moved in, and there was a lot of singing around it before Walt sold it in a pinch. Almost absently Troy chorded the line "Be it ever so humble," and smiled at Bebe.

She said, "Remember when the troop trains used to roll by the house and we'd go sit on the roof?"

"You hurrying into your bathing suit, as I remember, and built like a lead pencil. And we'd sing 'Remember Pearl Harbor' and wave."

She had strung hollyhock blooms with a needle and thread to wear in a lei around her neck. She wanted to look grown-up and beautiful for the boys going off to die for freedom. If the train passed at a good speed, sometimes the soldiers whistled.

"Now lay that thing aside," said Mama, pouring the coffee. "It looks like some kind of play toy. Anybody need canned milk?"

"Earl borrowed the guitar for one of his boys to try but he never did learn it and now it's been back in some cedar closet so long it will stink forever," said Troy. Suddenly he reached across the oilcloth table and ran his fingers, warm from the coffee cup, across her forehead. "You're getting a wrinkle." His skin was slick and hard from fretting the mandolin.

"You've got a few yourself."

"It's been no time at all, Bebe, no time at all."

She had to pause and work out their ages by addition and subtraction. Since she was forty, Earl would be forty-five and Troy forty-two, though he seemed no older than the boy singing off the roof in 1942, trying to do the guitar and the mouth harp all at once, eager to enlist. Together they went to the movies and were shocked by Japanese atrocities, though Troy could shave by then and sometimes left Bebe downstairs and sat with Peggy Aiken in the balcony. The way Veronica Lake blew herself up with a hand grenade! That evil white ground mist on Bataan. Alan Ladd parachuting into Germany.

She said, "I haven't been home for three years and you've never written me a line. Mary Ruth's Christmas cards and that's *it.* You could be dead in the river, Troy, for all I'd know."

Some of Mama's coffee splashed out to hear her say that—in the river.

"I don't write much but signs anymore. I've been busy trying to find how many words will rhyme with truck"—he laughed—"besides the first one that comes to mind."

"He works up new stuff all the time for Earl's radio show," said Mama. "Seasonal stuff, holidays and things."

There was something sad in it. All the pretend games she and Troy had played, the dramas they acted out on the railroad track for no audience. He'd written an anonymous column for the school paper, in insulting couplets, and Bebe had spied out material for him. "Comin' in on a Wing and a Prayer" was, for a while, the song that could choke him up midway. He planned to join the RAF and she the Waves. When she was "discovered" by touring screen stars entertaining behind the lines, and dubbed the new Madeleine Carroll, Troy would go with her to Hollywood and write cliffhanger scripts that would make her famous.

"Oh, Troy!" she blurted. "Where did the years go?"

"Now listen!" said Mama in a loud voice. "I am the Wrinkle Champ, so let's move on from that. I'm thinking about something. I been thinking ever since I laid there in Earl's bed this morning and felt in my bones that was Bebe tipping in so easy. Now are you paying attention? You done singing for a while?" They were.

"I'm thinking about getting on that telephone. Tomorrow's Monday and ought to be nice and clear, and here's Bebe, home for a little while. I'll call up everybody, see, and we can meet out at Hebron churchyard about the middle of the afternoon; everybody bring picnic supper. Daylight savings time and all, the women have plenty of time to fix; the men can come on when they leave the fields or get off work. We make the family reunion now instead of September while Bebe's at home—what you think?"

Troy said they'd never had it on a weekday but Mama, as

usual, couldn't stand the word *never.* Soon as somebody used it, her nostrils would start blowing out. "*Never* and *always*—dead people's words!" she snorted. And in their old vaudeville act, Bebe shot back, "You *always* say that!" and Troy chimed in with his line: "It *never* fails."

"Next weekend might rain," said Mama, unperturbed.

In 1965 when Bebe had been home for several days and they thought at first Walt Fetner's heart intended to fix itself, Mama and Earl had dragged her over every washboard road in Stone County to speak to every far connection, every old man and old woman, every blank-faced child cousin. Mama had gone without sleep and must have been worn out, but she denied it, making Earl speed it up so they could see them all. At places where kin owned a telephone, she'd call up the hospital and check that her husband was doing fine. Troy hardly ever went inside; he followed the kids off looking for spots he remembered—a cave, an old cabin falling in, the whitewash pits. "Remember now," Earl would tell Bebe when they parked by a rusted mailbox or a pasture gate and unfolded themselves from the car, "remember, you may never see so-and-so again." That *never* made Mama wheeze and say to Bebe, "But don't act like the last time, honey, act like the first."

Still, Earl was often right. Old so-and-so was apt to be eighty-nine, or have heart dropsy bad, or his boy had not written awhile from Saigon, or the next son was planning to move to Charlotte and father all his children at that great distance, or everyone came from stock that died off early without cause.

Troy reached for his mandolin and strummed a loud flourish. "How about it, Bebe? You up to seeing everybody?"

"It's easier than driving from house to house. Sure, call the whole bunch together, Mama. Let's see them all at one time for a real old-fashioned family reunion." She wondered how many of the 1965 faces were still left, whose goiters had won and whose land gone for taxes, and which ones she'd have to tell good-bye again. Act like the first time, honey, not the last.

Mama peeled off her weskit with the stained shoulder, let the placket gap wide in her flowered dress. She was counting whispered names on her fat fingers. "All the Fetners and Morrisons," she said, Morrison being her maiden name, and soon tipped over into the twenties with her counting. "And the women can bring food and the men their tools. And in the afternoon before supper we'll work the graves so it won't take but a little raking in September."

Oh, Lord. Bebe had forgotten that part.

"And here it is close to Father's Day—now that's real sweet. We'll take your daddy something." She always sounded as if Walt Fetner might sit up in his grave and accept it with both hands. "I'll ask Lorene to bring her Kodak. We can have singing." She reached past Troy's mandolin to press his forearm. "You can even bring that little toy thing with you for the singing." A concession. She gave that snapping nod which seemed far too forceful for her wattled neck.

"Something like this?" Troy struck a few chords and began singing one of Earl's advertising jingles:

If you want a used car
That's a perfect gem
Go choose it at Earl Fetner's,
Get a Pearl from him!
Ruby, Jade, or Sapphire
With their sil-ver-y chrome—
He'll finance your jewel,
You can drive it home!

Value that is priceless
At a price that's low;

Straight drive or automatic,
Guaranteed to go.
Best cars in the world!
See them all at Earl's!
Don't take imitation—when these are real pearls!
Get a priceless bargain at Earl's!

Once Bebe recognized the melody, she made Troy sing the whole thing over while she hummed alto. The tune was "Up a Lazy River," and Troy said when he put it on tape for the Greenway radio station, they used a few car horns for background rhythm and beat.

They even got up in Mama's kitchen and did the old jitterbug steps while going through the tune. Troy was the best dancer in high school and dated this skinny girl, Peggy Aiken, who was double-jointed; he'd throw out his knee and she'd do a backflip when the bass fiddle dropped into boogie.

They, too, started at that pace, with Bebe grinding both hips. But soon they danced slow as Kim Novak and William Holden, almost soft-shoeing on Mama's rough linoleum, until her slotted spoon shook off its nail and fell behind the stove and she made them stop and eat up that sliced cantaloupe before the fruit flies found it.

8

Bebe

June 17, 1968

Bebe woke early, not sure if it was late twilight or early dawn, and thinking at first the sea had come to a stop.

Instantly she saw her old bedroom. All the years came loose and fell. Lying there she might be any age. No wonder she had forgotten, while asleep, what caused that odd tickling in the brain, what lay ahead for her in this coming day or coming night. Maybe Christmas or the first day of school. A birthday party. Maybe her tonsils were coming out.

She slept again and dreamed of a crowd of people filing past the back of football bleachers. They were paying a penny each to look at a large hooded snake which lay coiled in the shade under the stands, and which sometimes struck toward them as they passed, or toward the man collecting their coins. She could not understand why she was there, marching by to look at a cobra. It lay in a deep green circle, the serpent's tail thrust down the serpent's throat. Although she did not speak her thought, the woman ahead of her in line threw back her cloak and said, "Don't worry. It's not really a cobra. It's only a puff adder."

Bebe woke, frowning at the pointless dream. The room had

lightened by then and she could remember how old she was and that today was the family reunion at Mount Hebron. The room was in Greenway; east she could locate the beach with Jack on it, Mickey and the Pinheads off to one side in a kind of parenthesis.

Overhead the old water stain still looked like a bell with a melting clapper. And to her right was the same window where Bebe was down on her hands and knees with a razor blade when she heard Jack rustling through Aunt Tyna's shrubbery that night.

She sat up, surprised at first to feel folds of cloth sit up with her. Grace Fetner had insisted she borrow a nightgown. ("Bebe, what if there was a fire?") She lifted its hem and took minuet steps to the window, but now Tyna's house had turned gray and half the bushes had died and the chained dog was sprawled in the drip space trying to get cool. A loud radio next door might even be playing Earl's automobile songs. Somebody had already hung out diapers in the sun.

By closing her eyelids down to cracks, Bebe darkened the scene, made Tyna's house appear shadowed. Just like a movie. And the organ music ominous. May, 1950. The girl on her knees at the window wearing white piqué was twenty-two and thought she looked something like Alice Faye. She was five feet seven inches tall and slim and lightened her short blond hair, and tonight her gaze was intent on her own left wrist and its stubborn pulse. Beneath the window a row of mock oranges Tyna Sherrill had fed with chicken manure bloomed thick, smelly now in a different way. She could have puked at that smell, because she had been sitting at this same window three nights running, and this was the third one she'd tried to kill herself. The first two nights had ended in disappointed tears. You couldn't keep crying forever, though, and by now she was about to come down with the giggles.

The problem that was driving her to suicide? She was pregnant. Eighteen years later, the Bebe who watched the scene *did* giggle. An ugly joke, but still a joke. If I could look down from the moon, I know I'd laugh.

She was working in 1950 at the Greenway Hardware Store but the father wasn't Mr. Sloan, no matter what kind of a crazy story Earl had heard. It didn't matter, really, who he was. She had fallen out of love with him faster than she ever fell in. And for three nights she had been sitting by that very window saying all kinds of final things to the stars and trying to get up nerve enough to slash her wrists.

She'd already tried cutting both arms in the bathtub, the one with the camel feet, so hot water would speed the flow of blood. But the steaming tub raised hopes it might bring on her period, too, and she kept bathing and hoping and putting it off. By now Bebe was nearly scalded all over, giving her body a little extra time to keep its promises.

She didn't know, either, if she could cut deep enough. She had rummaged through Stone County Library without finding any book that said how deep such a cut had to be. In *Gray's Anatomy* she had read all about wrist structure, which was pretty tiresome since it skipped from bones to muscles to blood vessels without giving you the whole wrist in one place; but it looked to Bebe you had to cut down pretty deep—and so far she hadn't been able to brave more than the first nick.

So she was kneeling on the floor by that open window, getting ready to slice down one more time, when she saw something glitter in a crack between two floorboards. A hairpin, maybe, or a dime. Not really thinking about it, she gouged into the crack with a corner of the razor blade to pry it out. And, poking around to dig the thing up, it hit her that from care for her fingers she had been using a safety razor blade (Earl's) to kill herself with, and she looked at the damn thing chopping into the floor as if it were butter, and then she just laid her head down on the windowsill and laughed till her lungs hurt.

By the time a bush began to thrash around down below, she was limp as a rag. Didn't even move; just rolled one eye down and spotted the soldier. She thought he was AWOL, or a deserter, and had dropped off the passing train. He pushed through to Tyna's porch, rattled the front door, wiped off a window and tried to see through the glass. The house had been closed for months and Bebe couldn't remember any of Lester or Tyna Sherrill's kin in the army. She left the razor blade deep in the floor and leaned out to see better.

The soldier came flailing back through the shrubbery, backing up to see if the second floor looked deserted, too. Why anybody would be a career soldier, Bebe didn't know. Not a thing was going on in the world anymore.

She called down, not loud enough to wake Troy or Earl, "Listen! They're all dead!"

He turned his face up, trying to find her. He looked like that soldier John Lund played in *To Each His Own,* and she was feeling a lot like the unwed Olivia de Havilland. He pushed a limb of mock orange out of his eyes. Bitter. He looked like John Lund, but bitter.

"Well, you're not dead, are you?" he said, still turning his head this way and that.

Wasn't that a laugh? Bebe giggled. "No, not yet," she said.

(In her bedroom Bebe, forty years old, had to laugh again just thinking about it. How things were intertwined—what he said, what she said, what went before and came after. What she thought now, at forty, was that if there was God and He laughed on the moon, He might also make up such patterns for nothing but the fun of it, and leave them lying around just to see if anybody paid attention.)

So Bebe said no, she wasn't dead yet. She was careful not to get cut *now* on the razor blade, rising on her knees till the soldier could find her face in the high window. Maybe he thought briefly of Alice Faye. Yes, he had a very bitter face. Dishonorably discharged—but framed, of course. Too loyal to some buddy to tell the truth and clear his name. Every dime stolen by prostitutes. A piece of old Nazi shrapnel still floating in his skull. She felt as wise as Myrna Loy when the vets came home from World War II, and gave him an understanding smile which he probably missed in the dark.

He said, "You couldn't come down here and tell me what happened to Aunt Tyna, could you?"

So she knew, then, he was one of the Sellars orphans and Tyna Sherrill had set buttermilk on his mother's coffin. She said she'd be right down, swung barefoot onto their back-porch roof. She was wearing a white dress because she wanted to be a virginal-looking corpse, but three nights of pacing and blubbering had nearly ruined it. Bebe thought the soldier could probably see all the way up its skirt to her Sunday underwear. She had put that on so Grace Fetner would not be embarrassed to have the undertaker counting safety pins.

Around the corner on the Fetner roof, her ladder was laid flat between two chimneys. She'd bought it at the hardware store for times she might want to slip out with . . . well, it didn't matter who he was. He hadn't deserved her, anyway. They had only used it twice.

The soldier asked the dark if she was all right, maybe thinking she "fell off the roof," and that set Bebe to giggling all over again. Every month Mama called it that, falling off the roof. Mama didn't think girls ought to wash their hair that week and said if you canned any peaches then, they would spoil.

Beyond the soldier's view, she backed carefully down the ladder, came up on the far side of a lilac bush, and made him jump. He gave her the meanest look. Bebe thought, then, he might hit her. Even leaned forward, thrilled. She wanted someone to hit her for having a Kewpie doll growing in her stomach. She laid open her face to him. He pulled off his army cap, slapped it in one palm, put it on again.

"I'm Beatrice Fetner," she said, "and if Tyna was your aunt, you've got to be a Sellars. Which Sellars?"

He was the oldest boy, the runaway one who had hung high in a sweet gum tree that famous evening, over the river. People said Jack had seen it all—his daddy drunk and washing himself and singing, and his mama wading out from the bank with an ax dropped on one shoulder. For hours afterward nobody could get him down, even when the body had been hooked downstream and sent off in a hearse, after Serena Mae had gone off in the sheriff's car with two fingers pressed on her twitching eye, even when Aunt Tyna and the deputies stood there and begged. He just hung up there, frozen, hugging the limb with his arms and legs. When the deputy shinnied up the trunk, he finally let go and fell into the river himself and everybody got wet fishing him out.

Bebe couldn't think of anything to say to a boy who had seen that. So she started in on how he could probably get inside the Sherrill house if he wanted to, by borrowing her ladder.

"They're dead?" he asked.

Tyna the year before with a heart attack. Lester from stroke on New Year's Day while he was beating icicles off the porch roof with a broom. Jack nodded at the dark house. "They got anything of my mother's?" Bebe didn't know. (Not till a year later did she tell him completely how his mother died, how she screwed out the light bulb and laid it neatly on the shelf where they kept sheets and towels for the insane, so the closet was black-dark at the end; how there was plaster under her fingernails where she raked a hand down the wall while she choked, how she messed up her clothes like a baby while she died. He had read she was dead from the Greenway newspaper files, but Bebe finally told him the details.)

Jack propped the long ladder but the first window was locked. Bracing, she waited at the bottom. What if Troy came? "That one's on the hall," he called down softly. "They ever take the kids out of the orphanage?"

She shook her head no. "Some got adopted. Some just grew up and went away." Lester wouldn't take a single one into his house if Serena Mae *had* been his wife's sister. She visited at first, later sent Christmas boxes. "Nobody came home in 1949 when—"

He slammed the ladder into the house. "I know she's dead. I looked that up in the newspaper office this afternoon." He climbed the ladder and rattled a pane, but that one was locked, too. From the top he called, "Did they bury her in the rain?"

"No." It was August, dry and dusty. She told him there was a big crowd all up and down Connor Street and even the train slowed down to see what was going on.

"I'm sure as hell of that," Jack said. They dragged the ladder to the back of Aunt Tyna's house, where it was darker. Bebe almost fell over a yard spigot and when he reached out a hand his thumb stuck in the hollow of her neck. He rubbed it there, stroked the tense cords on each side. "You scared of me?"

She whispered, "Yes."

He dropped his hand and climbed to the third window. If this stranger should murder me, Bebe thought. The pity of it! The grief to the Fetners, who would be untouched by any shame. Troy might sing about her, the way they did about Naomi Wise. It would solve everything. And he came from murderous blood. That was the pattern she thought God had sent her then; everything fit together. If God was on the moon looking down, He must have laughed to see how she guessed wrong.

Overhead, the window rasped. Jack stuck his head and

shoulders deep inside. Bebe hung on to the bottom of the ladder, knowing it really was the last night in her life. She had never been able to feel that with the razor blade, and now she was stunned by the very idea and began to stare at everything and to take deep drafts of the mock orange.

She could, then, have jerked on the ladder and called her brothers for help. Instead, full of rapture, she put her bare foot on the bottom rung and started to climb. To *ascend.* The word rang in her head. When Jack crawled inside the house the wood shook under her, and once she flattened herself against it and laid her cheek on the next throbbing rung. If she fell into the lilac, it might kill the baby but not her, and she'd have to lay in the clinic and answer questions. She thought it a miracle that she should be climbing this ladder she had bought for another purpose entirely; and now it had become as purposeful as the one Jacob saw when he slept at Bethel. She was smiling when she reached the windowsill. Bebe stopped there and fluffed her hair with one hand.

In the dark room, Jack was moving. "You plan to help me in?" she whispered loudly.

Something flat and black fell from the wall. She trembled. A door? It creaked back into place. By herself she swung through the window and demanded to know if he wanted to leave the ladder out there in plain sight for everybody. Jack never said a word, loomed out of the dark, helped drag it inside. Bebe had to run open the hall door to make space enough to lay it flat on the cold floor, and it made a great racket sliding up the wall.

She could see nothing. The smell of mothballs was strong. "I've never been in this part of the house." Only downstairs, borrowing sugar for Mama. Once she and Troy got a quarter for beating Tyna's hall and parlor rugs. Troy took thirteen cents of it, which wasn't fair. Bebe couldn't get any answer out of Jack. "Is it a bedroom, I guess?" Silence.

"Did you go to the funeral?" he suddenly said. He was around the corner, a voice from the hall.

"Sure I did." She tried to think of something to volunteer about the occasion but there had been almost no flowers and the crowd had been curious, first, and then angry.

An ugly laugh in the darkness. "What did they sing—'Rescue the Perishing'?"

Bebe didn't know why he had to ask that. Music had been a real problem to Tyna—said she never noticed before how many hymns had rivers in them. Said all she could find in the book were rhymes about crossing Jordan, gathering at the river, and washing in the blood of the Lamb. Bebe swallowed. "Tyna got this quartet and they stood on the porch and sang. It was all men. They sang 'Where the Roses Never Fade.' "

Again he was laughing. "How does that song go?"

She stood in the mothball smell, terrified, and tried to sing it properly in case this was *her* funeral. "I am going to a city / Where the roses never fade / Here they bloom for but a season / Soon their beauty is decayed . . ." but Jack was laughing too hard to hear the rest about how the streets would be laid with gold and the tree of life blooming.

"My poor mama!" he roared. "My poor mama!" Then he stopped laughing in the same instant, chopped it right off, and didn't move. Bebe couldn't tell where he was. She put out a hand and touched nothing but the dark air. She felt she was floating in it.

"Jack?" He might be walking on a soft rug but she couldn't tell. "Say something so I'll know where you are."

It was like being shut up with a nigger, she thought, him so black and the rooms so black around them. Then, in the doorway, she spotted the quick shine of his buttons and teeth. He said softly, "When I was little, we'd come to visit here."

"I didn't live here then," said Bebe nervously.

He faded and his voice came from another dark place. "Or Uncle Lester would drive his T Model to the river on Sundays and blow his horn at the bottom of the path. He wouldn't get out, but Aunt Tyna did and she'd send me to fetch Mama for a little ride." Jack slid into a far corner like something on casters. "And we'd ride fast on the highway, over the river bridge to the creamery. Aunt Tyna wanted her to leave and let the courts get her child support but Uncle Lester was strong on sticking it out till death did them part. They'd send me inside to eat ice cream while they talked in the car. I tried all the flavors those Sundays. Coconut ice cream—you ever had that?"

Stepping over the ladder, Bebe felt in the thick dark for a chair. There was a table with an icy marble top but she thought that might break if she sat on it, carrying as she was a tiny fetus heavy as lead. She pushed the table against the wall. Her fingers made out a crocheted scarf on it, star shaped, like fishnet. She could see Jack's full outline now, in the bedroom door. He had good shoulders, she thought, to be no taller than he was.

"Then there got to be too many kids to fit in Uncle Lester's car." He walked into the hall. "Next time I had any ice cream I had to pay for it myself." She heard him going down the stairs.

He didn't come back. There were cricket noises in the walls. Below, a door slammed. Teacups shook in their saucers and there was one high tinkling noise; she thought he had probably walked through the lone chandelier and felt it tremble around his head. Bebe groped out of the room and down the hall, jerked back from the stairpost, which felt to her hand like the seamed head of a wooden baby. Everything grew quiet except her thunderous body. What a breath! Her stomach growled; her heart was rolling in her like an engine on the rails. Both knee joints popped with the first step. "Jack Sellars? Where are you?" Waiting at the foot of these stairs, she thought, with a pocketknife in his hand. Now she was *descending,* one step at a time. Kathy Fiscus. Mary Carmichael. Naomi Wise. Bebe Fetner. It was a good thing she was wearing her Sunday dress. She hoped the police could tell tearstains from plain water, as long as they were on the cloth already.

Almost sinking slowly, she stopped halfway to look back at the dim light which rose to the top of rooms and clung there like smoke. When she couldn't find another tread her bare feet tickled on that downstairs rug with its mustard and vinegar flowers which she and Troy had hung over Tyna's clothesline to beat. She called out sharply, "Don't you go off and leave me inside this house!" If she was going to be murdered, she wanted it out on the lawn in the daffodils and discovered by morning, not left in here to molder. Tears rushed to Bebe's eyes at the thought of herself dead in the dew. A rose that would never fade. "Jack?"

To her right, a hinge began to squeak in rhythm. She found that open arch with her hand and could make out a round table, then a lump in motion. A rocking chair with some flickers from brass buttons as they moved in the dark. The lump said, "Once there were two of these chairs. She gave the green one to Mama and none of us were allowed to sit in it. The only decent piece of furniture in the house. Mama made some kind of dress for it out of newspapers and straight pins, and that way it was always in storage." The squeaking stopped. His head looked paler than the chair's back; Bebe couldn't see anything else.

"Come over here," he said.

She took a deep breath, got ready, and moved. *Now.* She stood by the chair to one side, not wanting him to rock on her toes. No victim wants his toes rocked on extra.

"What did you say your name was?"

"Bebe Fetner. That's short for Beatrice." Almost bowing from the waist, she tried to see what Jack Sellars looked like.

His eyes had been blue. Was the nose long, chin round, cheeks sunken? Were his eyebrows bushy or thin? She couldn't call up anything but John Lund in a flier's uniform in the wrong war.

"You better go home, Bebe Fetner." He put out one hand and his fingertips fell on the curve of her hipbone. Pelvis. Cradle. Four fingertips. She could feel each one resting there and how warm each one was. "Right out that front door," Jack said softly. His hand flattened and in no time at all had slid around and spread itself over her kidney, whose shape she could suddenly feel glow under the bone. She thought if he pressed down he could go right through her, could hold her spine like a baseball bat. It was the queerest feeling. She was afraid she would wet her pants. She had trouble thinking about dying and her kidneys at the same time and would never know, even now, which thought produced the slight, involuntary shudder which ran over her, standing there.

"Do you inherit this house? Are you going to live here?" She caught herself looking into the future.

"Not on your life. I got out of the army and came by for one look, that's all. Now I've seen everything but my mother's grave." Was his hand pressing? "So tomorrow I leave and I'll not be back. You better go home where you belong."

Yes. There was weight against her back. And she might have stiffened against his hand and drawn away but for the curiosity about the nature of her own skin, which felt like Jell-O. He could have driven his whole hand through her, found the near-baby and pulled it out like a doll from a box. *What's this? It's a tumor, you fool; put it back.*

I am going to have to kill my own self, she thought, letting him pull her. Just the way Mama said: If you want anything done right, you have to do it yourself. She was smiling as she touched his shoulders. With his two hands he brought her sideways onto his lap and they were rocking together in Aunt

Tyna's chair. The army cloth was scratchy. He drew Bebe's face next to his, one of his ears hot by her eye. He still had on his damn army hat so she flung that into the dark. Then his mouth was all over hers, hard, a jawbone. She dried up from terror as if someone had suddenly ground a shaving mug in her face and she did pull back then; but he would not. The wood frame of the chair scraped her elbow. She pushed him and grunted. It was as bad as kissing a skull and she was afraid again.

Then his tongue, which should have felt hard as a shoehorn, dropped wet and warm into her mouth. His hold on her eased, less needed, for Bebe had already begun to sink into him. His taste was not pleasant, sharp from tobacco, yet she was starved for it. Something caught her breast but, right then, it could have been anybody's hand, some passerby; she was not thinking of that yet. In a minute she rested her face in his neck, rocking, and his breath blew down the roots of her hair.

Very softly he said, "Turn this way. Bebe? This way, Bebe."

It hardly seemed real, her slow uncertain movements, the awkward shift until she was still in his lap but astraddle, and the chair swaying very slightly. He put one hand up her white dress, he put two hands. "Now kiss me." There were tongues in her everywhere.

She tried to say down his throat, "Now! Oh, now!" but he kept on until it was way too late for her.

Then they got down on the floor and he raped what was left of her—Bebe didn't care—and they fell asleep thrown down on Aunt Tyna's rug like a pair of old broken balloons.

Jack got her back into her own house before daylight; Bebe hardly remembered the ladder this time, nor how they got inside.

She felt drunk. Laughed and said astonishing things which

she later forgot. He climbed to her bedroom first and held out his hand; she remembered that part. She started to say, "Don't step on that razor blade." Let it go, she thought.

Inside her bedroom. She was singing and didn't care if Troy woke up or anything. "Shhh," said Jack. She sang, "There will be peace in the valley for me," and she meant a sexual valley, but he shushed her. She pulled his shirttail out and goosed him under the arms, laughing. She goosed him hard so the smell of him would be under her fingernails. "You trying to wake everybody up?" he said.

Walt Fetner would make him marry her and *that* would be some solution, she thought, but she couldn't concentrate on that. "Spend the night," she said.

"You know I can't." He switched on the pink lamp by her bed and they stared at each other, almost shocked to put faces to their recent movements. Bebe looked away. Jack wasn't really handsome except for those glinting blue eyes and, God knew, she was too used up to be pretty and wouldn't even look like Alice Faye's distant cousin. He didn't look much like John Lund, after all. His hair was darker and his features sharp. The bones on the bridge of his nose and along his jaw looked as if a file had been used to stroke them an edge. No wonder his mouth felt cruel at first. One of his eyebrows kept flying up by itself and had cut a wedge-shaped wrinkle in his brow. He wasn't much taller than Bebe and not nearly so big as he'd seemed in the dark. His eyes were the bluest she had ever seen and, being the color of the sky, they looked capable of seeing much farther than brown eyes could, right through the roof of the world.

She grabbed a brush from the dresser and started working on her hair, which was honey blond then, with a peroxide streak on one side.

"I'm going in a minute." He looked at the football pennant

over her bed. The snapshots of Guy Madison and Gable and Cary Grant, which were autographed and had turned yellow on her wall. There was a pink silk cushion a sailor had bought her on a weekend at Wrightsville Beach. She had put up glass shelves, buying brackets at a discount from the hardware store, on which sat two cups and saucers with a design she liked. It seemed very childish now. She brushed so fast her arm ached. She had Kotex boxes sitting out everywhere, for luck, and a sanitary belt hanging in plain sight on the closet doorknob, with coffee-colored stains on the elastic. A bitch or a heifer, that's how she felt.

Jack lay down and put his head on the sailor's cushion. "Just come here one minute and I'll go." Bebe shook her head. Her scalp was stinging.

"One minute. A peaceful one. I was too fast before."

Bebe said she wasn't coming. The next minute she lay atop him, not making love, not even kissing, too tired for any of that. Jack lay spread with her head under his honed chin, her arms wide on his wide arms. His thighs wide, too, and hers between. It wasn't comfortable. Her gaiety had vanished. She stared at the wallpaper.

"Next time I'm here, I'll look you up."

"You're not coming back." She had a good view of his warty Adam's apple. I am going downhill from now on, she thought. Next thing I'll be peddling it in the streets. She would have to move to a bigger city. She couldn't make a decent living in Greenway, indecently. "Besides, if you do come back I won't be here."

"I could bring you a present."

"Big deal. Keep your old present." Under her mouth a patch of skin the size of a quarter smarted and burned. Beard burn. I am going to turn out to be a tramp, after all. She rolled off him into the cool pillow and turned her face to the darkest wall. She was suddenly so sleepy her body had liquefied so if she'd had the energy it would have flexed at odd places. Bent between wrist and elbow, for instance.

"You're not angry?"

She wouldn't have answered him for a diamond bracelet.

He sat up. "See you tomorrow before I go?"

"You know where I live." If she never saw him again it would be too soon. She was drifting toward sleep, pausing only to decide that tomorrow night with the razor blade would be *it*. Next thing he was saying to the back of her head, "O.K. I'm gone."

Half asleep. "All right."

"You're pretty." He touched one finger to her spine, low, and let it slide slowly down the vertebrae. She opened her eyes and stared at the bedroom wall. His finger ran down her backbone like a stick on a picket fence. It moved on all the way, and the hand, too, like a saddle, held there, getting warm. I will be damned, Bebe thought, coming awake. He can do it any time he pleases. She was astonished at her own response.

He said, "Good-bye, then, Bebe Fetner," and the bed shook and he was out the window before she could even get up and ask him what was so damn special about *him?* He slid down a porch post, she guessed, and got paint streaks on his uniform. She went to sleep still dressed, the lamp glaring.

Next morning when she woke the white piqué dress was stained and her stomach felt as if it had been marched on. At first she thought Jack had hurt her deep; she was aborting; she swallowed four aspirins and hunched around the room holding herself and moaning. Then she saw it was only her regular menstrual period, after all, late but quite normal, jarred loose and set flowing while she slept.

At that she locked herself in the bathroom and cried so hard the ache in her loins spread through her chest and locked. Her scraped face swelled and felt prickly when she moved her jaw. A pimple took shape by her nose. She wiped her whole face with alcohol and took a hot bath with Lysol in the water to kill any germs he had. She sang "Blue Skies" in the tub, with a Crosby warble.

Then she took a second bath with scented bath oil and shaved her armpits and her legs all the way up to the pubic hair. She was beautiful lying in the water. She thought she might lie in bathwater for days and soak and drain and soak and start life over fresh as a newborn.

Troy beat on the bathroom door and then Earl beat. But Bebe just lay there singing and spreading the wet washcloth over herself in different locations till the palms of both hands were shriveled.

Then she put on a pair of old blue jeans and a bathing suit halter and a shirt over that. She went down to the kitchen.

"Earl said you was dead in the bathroom." Mama pushed cups along the table to make room. "You can dry your skin like that."

"I got the curse," she said.

"You know it's safer those days to just *wipe off,*" sniffed Mama.

Yesterday the coffee had given off a stench that meant morning sickness. Now it smelled wonderful. Bebe carried a cup to the hall telephone, calling back, "No, it's not my Saturday to work and I'm sick of the hardware store anyway."

Then she called up somebody and wrapped her shirttail over the telephone mouthpiece. In a deep British voice she said, "This is just a friend and it's all over town about you taking Bebe Fetner twice to the Great Pines Tourist Court." There was nothing but a choking noise in her ear. "And here she is pregnant and already telling people whose it is. You better marry that girl quick before her daddy lights out after you. Or her brothers."

She hung up. *Blue skies smiling at me / Nothing but blue skies* . . . Lit a cigarette, drank coffee. In a few minutes the telephone rang. She let it sing out four times. Then she picked it up and waited, trying to blow smoke upward in a ring. No, she couldn't. She propped her bare feet on the embroidered spread and the kerosene lamp sloshed around. No. No, she couldn't even take supper at his mother's house. Bebe told him, sighing, that she had just got up and wasn't feeling too good these mornings. While his words got faster, she slurped up coffee and belched for him once or twice. She scraped her nails over the mouthpiece, claimed she couldn't hear half of his question and made him ask it three times before she let him know she wouldn't marry him if he was the last son-of-a-bitch on earth.

She hung up. Laughed. She jerked the umbrella out of its crock and pranced down the hall, a majorette, and high-stepped around the kitchen table.

Mama stopped rinsing cabbage leaves to watch and held out her hand so Bebe could leave her coffee cup in it second march around. She'd been listening to the telephone conversation. "Bebe Fetner, just what has got into you?"

That was the funniest question she had ever heard. She started laughing, fell on the icebox handle laughing. She grabbed Mama and hugged her. Mama felt different. Big as she was, wide and heavy as she stood, Bebe saw that one hot wind could carry her off, that Mama might die before Monday—of nothing, really. She hung onto that fatness and shook her, half between laughing and crying.

Then she ran out the back door to the toolshed and moved lumber and sawhorses till she could locate Troy's old bicycle. It wasn't in bad shape since he still used it to keep his weight down, but the back tire was flat. By the time Bebe pumped that up she was sweating and had an ache at her navel.

She threw the pump into the shed. Mama came out on the porch and waved a knife at her. "You ride that thing now, Bebe, you'll get the cramps. If you don't get them this month, you'll get them next." She thought there was retribution in the cycle.

"No I won't."

"Well, button up that shirt. People will think you're some hoor."

"No they won't." Bebe looked at her over the bicycle handlebars, across the porch rail with buckets of ivy on it in a line. Mama did not stand much higher than their leaves. She shook the butcher knife at Bebe like a sharpened finger and said in a threatening voice, "Your daddy's gone uptown. He's getting a tooth pulled."

Bebe threw a leg over the bar and sat down very tenderly.

"You'll be back around twelve?"

"Sure."

The long ride led through the main part of Greenway, past the stores and the Playhouse theater, down the sidewalk by the Stone County Courthouse, where old men sat on the wall and leaned back against the swinging chain fence. Two pyramids of cannonballs were stacked on the courthouse lawn in front of two plugged cannons. Once, in honor of homecoming game, Troy took two mannequins from Penney's and set them downhill on Waverly Avenue, and rolled the black shot down the street like bowling balls. Had to work at Penney's all summer for nothing, to pay for the damage.

Bebe had to pedal to the very end of Waverly outside the town limits to reach Oakdale Cemetery. Steep hills she pushed the bike alongside the curb. She was sore and the folds of her jeans kept rubbing her . . . none of the words seemed right. She knew the names men had for that part of women, but she didn't use words like that then.

The outdoor clock at the bank said 11 A.M. Bebe was tired and beginning to wonder what she'd do if bloodstains seeped through her pants. Mr. Sloan was changing the slope of his awning in front of the hardware store. She stopped in the street although she had seen it rolled up and down a hundred times. I don't think I can work there anymore, she thought. Mr. Sloan threw his stomach in and chest out as she coasted by, and waved. She passed gracefully, as if it were the first time, honey, not the last.

The lower part of Waverly was split by grassy islands with three boxwoods at both ends. In the middle of each stood a granite slab with a brass plate listing which Greenway soldiers had died or survived which wars. Bebe rode by the Civil War, and the Spanish American, the First World War, with Walt Fetner's name on it, and the Second, thinking her daddy's tooth was out by now and he wouldn't be able to eat anything but soup.

Oakdale was Greenway's biggest cemetery because it was interdenominational and even Catholics could sleep there so long as they were white, and city taxes were paid to keep the grass mowed. The grounds were acres wide, with winding drives and curbing painted white by city workmen. On Sunday afternoons, people drove through just to see what was blooming and guess who was lately dead. The blacktop road swerved into pockets and looped over slopes and between Lombardy poplars. Bebe began to pedal furiously, knowing how quickly a curve or a high mausoleum could hide one person from another's sight. She had no idea where Serena Mae was buried. She whizzed downhill and took the wide turns, zipping past Grandma Fetner, who wouldn't lie at Hebron because they were mad at the preacher that year. She passed a classmate who got nephritis in the sixth grade, and a cancerous neighbor who died so slowly in public everybody was glad to see her go.

Few people in Greenway feared the graveyard. On Sunday mornings, a garbage truck drove slowly through to pick up the condoms and beer cans before church let out. Bebe herself had necked in the cemetery more than once, and an enterprising tenth grader had here laid her hand on his swelling fly. His solidity was a surprise. Until that night, she had wondered how males could unfold themselves enough to make entry and why all that softness would not tumble out again.

Bebe stopped the bicycle. That had to be Jack Sellars, uphill, the back of his uniform to her. Nothing in front of him but a patch of grass; the stone must be laid flat in the ground, between his army shoes, and he looking down upon his mother's name. Bebe dragged Troy's bicycle off the road, leaned it against a small copy of the Washington Monument. Then she leaned, too. So tired, and sore, and sweat stinging on her scraped chin and a fold of gauze thrust into her . . . softest place. Yes, he had nice shoulders. She leaned on the granite, panting.

Then she stepped out between two graves and, seeing he had not turned, screamed uphill, "*Jack Sellars!*"

He swayed forward as if struck between the shoulder blades. Bebe grabbed for a handlebar, thinking how quick she could ride out of there and get on a train and go learn how to dance with Gene Kelly.

He spun, looked down the slope. She threw back her sweaty hair. She had planned to look cool, blond, and tall; she needed a Vera-Ellen dancing dress split up both thighs. She walked toward him from the granite column.

Perhaps Jack saw a tangle-haired newsboy, the way he squinted, bent to the left, shaded his eyes. Took a few hesitant steps.

Oh, let him run! Bebe thought. Let him be the first to run!

He was striding. He said something she was too far away to hear. She hoped it was her own name. The sun was behind him so he seemed to be walking out of the light. She could not wait forever to give him his chance to run, so she ran. Her arms flew at each side as if unstrung. At last Jack was running, too, and with no grace at all their bodies struck each other, hard. Bebe rolled off to one side and almost fell.

But Jack was between her and the gravebeds and caught her so hard both feet left the ground. He lifted her high. Bebe turned one cheek against his forehead and the tickles of his army haircut. There was such pressure in her throat and chest she lost all track of what it might be—tears or joy or nausea? It was the same when Bebe was six and went tensely to the first day of school and knew that, from then on, she would be molded and changed. *I am bringing you, Miss First Grade Teacher, my whole life up to now.* And she did change it.

Bebe whispered, "Jack?" as if she were checking on who he was, since she had plunged up the hill to him, clanging her whole life behind her, such as it was. She drew back slightly and looked at the smile wrinkles drawn around those blue eyes. Did he know? No, he had yet to hear the clatter attached to Bebe like a comet's tail. When she kissed him it was more that her mouth struck his, demanding attention. She so much wanted him to feel the great load of all she could not say.

Maybe Jack felt some of it. Looking puzzled, he let her slide down, held her lightly. He stared over her shoulder, his blue gaze altogether gone. Then it flicked back and he said, "Good morning, Bebe Fetner," and smiled. He touched her face with one extended finger. "You got a raw place on your chin—mine?"

"Yours."

With his arm around her waist, he led her so they walked paired up the hill together. "Show you something," he said.

At his mother's grave, Bebe knelt to run her finger over the letters. Gravestones ought to be read with the flesh, she had always thought; eyes aren't enough. SERENA MAE WILLETT SELLARS. BORN AUG. 1, 1904. DIED AUG. 10, 1949. Maybe she decided on her forty-fifth birthday she'd had enough years and began measuring linen closets. Beside her slept JOHN ALQUIST SELLARS. Hacked to Death in 1935, though it didn't say that, of course. Bebe glanced around but Lester and Tyna Sherrill had been buried on a different hill. There were no other Willetts and no Alquists, just these two people paired off and filed away in this grass forever. There were no flowers on either grave.

Jack pulled out two pieces of cardboard held by a rubber band, took them apart, and showed her the yellowing picture of a young woman whose face looked thin and breakable and whose wide eyes—Bebe guessed—had also been as blue as beryls. Jack tapped his fingernail on that fading innocence. "Could you believe it?" She could not.

Anger came over her then and she frowned at the sky. That it could happen, bad enough; happen at twilight with nothing around but whippoorwills, terrible; but happen for a boy to watch? She thought angrily toward the sky: You really did mess up there.

Jack rewrapped the photograph and put it away. "What made you come out here this morning?"

She couldn't find the right answer and decided to be flippant. "Well, I know I'm not pregnant, so that's out."

Again he examined her chin and smiled. "You look good in the daylight," he said.

"You ain't bad," she said, suddenly embarrassed.

They began, aimlessly, to walk. In the next family plot lay a little girl, four years old, no reason given. The hot wind whispered in the mimosa trees. Over an aged mother, the children had put up a slender stone with the motto "Heaven is richer."

She showed him the grave of the local atheist, who had always been a good boy until he went to Chapel Hill and read the wrong books. "Grave upon my tombstone deep / Death is but a little sleep / And to me this life did seem / Smaller, passing, fitful dream." They passed on, reading epitaphs aloud. "This man was ninety-eight years old," Jack might announce, and she'd answer, "The whole family's here and died close together. Must have been an epidemic." All this sadness was sweet to Bebe—how we come and go and mimosas bloom—and she caught Jack's hand and squeezed it.

"Whose big stone box is that?"

"Allen, the cotton mill Allens. Practically our founding fathers." Up close, the gray mausoleum looked almost frivolous, like a gingerbread house that had molded in damp weather. Walt Fetner's hard work on a spinning frame, often when he was hung over, had helped ship some of this stone all the way from Italy so the Allens might wait out eternity in finer quarters than their neighbors. She showed Jack the brass plate by the door: Thomas and Nellie Grimes Allen, Mildred and Sam. "One daughter ran away and was never heard from again," she said, and in that instant knew she would never spend another night in Greenway.

Jack pulled her to the shady side of the mausoleum, dark under magnolias and cedars. He tried to slip a hand down the waist of her jeans. "No," she said.

"What did you come for, then?"

Bebe shook her head. "You opened me up and made me bleed."

It seemed he was trying to read her face. "You always come down like that, to anybody that stands under your bedroom window?" She said nothing. "You didn't know one thing about me," he persisted. But it seemed to her, now, that she had known everything and had been acting on that knowledge in advance of recognizing it. She knew no way to explain such a peculiar thing.

"But it was *you,*" she said firmly. He shook his head. Bebe caught his hand and pushed it under her shirt and onto her breast, deciding that was probably why she had worn the swimsuit top in the first place. She felt abruptly dizzy. It was true. Simply by touching her, anytime, he could scramble her up inside.

Openmouthed, he kissed her on the neck. "You are going to get hurt trusting people like that."

Big deal, she thought dreamily.

He said at her shoulder, "I was going to come back today and knock on your front door. And start over."

Bebe would never know if that was true or said only because her breast lay in his hand like a gift. He held her gently and breathed into her ear. How was he made and put together? She pressed at his waist and on his back. When he lowered his head to nuzzle at her breasts, she cupped his prickly skull. She wanted to grind the tips of two fingers inside his ears. He said something but Bebe's skin blotted it up. She framed his face and brought it to her own. "What was that?"

He was flushed and fast of breath. "My bus. Leaves in an hour."

His wide blue eyes were very near, the sandy lashes, some crooked blood vessels. She closed off the vivid color with her thumb and rubbed his wrinkled lid. Her throat hurt. There's no way to know what lies behind a look nor inside a body, no way at all. "You can't go."

"I'm going." He pulled back. "I'm glad you came, though."

"You would just *leave?*" Loose from him, she felt suddenly withered. She slapped the front of her shirt together, looking down at the scattered magnolia leaves, tough as cardboard dropped in the grass.

He said seriously, "You're the only good thing that ever happened to me here. I'll never forget you."

She was furious. "Well, big damn deal, Jack Sellars!" She turned to go back to the bicycle, weighing nothing at all except in the throat, where some stone had lodged.

To her back he said, "Bebe?"

She stamped around the corner of the mausoleum. Out of sight, she heard him say, "Would you want to come? You wouldn't, would you?" She went by the brass doorplate and the concrete door with its jailer's window and turned the other corner and pressed herself to that stone wall like a leaf driven flat by the wind. She had planned to cry there, but it wouldn't come out over her dry tongue.

Then he shouted, "Bebe? Please come with me."

So she could cry after all. She circled the building and fell wailing on his back. If some reporter had come up with a microphone then, from the Pathé News, and asked her if she loved Jack Sellars, she'd have cried: "No, of course not!" How was that possible so fast! He couldn't have loved her yet, either. Bebe would have told the microphone that she was only fighting to survive—that right then it seemed her body could not survive apart from his, that touching him was as urgent as food or water once had been. That he was her medicine and her transfusion and that she grabbed onto him from selfishness and greed. That it even disgusted her a little! And that he might hang on to her for fifty other reasons she didn't know and didn't care to know.

Nobody asked Bebe then. And by the time somebody did, she had begun the slower act of loving him, which wasn't completed yet.

They left Greenway with Bebe dressed just as she was and Mama was right—the bus driver thought she was a hoor.

From the terminal she called home and told Mama she was

getting married and would write her a letter, and where they could pick up Troy's bicycle.

"What is it doing *there*?" screamed Mama, and started crying.

Walt Fetner came to the telephone, his mouth swollen and full of blood, and yelled a lot of things Bebe couldn't understand.

"Tell Earl and Troy good-bye." He gurgled. She managed to say, "His name is Jack Sellars," and Daddy said, "*Jesus Christ!*" "No, Sellars," said Bebe, sniffling.

In Winston-Salem Jack said they would get off the bus and spend his severance pay from the army in some place that had inner-spring mattresses. He bought her some dresses. Bebe could have used a little sweet talk but he was the quiet type and she had to figure everything out by the way he rode on the bus, always with one hand touching her somewhere.

That night she lay in bed wearing nothing but a sanitary belt and a pad and he had to come by friction alone, cursing under his breath. She was afraid. A stranger, bearing down on her in the night. Long after Jack fell into his deep sleep, she lay in the squeaky bed and tried to remember who she was. He had only to turn and brush her in the dark and saliva would rush in her mouth. She was very frightened and did not understand herself.

The second night they were still in the Winston-Salem hotel and he hadn't married her yet, nor mentioned it. He said at her hair, "Take that damn thing off."

"I can't." Of all the movies she had ever seen, there wasn't a one to help her now. She didn't believe Claudette Colbert ever felt like that about Clark Gable, or had been in such a fix.

"You can take it off," Jack said in the dark bed. He ran his hands over her. "When you start wanting me bad, that flow will stop. It's like changing gears."

Angry, she hit him. He grabbed hold of her hand, too tight, and then rubbed it with his chin. "I promise you it's true."

Bebe got loose and rolled away. "That's all you wanted me for."

"It's a lot." He caught her hand again. "Touch me one time."

"I won't."

"You will," he said softly, "when you're ready."

She tried to lie stiff as a broom handle while he was tracing the shape of her with his slow fingers. "I keep thinking I'll wake up in the morning and you'll be gone," Jack said. She couldn't think of a single place to go, even Hollywood. Then he pulled that hand around himself and held it there and lay long against her, groping for that elastic band she wore. She kept still, amazed at the feel of him. Was it possible for an ordinary hand to be *hungry?* He kissed her very slow. She thought: He's only a stranger and knows things I don't even know about myself.

She lay in a dream, a white slave, sold to the sultan when she was really a bright girl reporter for *The New York Times,* helpless now in his Baghdad palace. Whatever the sultan said to do, she'd have to do. "Yes," said the sultan, "and now here," and moved her hand. By then the Turks were removing the last of her cheesecloth costume, touching her here and there with their oily hands. She was drugged from their spicy wines. "I'll be gentle," the sultan said, and pulled her over till she sank on him and he whispered, "Now. Stretch out and lie still." But she could not keep from moving. "Shhh," Jack said then. "We have years. We can sleep and start over." He moved very slightly. "There's nothing we won't have the time to try."

Bebe knew then he would marry her. No point in pretending, then, or in hiding her need for him. When things stopped feeling this good she might lie, but not now. So she moved and they hurried and Jack stopped being gentle and afterward both slept deeply with only her foot touching his foot.

Next morning, in Forsyth County Courthouse, Bebe married in daylight a man named Jack Sellars she had known two days chiefly because he inhabited the body which, in the night, inhabited hers so well. Maybe that wasn't the best reason to marry. Maybe those who talk about common interests and compatibility had something on their side. Bebe would never know about that. Had never cared. Jack made her own body sweet to her, and she couldn't bear to have that feeling stop. And it never did. It had waxed and waned; she had sometimes wanted others, and no doubt he had as well. At forty, Bebe could watch Mickey swagger down the beach and know just how he'd feel sliding into her; she could imagine rising to him and swinging both feet high. Could have, she thought, screwed a lot of men and liked it every time.

But even now, after all those years and at her age, when she lay there in her old bed in her old room in Greenway, smiling, and slipped both hands down between her legs, they were only substitutes for Jack's.

Treva Fetner was the world's best housekeeper. She couldn't leave for Mount Hebron Monday until every dish from lunch was dried and put away and she had set out a bowl of ammonia and water on the kitchen table to banish all odor of food. Then, while Earl fumed (but admired her singlemindedness), she had to sit down for the 1 P.M. television show of household hints. She copied directions for making a pomander ball. At last she allowed him to load the car trunk with her foil-wrapped packages and they set off for Connor Street.

Bebe was waiting on the front porch in a pair of shorts and a see-through blouse. "She's the guest of honor," Tweet murmured severely. Also, she let her cuticles grow every which way.

"Looks good, too." Earl grinned.

"If you would just fix that tooth." She leaned out to wave joyfully to Bebe and Mama as they carried out food in a cardboard box with only a clean dish towel thrown over the bowls. Then the foursome drove down Connor Street in one of Earl's 1968 "sapphires," with air-conditioning and windows which rolled up and down from the driver's instrument panel. Tweet had her hair in big rollers under a shower cap and wanted Bebe to comb her out before the reunion crowd arrived. "You don't have to roll yours much, do you?"

Bebe said, "Trouble enough to comb the stuff."

"Earl, she has *seen* the window," snapped Mama, to make Earl stop playing with the switches.

Tweet leaned over the blue seat. "You put anything on your hair, Bebe, to keep it so blond?"

Bebe lied and said no, so Tweet lied and said she didn't either. "I hope those kids won't drive too fast," she worried to Earl. "I'm not even sure Kenneth knows how to get there. Earl gave Kenneth the fastest car he handles as soon as he turned sixteen."

Earl stopped sideways in two parking places to show Bebe a new office building seven stories high. "This is where the old Herb House used to stand—remember that, Bebe?"

She remembered its big sign: THE HERBARIUM OF WALLACE BROS. The Fetners all came uptown to watch it burn in the thirties, and that sign crinkled up in the flames like a card on the fireplace logs.

"This town is growing," Earl said as he drove away. "You and Jack should have considered it."

Tweet pulled out hairpins. "I don't know why Troy wanted to move off by himself that way."

"Troy!" Earl flapped his snuff-brown hank of hair.

Mama said to herself, "My foot feels so numb I wonder if I'm getting what Jiggs got."

"Jiggs who?"

"Gout, that's what it was. I wonder how gout gets started."

"Earl thinks it has had a bad effect on him, living out there. And Mary Ruth is just not the same person."

Mama said she had never known a soul to have gout, though, except in the funny papers.

"Bebe? Did you hear I was in politics now? I'm the Stone County manager of the American party? For George Wallace? I bet Mama wrote you. I bet she sent you the piece from the paper."

No, she didn't. Never the singer Troy had always been, Earl nonetheless offered the campaign lyrics set to the tune of "Are You from Dixie?" "Are you for Wallace? / Well, we're for Wallace! / He will fight to keep America strong!"

It made Bebe think of Mickey McCane. She said to Mama softly, "Wallace is so common."

But Earl heard. "Common *sense,* you mean. Little more of it and we could stop the federal government from trifling with our children's education. Tweet and me worries all the time." He patted her, next to him on the front seat. "Don't we, honey? You'd feel different, Bebe, if you had any children."

Fearful Bebe's sore point had been rapped, Mama leaned forward and asked fiercely in Tweet's ear, "Did you bring a can opener? Ice pick? You got a ladle for the tea?" Tweet nodded her mousy coils of hair.

"You've got to admit Wallace is a man will say what he thinks, Bebe."

"If you call that thinking. Troy rode me by your car lot, Earl. It's really something how the business has grown."

"Troy!" he said again. He turned onto the Hickory Highway. "You ought to talk to Troy while you're here. Draw him out. He's got . . . got things on his mind. He's not ambitious like he ought to be. He might be getting mixed up with the wrong people."

"That's not all he mixes," said Tweet.

"What people?"

"People that didn't grow up here and think they know it all. He is just down on everything. Moved way off in the woods. He just sits out there and thinks too much."

"Even Earl can't talk to him anymore," Tweet said.

As if Earl ever could. One time Earl got him a job at the chair factory that Troy didn't want, and Troy wouldn't take it and they had a big fight in the backyard. Daddy was lying in the hospital with his first heart attack, the mild one, and Earl said Troy was worrying him to death being shiftless. It nearly landed Earl in the hospital, too. And overnight a set of mock Burma-Shave signs went up by the road at 217 Connor Street:

BUSY BODY

BUTTED IN

BUT GOT

HIS BUTT

BEAT UP

The early shift going to the mill got a good laugh out of that.

Tweet said, "Troy's not a drunk or anything. We wouldn't want Bebe to think he was a drunk."

"No, but he's steady." Earl lit his menthol cigarette and said thoughtfully, "I'm going to send you and Jack some literature. Newspapers and TV—you can't believe them. They try to take pictures of Wallace sneezing, picking his teeth. They hate him. He says what everybody knows at heart and they hate him for that."

"How about Troy's job? Does he like it?"

Earl said grumpily he made fun of the whole business all the time.

Mama was moving restlessly in the backseat. "How about the lemons?" she demanded. "I just know you left the lemons."

Turning off the state highway, they rode by Greenway airport with its dozen small planes that seemed to be covered with crepe paper.

"Four bucks, they'll fly you over town," Tweet offered, but Earl drove his four dollars by at a faster speed. Bebe remembered when the runway was in corn and sweet potatoes and Alley Bost plowed it taking turns with his mules.

The next road was unpaved and dusty. Gone were the tenant houses of weathered black wood. They passed shoebox homes covered in brick veneer, some with pedestal glare balls or plastic chickens squatting in their sunbaked yards. A tire stuffed with petunias. One pink flamingo upright in the clay.

Another turn and—thank God! Something had stayed the way she left it. The powdery road still wound narrowly under thick oaks; a rusted barbwire fence on her side fell over years ago. Bebe rolled down the window, manually, not caring about Earl's air-conditioning. Weeds grew, oil-flecked, between the shallow ruts through the green, quiet tunnel. If Bebe believed in a Heaven and some way to get to it, she'd believe in a way like this. And you'd walk it, by yourself, late on a summer's day and God would wait at the end with a hand to shade His eyes, calling, "What took you so long?"

"You'd think," Earl complained, "they'd pave this thing."

Bebe saw the last bend coming. They swung it and the small white Hebron church, where it ought to be, sat six feet back from the road's edge, with a single wooden step to its broad blue door and a thin spire like a sharpened pencil. The name sign was still wired under warty scar bark on a low limb of the black gum. At the real Hebron they buried Abraham, Isaac, and Jacob. King David lived there. It was one of the cities of refuge.

Years before on surrounding farms, Morrison children and Fetner children and Alley Bost's children (and, if you went far enough back, Allen and Grimes children) grew up and played together, and on Sundays sat neatly in this church, males on the left side, females the right. Some of them married each other and moved into town but could not feel at home in the brick and stained glass of First Church, or Second Church, whose names even sounded impersonal; so mostly they gave up church except for holidays, and then they drove back to Hebron. Their children—Earl's age or Bebe's—often had no real church at all except for the summer revivals. But they admired the look of this one, so much like a toy, like a copy from history books or off Christmas cards.

For a minute after Earl parked, they sat still, pleased with how peaceful it was; then Tweet said, "This place doesn't seem real, does it?" meaning a compliment.

They were the first to arrive. Bebe combed out Tweet's hair in the car but Tweet thought the style was too loose for her face, and tamed it all down again. The women moved to the open-air shelter where picnic supper would later be spread. Kenneth Fetner roared up next in a ruby red speedster and helped Earl unload both cars. Bebe swept twigs off the long table under the pine-slab roof, half hearing Tweet and Mama talk about the preacher (too young), mosquitoes (knew they'd forget something—repellent), and why it wouldn't rain (no dew on the grass that morning).

"I guess the Loftins will come and I dread it." Mama slapped down spiderwebs from the rafters. The worst thing she could think of was to eat a living spider.

The Loftins were the family savages. Not a superstition or

tall tale they didn't believe. If ever a flying saucer passed over the southeast, some Loftin would see it in his third eye before the radar did. All of them, even the babies, got premonitions. One Christmas at the Fetners' house, Wesley Loftin threw salt over his left shoulder and it got in Troy's eyes. They were all crazy about salt. They cited some rule about putting a little salt on everything you owned every New Year's morning; if you didn't do that, somebody in the family would die before the year was gone.

"Honey," Mama used to tell Bebe, "they'd even have the bees salted." The Loftins did things like that all the time and then claimed credit when the rest of the family survived. Bebe wondered how long they could keep up those old ideas and look at television, too.

Tweet said, "You take a walk, look around before the crowd comes. I plan to scrub this table."

"You remember where your daddy is?" She remembered. She heard Tweet ask Mama how her hair looked and then turn down the advice, insisting, "No finger waves, Mama; finger waves are *out.*"

Mount Hebron churchyard was small, not grassed except by luck, in patches. Abelia bushes by the side choir door had been sheared this spring, as usual, round as yeast rolls. Behind ran the dry stone wall around the sloping graveyard, and at the bottom of the hill lay a large, spring-fed pond, which the congregation dug so there'd be water if the church caught fire and also for baptisms and youth swims. How typical that was! At Hebron, they'd always felt half of Christianity was being efficient.

The cemetery wasn't a bit like Oakdale, where Jack's parents lay. Very little shrubbery. Whatever grass grew must seed itself on the wind and dandelions got the best of that. Family plots were sometimes outlined in bricks or cement blocks or field stones. One time Miss Nannie Furman, who was the very one to think up something queer, saved quart fruit jars and filled them with sand she'd dyed with food coloring—red and green and orange, mostly—and set these in a low wall around her mother's grave with the lids buried deeply in the earth. They shone like four rows of traffic lights and in the hot sun the colors aged and streaked and the contents looked melted. Somebody finally talked her out of it after boys began stoning the red ones so the spilled sand gave the effect of blood seeping from underground.

Again Bebe felt the old sweet mimosa sadness.

Just going home at all was a way of admitting inside that you moved toward death. You don't even have to visit graveyards or mention the word, she thought. Just your old house and the people in it are enough to make you know: *The wheel is turning. I am on that wheel.*

A new car arrived. Teenagers Kenneth knew but Bebe didn't raced through the graves, towels flying, and threw themselves and their inner tubes into the muddy pond. Tweet screamed from the top of the hill to watch out for snakes and snapper turtles. They didn't care.

Walt Fetner's grave was near the rock wall. January 6, 1965. Maybe the Loftins didn't salt all the bees that year.

He was uptown one Saturday having his hair trimmed when his heart choked for want of blood. Now if that barber had been a Loftin, he'd never have lifted a scissors after that. Bebe came home from Durham. It wasn't his first attack, so naturally they thought he knew how to recover, although Mama didn't feel they were giving him enough medicine. Just to let him lie there and get either better or worse, she thought, was refusing to take sides. But he did get a little better and could eat and ask Bebe if Jack had gone crazy yet. Then a clot moved, and it rolled down his bloodstream like a musketball and plugged up his heart. Bebe was with him when he died. Seems that she knew one minute before it happened, and Daddy knew, too. He was like a grandfather clock ticking; then some hand she couldn't see reached in and blocked the pendulum, and he stopped. His eyes looked dreamy and lazy; he didn't seem to mind.

The bare space on Bebe's right was where Grace Fetner would someday be buried. It didn't look wide enough, but she might be skinny by the time she died. Bebe was only eight when Bertha Roseman, to the left, gave up to cancer. It ate her to the size of a little child.

More cars were parking on both sides of the sandy road. She heard astonished voices cry out, "Maude? Is that you?"

"How in the world, Vince, have you been?"

"I'll be dogged, Will."

Rolling through the churchyard, an old Nash finally nosed its way into oak shade. Troy and Mary Ruth climbed out, Troy wearing his squealing son wrapped around his neck like a scarf. He whirled so the boy grabbed for his nose. Mary Ruth, who'd be pretty if she weren't so pinch-mouthed, said something that got Randy set down on unsteady legs—he was nearly three—and Troy rummaged in the trunk for his mandolin. He saw Bebe and waved it. Mary Ruth called him back to carry a Thermos and three covered bowls to Tweet and Mama. She called, "Glad to have you home, Bebe!"

Set free, Troy trotted all the way around the rock wall and climbed inside where she sat by Daddy's grave. He was sweating, his face redder than one of Miss Nannie's fruit jars.

"Know what I do sometimes?" he panted, dropping cross-legged by the headstone. "Come out here late at night, empty a shotglassful, a small libation, on Daddy's grave. Sing him a song. 'That Silver-Haired Daddy of Mine'—remember that?"

Bebe laughed, because Walt Fetner had taught all three of his children the words. Said it was the most satisfying song ever to come over the radio.

Bebe told Troy that Mary Ruth looked good and how fast Randy was growing. "Does he have anybody to play with where you're living now?"

"I see Earl's been priming you." Troy grinned. He tuned up and sang in a bluegrass twang:

> *If Jesus appeared in a stable today*
> *The Mental Health Clinic would take him away.*
> *They'd put him in day care and foster households,*
> *They'd teach him to pee in a porcelain bowl.*

Mama screamed downhill, "*You cut that out!*" especially when she noticed the teenagers listening from the pond.

Bebe tried not to laugh. "You have been drinking."

"And drinking." He nodded. "Earl gets after me and Mary Ruth gets after me. Don't you start." He struck a sour chord on the mandolin. "I hate cars, you know that?" Lying back on a few tufts of grass, he squinted into the hot sky. "If I could be Randy's age again, I'd have the sense to stay that age, and live out in the woods and keep it simple."

"And never grow up?"

He said heavily, "And never grow down."

He reached for the mandolin again and backed up until he was propped against Walt Fetner's tombstone. "So what you want to sing?" He managed to grin. " 'Great Speckled Bird'? 'Lily of the Valley'?"

"Earl said you'd got hard to talk to."

"I've got hard for *Earl* to talk to." Troy tested a string and retuned it. "Earl's done the changing, Bebe. Someday you try to figure out how Earl is modern and hates the blacks, and I'm old-fashioned and don't. That's part of it."

Bebe was surprised that a second Fetner should even care. And that Earl and Troy should be having their fuss over race relations? Not to be believed. She wondered what Walt Fetner would have thought. A strike to get more money in his pay envelope was one thing, ward-heeling because of the easy comradeship it brought was one thing, but even the war had been too far away and large-scaled for their supper conversation.

And she was the same way. When Jack first bought the TV, she made resolutions about keeping up with current affairs. Soon she was bored. The evening news looked like a rerun every night, and the pattern of one day repeated the one of the day before.

"Let me get this straight; the problem is that he's working for Wallace and you're not? Is that it?"

"Oh, in a way." Troy shrugged. "What did you say you wanted to sing?"

Randy Fetner, in his underwear, headed for the pond. Troy yelled, "I've got him, Mary Ruth," and followed the boy to the water's edge. They looked alike. Randy was his late son. Troy married once before and it didn't work out. A daughter lived in Texas that he hadn't seen in ten years.

When he came back Bebe asked him to sing "Where the Roses Never Fade," and he did it so easily he must not have remembered where they had heard it last. Bebe joined in, very softly and pretty flat. Zorro would whine and paw at his ears to hear them. They watched Randy paddle in the shallows.

Mama expected thirty-five to fifty people at Hebron. Early arrivals were already walking the aisles between graves, nodding toward stones on this side and that because it was impolite to point where a dead man lay. Bebe spoke to them all, even the ones she had half forgot. There went Uncle Rollo Morrison,

Mama's kid brother, and his guinea pig wife with her Kodak. He was an electrician, learned it in the Signal Corps. Met Lorene in Arkansas.

"Hold it right there, right still!" cried Lorene, and snapped Bebe's picture. Their son, a student at Wake Forest, stood to one side and looked embarrassed to be there. He had hair as long as President Lincoln's.

Walking back to the shelter, Bebe could tell the Loftin family had arrived. One wiry girl was doing handstands while some Loftin screamed, "Don't do that, Sue! Your liver'll turn over and you'll die!" If it hadn't been for Loftins, how could they have kept their livers right side up so many years? Tweet rolled her eyes at Earl. She could not stand the Loftins, who were unsanitary in their habits and claimed conjur might make people sick as easy as any germ.

Mama hurried to Bebe, afraid she'd get the names wrong. "Bebe, I know you'll be glad to see Fred Loftin again. And Versie, of course. You remember their girls? Alma and Lou and Merle? Merle's married and lives up at Hiddenite. Which one's your husband, honey?" Merle, who must eat a lot of butter and pie, pointed out a chubby man with a fishing pole.

Versie Loftin, a tough whit-leather woman, her skin and hair almost the same shade of brown, looked more Cherokee than the rest of the family, though they all claimed a little. Bebe had always considered herself a lost princess, like that girl in *Broken Arrow.*

She remembered Versie by her popeyes, which were green and came at you like traffic lights. Students on passing school buses said Versie was a witch.

"Bebe, I knew you were coming because I been dropping forks all week," she said. She felt all over Bebe's hand for lumps. A few steps at a time her husband, Fred, edged away. He never did talk much. A dimestore rabbit's foot hung on his watch chain. The Head was his lucky sign, so Versie always said. He fished when the zodiac sign was in it, planted wondrous corn and cabbage then. This time he nodded and stepped aside and even pointed a hand so Bebe could see old Mamie Loftin, who must have been a hundred, bent like a sparrow inside a huge upholstered gray chair somebody must have carried to Hebron in a pickup truck. Bebe thought Mamie might not be sure where she was. Her eyes seemed to look straight through the glass bodies of everyone. Bebe bent down and spoke loudly and said her name twice, but still couldn't tell. Mamie didn't move and stared straight through the buttons on Bebe's blouse. One bony hand flew lightly up and down in her lap. She might even be back in 1890, carding wool. Bebe shouted, "*Good to see you, Mamie!*"

Versie laughed out loud. "Well, Bebe, that will do her good for a week!"

How would they know?

Fred had worked his way back to the truck and begun unloading rakes and scythes and hoes. The men knew it was time to work if the Loftins couldn't find any sign against it. More men had come than Bebe expected—just walked off from work today with some excuse. Each chose a tool and walked downhill into the graveyard, Earl with a hoe. Even Troy, carrying his wet son to Mary Ruth by the armpits, picked up a bucket and steel brush to scrub lichen off Daddy's tombstone. Half the cemetery must be Morrisons or Fetners from the way the group spread out across the hill. Younger women unloaded trowels and potted plants and there was some talk about whether cactus would seem disrespectful. Alma and Merle carried geraniums to plant over Will Loftin's head—old Mamie's husband, dead fifty years. Could Mamie possibly remember him? How he felt moving in and out of her body, long ago?

Bebe even wondered what her body would be like when a woman lived to be a hundred. Did everything grow back together except for a little hole to pee through? Old women were nearly hairless—she had seen Grandma Fetner naked once—and so bony, the flesh looking more and more like a dress they would soon discard.

Grace Fetner had brought ground cover plants in a berry box. Ajuga: bugleweed. It bloomed blue in the spring and in winters—Mama said—grew flat to the ground and turned purple. "It might look sort of . . . royal." Mama smiled, handing Bebe the box. Bebe was thinking of bugles and Gabriel with his. She followed her brothers and, as they cleared, began tipping the little plants out of their box and setting them evenly like a quilt pattern. Next door, Lorene had dwarf zinnias in Dixie cups.

Half a threat, Earl said, "I sure know how Daddy would have voted if he'd lived till nineteen sixty-eight."

"Do not," said Troy.

Bebe decided to interrupt. "Earl, if you had a Cotton Club up here would that be a false name for the KKK?"

Earl said it could be. "We got coon hunters' associations, things like that." He laughed. "Let Earl Warren put *that* up his ass."

"See, Bebe? You don't have to drink to rot your brain." Troy was laughing, too, but his tone was acid.

Earl leaned on his hoe. "So who would you like? John's baby brother? That one's out. Eugene McCarthy? Thurgood Marshall?"

Troy scrubbed the tombstone hard enough to grind away its surface. "Since Bebe's home, let's get along if we can."

Earl couldn't leave it alone. He dug up a thistle and left a crater. "I know how Daddy would have felt, that's all."

Bebe told them both to knock it off. She remembered the

good time Walt Fetner had when he struck the mill and made the Allens pay a decent wage, though he drank up his wage increase and considered it a gift from the upper classes. He'd always worked their ward for Roosevelt; a crippled guy; had guts. But Hubert Humphrey? Eugene McCarthy? He'd worked for a dozen foremen as slick as Nixon was. He wouldn't buy snake oil from a drummer like George Wallace. She said, "You boys quit fussing." She stuck ajuga where the thistle had been. "This November, Daddy would have gone fishing. Took him a Loftin to spit on the worms and stayed till midnight and had to be carried home." *Sleep well, Daddy.* She covered the plant almost tenderly. *You're not missing much.*

Slowly, perhaps against their will, the men relaxed. "That was a good ad yesterday," Earl forced himself to say.

And Troy, "Glad you liked it." He dipped the scrub brush, hummed softly "Sweeter Than the Flowers." Then Bebe put an alto under his first verse of "Can I Sleep in Your Barn Tonight, Mister?" and they were off, squatting on their haunches over Walt's grave, singing loud, grinning at each other. Earl was the only one left chopping weeds in the hot sun, and at first he wouldn't join in. But you could hear the others picking up lines they knew. "For it's cold sleeping out on the ground." They finished the song and Troy tightened a peg on his mandolin.

"I hope," Earl grunted, "you have not been out here drinking over our daddy's grave."

"That would dishonor him?" Troy strummed, gave him a sidelong look.

"Just don't you act up, Troy Fetner. I've got my children here."

Naturally that sent Troy straight to the rock wall, on which he started marching up and down and making the mandolin vibrate and the air vibrate from music. He played "Sweet

Fern," and picked up some help on the chorus. Men's rakes rasped on the sand like brushes over drumheads while Troy played. Even the teenagers, riding inner tubes like beetles on the pond, had joined in the songs, warbling sometimes, making fun, giving weak imitation yodels. Walt Fetner could really yodel and it sounded like his voice was out of joint—little they know, thought Bebe. "*Eeee*-haw!" the kids called from the water, faking it for Nashville. They had never lazed on porches on summer nights, blowing combs through cellophane, watching the low moon, hearing the train blow far down the track. Blow songs. "Freight Train Blues." "Wabash Cannon Ball." The songs which she once thought were all about Bebe were—to these youngsters—about history. She hummed, as a trial, "Hear the train blow, love," and it still seemed to be written for Bebe. Troy caught it and found the key. "Build me a castle / Forty feet high / So I can see him / As he rides by. / As he rides by, love / As he rides by / . . ." and Troy's tenor went arcing over the words and even Lorene, who had maybe learned the song in Arkansas, joined in, and the college boy, too.

Between stones in the graveyard wall a lizard showed his slim blue head and kept it out while Troy was marching on his roof. Still singing, Bebe watched the lizard flick his sharp tongue; maybe he sang, too, and they couldn't hear. That lizard might never have heard a human sing before, outside of church. Most creatures sang—the bugs, the birds, hounds and tomcats, roosters and bulls—but from one generation to the next they might all forget that humans could. The lizard had stuck his head into the sun to marvel, Bebe guessed, and she raised her voice. "Roses love sunshine / Violets love dew / Angels in Heaven / Know I love you."

Troy led them next in "Pins and Needles," "The Wreck on the Highway." He stood on the wall now, his long legs spread, and wailed like Roy Acuff. They sang "Beulah Land" and

"Wait for the Light to Shine." The busy women, too, had lined up beside the food tables, their high voices making a violin section: "Wait for the light!" Even Earl came in on that baritone echo: "Shine-shine-shine."

Troy bent at the waist and stage-whispered down to Bebe, "Now that old Earl mentions it, wouldn't a little booze go well about now?"

"I'm sure you've got some," Earl snapped, singing "Shine-shine-shine."

And they sang on, red and hot in the summer sun, their voices close to a shout. They felt alive, for once, at the top of their lungs and joined together by bonds their voices could only represent, and began unconsciously to lean close together and lock arms. "I've got that joy, joy, joy, joy, down in my heart / Down in my heart / Down in my heart / I've got that joy, joy, joy, joy, down in my heart / Down in my heart to stay." Bebe saw Mamie Loftin's big chair under a tree like a boulder. Even her deaf ears could hear this mighty roar of praise. Perhaps her spindly flying hand was keeping time.

When their throats finally got dry, the laughing women carried buckets of water up and down the graves. In Bebe's floated a dipper made from a long curved gourd, carved and varnished some tiresome winter, marked by a pocketknife with suns, moons, stars, and daisies. "Going to eat soon," the women warned. The cold well water tasted of the earth. Bebe's ajuga was all safely in the ground and Troy, mandolin hung around his neck, carried pails of water to settle it gently over their father's bones.

Earl swiped his forehead, happy. "You're really good on that mandolin, you know that, Troy? Listen, I never mean half what I say."

"What Fetner does?" Troy held the mandolin high, tried to see through the openings in its box, and he said, "Versie just told me if you put a snake rattle inside, the strings won't ever get damp. You ever heard that?"

They hadn't but, like Troy, stared at the mandolin and wondered. Where do these ideas come from? Bebe wondered. Who's to say it isn't so?

She stacked Lorene's used Dixie cups inside the berry box and carried them up the hill so they could be used for other flowers in another season. There seemed no place to put the box on the carpeted floor of Earl's sapphire, so she stuck it inside Tweet's litterbag hanging from the door handle. Old Mamie sat motionless in the plump chair where she was left, as if their music had blown past her on the wind. She looked to be sleeping, but no, her open eyes were staring at the pointed spire of Hebron church.

Alma Loftin stood by the choir door snapping off small twigs from an abelia bush. There was a white froth on the stems. Bebe had heard Jack complain of it—some kind of scale or fungus.

"Frog spit," Alma told her, frowning. "And poisonous. I wouldn't want some child to get it." She scooped a handful into the blackened oil drum in which they would later burn all the trash. A quartet was forming near the pond. No mandolin now—just the men's voices over the throb of Snapper Dobson's bass. Snapper was skinny, with an Adam's apple of amazing size, and his bass voice made foot soles on a church floor tickle. They sang "Will the Circle Be Unbroken?" Bebe breathed that echo. "By and by, Lord. By and by."

By now the food was spread and kept covered on the long pine table and Tweet was alert for flies. Bebe peeped under napkins, just like the other children. "This world is not my home," sang the quartet. "I'm just a-passing through."

But they would eat well, passing. Fried chicken, ham biscuits, potato salad, chess tarts, many sandwiches, deviled eggs, candied yams, ambrosia, a dozen cakes and pies, relishes, piccalilli, watermelon rind pickles, brandied peaches, coleslaw, baked ham, roast beef, cheese straws, pulled mints, sliced cantaloupe, cookies and pecan balls, pralines and brownies, jelly roll, grated sweet potato pudding. Bebe was tempted just to stand there and smell for an hour.

"Leaning," the men sang. "Leaning on the everlasting arms."

At the end of the table were three washtubs: lemonade, tea, and the last with block ice and a pick. Lorene and Mama, sitting in the grass, compared their swollen ankles. Letty Jean, Clara, Barbara, Diane, and Faye (Bebe learned from Versie) were the names of girls drying now their long lank hair and also sniffing at the food. Versie took her, too, to meet Christine, who had married Jerry Loftin last year. Everybody made her admire their angry-looking baby. Not nearly so handsome as the one on the bus but he had so much movement to look at here, and his looks were flying.

Mama struggled to her feet. "See how nice the graves look now! Bebe?" Daddy's grave seemed splotched with the new plants. Sticks and weeds had been piled up near the pond. Morrisons a hundred years gone now had their boxwoods pruned. Around the headstones had sprung up petunias and yellow marigolds and iris with their spears slashed back. Some of the stones were still wet from a Borax scrubbing. Even the plastic wreaths looked better since they had been dipped into the pond.

Mama whispered, "Don't you ever bring me any of those stinky marigolds. Or that cactus, either."

Bebe watched Troy climb over the stone wall to talk to somebody hidden in the edge of the adjoining woods. A Negro man—she had to learn now to say "black," having spent years learning not to say "cullid." Bebe remembered, then, that the

Wilkie farm lay near to Hebron church and all of them were cul—*black,* except the baby girl, who had freckles and hair and eyes the color of gingerbread. Was she supposed to call Phibby (Phyllis) black even though she was not?

Troy used to squirrel-hunt with Blake Wilkie. A generation back they had all been neighbors and had threshed each other's wheat. They all came to Daddy's funeral. Bebe imagined they must sit around nights now and laugh to hear Earl Fetner had gone into politics and on the Wallace side at that. Mrs. Wilkie came in to help Mama when all three children were born; she was the first one beyond the doctor to get a good look at Earl Fetner's ass. Surely the Wilkies could never take him seriously.

Lorene said, "Let's call them all to eat." Tweet added darkly that mayonnaise would *spoil.* She gave the teenage girls some pans to beat like tambourines. Letty Jean ran back and forth behind Mamie Loftin's silent chair, hollering and beating. ("Her *mother* was nervous," Aunt Versie said.) Like magicians the women began whipping their hands over the table, jerking off foil and wax paper, slicing desserts and thrusting spoons into bowls.

Just then somebody really screamed. Letty Jean's call rattled off in her throat.

For one instant all the men were stopped by that shriek upright where they quit working, the quartet open-mouthed halfway between "Leaning" and "Jesus," a field of carved monuments. They broke into movements. They ran; everybody rushed toward the pond. One of the children pointed. They saw a thrashing far out in the water, two white clubs that beat on the surface, dropped underneath, then pounded again.

Bebe could hear Mary Ruth: "Where's Randy? Where's Randy?"

Troy had leaped over the wall and already fallen prone into the water as the others poured downhill, and Blake Wilkie charged after him, slinging his felt hat behind him in the woods. Fat as she was, Mama cleared the stone wall in one jump, said "*Uh*" as she came down on that pinned leg; and ran into the pond like a driverless truck. A tire tube floated near the spot where the water moved more quietly.

The girl who had pointed was crying to anybody who would listen, "I looked out? I saw this tube? This little boy in it? I said, 'Little boy?' He just slid right down the middle hole! I looked out? Saw this tube? This little boy in it?"

Across the pond Troy swam with long, fast strokes. Bebe could hardly believe its bottom dropped off so fast. He still had on his shoes. Mama was just walking through water deeper at every step, her waist going out of sight now. Bebe plunged in and grabbed her. She drove on, leaving her wet apron in Bebe's hand. Swimming hard, Mary Ruth passed them both. This time Bebe squeezed up the flesh on Mama's back by handfuls and yanked hard enough to tear it from her bones. Earl thrashed in to lead her to the bank. In the tepid water Bebe stood to watch Troy dive, dive twice, then come up with the boy slung muddy on his shoulders in much the same way they had arrived. Mary Ruth splashed to them, beat on Randy's back all the way to shore, talking to him, calling him.

Troy stumbled with his load out of the water. He grabbed Randy's ankles so he hung upside down, as if newborn. None of the Loftins said one word about his liver turning over. While everyone watched, silent, Troy thrust a finger down the boy's throat. Mary Ruth was moaning.

And Randy blew out water, mud, and strangled noise.

The whole crowd, then, could draw in a long breath without stealing any oxygen he needed.

Hung in the air, Randy wrestled until he was handed to his mother, who folded over him as if she might cup him inside. Bebe's legs and shorts were heavy with water as she climbed wearily ashore. Mama, backed up against Earl's shoulder, closed her eyes. Bebe could see the quick tears.

Tweet said, "Troy, you better let a doctor check him."

He nodded, led Mary Ruth toward their car. Earl ran ahead to move them all into his newer, faster one, and the sapphire roared out of Hebron churchyard and down that dusty road. Bebe turned. Blake Wilkie, wet to the thigh, had started for the woods to find his hat. She called him back. "Thank you, Blake." He nodded. "Take dinner with us?" No. He said he was glad about the boy.

"Go get your people and come eat with us, Blake. You know you're welcome."

"No, thank you." Blake had let his hair grow bristly. There was a glaze over his face when he talked to Bebe and she saw that he did take Earl seriously and was no longer their friend in the old way. His reserve shocked her and she put out a hand to his arm. He stared at it until she took it away. She wanted to tell him, "Look how quickly Earl took the boy to the hospital!" A man who did that was all right. But Blake had already seen that.

Instead Bebe said, "I hope to get by to visit you while I'm home." She'd like to see Phibby and told him that. Blake said Phibby had moved to town now. His dark face had changed more than any other she had seen today, and not from aging. Acceptance was gone. From now on, Blake Wilkie might make judgments.

Uneasily, hopefully, Bebe said, "I like your haircut." Almost said hairdo. He nodded. She knew no way to bring up how common and trashy George Wallace was, so she wound up helping him find his hat, outrunning him, in fact, so she could be the one to bend down and pick it up and brush the leaves off and lay it in his hand. She didn't know whether he understood that or not, walking off in the woods so quietly like that, not setting it back on his head.

Slowly, Bebe turned away. Everyone was talking softly now, wandering up the hillside, outside the wall, far away from the tombstones. Hardly noticing what they did, awed children filled their cardboard plates and ate, stared at the quiet pond while their jaws were grinding. Soon all of them started to eat. A honeybee still struggled in a bowl of beet juice. Nobody mentioned it, or ate a beet. They tended to cluster in families.

"You'll remember this visit for sure," sighed Mama, wringing out her skirt. "Ought we to go on? Go to the hospital?"

"You'd only be getting in the way," said Versie.

"Can't there be brain damage after a close call like that?" Lorene wanted to know. She asked Merle's husband, an orderly at Stone County Hospital; he said yes. Alma Loftin pointed out a small grave in the east corner. *That* Fetner drowned, she thought. It didn't say so on his gravestone but people knew. Eighteen fifty-seven. In a millpond, she thought.

Her mouth full of cake, Versie said proudly, "I never worried for Randy, not one time. I've heard no death tick in the walls. The clocks are running, none of our doors been blowing open in the night. No dreams, no stars shooting. I had every faith Troy would pull him out in time. In fact . . ." She chewed and gazed at the sharp steeple. All awaited the good omen or lucky dream she might remember.

But Fred Loftin interrupted her before she could get her thoughts together. "Fix Granny a plate, I'll carry to her."

They examined the picked-over food. "What looks easy to chew?" Mamie, in her upholstered chair, had not let out a sound the whole time.

Versie piled a plate of banana pudding, deviled eggs, cake. "Lend me your pocketknife and I'll take some chicken meat off the bone." She chopped a fried breast into slivers the size of almonds.

"Give her some mints." Merle passed the tray. "They go down to nothing in your mouth."

Versie handed over the full plate. "I'll bring her some tea, Fred. What ice is left."

Old Mamie Loftin, twisted in the big chair, had leaned her head way back but it couldn't be the spire she was watching, after all. Bebe glanced up expecting a buzzard or hawk, but the sky was an empty, glaring blue, like aluminum.

Fred touched her gently on one arm. "Bet you've been feeling forgot!" He bent a little closer and for a minute it looked as if he sniffed, dog fashion, at her white face. The plate tipped. Eggs, pudding, chicken bits mixed in the grass. "Versie?"

"I told you I'd bring—What's the matter?" Versie stooped by the gray chair and set the tea glass by her shoe. "Is she gone?"

"Been gone. Feel how cool she's got."

Versie ran her fingers onto the corded neck in search of a pulse. "All the time we ate!" She exhaled, looked at her own fingers, absently wiped them on her skirt. "All the time we ate! I been just talking and laughing over there. You think the excitement? Seeing Troy's baby nearly drown?"

"You felt of her." Fred shook his head. "I don't think she lived much after we got here and set her down in this chair."

Stiff as a board, Versie stood behind the chair to study the upturned face, stepped this way and that to see how the chin had dropped and one set of fingers been laid in the other set. She noticed Mamie's wide gaze, followed it skyward, strained up herself in the glare. Again, she peered in the dead eyes and then, very slowly, spread one lid wider with her thumb and forefinger. "I wonder," she whispered, looking into it as through a keyhole, "I wonder what she saw."

• • •

"That sure did hack the Loftins. Having her die and them not warned in advance." Mama wiped off her kitchen stove and left the rag there in a wad. "Was that the phone?"

The operator was placing Bebe's call to Jack at night rates. She had been waiting in the hall and could not wait longer for the reassurance of his voice, snatched up the receiver, only to hear how different he sounded on the telephone. "Hello? Hello?"

"Hello, Jack?" She asked it uncertainly. As soon as she got a clear picture of how blue his eyes were she began to miss him. Either the ocean's roar or a singing in the wires came into her ear. "Are you all right?" she demanded. Jack seemed relieved to hear from her.

"Hey, Bebe! When you coming home?"

It was two places: home, the way time lay either ahead of you or behind.

No, he answered impatiently, of course the Pinheads hadn't come and yes, he had been lonesome. A few families touring the coast stayed overnight and brought loud radios, including one sucker who claimed to have a map to Teach's treasure. He sounded very far away. Bebe felt she was calling him up from yesterday.

"There's one more, too." Jack almost apologized. "This kid rode up on a motorcycle. He's dropped out of school to see the country, he says. I guess his draft board's after him. A nice boy even if his hair *is* long. He wanted to sleep out on Pickle Beach and asked what I'd charge for that."

"Right out on the beach?"

"That's just what I said, so I've put him in a trailer. It was empty anyway. That seems all right."

"How much are you charging for just one?" It must be the ocean, surely, not the wires, beating on Pickle Beach.

"Bebe, the thing was just sitting there empty."

"Free?"

"He's not but twenty years old and already give up on everything."

Free. "Well, finding a generous man must have cheered him up a lot."

Jack said, "This boy thinks all the babies born in the next ten years might be the last ones now that we've poisoned the air and water."

"How's Zorro?"

"What are they doing in schools these days to mix up kids like that? He's fine, just fine."

She couldn't help asking, "This boy isn't crazy, is he? He's not going to put a knife in you while you sleep?" The tide must be high and every window open. She felt homesick.

"No, he's not crazy." (Shouldn't have said that, Bebe guessed.) "What's been happening in Greenway?"

Bebe told him about the family reunion at Hebron but all she could get across was what happened, and not how it felt to her, happening.

"At least Mamie Loftin had a long, full life."

Those were Tweet's exact words, too. To Bebe, mostly, it looked long. "And Blake Wilkie came by but he wouldn't even eat with us—that's right, you never knew Blake Wilkie. Anyway, Earl is in politics now."

Not liking what little he knew about Earl, Jack said, "Your dog is stinking up these rugs. Should I hang them out?"

"Hang them in the sun." Bebe stretched one foot but couldn't quite reach Mama's conch shell with her bare toes; seemed she'd feel better if she could. "Jack, all this has given me the blues."

"Come on home then," he said, but she kept on.

"It is depressing here, and then it's happy, too."

"Mamie dying like that, no wonder you got depressed."

That wasn't it. She couldn't explain. It was the mixture of both feelings, happy-sad, so they spilled into each other until she could hardly tell the difference. All that singing, so full and loud; she could have flown up to Glory on that noise. Yet at those best moments, things seemed already to rush away, to be fading, even at the center of praise to be halfway gone.

"I look at something and it's halfway gone," she blurted.

"You hurry home. I'm halfway gone with you not here to look." Quickly Jack coughed. "Besides, your damn dog is giving me a fit."

They talked some more about when she'd come and he'd meet the Wilmington bus. He'd been invited for Pauline's clam fritters and Willis's color television. Sometimes he fed the boy in the trailer, who didn't seem to have much money and didn't seem to care.

Bebe broke in. "You're not riding his crazy motorcycle, I hope?" Couldn't get away from that word *crazy.* Jack had once owned one and she'd always been scared of how fast it went.

"I would if he'd let me."

Saying good-bye, she asked abruptly, "What's his name?"

"Foley Dickinson." Bebe could have had a boy almost that age. She'd never have named him that.

She hung up, walked to the front screen, and looked through the blaze of the streetlight to the twin black rails disappearing in the dark. "Mama? When does the train come by?"

"They don't run like they used to. There'll be a freight, quarter to nine, thereabouts."

Bebe wandered outdoors to the tracks and laid her penny flat on the black rail in the old way. One summer night a man dropped off the train at the Connor intersection and hid on their back porch where the icebox was, and had himself a meal of ham and radishes. When Daddy got home from late shift, the hobo was squatting by a low back window though there was nothing to see in that room except Mama asleep in her cotton slip. Daddy walked up behind him through the privet; it was a surprise to them both. The man turned and screamed—"Screamed like a woman," Daddy would say. "It confused me." He struck out at the stranger but his fist hit nothing but air. The man took off running down these same tracks. He was a black man. The Greenway police borrowed bloodhounds from the county prison camp and tracked him to the icebox and the window and for two miles by the tracks, but never caught him. All next day Troy and Bebe made casts of everybody's footprints using cornstarch and soda and water mix. Troy pulled up fingerprints on cellophane tape. They set out more food for bait so he'd come back the next night and they could see for themselves how a criminal looked.

The train came into sight, cutting the dark with its single eye. Slower than Bebe remembered. Smaller. Nothing but thirty-two boxcars and a man walking on their roofs who wouldn't wave back. Her penny had fallen off and she couldn't find it in the weeds and gravel.

Bebe called Mama through the moths on the screen door. "You want to ride out to Troy's with me and see how Randy is?"

"You go on if you know the way. I'm right tired."

That made Bebe search her out in the dark bedroom, spread out on the counterpane. "Your hip is hurting."

She lied and said it never hurt except when she was constipated. "You go on, now."

"No wonder, jumping that wall the way you did." Mama was sixty-nine. Bebe sat on her sprung mattress and touched her bobbed Nucoa hair which used to be blond and turned up in a roll all around her head. Maybe her head had always been small and that brim of hair had made it seem larger. "I could just call them." But Grace Fetner wouldn't have that.

So Bebe took the two-tone car Earl lent her (half ruby and

half pearl, she guessed) and drove out the bypass to find Troy's house. Mama's directions were to turn off onto smaller and smaller roads and at last go down a bumpy wagon track beyond the mailbox with FETNER lettered on it in red nail polish. With these bumps, Bebe thought, no wonder Troy's car is so beat up. Once she bounced so hard her head struck the ceiling of the car. With no warning at all the road turned uphill and the ruts changed into ditches on one of those sudden steep inclines that proved how close the Blue Ridge Mountains were. She felt safer creeping in low gear.

But there was no house on the crest. She braked going down again. Thick forest grew on both sides and the potholes hid tough roots of sweet gum and maple and oak, washed naked by the rains. Ahead, on the left, shone a single dim light. A small lamp in Randy's room, perhaps, so he wouldn't feel underwater in the dark.

The turnoff was marked by a pair of white stakes. Bebe parked in crisp leaves where her headlights picked out an A-frame lodge, brown and brown-roofed, with no front windows and little trim. In the night it might even look like a woodpile or old sawdust mound, and you'd drive right by. She switched off her lights.

The lamp was shining from the back. She could hear voices. Knowing Troy, she decided there probably wasn't a front doorbell. Slowly Bebe picked her way around the house through saplings, stones, drifts of leaves. Her heel dropped into the tunnel of some mole. She could see a screen porch at the rear. Downhill beyond that came the sound of running water. The sudden cool air felt almost solid. She stepped toward the square where porch light spilled and opened her mouth to call. Then she saw four people on the back porch instead of two, eating off a card table. The two white ones were Troy and Mary Ruth. The dark faces belonged to Blake and Otis Wilkie.

Bebe couldn't move. Not that she was prejudiced, exactly; they'd have eaten together at the picnic and nothing thought about it. But supper in Troy's house . . . Her surprise lasted one minute too long and turned her into an eavesdropper. "Eavesdrooper," Walt Fetner called it, as if spies hung from the edge of people's roofs like possums.

"So what did the sheriff say?" That was Troy, whose back was to Bebe.

"Said any man, any color, would do that was a polecat. The sheriff's all right."

"It had to be Friday night," Otis said. "We all went to my brother's wedding up at Mocksville. Chained up both dogs."

"Who do you think it was?"

The two brothers looked at each other. Blake finally said, "We got a long list."

Mary Ruth, still pinch-mouthed, offered to bring more coffee and stopped still a minute, staring into the dark tree limbs. Bebe had a funny feeling Mary Ruth saw her and couldn't decide what to do about it, so she yelled out, "*Troy?* Is anybody home?" With much noise she crossed into the light.

Troy came down the steps with both hands out to grab one of hers. "Didn't hear you drive in, Bebe. Come on in the house. Some old friends of yours here. Did you eat? I can put another steak on the fire." He hugged her. They went up high back steps and Mary Ruth, too, put out her arms. How tender all this touching felt. Somebody died today and nearly died. Bebe almost crushed Mary Ruth—whom she didn't much like—thinking: How warm and sweet our bodies are! If Jack was here I'd take him straight to bed.

The Wilkie brothers, on their feet, seemed nervous. Bebe stuck out her hand and got a quick light shake from each one. "Blake, you got gone today before we could really talk. Otis, how's your mother? I hear Phibby's moved to town."

They were all fine, everyone, just fine, no matter which names she tried. The two men shifted and nodded.

"Mama was just talking tonight about your mother and how she came in when we were all born and helped so much." All right, so Mama never mentioned that. Big deal. She should have.

Troy made them all sit at the table to have chocolate cake and coffee. Chocolate? Was God on the moon grinning? No, thought Bebe, that's *my* silly pattern, not His fault.

Otis, too, had frizzed his hair and wore a loose multicolored shirt like somebody from Samoa. Blake had on a white shirt and tie.

"Is Randy asleep? What did the doctor say?"

"Says the only bad effect is the fear he'll have for a while."

Otis gave Blake a quick, hard stare. She felt a mountain of thoughts about fear cross over the table from one to the other. Maybe that's why she asked Troy, "Why didn't you warn me Earl had gone in for politics? He's going to make a fool of himself."

Silence. The Wilkies didn't even nod. Mary Ruth left to get cake and coffee. Finally Troy said, "You can't stop anybody from doing that."

Softly Blake said, "It has helped his used car business," and then Otis giggled.

"Well, I'm sorry about it," she fumbled.

"Don't let it worry you, Mrs. Sellars," said Blake, who had never called her anything but Miss Bebe in her whole life.

"But we Fetners have never been like that!" she declared. Nobody would face her. Otis had taken an interest in a wart growing near his wristbone. For no reason at all Bebe wondered if the Wilkies ever knew the man that ate their ham and radishes, knew him for years and never told.

Mary Ruth served the cake and coffee, pulled a fifth chair where she'd straddle a table leg. She looked tired. Her brown hair was cut short in a high frothy crown with short wisps on her brow. She didn't like being seen in glasses though her eyes were shrunk and the bridge of her nose dented. "I've never been as scared as today. It aged me." She frowned at her plate, not eating. Maybe she was figuring out Randy's horoscope; Mary Ruth was an astrology nut. As Mama said, she used to be a Presbyterian until she went off to teachers' college and got too educated for it.

The Wilkie boys gobbled their cake. Mustn't say boys, either, Bebe thought. She would never get the new dos and don'ts straightened out. It struck Bebe forcefully that she had no notion how to make conversation under these new rules. The Fetners and Wilkies had been laughing and talking for years, but she couldn't remember a single subject in which Blake or Otis was especially interested. What had they talked about, then?

"How are your crops this year?" she tried.

"All right," said Blake.

They don't know me, either, Bebe thought. Did they go to the movies much? She couldn't think of a soul, suddenly, except Butterfly McQueen.

Otis said easily, "You've lost some weight, Troy."

Troy. She got Otis going for all of two sentences about the weather. She wondered if she could say she was sorry Dr. King got shot. I can't say that.

"I walked over to the graveyard about sunset and it was good to see the honeysuckle gone," said Blake.

Bebe, delighted, asked if Otis still preached and did funerals in his spare time.

"I've give that up," he said succinctly, holding the silver-plated fork as neat as a lady would.

And Blake said, "Like Earl, we've kind of gone into politics ourselves," grinning.

"In a way," added Otis.

She had seen shirts like his on TV and remembered the name: dashiki. "That was too bad about Kennedy," she said, hoping to ease up to the subject of King after all.

Blake said he meant more local than national politics. Bebe tried to catch Troy's eye but he was smiling at his cake plate and wouldn't look up. "A terrible thing," said Mary Ruth politely.

"Troy, who's your pick for president?"

"I think whoever's president we are coming to a bad time."

"Coming to or staying in?" Blake finished his cake. "No, that's not fair." He said to Bebe, and it seemed the first honest open thing, "I'm mad tonight, pay me no attention."

"Stay mad," said Troy.

Mary Ruth was squirming in her chair. "This icing is too sweet," but Otis said it was just fine despite the fact his mama was known to make the best cakes in Stone County, or used to, baked in a woodstove. Bebe tried again to find out if she was well but he'd only say she got heart flutters late at night and couldn't sleep. He was bolting his last crumb of cake and his brother got instantly to his feet and said they must go.

"Will you give my best to your mama?" Bebe wondered why even *that* sounded awful. Best *what?* She felt the Wilkies themselves had somehow trapped her into saying all the wrong things and she wished they hadn't come. When Mary Ruth offered to show her through the house, she was glad and jumped up. Troy walked with the two men down the back steps.

Bebe called, "Need me to move my car?"

Otis said, "No. I'm parked down the road a ways," although she couldn't remember passing any parked car.

In a low voice Troy said to the Wilkies, "I said I'd look into it. I'll see there's a warrant and you ask the neighbors. Don't you worry. Don't let your mother worry."

That's all she heard before Mary Ruth led her into the house. "The inside's not finished. I doubt it will ever be finished." They passed into rooms starkly simple with dark beams, slanted white walls which—Mary Ruth said—made picture frames look silly. "Troy's supposed to be finishing the house. He keeps Randy while I work, and he puts in tile now and then or builds me a shelf. He writes all those jingles here at home."

Bebe spotted at once the contrasting verbs: I *work;* he *writes.*

In front of a large brick fireplace with untidy bookshelves sat a black leather chair and hassock which must be Troy's. The draperies were printed with the signs of the zodiac. Mary Ruth was a Capricorn and Troy a Sagittarius. Bebe said the design was pretty and brief enthusiasm flared in Mary Ruth's face. "I had to order them," she said. "Silk screen."

Troy joined them in her small, well-organized kitchen, one of the few rooms with windows. "Mary Ruth can see the creek from here." Bebe could tell from her eyes that she never watched that creek. "Uh, Bebe, there's one thing. It's none of Earl's business that Blake and Otis were over here tonight—is that all right with you?" Although she nodded, he kept explaining. "Not that I care, but the Wilkies do, in view of some of Earl's new friends. Friday night somebody that knew the whole family was gone drove up to Blake's house and poured kerosene down his well."

"Oh, Troy! I'm sorry!" She wished now she'd said it about Martin Luther King no matter how dumb it sounded. "Who would do such a thing?"

"Who knows? Their kids were early to integrate when it was still freedom of choice. It was easy to remember the name—there were so many Wilkies popping up in every grade." Bebe had forgotten to ask about all the kids. "Then Otis is on the Good Neighbor Council, though that's often worth less than some sewing circle. Well, Mary Ruth, it *is,*" he added when his wife frowned. Troy took a bottle of bourbon from under the kitchen sink and slit the seal with his thumbnail. Mary Ruth made him store it there, Bebe supposed, with Clorox and drain cleaner. "You asked about Phibby. She's a teller in the Greenway Bank now, and her husband works with a community action group. He's pretty hotheaded about the lack of jobs for blacks. He once said the best community action would be a bomb under Allen Cotton Mill, and the newspapers picked that up."

"A bomb!" Bebe was really shocked.

And Troy broke out laughing. "Come off it, Bebe—who do you think you are? Remember the strike? Remember the dynamite and the bridge? Remember how Daddy—"

"I remember, I remember." Somehow it didn't seem the same.

Mary Ruth said crossly, "Troy has to take all this stuff to heart like some hobby."

"Mary Ruth thinks anything really important should be taken to the cash register, the way Earl does." Their tension made the air swarm.

It seemed important for Bebe to say flatly, "Earl wouldn't have anything to do with putting kerosene in a man's well. Especially Blake's."

Reaching to a shelf over his wife's head, Troy set down two glasses. "Suppose it was done, though, and afterward Earl was told about it. Told who and when and how. Suppose they were friends and customers and belonged to his—ah—raccoon hunting association. What do you think he'd do?"

"He'd call the law."

Yanking an ice tray from the refrigerator, Troy made a noise like a whispered laugh. He held the tray under the faucet. "Honey, you been gone a long time."

"Three years since the last visit."

"Three years can be long, you know that."

Mary Ruth's mouth was puckered. "Want to come upstairs with me and look in on Randy?"

"Have us a drink poured when you get back."

In the smaller bedroom, Randy slept belly down on his low bed. His mouth was open, the lower lip folded double over a round wet spot on the sheet.

No wonder Bebe's voice got soft—she was softer all over—saying, "Last picture I saw of him was right after he got out of the incubator. Troy said he looked like a naked bird."

"I wish you would talk to Troy," breathed Mary Ruth. "He can be more of a child than Randy." On the wall over the boy's bed hung small glazed cherubs, so set on the slanted wall that when he looked at the slope they must seem to swoop in the air.

"I doubt Randy remembers much of what happened today," said Bebe. "It wasn't really Troy's fault he got out in the water like that."

She shook her head. Her hand, very white and blue-veined, was curled on the bedrail. "I didn't even want to put him in the bathtub tonight but Troy said not to borrow trouble, try it and see. He played with his ducks like nothing had happened." With one finger Mary Ruth probed a dimple in Randy's elbow. He slid in his sleep; both knees dropped and his rump flattened. Where he had slept on it the hair was matted like yellow lint. "I can't stand living off by ourselves like this," she said, and led the way to the stairs.

Troy waited with bourbon and water on the porch and put Bebe in a folding webbed lounge with cigarettes and an ashtray. In a high voice, Mary Ruth asked, "Don't I get a drink?"

"You don't drink."

She headed straight for the bottle. "Maybe tonight I do. It isn't every day a mother nearly loses her son. Maybe I need a drink." She poured more whiskey than water in the glass. "Maybe it's time I found out what's so good about this stuff."

Carefully, Troy said, "Better thin that down a little more."

But she stared out where the creek couldn't be seen in the dark and took a long mouthful. Her eyeballs expanded a little when the taste hit. She gulped and let it go down, opened her mouth to take in some air.

"Told you so."

"Smells like something that went bad in the refrigerator."

Nothing could ever go bad in Mary Ruth's refrigerator. Bebe had seen inside while Troy was getting ice—mostly cottage cheese and lettuce, so no wonder they were all three thin and nearly electrified. Mary Ruth got a second swallow down. "How can anything so cold end up feeling so hot?" Troy laughed. "They say Capricorns shouldn't drink," she said sullenly.

For a while they listened to the crickets and a far-off whip-poorwill. Still thinking of the Wilkies, Bebe said lazily to Troy, "I knew this nun once named Sister Marguerite and she said one reason you couldn't get reincarnated along family lines was that whites would stay white and blacks would stay black, instead of switching colors on the next go-round and maybe learning something."

Troy guffawed and broke her mood. "Listen, I would come back from the dead to see ole Earl work on the garbage trucks."

In a quick parade Bebe pictured Earl darker and kinkier, then Treva, sterilizing somebody *else's* kitchen, and Mary Ruth in an Afro casting horoscopes from a crimson tent, and Mickey McCane singing sermons at the House of Prayer; and she leaned back and laughed at the justice of it.

Mary Ruth took a big draft of bourbon and didn't laugh.

"Don't get mixed up with that cycle business," she said soberly. "Or the Catholics, either. Let me lend you a book—when's your birthday, Bebe?"

"February twenty-third."

"A Pisces—should have known it. First decan, too." She said in amazement to Troy, "This stuff isn't bad when you get used to it."

Troy, bored with astrology, leaned back, the wrinkles fading from his face till he looked like Walt Fetner used to when he wasn't drunk yet but just lazy and contented. ("So what if I don't go in to work tomorrow—will the mill fall in?" he used to ask Mama, pushing his shoes off with his toes.) Troy said in Daddy's voice, "I own a hundred acres here, Bebe. Some has been cut over for timber, and only ten by the creek are cleared for farming. If you listen in the summers, you can almost hear things grow. By the time Randy's twenty, the woods will be thick again."

And I'll be fifty-seven, Bebe thought.

"That's going to be a good thing," snapped Mary Ruth, "since it's all Randy has to play with now. Trees."

"You working any of the fields?"

"Putting it all in orchard. Someday I'm going to thin out this hillside"—he waved toward the sound of water—"and in the spring we'll be able to look through and see the fruit trees bloom."

"Won't that be wonderful?" said Mary Ruth grimly, and poured more bourbon into her glass. Mary Ruth stared through the screen as if she could see the creek right through the matted dark, every ripple and sandbar in it, and maybe see her son drowning there. Her eyes were pinpoints. She might even see tadpoles milling in pools and the rounded stones rolling slightly in the bottom mud, and not like any of it. Bebe lit a cigarette. Time she got home to Jack.

"How deep is the creek?" Maybe Mary Ruth would answer her in inches.

But all she said was, "Every spring it floods and I'm always uneasy about Randy. The current . . . that's one reason today was so bad. I've pictured him falling in that creek a hundred times. Being swept away. I even dream of it." She made the ice turn slowly in her drink. "I'm out there picking blackberries when suddenly the water carries him past me. He'll be sitting on the surface like some roller coaster, but crying and reaching for me. And I stand there eating blackberries." She stared into her glass. "Seeds in my teeth. Juice everywhere."

Bebe reached over to touch her hand, which swung away and carried the swirling drink to her mouth. Bebe wasn't even sure she dreamed of Randy at all; the dream might be about Troy, who wasn't in it by name. They seemed to be passing through their quarrelsome years. Everybody thinks of divorce sometimes. Bebe did. After the operation she looked like a witch and felt like two. Jack did everything the doctor said that was supposed to make her feel like a whole woman. The more he praised her, the surer she was he lied. He wore himself out understanding her. Bebe got damn sick of being understood. Understood, big deal; who needs it?

"Randy might dream about the creek, too. Now." Mary Ruth made herself another drink. "He's Cancer, like Earl."

"If we don't keep scaring him," Troy said flatly, "he'll forget. That's what the doctor said." With effort, he smiled at Bebe. What had scared him as a kid, he said, and in dreams, too, was the water backed up behind that big dam on the Katsewa River. "You know how it feeds out those holes and falls down the face of the dam? And I'd heard about water pressure. I thought if you fell in on the high side the pressure would somehow squeeze you through those holes. Your body would come out like something mashed in a clothes wringer and slide down that spillway no thicker than a snake."

Bebe was reminded to send Troy to the car for a bag of seashells for Randy, along with sand dollars and dried starfish she had brought him from Pickle Beach. While he was gone, she told Mary Ruth they needed to take a vacation. "Come down where we are, maybe."

That gave her a laugh. "What does Troy need a vacation *from?* He and Randy are just little boys together. All day they walk in the woods and find bird nests. They go wading or whittle. I pay for the meat, I carry it home, I cook it, then I do the dishes. I'm the mean mama that makes them brush their teeth. Even Troy's orchard . . ." She stared out, saw that, too. "He's not got but six trees started." Getting up, she emptied Bebe's ashtray. She was shorter, maybe five feet two, and thin as a pullet. "Mostly Troy sits out here on the porch and visualizes how the orchard is going to look. . . . I was just telling Bebe," she said as Troy carried in the bag of shells, "what a great visualizer you are."

Troy spilled the shells on his lap so Bebe could tell their names, and held them to the light, murmuring, "Your beach—I guess it's not integrated? Blake and Otis, for instance, couldn't come?"

She had never thought about it. "Well, Blake and Otis, *sure.*"

"Since you know Blake and Otis. But a Negro family you didn't know? That drove up carrying the right amount of money?"

She said defensively it wasn't *her* beach. "We just manage it for Mr. Bennett and he never said one way or the other."

"Probably couldn't, then. Not even Blake and Otis. Not even Phibby, who could pass as a Florida suntan." He stretched his long legs and shells rustled in his lap. Toward Mary Ruth he said, "Bebe and Phibby used to have this game going, during the war, U.S. spies of some kind. When we'd come out to Hebron, Bebe would sneak off to the woods to see what secret message Phibby had left in some hollow tree, under a rock."

Wrapped up in wax paper. Signed Roger or Mayday or X-29. Sometimes they had written in code since both owned the same cheap New Testaments and could use that for a key. Smiling, Bebe said, "Then Earl and Troy found our drop, and they started putting in notes of their own. 'We Nazis know everything.' Stuff like that. They'd write down things nobody could know about Phibby and me unless they were watching every move. Scared us to death."

"Till we went too far."

Both were laughing. "First time I found a paper that said 'Fuck you,' and then explained how in a *poem,* I knew who one Nazi was."

Not smiling, Mary Ruth said, "Well, you'd hardly know Phibby now. I doubt she'd speak. You've never seen the money she must put in clothes just to sit in that little bank teller's window. Way she dresses, you'd think she was Lena Horne."

"It's her money," Troy said softly.

"You teach any of the Wilkie children, Mary Ruth? I forget how old they all are."

"*All* is right. That is a stairstep family. No, but I've got other colored children in my class, poor little things." She rubbed the dents in her nose, as if they were scars she had earned honorably in classroom wars. "They have a hard time keeping up. I don't know what they expected."

"Expected to be taught maybe," Troy said. "Like anybody else."

Instantly Mary Ruth's face got patchy red with hives and her eyebrows dipped, making her weak eyes even smaller. "And I teach them, Troy Fetner, I do a damn fine job teaching them.

But I can see what they score on achievement tests. There's not a one that isn't a grade or two behind the white children. That's a fact. It's in the records."

"Written down in black and white. Not a *one,* Mary Ruth?" He hummed a song Bebe knew and Mary Ruth didn't: *There's not a friend like the lowly Jesus. / No, not one! / No, not one!*

To Mary Ruth it was just another tune. Her voice grew louder. "Maybe it's environment, maybe heredity, maybe dirty rotten luck—but still, it's a fact. Maybe their schools were bad. Maybe their teachers got better pay for MA's that weren't worth the paper they were written on. A lot more pay than I get, for instance." How delicious her drink had become! She drank for energy while Troy kept humming: *Will he refuse us a home in Heaven? / No, not one! / No, not one!* "I don't claim to know the causes. I'm just stating the fact. And I'm *not* prejudiced!"

Quietly, he said, "Maybe not. How about the Rustin boy that got into Duke with that fine SAT score? Environment? Heredity? Is he a fact?"

"I knew you'd mention him."

"Just like I knew you wouldn't."

Honestly! Bebe thought. If I was col—black, it would do me good to know how much time white people spent talking about me. Do they have the remotest idea how they dominate by not being there? She had heard all this in Durham, Winston-Salem, all day long at the café, and hours already from Willis Buncombe. For Troy and Mary Ruth, race seemed only a substitute, their real quarrel still locked deep inside. Sometimes Bebe wondered how the big quarrels in this world would ever be settled with so many little ones mixed in. She waved her empty glass.

"I'll face up to smart and dumb," Troy said, taking it but watching his wife. "Blake's got one boy himself that's dumb and clumsy besides. Dumb people can manage. Why can't a dumb black get the same deal as a dumb white? That's all I'm asking."

"Percentages," hissed Mary Ruth. "And what happens to Randy when all I've taught him comes up against what they know? Have you ever been cussed by a seven-year-old? I have!"

Absently, Troy snatched her glass as well. The new drinks were very strong. Bebe pictured herself, drunk, falling downhill in Earl's borrowed pearl and not living long enough to make love to Jack one more time.

"One of Mary Ruth's troubles," Troy said to her in his sweetest voice, "is that she got all this education and can't really tell smart from dumb. She thinks, for instance, Earl is smart." He marched down the back steps and into the night.

Mary Ruth showed her teeth. "He's doing that to spite me." She called to the dark, "Go pee in the bushes; see if *I* care!"

Irritated, Bebe said in a rush, "It might do you a lot of good to go pee in the bushes with him."

"Talk about gall!" cried Mary Ruth. She stood up with some care, said coldly, "I am going to check on my son that nearly drowned today." The liquor had settled unevenly in her feet, one of which flew off to one side. She left in a ladylike stagger. Bebe could not decide whether to tiptoe away this minute, go home and work jigsaw puzzles with Mama, or wait and apologize to Mary Ruth. No wonder they were both on a ragged edge, after what happened. She called, "Troy?" No sound but a million insects. She'd finish the drink at least.

When Troy first got home from Korea, the Fetners thought he'd go to school on the GI Bill. "What for?" he said to Mama. That flustered her. "Why, to get ahead, of course!" Troy said, "I *am* ahead and that's just what I want to stay ahead *of*."

He came home from the army married to a plump, dark girl

he'd met when his unit landed in San Francisco. Sally claimed to be part Italian but Mama said it was plainly Jew. They liked Sally, though. "She'll help Troy grow up," Mama said. "Jews are ambitious."

If Sally saw a dress in a magazine she could make one just like it on her sewing machine. The same with food. A Technicolor molded salad—and she could whip one up without a recipe plus stitch up the hostess pajamas on the facing page. When Troy took Sally to restaurants she would nibble slowly the dish that interested her, separating ingredients and proportions in her mind. Tweet thought, at first, she had found a fellow spirit. Her talent even impressed the Loftins, and Versie said Troy's wife had second sight, but not much.

Actually it was second *hand* sight. She ran a messy house. The ability to duplicate was Sally's true way of living. She was like a lizard who could lie on a summer leaf and be green and then turn brown when the leaf did. From printed examples, Sally knew just the life she wanted and how many electrical outlets she would need to make it work. Soon Troy was traveling the western third of the state selling insurance while Sally's house was filling up with rotisseries and hair dryers and sunlamps and waffle irons. "Everybody has one," she'd say. Everybody wore it, ate it, owned it, needed it.

The more Troy earned, the quicker Sally spent his commissions on things that plugged into walls. Electric shoe polishers and toothbrushes. Washer, dryer, dishwasher, ice cream freezer, corn popper. Floor scrubber and polisher. Drill, hedge clippers, manicure set, refrigerator, freezer. Mixer and blender and slicer. Steam iron, toaster, fry pan, griddle. Razor and vacuum cleaner, sander, soldering iron, a reducing couch to vibrate her hips, a hobbyhorse electro-exerciser, a family massage unit. Coffeemaker, heating pad, vaporizer. A steam hair curler, television, radio, hot plate, sewing machine, and phonograph. First fans, then window air-conditioners. She owned a gizmo that heated the winter water in their fish pool and one to turn on the curb light every night at sunset. She had wall clocks in every room and all of them hummed instead of ticked. When Margaret was born she added sterilizers, a humidifier, and bottle warmers—the portable one plugged into the cigarette lighter of their car.

And Sally was just getting started. She wanted an oven that would clean itself with sonic waves. Soon she planned to tear up the floors and install radiant heat in copper pipes. She expected, in time, an outdoor swimming pool: heated, filtered, chlorinated, and at last glassed in. A neat yard followed by professional landscaping. A porch to become deck and patio, a bedroom which would enlarge to a master suite. Sally saw her life stretching ahead with each year larger and smoother than the last, and humming with current.

To Troy, the big joke was that everything Sally bought had to be operated, cleaned, repaired, traded in. Her conveniences wore her out, he said. Sally asked which century he wanted to live in. Did he ride a horse to work? Shoot game for the table? Plant hay for his cows? When he turned back to the olden days, she said, she might go, too. Troy said she was owned by appliances. She said if she knew where to buy one, she'd get him for Christmas a Nothing Machine which would just sit there and look pretty. He offered to buy her a robot husband and she could run him on High till he rusted.

(Mama wrote Bebe that Troy had at last settled down. Way down. Down in the dumps.)

Bebe listened but there wasn't a sound from Mary Ruth upstairs nor Troy outside. They might be standing somewhere separate in the dark, planning what mean thing to say next. She felt a little tight, and lonely. She got up and made herself a drink of straight ginger ale and, on the lounge, raised it and toasted Jack in an eastward direction. Who says old Bebe don't know when she's had enough?

The rest of Troy's story, the inside part, none of the Fetners knew for sure, though Bebe could guess and make up the missing parts. She even liked that best and sometimes Troy's face shifted in certain imagined scenes to resemble Robert Taylor's or Cary Grant's. Sally had looked like Gail Russell, overweight. The best she could do for Mary Ruth was emphasize a resemblance to Vera Ralston.

Something had happened to Troy in Korea. Maybe he counted too closely the deaths that were paid for an invisible line of latitude. Maybe somebody's pain or his own affected him, or the waste of that countryside, or nothing but a series of thoughts that recurred in him while they were capturing hills, losing hills, storming the same slopes again. He started to look to himself the way ants in an anthill look: mindlessly busy. The army—bustling and senseless. At home again, driving the mountains, he'd imagine how beetles must labor to climb over twigs. Everything shrank in importance. At first he was troubled by some vague sense that he had been misled, been promised better things, but even his disappointment shrank until it, too, could hardly be taken seriously. Sometimes he stood in his backyard and listened with disbelief while Sally's electrified house thrummed to sustain itself so the next day it could do it again. He was reminded of how, as a boy, he had watched through a plate glass window while a roomful of machinery bottled Coca-Cola. The house bottled nothing. The circuits were closed. So far as Troy could see, all of the circuits were closed.

He fell back on the practical jokes of his high school days. When he filled out forms that requested his college record, he wrote in: "Korea, Clash of 1952." Once he had secured a man's signature for an insurance policy, he'd revise in the outer office the secretary's THINK sign, adding *or thwim.* He sat on his porch with the Stella guitar singing dirty limericks about the neighbors. One Sunday night he broke *into* the jail and was sleeping in a cell when the sheriff arrived next morning. It did not, however, dawn on the sheriff thereby that there was something laughable about his job.

Sally had trouble even quarreling with him, he was so quick to turn the whole subject into a joke, or to agree with her easily since the matter was unimportant. He was happiest with children, including his daughter Margaret. Otherwise he was happiest making small practical jokes at the expense of citizens of Greenway, a joke being a trick played on the mind, a way of dramatizing how someone expecting a certain meaning could be yanked away to another. When the feed store hung out the sign EASTER CHICKENS FOR SALE, Troy added: *Cheep.* They liked it so well they left it that way. Later he painted a subline: *Our Coop Runneth Over.* The highway department was not as flexible. The sign they posted read CROSS ROAD and when Troy appended in parenthesis *(Better Humor It)* they took the whole thing down and started over with Ⓧ.

Sally was not amused. Sometimes Troy played his pranks instead of selling insurance, like the workday he spent standing in front of the photographer's holding a placard: *Someday My Prints Will Come.* She served him TV dinners straight from freezer to self-clean oven and had to buy everything on time.

When Mary Ruth Packard came to Greenway to teach second grade, Troy's daughter Margaret was in her class. They met by accident one Saturday in Allen Municipal Park. Troy did not know the teacher was considering the small zoo as a field trip for her class; he assumed she loved animals. Mary Ruth had no idea that once a year some vandal unlocked the wire cages and turned all the inmates loose, and that Troy was the vandal. They talked about Margaret, then about being penned up, caged, bound, and held down. She meant the school routines and also the unjust tyranny of men. Troy thought her sense of freedom would be a healthy thing for Margaret, whose love for battery toys that walked, talked, and lit up was a worry to him.

It would have ended there but Sally heard they'd been seen at Hardee's Drive-In eating apple turnovers. She, herself, had been working hard at that very time thawing a three-course meal and baking a Betty Crocker cake. She had less time to make meals from scratch those days; Troy said it was because she spent all day just turning things from On to Medium to Off.

"It's just like you to pick the laziest way," Sally sneered when Troy got home. "You don't have the gumption to go looking for a woman. No, you'd have to screw the one most convenient. Your daughter's own teacher!" She had already decided if she was to have a swimming pool, she might have to move back to California.

Troy said that wasn't so. It was perfectly innocent. He added that if General Electric sold automatic screwing machines, she'd possibly get passionate.

"Thank God," said Sally (perhaps meaning General Electric), "my sister don't live here." She began to picture herself with a generous separation agreement, living in a high-rise apartment with vinyl furniture and glass coffee tables. She set out Vienna sausage by the electric can opener and went upstairs to use her sunlamp.

"Switch Injun on warpath?" Troy hollered. She wouldn't answer.

Next week Troy drove to Mary Ruth's boardinghouse to apologize for the gossip his wife had spread all over town. Thinking the school board might fire her, those stuffy old men, she began to cry. Troy thought she was saddened by his problems. He played his ukelele and his Hohner mouth harp to show that his spirits were still high. Mary Ruth heard the tuneless thrumming as a clumsy effort to cheer her up and was touched, the way a red apple left on her desk could move her sometimes and almost persuade her that she liked teaching. She didn't, really, since these rural children had already been ruined by parents who didn't know the first thing about psychology.

"You're just like a little boy," she said. "I can drive if you want to play your guitar a little bit."

Troy was delighted when she called his instrument by the wrong name. Sally had once threatened to buy him an electric one, with amplifiers. The landlady watched them back out of her yard and went in to telephone people. Troy sang the song about the little old lady that swallowed the spider, and a bird to eat the spider, and then a cat, and so forth.

He liked it that she was driving while he was free to make music. An ideal male-female relationship. Observe the cardinals. He made her park by the cornfield beside Earl's house and quickly hand-lettered a sign and propped it near the used cars: IF YOU DON'T SEE WHAT YOU WANT, IT WAS TOWED AWAY.

He'd settle down, Mary Ruth thought, with the right woman's influence. Not that she was interested. Frankly, the size and rough texture of men had always frightened her.

"Mary Ruth," Troy said, "I sure do like that story Margaret says you read her class." *Peter Pan.* It was the prettiest story Troy had ever heard. The boy who wouldn't grow up.

Mary Ruth's mind was on her job. Would they fire her for the talk of a maladjusted wife? She drove until it was dark, thinking about how she would answer the school board when they called her in. "Mr. Fetner," she'd say, "is as harmless as a child. And if I were a man, you'd never have said a word. This double standard!" When it became hard to see without her glasses she pulled down a small road to give Troy the wheel.

Well, I'll be damned! thought Troy. Old Sally put ideas in her head! Might as well have the game as the name. He wrapped an arm around her.

Just like a little boy, she thought. Her horoscope for the day had urged warm response to potential new friends. He just wants a mother, she thought, recalling the psych course in which she had earned straight B's. Troy reached out the car window and caught her a lightning bug, the way Tom Sawyer would. He was thinking that, for all he knew, toads offered vows when they copulated, till death did them part, and then lived on a couple more months. So many solemn ceremonies. He was smiling as he let the firefly loose inside the car.

Almost a girlish smile, thought Mary Ruth. Mary Ruth liked girls better than boys and had gone to a girls' college. Girls could read better even in the second grade. The only book she had ever read more than once was *The Second Sex* by Simone de Beauvoir. Though what Simone saw in Sartre, Mary Ruth would never understand. She turned her body away from Troy's hard ukelele. The movement made Troy's bending head fall toward her shoulder instead of her mouth.

So that's it! thought Troy, surprised but always willing to please. He unbuttoned her high-necked blouse. Maybe it's because she's so flat-chested. I've gotten with cotton what Nature's forgotten, he thought, moving pads out of his way.

Babies. Men are such babies, she thought. Before she could stop him he had burrowed inside and rooted for her small breast. If a man got the curse it would just kill him. She tried to draw back, which elevated her nipple just enough. "Now, Mr. Fetner," she began, and that sounded ridiculous. Mary Ruth tried not to laugh.

But Troy could feel the smothered tremor in her chest. All right, he thought, if that's the way she likes it—with the mouth—she'll have it with the mouth. He began making lower access with his hands. Mary Ruth was astonished and at first could not move. This surely went beyond comfort or grateful kisses, and yet it was never how she had imagined rape to be; she could think of no word to call it. She began to protest and twist and pull back, and her clothes kept opening downward.

She had never had it that way—with the mouth—before; in fact, she had never had it any way at all. Nothing prepared her for the way her body suddenly leaped free of her mind, cut loose her Bachelor of Arts degree and forgot about it. While her body was having a good time at some distance, her mind chattered: *What in the world this is terrible I never Oh I can't mustn't he doesn't dare there does he? Stop it this instant!*

But her tongue had come unlatched from her brain and would not speak a word. Mary Ruth closed her eyes rather than glance down at what her body was doing all by itself, what it insisted on doing. How delighted it was.

When her body had finished and not before, it allowed her mind to take hold again, close it and cover and button it. Troy went off into the woods for reasons Mary Ruth did not even care to imagine.

She slumped at the steering wheel. There had flashed into her mind the plot of some dreadful book her father had once read and talked about endlessly, about Martians, how their heads detached themselves from necks and scampered around on small spider legs and chose whatever inert body might suit them at the time. She tried to remember who had written such a crazy book, testing her mind to see if it still worked after being disconnected. Edgar Rice Burroughs. A man who could think up Tarzan could think up anything. A man immature as her father would read it.

The car door slammed. Knowing where Troy's face had

lately been, she could not look there. She heard a match strike. They sat in silence and the lightning bug Troy had brought inside the car flashed bright and dark on the dashboard.

Troy could not figure out just what words were required of him. To tell the truth, he expected the teacher to thank him for the lesson. Her hands were shaking, doubtless from passion for him. He pictured the two of them camping out in the Great Smoky Mountains, making love (*his* way next time) under the heavy stars. He said, "What do you want to do now?"

She had no idea what grotesque physical act he might have in mind, and shivered.

"I guess Sally will leave me any day." Still Mary Ruth was silent. Poor little thing never had a minute's fun before, he thought. He found his flask in the glove compartment. "You want a drink?" She said she didn't drink but didn't mind if he did. *That* was something, Troy thought, taking a long hot swallow.

She was staring at the movement of his throat. Clearly he was calm and confident and had evidently made up his mind to marry her, since only love on his part could have led to . . . led to *this;* and could she have ever let him unless love were starting in her, also? She had never let anyone else. No one had tried very hard. How precious her body must be to him if he could kiss it anywhere. He would adore her, care for her. She would not have to teach school anymore, but would teach Troy insight and maturity. She reached across shyly and rubbed his blond hair. Troy leaned over then to kiss her mouth, but the very idea made her jerk back and . . .

"Bebe? You gone to sleep?"

Bebe was so embarrassed she nearly spilled her drink. To be caught making up stories like this, on Troy's own porch, and on such subjects! As if she could know what had been in their minds when even Jack's was a mystery. Gawking at Mary Ruth, she wondered if it could really have been that way. She still looked as skinny as a teenage boy. No hips at all.

Mary Ruth sat by her. "Troy's still outside?"

Bebe nodded. Maybe too far outside. Sally did leave him and went back to California with Margaret, married and moved to Texas and was running on AC/DC down there. Troy worked in the mill for a while, still baiting Earl with his jokes about the auto business. Leaving signs on certain models: *Special Feature—Windshield Rejects Parking Tickets.* People chuckled over some of them. As an experiment Earl ran one of Troy's ideas for an April Fool ad, under the title "It's Time to See Earl *if*": There was a long list of *ifs.* "If the last time you took your present car to a mechanic he told you to keep the oil and change the car." Things like that. Somebody invited Earl to join the JayCees because he was so original. And after a while Troy worked for him most of the time, and drifted into marriage with Mary Ruth.

Who said to Bebe now, "Troy is so selfish. All men are selfish."

"Come on now," said Bebe mildly.

Mary Ruth was still drinking. "I am the strong one in this marriage, let me tell you that, Bebe."

"If Troy's not strong, why didn't Sally change him? Why can't you change him?"

"That's not strong, it's stubborn."

They could hear Troy at last, coming uphill through the thickets, humming a song. "He's been down to look at his precious creek. He's afraid somebody else upstream will pollute it. He'd be happier if he could live on some island, miles at sea, and never have to work."

Bebe smiled. And pick coconuts. And sing in Hawaiian.

"You two have a good talk?" Troy left the screen door

cracked. Mary Ruth got up to slam it so the moths wouldn't fly in. "Wipe your feet," she said.

"We had such a good talk I'd better go home while I can still drive."

Troy seemed to have forgotten the quarrel, so quickly Bebe was not even sure how long he'd remember the kerosene in Blake Wilkie's well. "If you wrecked Earl's car he'd let you pay it off, Bebe. He's got an easy credit plan—one hundred percent down, no payments."

"I hope we can really have a good talk while you're here, Bebe," said Mary Ruth, who had forgotten nothing. "Sometimes it takes a woman to understand another woman."

Understanding. Big deal. Bebe had outgrown that. She stood up to find her pocketbook and Troy opened the door and left it cracked again. "Throw me your keys, Bebe, and I'll back you into the road. There's a bad stump." He pitched them hand to hand, watching Mary Ruth fumble with the hook on the door. "Honey, you all right?"

"A little dizzy," said Mary Ruth, drawing herself tall.

"No bigger than you are, you'll feel that stuff quick."

She couldn't resist saying, "Besides which, I lack your training and experience."

She and Bebe went out the front door and waited while Troy lined up Earl's car in the road, its headlights making the bushes ahead a sudden, brilliant green. The leaves looked wet. Mary Ruth said, "I'm glad you came, Bebe. Did me good."

Bebe whispered, "Let Troy do you good, honey," and said louder, "I'm glad Randy's all right. That will ease Mama's mind."

Waiting in the yard, Mary Ruth had got dizzier. She pressed one hand on a tree trunk. "I might be sick," she said thoughtfully. "I just might do that."

"Troy!"

Quickly he had both hands on her shoulders while she bent to vomit at the base of the oak. He muttered, "Bebe, she never drinks."

"Of course."

He told her to go on home, Mary Ruth would be fine. In Earl's car she looked back at them, paired and bent forward as if they were searching for something on the dark ground, Mary Ruth's wedding ring, perhaps. Now was the time for Randy to call out the way children did on cue in movies and television, so they could walk in together and look down on him while he slept.

Seeing how the road and trees looked like a dream landscape the lights opened up, Bebe drove cautiously. She was a little high on Troy's bourbon, and her tongue felt like a pincushion. She kept wondering which bastard poured kerosene in that well and wishing she'd said something good about Martin Luther King or . . . well, George Washington Carver wouldn't do? She didn't know enough to decide who would have been right. Or, crazier yet at 2 A.M., Bebe wished she could drive into Greenway and find a Negro boy or girl and buy him or her an ice cream cone, either vanilla *or* chocolate, or even both. The thought was tangled. Mary Ruth's not the only one that's dizzy, Bebe thought.

She crossed Troy's creek on a wooden bridge. She couldn't see even six fruit trees. So she was simpleminded with her ice cream cones! She wished the whole world were simpleminded and in tune with her, but it wasn't, so maybe she'd be better off smart like Jack, and bitter. There wasn't an eyelash-difference between her laughing and her crying, result of Troy's liquor, too. I'd give a lot, Bebe thought, to have been drunk just once with my daddy and found out if we were alike or different.

When she got home and climbed up Walt Fetner's cement

chunk without a slip, she found a note from Mama stuck on her room door with flour-and-water paste.

The Western Union called. Telegram from Jack. Those people (he said you'd know who) are coming early on Saturday and can you come home after Mamie's buried in time to get things ready. Don't call back save the money since he's already called Mr. Bennett twice today he says. But wire him when to meet the bus.

Bebe was glad. Time to go home. Time to go home from home.

The Pinheads were coming. Jack is mad and I am glad and I know what will please him.

She left the note glued there and pressed against the inside of the wooden door and thought about Jack and how no woman ought to get high and then have to go to bed by herself. Memo: Never get drunk with Mickey. Oh, she wished she was home and was home and she wished she was home.

Inside a whirlpool of air she undressed, then lay in a bed which was spinning very slowly, making her head turn inward like a spiral, like a conch shell. How easily the whirlpool moved from the outer rim to the core; she had only to let go and ride it into the point at which she would bump into her own soul in the deepest dark. Bebe opened her eyes and watched the room turn inward, too. I think I am lying on a screw that is being slowly tightened deep in the wood and the house biting down to the bottom of Stone County where the lava is. I think those are helicopter blades, moving, under my mattress. I think I could turn in reverse direction just as well, and the blades might lift me and send me wheeling out into the night sky till I looked down on the nice clean graveyard we got ready for Mamie. If I descended at Hebron, I could bore her a resting place like a drill and it would have sides so smooth and polished you could paint pictures on them and the colors would shine.

I can turn so easily and gently in this bed as to ream out the giant ear of God. Yes, I think He has an ear and is shaped like we are. Jack says that's simpleminded, but isn't it simple to think He's got no shape at all; or believe some sun blew up and made all this and Bebe, too?

Just before she fell asleep she began reciting the telegram she ought to send back to Jack. It sounded like a song she and Troy might sing with his mandolin, and the more she ran it in spirals through her mind, the sillier and happier it became. "Who do you call on but the simpleminded when the simpleminded come?"

The song orbited. Bebe went looping out into space, end over end, and all the stars were falling the other way.

9

Jack Sellars

June 16–17

With Bebe gone, Jack spent his days outdoors on the beach, thinking he might discover what she loved about it. Zorro ran alone a long way up the strand.

What was it Bebe saw as beautiful? The sea changed colors, sure, but was mostly dark gray, nearly solid. He thought it resembled cold but unset gelatin, as if people could walk out to distant ships and not sink in over knee deep. Until, with no warning, a fissure appeared.

Day and night, that endless wind! Sometimes with water mixed in it, sometimes sand. Only a feathered bird could bear that wind. All soft-skinned fish hid deep in thick water and whales dived down. Nothing but people stood in the open to get stung.

And gulls at Pickle Beach were not like ordinary birds but would eat anything, like buzzards over the Katsewa River. Sharp-tailed terns dived headfirst into the sea as if to dash themselves to bits, maybe trying to escape the wind. Bebe would probably say: They do what they're meant to do.

Nights were long with Bebe's half of the bed so empty, and

the overland breeze dampened everything. Daytimes it fooled Jack and kept him in the sun too long. His cool skin burned, got dark, reburned.

In one way, though, the scenery suited how he felt. Such loneliness in so much space! He stood on the sand no taller than a finger. In the dark, not sleeping, he heard how close he had always been to being washed away, blown away.

And something else happened with Bebe gone. He waited so steadily for her to come back, watched for her on the beach, listened for her step in the house, that at first he mistook that constant waiting for upset stomach or a case of nerves. At last he recognized the feeling as a case of anticipation. She had made him not only look forward to her return, but trust in it. He was not accustomed to trusting the future to bring him his desires.

While she was gone a part of his mind made the comments Bebe would have made. He picked up shells he knew she would have called to his attention. Let the dog sleep on their bed, as Bebe did.

One night he took his mother's picture from the strongbox but found himself thinking of Bebe's face more than the scene in the river. Deep in the box, too, was a folder that nun had given Bebe and she had stored here without his knowledge, as if it were every bit as precious as money or insurance policies. The folder described the Carmelite nuns of Dijon, France, and he doubted Bebe had ever read it all the way through. But penned on the cover by the nun was her suggestion that Bebe learn about Mother Marguerite of that group, the French Saint Theresa, who once had said, "The interior life consists in very few words and a very great tendency to God." Wasn't that a Catholic for you? Always greedy for Protestant souls, even waitresses.

Jack oiled the chains of the porch swing and repaired the screen door. Nights he lay stiffly, afraid to sleep and have the dream without Bebe there to wake him. When Zorro whined, he reached down to pet him, because Bebe would have.

He planned to tell Bebe all this when she came home since he'd let the years go by and not told much. Walking on the beach, he rehearsed to the dog. "Bebe, if it hadn't been for you I might have . . . have gone really sour and made somebody pay. It's you, with no better sense than to trust me, that made me trustable." Trustable? There couldn't be such a word. Bebe wouldn't care. You and the dictionary—big deal, she'd say. Jack smiled at the quiet sea. Maybe it *was* beautiful.

Sunday the tourists went back to their jobs. That afternoon Jack came home from losing to Willis at blackjack and saw the front door standing open. All he could think was the Pinheads were early and loose in his house, slobbering wet orange crush on everything.

He left Zorro in the car, took the steps two at a time, and ran through the empty rooms. Nothing. Second time through the kitchen, he saw a paper stuck on the chrome handle of the refrigerator. Big capital letters in pencil. I HELPED MYSELF TO ONE OF YOUR BEERS. Jack jerked open the door. The only tall beer was gone and in its place, atop another note, a stack of coins. This note said, *Why did you get mad? What made you think I was some thief?*

Jack left the money there to chill and walked to the porch. He could see a boy, naked, diving in the waves. Boy? Straight blond hair as long as Bebe's hung below his ears. What looked like a box on the sand must be his folded clothes. He was young, hard-muscled, tall. Beyond the breakers he floated on his back.

Jack watched from the swing. The boy took his time, riding waves to shore, going farther out, sliding to land again. Then he carried his clothes into the surf, sat down, and squeezed the cloth in the foamy water. He squirmed into the wet pants, facing the road so anybody could see him naked. Denims sliced off at the knee and raveled. A flowered shirt. No underwear. The boy stretched and strolled toward the house, thirsty for his second beer. Were there more teenagers out of sight?

He hadn't seen Jack until he reached for the screen door and Jack said, "Where's everybody else?"

His face got very still. "You'll have to ask them," he said finally, showing a set of perfect teeth. His eyes were squeezed so tight against the sun Jack had to guess their color. He came inside, one hand pushing air toward Jack. "Before you ask, I'm harmless and I wear my hair this way because I like it. Looking for no trouble."

He looked like the kids in Bebe's old café, with their long hair and sideburns. Jack got excited. He thought, with a few more beers, the kid might discuss Socrates. Someone to talk to at last! Not Willis and his lies, not Pauline's Methodism or Mickey's brag, but Jack's postgraduate work delivered by extension. "You by yourself?"

The boy nodded. "At first I thought the house was empty and I'd just stay a few days. I saw somebody lived here when I got inside. Find my note?"

Empty? With all Jack's improvements? The centipede grass, that row of cedars?

The boy said quickly, "I wouldn't have hurt anything."

"You traveling by thumb?"

"Got a motorcycle. It's under the house, inside that plastic. This sea air is murder. It'll probably rust glass." The boy was used to winning arguments with that smile. He played it the way Willis played the last card of a straight flush. Jack grinned, too. He hadn't left that orphanage and ridden a train out of Troutman for nothing, living a year on his own smile and the soft hearts of old ladies.

"Well, open us both a beer. No charge this time." He was

surprised at himself. Perhaps he was being friendly on Bebe's behalf, saying what she would have said.

From the kitchen the boy called, "I'm Foley Dickinson. You on vacation here?"

"Live here all the time." He was tall as a basketball center. Jack took the beer and shook his wet hand. His fingers felt as if they might wrap around twice. "Jack Sellars. Where you headed?"

Just seeing the country, Foley said, while there was still a country to see. When he dropped out of Boston University snow was on the ground. He started riding south toward the heat. Sometimes he'd stopped to work awhile. He was going around the nation's edges first, then would ride here and there into its heartland.

"You flunk out of school?"

"No, my grades were all right." He closed his eyes while he drank. He was healthy, handsome. For a minute he almost looked like Bebe; that's how lonesome Jack was. It may have been his yellow hair. Foley said, "Everybody goes to school to learn to pay his own way and not burden society. Some go to college so they can learn to pay six, eight, ten other people's ways, and still raise a family and file a nice tax return. That's why my father sent me to his alma mater. I got tired of learning that." A lot of beer went down his throat at once. He'd had practice in some high-priced fraternity.

Didn't sound like some Marxist radical. Jack relaxed, though he was almost disappointed. *Darkness at Noon*—he'd read that and never had a chance to try talking dialectic, or even listening while somebody else did. He caught himself pronouncing his words carefully, seeing they had strong *d*'s and *g*'s on the end, because Boston University had sent him an accident of value, somebody educated to talk things over with.

"I thought your generation planned to end poverty and

didn't mind bearing the rich man's burden." He was proud of that. Rich man's burden.

Foley just smiled. "I got to the place I could pay my own way and that seemed a good place to stop." He propped his feet on Bebe's new cushion.

"Wait till you get married. You'll wish you'd stayed in school."

"Let's both wait," he said.

Politics? All the kids were interested in politics. Jack asked about Foley's pick for president and he said Clean Gene McCarthy. No realist, then. Did he like to read? Yes, Foley said, although film had made books obsolete. That would be just my luck, thought Jack. A lifetime late I come to books and they're going out of style.

Foley got a little wary. "You live alone here?"

Maybe he thought Jack was a fag and would charge high for the beer. Jack wanted to say they had fags in the olden days, too, but decided to let Foley off the hook. "My wife is visiting her family for a few days."

Looking relieved, he asked about spreading his bedroll on the beach. He sounded like Jack at the back doors of widows' houses in 1936. *Could I rake your yard for my breakfast?* He'd got all the way to Ohio asking that, but this was 1968 and nobody needed to pledge work. Jack offered Foley a trailer and, to show that he read *Time* magazine, said he wouldn't allow any pot smoked on his property.

Foley was tickled. "Don't want any Afro-American girls in my bed, either, I guess?"

Jack started to say he'd had black women in his day and they were no better or worse than white, but Willis had been on his nerves about this so long he couldn't tell racism from neutrality. He just sent him to an empty trailer with part of Bebe's casseroles and frozen cake. Foley was mildly grateful. He'd expected housing, the way Jack had known he'd get breakfast even if there was nothing to rake but hard-packed dirt around some woman's house. Thank God, he thought, Bebe isn't here; she'd pet this boy to death.

Zorro had to be called back from chasing Foley to the trailer. Jack finished his beer in the swing and thought about who he might have become with an education from Boston University. What if he'd had that and Bebe too? He was jealous of Foley Dickinson. He bent the beer can to nothing but it was no fun with that flimsy aluminum they used nowadays.

Then he went down to the greenhouse to see what Foley was riding. A black and silver BSA Thunderbolt, 650 cc, with four gears and twin mufflers and a speedometer that went up to 150 mph. Must have weighed 450 pounds. He had welded on an extra spotlight and rigged a leather mailman's pouch under the seat. Jack climbed on, squeezed the clutch, waggled the front wheel in the thick sand. It felt good. Once he had owned an Indian. Could he handle this one? He rocked on the handlebars to test the suspension, even thought about searching the saddlebag. That long hair and all. Booze was one thing but this grass, this LSD . . . He thought there was something womanish about drugs. Little maiden aunts getting stoned in their parlors off patent medicines and cough syrups. *It helps my neuritis. It gives me religious insight.*

That night Jack was half asleep when somebody idled a B-29 under the bedroom floor. Zorro scrambled whining over the pillow as Foley Dickinson rode onto the highway, wound up his engine, roared back and forth awhile at top speed, a mile on either side. This was the first noise made at Pickle Beach that unstopped the ocean from Jack's ears, and he grinned as the growling waxed and waned while Foley raced something invisible past the house.

Monday morning the BSA was parked under the plastic

again with Foley's boots upended on each handlebar. They were black and had six buckled straps and padded ankles. Their smell filled the humid air. A Cycraft helmet, too; he slipped it on and snapped the chin strap but it was too small and clamped his temples. Felt as if some thumb and forefinger were pinching there and might pick Jack up and throw him in the sea. When he thought about being twenty and in college with the whole world ahead and only good memories behind . . . well, did Foley Dickinson know how lucky he was? Could he possibly know that?

Jack watered his tomato plants before they wilted, then walked to the surf and waited for Foley to invite him into his trailer so he could explain how well off young people were. He'd said he was paying a long visit to his native country, studying America and its people with his own eyes before smoke and violence stopped it all. Wasn't Jack evidence? Didn't he want to study Jack Sellars?

Foley didn't call. Not even when Jack went wading and could see Foley at the trailer door. Not even when Jack picked up interesting things from the ocean's edge and held them to the light or offered them to Zorro to chew.

The sun was giving him a headache. Or perhaps he had endured the dream and did not remember? Serena Mae used to get headaches. She would look up from supper, alert, that awful expectancy in her face. The children could almost watch pain begin and run across her head like a crack down an egg. As it went through her eye the lid would twitch. Very carefully she would slide back her wooden chair and carry that head outdoors like something full and barely balanced on her neck. She'd walk stiffly to her dark place by the river, shaded by creeper and muscadine. She wouldn't sit on the rocks for fear of copperheads, but would take up the hearth broom of corn husks she kept in the grove and sweep back leaves and twigs, sinking at last to the damp ground with her back against a tree. She'd close her eyes and the left one would keep twitching. Sometimes she laid two fingers on that jerky lid. And she'd wait. It had something to do with the river. In the Bible, didn't lepers bathe in rivers? A river kept pouring by. The current washed endlessly past. Wood chips on the surface rode out of sight. Sometimes Mama sat all day till the hurt drained out of her, downstream. Jack got in the habit of climbing the sweet gum tree so he could look down on her leafy roof and see her shoes stuck out in the sun. It turned out to be a bad habit.

Foley Dickinson finally came out of the trailer, waved, but took his swim at a distance and dried off in the sun, back turned. He made a skirt with one of Bebe's towels and ran toward the trailer, sometimes leaping high to aim his bare heels at each other. At his age, Jack had been in twelve states, could work at anything, could tell from a boxcar if his size hung on somebody's clothesline. The things he could tell that boy!

Later Jack carried a quart of milk and two eggs to Foley's trailer.

"Come in, Mr. Sellars." He was in the kitchenette writing in a black ledger. There were others like it stacked on the table by a cardboard box. He still wore the towel.

"Brought you some breakfast." They were ruled record books for office use, bound in black, with a mahogany-colored spine and gold trim. Fancy. Jack's jealousy was keen. I bet Foley never saved Blue Horses off notebook paper in hope he might someday own a bicycle.

"Just be a minute," said Foley, writing. "Wanted to put you down, Mr. Sellars, and the house and that birdbath." Moving closer, Jack watched his ballpoint pen skip rapidly across the page. The letters were tiny.

"You keeping a record of your travels?" It seemed like a joke if Foley's generation was really the last before apocalypse. Who would read it?

"Not exactly. Just things I want to remember." He rubbed his eyelids before starting to boil the eggs, tore off a paper towel and pressed it to both eyes. They were bloodshot. "Want an egg?"

"I've eaten." Jack accepted a cup of coffee. "Is it part of your schoolwork?"

"No. They weren't teaching me much I'll remember." Foley gave that polite smile. He had such good manners Jack saw he would never get to know him. He poured cream into his cup.

"Could I read some of it?"

Instantly, "No." Another smile. "I'd rather not."

Jack stirred his coffee paler. Stuck-up college boy.

Watching him, Foley said, "I don't let anybody read them. It's nothing personal."

"How long you plan to stay?"

"I won't impose on you long, sir," said Foley stiffly.

Bebe, he thought, would just say whatever was on her mind. Jack decided to try it. "No hurry; that's not what I meant. I don't have many people to talk to here, and I don't have your education but I was hoping . . . you know. To talk some? Is there a real generation gap?"

"Damn right." Foley grinned.

Jack thought it was worse than that, a human gap, ancient, wider than time. Jack almost struck his forehead, he was so frustrated at knowing things he could not say, swarming with questions he did not know how to formulate.

"I still believe in talking, though," Foley added. "That's one reason I took this trip—to hear what people have to say." He rubbed, instead of his ears, both eyes. It might be a nervous habit.

"Say about what?"

"About our decline. About entropy."

That sounded like some slow wasting disease. But words defined were not what Jack wanted except as a starter; he wanted to hear what professors had learned of the *why* of things, whether the worm underfoot was linked to him by chance or design and, if haphazard, how luck became so intricate. He wanted the Boston University scholars to draw him a line between what was and was not premeditated. Slowly and vaguely he tried to explain this to Foley, who laughed as he peeled his eggs.

"Paralogism," Foley said. A word, another damned word. "That's Kant's term for an attempt to draw conclusions about an existence which is completely beyond human experience."

Jack was embarrassed and angry. He could not remember who Kant was. "You give me a name for my question, O.K., but what's the answer to the question?" Perhaps he only needed to learn words, just words; the secret was in the words.

"Pass the pepper." Foley split the first egg, which ran orange on his plate. "What you want, Mr. Sellars, is a college bull session and I wasn't much good at that."

"Go on," said Jack.

Foley looked puzzled about where to go, frowned, said finally, "Philosophy for amateurs."

"You studied philosophy!" Jack declared. He, himself, had tried to read a digest of the world's great philosophies but could not get through its maze of language.

"Took a few courses."

"Well?"

"I had semantics, mostly."

The same maddening problem. "What are semantics?"

"Language, verbal signs."

"I knew it," sighed Jack. If you knew enough words, you

could pin everything down in a scientific way and control it. He sat there, satisfied, watching Foley fork the last piece of egg. "I'm going to Buncombe's store for cigarettes. You want anything?" He was silently saying the new word three times to make it his own: semantics, semantics, semantics.

"Got everything I need."

"You want to come along? If you're writing down experiences, you ought not to miss Willis Buncombe." What lies might Willis tell today about his crippled hand? Serve him right to have his lies solemnly written down. Serve him right to have Jack announce: That's only semantics, Willis.

"O.K." Foley scooped the last eggshell and drank half a quart of milk. He scrubbed the lids of both eyes again with his knuckles.

"You get seawater in your eyes?"

"Got something," Foley said.

While Jack found car keys and shut Zorro in the bedroom, Foley squatted to look at his obsolete books, stacked in orange crates Bebe had painted orange because it tickled her to have the color say the name. Wasn't that just like Bebe?

Foley said, "I might borrow something to read?"

So he'd stay at least another day, talk more about semantics, maybe. "Sure." Every book Jack owned was secondhand or cheap. Traded-in texts and old novels and parts of broken sets. A few volumes of some out-of-print encyclopedia, and wasn't that typical? If a fact didn't lie in the first five letters of the alphabet, he'd never track it down. Horticulture books. Zane Grey. Erle Stanley Gardner right beside *Othello*. Darwin. Jack liked Darwin. Books on mediums and life after death, which he thought even Bebe might like, but she didn't. *Reader's Digest* Condensed Books because they looked like a lot of pages for the money. Field guide to birds. Used paperbacks. He owned books on cells and DNA and heredity, Toynbee, the Greek histories. The ancients had taught themselves just sitting in that rocky land beside the Mediterranean, without books to read. Jack admired that. Lately he'd been reading about human blood and seawater and how much alike they were. It gave him the creeps.

He saw Foley scrub his eyes again. "You might need glasses."

"Maybe."

Driving, he watched Foley lower the visor and squint in the glare. He tried to engage him in conversations college boys would like. Did Foley believe in situation ethics? Yes. Had he been to Haight-Ashbury? Not yet. Should people bus students to integrate schools? Yes, until housing patterns changed. Would Humphrey win the nomination? Probably. What about Robert Kennedy's murder? A senseless killing; we were all to blame.

After a while Jack said, "If the glare's too much, I've got sunglasses in the glove compartment."

"Thanks." Foley put them on with relief.

"How long have your eyes been bothering you?"

"About a year."

"What does the doctor say?"

"Says I imagine it."

"Imagine what?"

"That I'm going blind."

Startled, Jack let the car go off the road and had to jerk back. "Are you serious?"

"He says I'm not."

"Is he a good doctor?"

"Not for me."

They were pulling in at Buncombe's store and Willis got out of his hammock and waved half a hand. Foley leaned forward, took off the glasses, put them back, whispered, "Is that something black around his neck?"

"It's a cut-up tire," said Jack, and explained Willis's ideas on arthritis. "And he's really missing some fingers, too; that's not your eyesight." He waved to Willis and got out. "You ought to see another doctor. Young as you are, Foley. Hear?"

"I might. There's something he's not telling me."

Willis could hardly wait for this new audience, toward whom he walked with an exaggerated limp. When they were introduced he called Pauline, who made everybody come inside to the drink box and began mothering Foley. Did his parents know where he was? He could dial them direct anywhere in the country now; did he know that? He could use their telephone.

In the next minutes, under the Buncombes' prodding, Jack learned more about Foley Dickinson than he'd pieced together all day. Willis once said that people who noticed his crippled hand would make allowances and he made sure the boy noticed before asking his nosy questions.

Where was Foley from? What did his daddy do? Foley put on a politer smile. The Dickinsons lived in Hagerstown, Maryland; his daddy was an orthodontist, very fat and good-natured; and his mother was his technician. He had three sisters, also good-natured. In fact, he was the only child who had ever given a minute's trouble, he said, almost bragging. One sister was married and taught piano, one was a decorator in Atlanta, and the third was still in high school and a majorette. His father hoped Foley would become a lawyer and someday he might. "At least in law," he said, "the bullshit is orderly."

Hoo hoo, hee. Willis, wheezing, told a tale about suing that contractor whose stupidest worker had dropped lumber off the tenth floor, knocking him down and crushing one hand. He described their slick insurance lawyer, a Harvard man, with his dollar value for each finger. His little finger, Willis said, had been priced so cheap there wasn't much point in anybody owning one. He wagged the remainder of the hand he had barely salvaged.

"Have a grape, honey," said Pauline, wiping the bottle on her dress.

Trying to top himself, Willis added, "I was afraid they might amputate that no-account little finger while they were at it and even charge me for taking the nuisance off."

He showed Foley his clocks—how the main wheel engaged the first pinion and its spindle turned the second wheel and so on down through the train. "The second spindle turns once every hour and carries the minute hand, and it takes a twelve to one gearing to drive the hour hand."

Foley wrinkled his nose. He said clocks were products of typical linear thinking and if they read Marshall McLuhan they'd get cured of that. He was blinking his eyes adjusting to the dim store and looked owlish.

Willis gave Jack a sour look before he yanked his stiff neck high in the rubber collar and lifted his chin. Next to black militants he could not stand a smart-assed college kid. "Of course you know about the atomic clock? You studied that in college?" Foley hadn't and probably didn't want to.

"You take cesium," said Willis flatly, as if he were going to insist that cesium be taken. "Each atom acts like a magnet and a beam of them passes through an alternating magnetic field—"

Jack said, "You got one of those, too, Willis?"

"Of course not," he snapped. "I keep up, that's all. Get us a Popsicle, Jack."

They ate while Foley explained his trip, biting the chocolate off his Popsicle first, then sucking the full vanilla square. "I feel strongly about ecology," Foley said. Ecology, thought Jack. Ecology. Semantics, semantics.

Willis thought he had a great idea. "Mostly," said Willis,

"you see retired people riding around the country because they want to see it once before they go. To see it before *it* goes—now that's a different thing! That's bigger."

"It's pitiful," Polly disagreed. "What does your mother say to that?"

"My mother never thinks of such things, ma'am," he said with that winning smile.

"I bet she does."

Jack examined himself in the shoplifter's mirror. He looked small and twisted in its silver circle. He'd been reading that two-thirds of his body was the same fluid which beat now on Pickle Beach, though the sea had grown saltier now than he. First there was a one-celled animal and then a metazoa and the metazoa was the first creature to wall off seawater within itself as a body fluid. And Jack still had it. He was a diluted tidal pool, shut off from the great ocean. He didn't like that kind of linear thinking because the line was so long, and he wondered if Foley's McLuhan had ever drawn it all the way.

"Just ask your mother sometime," said Pauline in a threatening voice. Foley was trying not to laugh. Willis said he had traveled over the country once. "When was that?" asked Pauline.

"Never mind. How's Bebe?"

Jack said, "She's supposed to call tonight." He stuck out his hand to see if the mirror would catch him stealing corn flakes. His hand, swollen with seawater, loomed up foreshortened in the glass. So we took the sea with us on land. You'd think it would look as beautiful to me as to Bebe—father ocean, mother ocean—that I'd walk in the surf and my blood would pound. "Pauline, this boy wants a good pair of sunglasses, Polaroid; put them on my bill."

Foley objected. He could wear his cycle goggles. But Jack bought them because that's what Bebe would have done.

Willis, learning that Foley kept journals, wanted to know what he'd written about Brunswick County.

"Not much so far."

"Jack, we ought to show Foley this little part of the world." Willis pointed his melting Popsicle. "You know how many tourists go every year to that place the volcano buried? That town in Italy?"

"Pompeii," said Foley.

"So here is America, Pompeii before the volcano, and one tourist ahead of his time." Willis gathered their ice cream sticks because Pauline was saving them for summer Bible school. The children stuck them in modeling clay to make little Calvarys. "By God," said Willis. "This boy is the first interesting thing to come down that road in years."

"They fit all right, Foley?"

The boy's face looked small behind the huge green lenses. "I appreciate it," he said. "The glare does bother me."

"Don't you have eyedrops or anything?" Foley shook his head.

Willis said, "Let's take him up to Fort Caswell and ride him around. I'll even put gas in your car."

"You'd better, since I left plenty in the jeep."

Jack had to pump it himself while Willis went to untie his brace because he was suddenly feeling better.

"The boy's a funny one," Pauline said by the gas pump. "Is he related?" No, just a stranger. They heard Foley laughing inside the store.

"Tell me the truth," Jack suddenly whispered, hanging up the pump. "How did Willis really lose those fingers?"

She stared and shook her head.

They went indoors for Foley, who was walking through the grocery aisles reading brand names and roaring with laughter. "Duz, Raid, and Joy!" he read from labels on the shelves.

"Gleem, Halo! Easy Off Real Kill. Ban Zest. Suave Dr Pepper Lays Betty Crocker."

By his table of clocks, Willis watched the boy melt across two mirrors, still laughing. "Mennen Breck Tender Leaf. Vitalis Vanish. Pet Silver Cow Arrid." Must have been a riot with the sophomores. Didn't have much trouble reading through dark glasses, Jack thought. They climbed into the car.

"You need a camera," Willis said.

"That's what my eyes are for," said Foley.

They drove through Fort Caswell, 142 years old, now turned into a summer campground for Baptists. "Now look at this. I just wish you had a camera." Willis pointed to church people swimming in hot mineral water in the same concrete pits where coast artillery stood in the Civil War.

"It's ironic," Foley said.

Semantics. Ecology. Ironic, ironic. Jack said, "You think the Baptists will inherit the bunkers in Vietnam, Foley?"

Willis perked up in case Foley should favor Ho Chi Minh and asked if he was a pacifist.

"I'm a nihilist," Foley said.

On the front seat, Willis—eyebrows up—tried to catch Jack's eye and draw comment. No luck. He pointed out places where hurricane Hazel had changed the coast and blown buildings off their foundations. They walked in Old Town graveyard, where colonists from Barbados were buried in the 1600s. When that colony gave up, the lords proprietors closed the area to settlement for nearly fifty years. The next century, though, there were big and beautiful farms: Kendall, Clarendon, Pleasant Oaks, Orton, Lilliput.

"Lilliput?" Foley wanted to see that. Its acreage had been absorbed into Orton plantation and Willis didn't know the old boundaries. Foley explained about Gulliver and Lilliput. In Lilliput, he said, the two political parties wore either high heels or low heels and the emperor wore the lowest heels of all. "Swift makes you see how insane all systems are," he added. "I think I'll go to the Democratic convention in Chicago and see it for myself."

"A great town, Chicago. I got hit by a streetcar there." Willis raised his partial hand, casually, and let it fall on the back of the seat.

Foley wanted to know if the ocean here was polluted yet. "It will be."

In places, especially at the mouth of the Cape Fear River, it already was. Waste washed to the sea from inland; there was little industry in Brunswick.

In Southport they made Willis sit on the Liar's Bench, which had been set near the water and paid for by public subscription. He wanted to carve his initials in the wood but there wasn't room. They drove to Shallotte and Holden's Beach and Ocean Isle, but Jack liked Gause's Landing best, a fishing village under big trees with drooping moss that touched the car's roof as they passed. It stirred memories of the Katsewa River valley and he was surprised this made him like it more instead of less. He caught himself looking for cool shaded spots by the water's edge which Serena Mae would have liked.

Foley took off the new sunglasses and rode awhile with his eyes closed.

Willis whispered, "What's wrong with him?"

"Some kind of eye trouble," said Jack.

"Is that a fact? Foley?" Willis turned to the backseat. "What kind of eye trouble?"

He looked asleep. "Things disappear. I look at a scene and parts seem to be missing. Sometimes I can see things move off out of range, just catch the blur in the corner of my eye."

"That blur business—everybody does that," said Willis, frowning.

"But have you ever turned your head fast enough to see what it was?" Foley asked. "To catch it?"

"Catch what?" Willis asked.

Jack said, "Forget it."

In Calabash they ate seafood platters and Foley carried extra corndodgers away in his pocket.

Willis knew one example of pollution that might appeal to Foley, Campbell Island in the Cape Fear River, three hundred acres enriched by bird guano.

"Bird guano isn't the same thing as pollution by man."

"Wait," said Willis. "In World War Two the island became an army target for bombing practice and now those bombs are still unexploded in all that manure and nobody can use the island."

"Crap with a bomb in it! Can we go see?"

"Well, the bombs are underneath. You couldn't see the bombs anyway."

"You'd have to imagine it?" Foley put on his dark glasses.

"You can't go over there. You want to just look at the island at a distance?"

"What for?"

Jack asked, "Is that the truth, for a change? About Campbell Island?"

"Sure it is." They had parked because all that milk and coffee was thundering in Foley's bladder and he had gone off barefoot into the bushes. "Put it in your notebook, Foley," said Willis as the boy came back to the car. "Live shit."

Just before dark, Foley took Zorro for a long walk along Pickle Beach. In the light drizzle he wore a windbreaker jacket with big printing on the back: NIETZSCHE IS PIETZSCHE.

Jack rushed to the ringing telephone. "Hello. Who? Oh." He grabbed an ashtray. "Hello, Mickey." There followed a long question about a possible lost fishing rod. "I'm sure I'd have noticed if you left it in the trailer."

"Ask Bebe, will you?"

"She's gone home, remember? For the week."

There was a silence. "I forgot," Mickey said. "I thought maybe she changed her mind." After a pause he described the missing rod vaguely, without much interest. "Maybe she found it cleaning up and put it someplace?"

"She'd have told me."

"Ask her when she gets home, O.K.?"

Jack said yes without mentioning when that would be.

Next time the phone rang it was Bebe in such a state he thought at first her mama had died, but it was somebody named Mamie so old she was able to perish the minute her survivors glanced away. Bebe sounded homesick. He changed the subject to Foley Dickinson. She was afraid he might be a nut so Jack didn't say the boy might be going blind by imagination. One year at exam time, some student came into the café and just wrapped his arms around Bebe and started crying. They had to send for help from the college infirmary. While they were waiting, the boy sat on his barstool and cried all over Bebe's chest. There was nothing Bebe could do but stand there and roll her eyes at people. She didn't even know the boy. "It's all right," she kept saying. "It's all right in the long run, honey."

Jack wanted her home so much he could hardly trust himself to say so. Her voice sounded far away. It was hard to hang up the telephone and stop the sound of her. "You hang up first," Bebe finally said. Jack told her to do it. He wondered how many switches would close between them, upriver, like slamming doors. "Good-bye then," she said abruptly. The telephone emptied of her voice. He went onto the porch and sat with her dog in his lap.

About 9 P.M. Foley tapped on the screen. He was riding to Wilmington, see what was going on. He wore the same lettered jacket and the smelly boots. Under one arm he carried the box which held his ledgers.

"Plenty to eat if you want something before you go."

Foley shook his head. "This thing fits in my saddlebag, but I don't want to carry it around all night. O.K. to leave it here?"

He could have left it in the trailer. Jack saw by Foley's grin that he expected him to snoop in the books, that he even wanted it, but without permission. "Sure."

Foley carried the box into the living room, where Jack got under the best lamp and lifted a book to show he'd be busy. He was reading about lymph and plasma and osmosis. Water goes where salt is—from memory, for all he knew, seeking the ocean. Jack had just learned that if his kidney ran for one hour like an open spigot he would die.

Foley placed his box high over the fireplace, in easy reach of his long arms, though Jack would need a chair. Bebe's cups and saucers tinkled. "I'll pick it up tomorrow."

That should give Jack plenty of time to read it all, he meant. Jack listened to his motorcycle start, cough out, and start again. The noise mounted until he kicked into gear and was gone. Jack skipped a chapter. Like a dust speck, Foley's box hung in his eye. Bet he'd left a hair or a piece of lint arranged so he could tell if the box was opened.

And he wouldn't have touched Foley's books, out of stubbornness, if Western Union hadn't called and read out a telegram in singsong:

ROSIE, SON, AND NURSE ARRIVING SAT. JUNE 22 FOR ANNUAL STAY LETTER FOLLOWS EARLY DATE UNAVOIDABLE MANY THANKS

GEORGE AND LAVERNE

"Wait a minute!" Jack said. The operator thought he was writing down the message and read it again, slowly. Jack dropped his book on an orange crate. He'd wire George back and say . . . Not yet? Tell him they had no room? They weren't expected till July!

Jack told the operator to get off the line so he could call Richmond.

The Bennetts were out. George's son, the high school fullback, explained they were at a Lions Club dinner. "Call him there," Jack told the operator. "Yes, it's an emergency."

He must have been sitting at the head table by the time it took. "My God, Jack, what is it? What's wrong?"

Nothing but his goddamn telegram, Jack said.

George started in about unexpected trouble at the home—the plumbing went bad and water poured everywhere. They were clearing everybody out a week early for repairs. Jack swore and George said it wasn't his fault. Completely unforeseen.

Jack hung up, paced, then called George back. Someone had to fetch him out of the banquet room again. This time George did the swearing. He had to make a speech in a few minutes about the eye bank; what in the hell did Jack want now?

"If it's a week early, how do you know the nurse can come? I sure can't look after them myself."

"That's all taken care of," said George. "And don't call me anymore."

"All right. If Rosie drowns while she's here, I'll mail you a postcard, hear? I'll ship you her body by Greyhound bus."

There was nothing to do—after George hung up on him—but wire Bebe and ask her to come home. Not that she could do anything. But he'd feel better when she was home.

Jack couldn't read about the bloodstream after that. He mixed a drink. He dreaded going to bed, for fear of the dream.

Maybe there'd be two women in the Katsewa River this time, with one saying, "Let's go, Rosie." Jack stared into the ashes on the hearth. Zorro chewed a throw rug until he got tangled and began to whine. Jack scratched the dog's spine while his tail stood straight up. Then he moved a table by the chair: cigarettes, ashtray, the bottle and more ice. He took off his shoes and threw them into the bedroom with his dirty shorts, near the unmade bed. Standing on a stool, he opened Foley's box and left its empty halves plainly on the hearth in case the boy should come in before he'd finished reading. If there were threads or hairs he could not find them. He was excited. The feeling was the same as when he'd stood on a ladder outside a classroom at Durham Tech. The man had been lecturing about fungicides. I can use that in my work, Jack had thought, listening. Later in the day, at the next window, the subject was photosynthesis. Air, sun, and water: that was all it took. He'd cut off an individual leaf and examined it for stomata. The bush came alive for Jack in that instant. He almost heard it breathe.

Taking a long drink, Jack stacked the numbered books in his lap in order, volumes two through five. There was no volume one. None was over half full of Foley's cramped handwriting. Jack opened volume two and began to read.

It started at an art exhibit of the usual long, thin sculptures, clay people fresh off the rack and stretched lengthwise, and figures with gaping holes in their sides. My eyes went out of focus. I could see holes, the space in the holes, better than what the artist had sculpted. I can't explain it. They use pictures to test for color blindness, and some can see a pattern in the red dots and make a red design while some can't. I saw the wrong pattern, that's all. The shapes became background and only the spaces counted. I felt queer.

Went back to art exhibit. Same effect.

I've noticed something about the paintings, too. My eye keeps going to the center of the canvas. No center is there, so what am I looking for? In abstract art or cubism, the whole space of the picture is of equal importance and should be seen as a whole. Nothing comes to focus or gives a visual climax. Artists used to have people sitting near the center, or something stronger or more vivid than the rest. My gaze keeps going there and, even in a collage, I almost see something in the middle where something ought to be.

I have a feeling of futility. What am I doing at college and what will I do when I get out?

Had eyes checked at the infirmary. 20-20. *Got a lecture about studying too hard. I hardly study, that's my problem. It doesn't seem to me they are teaching anything I ever wanted to learn.*

I have a name for my focus problem. Seeing Absence. Or maybe, Negative Vision. I seem to be, or my optic nerve seems to be, more interested in whatever's missing than what's there; and I swear I can almost see it, just a little. Could I be getting glaucoma? At my age?

The problem lies in perspective, maybe how the muscles focus my eyes. Some things look bigger or smaller to me, even when I know they are actually the same size. I tried this on a Cézanne. The apples kept shrinking, since they were only apples. He painted them on an enormous scale, but my eye rejects that and still I see only apples much smaller than his brush claimed they were. The infirmary is sending me to an ophthalmologist at Johns Hopkins. What if I have cancer of the eye? Maybe I'll need a cornea transplant.

Dr. Winstead has ruled out everything but nerves and still Boston looks to me flat as a pancake. He says to stop brooding, especially now, when snow has covered everything and made the city beautiful.

It happened in lit class today. I read aloud a lovely line from an Allen Ginsburg poem. The line wasn't really there and after the class started rustling and coughing, I looked and looked but couldn't find it again myself.

Dr. Winstead won't prescribe glasses or contact lenses. I thought of buying a pair at the dimestore. I carry a pocket mirror around and snatch it out in different lights to see if my lens has become opaque. I feel I could look through my pupil into my own head. Nerves, Dr. Winstead says. I don't have anything to be nervous about except the world situation which—God knows—is bad enough, and our poisoned country and the war and things like that. But people have lived through plagues and Indian wars and I guess we will live through all this. I feel depressed, though.

Went home this weekend to test Dr. Winstead's theory that I'm under great pressure from home to succeed and am rebelling on a psychosomatic level. My parents denied this. They both had to work on office tax returns and had little time to talk. In my bedroom, I tried to pick up a catcher's mitt off the dresser which hasn't been sitting there for about nine years.

"How is't with you, that you do bend your eye on vacancy?"—Hamlet, Act III, Scene 4, lines 116–117.

I'm going to use these journals for other subjects. Dr. Winstead says I have gotten preoccupied with an idea, need to be better rounded, take more interest in the external world. The funny thing is that's what I'd always done until it began to disappear. I'm no bookworm. Played basketball in high school, dated girls, repaired my car, listened to Jefferson Airplane, watched TV, worried about the war, worked part time, respected my parents. But I've promised to write about other subjects and stop thinking about vision.

ANOTHER SUBJECT: *I major in English and might be a writer someday. Viewpoint in fiction interests me. The last time they showed reentry of a space capsule on TV, the commentator called it "simulated." There it was, streaking like a wine cork with a tail across black space. But who saw it like that? No astronaut, or monkey, not a newsman, the control center at Houston nor aircraft carrier at sea. In fact, nobody has ever seen it from that angle nor ever will—even a twin capsule racing alongside will never have that particular sight in its portholes. What television did, in an objective news program, was use omniscient viewpoint! I sent them a postcard: "Greetings to Henry Fielding who is president of CBS. There is no way to elude illusions."*

I doubt I'll be a writer. All the books are written, and films are more popular. The hero is dead. We have no big subjects to write about.

All events are loose and separate.—Hume. Kropotkin.

Finally we reached that point in history where God was no longer around to spoil the fun. And the fun stopped.

Been trying to read a fragmentary novel about a main character who is no hero, but more like Osiris, scattered in pieces from page to page. Went to sleep.

Today I thought my philosophy professor made some statement he did not. He denied he had spoken the words in his lecture at all, although I had put them in my notebook. Here's what I wrote: "The purpose of philosophy is to help a man locate the one place he can stand still in, which will be forever true."

If you have a tumor in the eye, sometimes they burn it out with light, with radium; an interesting twist.

When Odysseus met Polyphemus, he called himself in the introduction ou tis, *No Man, the man without identity. It doesn't say how he looked to Polyphemus. In the mirror, the reality of my face is as clear as ever and, in fact, the shape of it oddly looks more important to me, although I don't know why.*

"Let every eye negotiate for itself, and trust no agent."— Midsummer Night's Dream.

Joined a fraternity. Faces looked alike. I had a good time and got, ha ha, blind drunk. Dated a Tri Delt and made out in my apartment and she spent the night.

I would like to see my own face before I was born.

In James Purdy's book, Alma was trying to write a memorial about Cliff and found that even his photograph looked almost retouched. The Army and Navy have developed plastic artificial eyes that won't crack. The business they're in, no wonder. NOTES FOR ENGLISH PAPER: *It is not necessary for the population to participate in mystic visions in order to follow them. (Prophets and Israelites, etc.) I, for instance, have never taken LSD, nor have most people I know, yet we all talk and think as though we have. Thousands of us are trying to move beyond rationality and verbalizing and toward essence, vicariously. Doctors must not realize that by maximizing the risks of drugs, they maximize their possible holiness. A bearer who touched the Ark of the Covenant fell dead. Every victim testifies to holiness. Half the great sexual thrill once produced by wars was the knowledge that wars made it possible to be destroyed. Ditto the Christians in Rome. Great risks make great causes. But in this decade, if we are all to be lost, down to the smallest snail, and in a relatively short time, war grows commonplace. We no longer run a risk but are run by risk. A man swallowing a pill or a sugar cube, at least, is not ingested by the pill against his choice. It's more attractive to many than the knowledge of being eaten alive by somebody else's stupidity: a dropped container of nerve gas, a stupid war, a nuclear button pushed, a growing garbage dump to live in, insane Vietnam. Existentialism: Camus and Angst. We are left only with courage. Tie this in. People on acid also see things that aren't there, and brag about it, but I guess I'm on a different trip.*

I think I'd like to sit under the bo tree like Buddha.

Bought a motorcycle. Took all my savings. Thought it would do me good to ride on weekends. That way, when the landscape blurs, I know it's a result of speed. My grades are slipping.

That Tri Delt thinks women are discriminated against and I have Victorian ideas. If she says a prayer at night, I bet it starts out: Lord God of Hostesses.

I tore out pages describing the countryside near Boston. When I reread entries, I notice an odd effect. If I write in concrete detail, how the grass looked, which bird was singing, I soon forget. But when I write no more than that a farmer waved to me from his tractor, that man stays on succeeding pages like a shadow, though he had no significance. He gets between me and my sentences like ectoplasm. I meant the journals to be about me and the external world. A single mention of a stranger who does not see but is merely seen one time dignifies him with mystery. The less I know about him, the more interesting he becomes.

My roommate said the first sensible thing about my eye problem. "Why don't you figure out what you're looking for?" he said. That's it. What is the absence? Something that isn't there but ought to be. Something I almost see except when I look head on. Something that used to be there not so long ago, that I miss but can't quite remember.

Home for the weekend. My father said, "I don't think the soul is immortal but sometimes I wish it was." I started explaining that I didn't either, that the soul was our word for the way the physical brain functioned, as a light was the result of a light bulb functioning. He stared at me. "What brought that on?" I said I was only answering his question. "I didn't ask you any question," he said, "and especially not that one." He's very scientific. Now he wants me to see a shrink.

Dropped out of school. No shrink for me. I am in Washington, D.C., and took part in a demonstration against the war. The answer to everything is to reform society. One black said under his breath that all the whites in the march were just "playing games."
A week in Norfolk. Something about the water rests my eyes, maybe the sheer size, the scope. Is that what I'm looking for? I feel my eyes are hungry, almost starved, and the ocean is not what they craved, and yet is not far from it, either. Such thoughts make me think I should have seen that shrink. Broke a brake pedal getting away from a truckload of bricks and am washing dishes to pay for repairs.

Robert F. Kennedy is dead. I can't stand it. Can't stand it. If we had a good society, this wouldn't happen.

I've never known anybody really evil. Misguided, or sick in the mind, maybe, or warped by environment or heredity, but I know if we could change those factors, people would be kind. I have some faults, of course, but most of them do no harm and I am certainly nonviolent. A man on a Norfolk street corner today was preaching sin to the sailors and they were asking him where they could find some. I'm sure that's healthier. I offered him my Playboy *magazine and he said he'd pray for me. A funny thing: I thought I saw Kennedy dressed in a sailor suit, walking with a girl. I followed them around a corner but they were nowhere to be seen.*

At Kitty Hawk, where the Wright brothers flew. Sat on a dune and tried to write a poem about Icarus. There must be 10,000 *bad poems about Icarus. I feel better by the ocean, though the salt air makes my eyes sting. The size rests my vision. Think I'll ride by its edge and trace the coast of this country. I think we're really doomed. That's what the preacher said, but he meant Sodom and Gomorrah stuff; he meant God would come back from the dead and do it. He talked about how the earth would crack like an egg and hatch out the millions of dead. And me they want to send to a shrink.*

Foley's journal went on and included his arrival at Pickle Beach. Jack was disappointed. He had expected more thought than feeling, more facts, more references to college classes and the specific wisdom of individual teachers. English, to Jack's mind, was a major for female schoolteachers. He read few novels himself and no poems at all. What disappointed him most was how little effect Foley's schooling had on his problem. He used his education more to explore his worries than solve them. Was it possible the more you learned, the clearer it became how bad off you were? Like the difference between a savage catching a fatal disease and an internist catching it?

Jack skimmed the other volumes with their scattered drawings and doodles, lines about Icarus, words of songs Foley was memorizing, lists, three versions of a letter to his draft board requesting conscientious objector status.

Jack thought that doctor had been right telling Foley to study the external world and stop thinking about himself. Nature was full of questions, too, but these locked a man closer into reality. At State Technical College, Jack had been introduced to Nature as soon as he came within earshot of certain classrooms. He'd been studying Nature ever since, could study it till he died without knowing how it worked. He could not, for instance, learn everything there was to know regarding one square foot of ground at Pickle Beach: the minerals, the insects, bacteria, fungi, plants, and so forth. It would do Foley good to concentrate on Nature instead of—what had he called it? Jack leafed back. Negative Vision. Seeing Absence.

Thinking of this, Jack got a stub pencil from the kitchen drawer and began printing, slowly and carefully, a separate entry of his own into Foley Dickinson's journal, volume two.

Plants flower at a certain time of year because they have some way of measuring length of day and night. Crocuses under a lighted driveway post will even bloom earlier. I don't know how the seventeen-year locust knows when his resting time is up. When a beehive is carried across time zones, the bees' sense of direction becomes confused and must be adjusted from Virginia to California. If birds are shielded from the sun and confused by mirrors, their clock and compass for navigating also becomes confused. There is one parasitic fern that grows under only one kind of tree, and puts down a long taproot to feed off its roots. How does it reproduce from one tree to the same kind miles away? I have read that the smallest beach crab can know the time of day from the angle its bodily axis forms with the position of the sun. Some people say when a tree or a plant is cut, it screams toward whatever ear could hear it on that scale. Some creatures on a twenty-four-hour biological rhythm do not change it even when moved by jet to the South Pole, and I read that if you photograph a plant once a minute and then speed the film, it seems to react to fear with stems and leaves as strongly as a dog or cat might with teeth and claws. Someday I would like to talk with you about these and many other things which I, Jack Sellars, do not understand.

It took a whole page of Foley's handsome ledger to hold Jack's large, neat words. He checked spelling and was meticulous dotting the *i*'s. He held the page at arm's length to see how the letters looked. He was pleased. Like his knowledge of Latin names on paper, the entry stood for his ability to know more than his tongue could pronounce. It gave him satisfaction, too, to get into Foley's book the way a boy gets under the circus tent.

I hope he can *see* it all right.

Jack stacked the journals carefully inside the box and then put the box carefully on the mantel. Maybe, he thought in a burst of sudden cheer, Foley would be able to see in the Pinheads the intelligence they did not have.

Mickey McCane

June 17

She didn't come. She isn't coming.

Mickey hung up his telephone. The first fear crawled over him, as it used to steal coldly up his body when he woke in too quiet a house and knew by the silence, even before he called, that his mother was gone again.

"Find your fishing rod?"

He almost answered Eunice by saying it was in the attic, which it was. He watched his black shadow on the wall, even made the outline of a rabbit and a wolf by meshing his hands against the light. "Bebe put it someplace," he finally called. Eunice was in the den sewing rickrack on an apron. She was always sewing and the sound of her scissors through cloth nibbled at him. From the doorway he watched her finishing up, tying a knot and biting thread with her teeth.

"I'm in my socks," he warned. Sometimes she dropped straight pins in the carpet. This time—she pointed—they were all stuck upright in the cushion by her on the couch. "I was using that cushion," he said. Obligingly she drew them out and passed it to him. One of the pins tumbled into the rug and was lost to sight. Mickey sat in the recliner no one else was allowed to use and slapped open his newspaper to read about local softball games.

"I went to the doctor today," said Eunice. Her gaze slid away. She opened the hassock and took out one of the endless squares she was knitting into an afghan. She said it kept her fingers from trembling. "About my headaches."

"If you'd quit some of that close work, your headaches would quit," said Mickey for the tenth time or so. "That needlework *makes* you nervous."

"Dr. Culver said we need a vacation."

Again? Mickey turned the page and folded it. "He said that before. So take one. Go up to Lake Lure like you did last year."

"He said *we*." Eunice swallowed hard in her skimpy throat.

"Nobody asked him to prescribe for me."

"My mother can keep the boys." It wasn't like Eunice to be stubborn. "Dr. Culver said it was his favorite prescription for a marriage, especially at our age."

She had told him all this last month. The second honeymoon business. She seemed to be telling Mickey in May, without coming out and saying so, that she might leave him *if.* If *what* he couldn't imagine. She had everything a woman needed. He had used her money well in the laundromats and took care of all details. No woman left her husband for *tension,* which was the best Eunice could claim. She had talked her problems over with her doctor, she said, that pansy of a man with the wet handshake. And he'd said the McCanes ought to take a trip and rediscover each other. He even wanted Mickey to come by for a talk instead of going off fishing by himself so much.

Mickey had only to look at the doctor's wife to see how much Culver knew. There stood his prescription, two hundred pounds, and she sweated all the time. Under her arms she was wet all the way to her belt, even in wintertime, and he didn't see the Culvers eloping to Florida. Mickey told Eunice that, in May, and drove out to the Cotton Club and shot pool with his friends.

She had been asleep when he got home that night but he shook her awake. "And nobody leaves me," he said. "I send you on a vacation by yourself, that's all right; but nobody leaves me. You hear that?"

And she had the nerve to say, "Your mama did."

He thought quickly now: My mother loved me. Rattled his paper. "I might take you up to Boone in August."

"You really mean that, Mickey?" He nodded and she smiled over her wool stitches. Even the smile looked wan. The thing about Eunice: she looked like a woman left out in the weather too long. Faded and bleached. Strangers in the grocery store had been known to come up to Eunice and offer her aspirin—that's how she looked. Her eyes had turned tan and between her tan eyebrows were frown lines so deep they must show up as ridges on the back side of her head, under her tan-colored hair. Some nights Mickey had reached through the dark and laid his thumb above her nose, but the skin was not even smooth when she slept. Suppose some little kid got left in the backyard for years and just laid around in the wet grass and worried? She'd get lighter and thinner and have those frown marks in her face.

Bebe's face and body, by contrast, were almost juicy. *Ripeness* was the word that came to him most—Bebe had become at her age all that had ever been in her to become, had mellowed; everything so undersupplied in Eunice brimmed and ran over in Bebe.

Mickey savored again in the recliner the moment Bebe had turned to him, that easy willingness, the free gift of her arms with their downy blond hairs. What she had said to him later he would not think about; that would be overcome.

He knew how to handle it. Never admit you are powerless; that was his first rule. Whatever a man insisted upon came true—not every time, but mostly. He had learned over the years some small insistent tricks to play upon his body. Had stood in the toilet, willing his slow erection, making a picture in his mind of how Eunice might whimper at its size, and behind her a long line of other whimpering women, frightened by so much strength and malehood, throwing their arms around his hips in amazement, calling it iron or steel, cringing, wincing, but slowly giving way, because they desired to be ruled.

Only the first time with Bebe would he need self-trickery; the first time would prove his vigor. That single joining to her would empower him further; he was not certain whose seed would pour into whom, but he felt she would be to him one endless aphrodisiac until he could enter her at will, even gently and slowly, could even be gentle himself in time, and at peace. Bebe would make him whole, he was certain, not knowing that the longing of one thing for its opposite is sometimes the pull toward wholeness, but sometimes not.

He flapped the paper, abruptly, and stared at Eunice. "I might do better than that. Might take you to Pickle Beach." Let Bebe see for herself what he had to put up with.

"You're kidding!" Eunice said. She almost dropped her knitting.

"I just might, I said."

"Is it a nice place?"

"Sure it's a nice place. Would I go if it wasn't a nice place?"

"And we'd be by ourselves?"

Mickey nodded.

"When?" Eunice was pressing; maybe Dr. Culver had told her not to take no for an answer.

"As a matter of fact, we ought to go pretty soon if we're going," he said, well satisfied with the effect on Eunice. He told her about the Pinheads but she was more interested in when they could leave, how long they would stay. "The Pinheads will be there the whole month of July." Next week then? Eunice said. This week? "The idea that somebody like that, not normal, has a kid at all is disgusting," said Mickey. "What kind of a mother is that?"

Eunice got up to telephone her family about keeping the McCane boys while they were away.

"They ought to be sterilized, people like that," Mickey said to himself.

10

Bebe Sellars

June 22

Today is Saturday. The Pinheads are coming. Today.

The thought was in Bebe's head when she woke to the ocean's steady music, as if she had been thinking it all night in her sleep.

When Bebe was little, Walt Fetner would tell her every new thought cut a line in the brain; that's why its surface was so wrinkled when everything else in the body was smooth. For instance, the more you thought about arithmetic, he said, the deeper the Arithmetic Line became. That scared her to death because she spent most of her time thinking about Bebe Fetner, and she was afraid that particular ditch was cut so deep it might split her mind in two, or break off a gray and lumpy island in her head.

This was the day. She felt relaxed and curious. She reached across the bed to touch Jack. He wasn't there. Was he still worried about the Pinheads?

In the kitchen, coffee was made and kept warm for her. She spread bacon slices on the griddle before carrying her cup to the porch to look for him. Jack sat on an inner tube and watched the mottled clouds where it rained to the southeast. It did seem to Bebe that his dread of the Pinheads' coming had eased. She had never understood that dread. A fear that Rosie was like his mother? Or Jack might be like her feebleminded son? It made no sense.

The night before, trying to explain, he'd said the Pinheads just demonstrated that people came in all layers and the layers couldn't be changed. Layers? He said, "They're as dumb to me as I am dumb to others."

Big deal. "And all of us," she'd said then, "are dumb to the angels and the angels are dumb to God."

"You still believe in God." It was a statement, full of wonderment.

Bebe was fresh from old Mamie's funeral, and stubborn. "Don't say the word *God* if you don't like that. Pick out some other word to believe in."

"Words." Jack laughed. "I'd better ask Foley to lend me one."

She decided he'd been reading Darwin all the time she was gone and could only look from A to Z, then to now, and left to right. The older Bebe got, the more she wanted to see the back of her own head. If she knew how, she could look around in a circle, a perfect circle, because she was certain the ring was there. Could even watch Mamie Loftin moving around it yet—or something like Mamie. She knew better than to say that out loud. The few times she'd tried, Jack had replied, "Write your nun a letter; that's more her department than mine."

She tried to gauge Jack's mood by watching him watch the sea. He might still expect the very worst to float ashore. Somebody on the coast watching Columbus sail west probably claimed he heard all three thuds when the boats dropped over the edge.

Bebe blew the whistle he was using to train Zorro. When

Jack turned, she pointed to Foley's trailer, then put on a robe and scrambled some eggs. She was sliding the platter into a warm oven when the light rain reached them.

Jack and Foley clattered up the back steps and burst into the kitchen. Foley wore his damp jeans wrapped on his head like a scarf, now snapped them out straight and stepped into the legs. "I was sound asleep. Morning, Bebe." He called her Bebe and Jack Mr. Sellars.

She thought: If I could once get those jockey shorts off him, I'd boil them in bleach. "Go wash your hands while I turn the toast." Foley liked his buttered on both sides, with cinnamon and sugar. Mrs. Dickinson probably lay awake nights for fear he ate bread with weevils in it.

As he chewed on a strip of bacon, Foley said, "Today's the day." Bebe sneaked scraps under the table to the dog. "What time you think they'll come?"

"Who knows?" Jack forked his eggs so carefully you'd think he was unscrambling white from yellow. "They flew into Myrtle Beach yesterday and some nurse drives them up the coast today. What time is it?"

"Little past seven." The clock had just finished putting on a show. Bebe tried to make Foley look at her. He had a smile like Sonny Tufts in that war movie when Veronica Lake's hair was all over her face. "Foley? Did you do it?" Last night she had given him one of their Pickle Beach postcards and a stamp and told him to write his mother.

"I will, I will."

The card showed the sea and sand in color, with their house blurred at the back, looking better than it really did. "I'm twice as old as you and I write *my* mother." No answer. Jack had told her Foley owned four diaries full of words and he still couldn't spare his folks a single postcard. Bebe thought: I would skin him if he was mine. "You write her after breakfast and I'll carry it up to mail." Foley wouldn't look. She reached across the table and spread her fingers in the air over his scrambled eggs. "That's the price of the meal. You hear?"

Just like Sonny Tufts, that grin. *So Proudly We Hail.* "I promise, Bebe."

"Now listen," she said. "Who goes out to meet them when they come?"

"Meet them? Nobody has to meet them," said Jack. "Let the nurse knock on the door like everybody else."

She was dissatisfied. "Maybe she can't leave them. I don't like the idea of her locking them in the car in all this heat. Why don't you plan to take the key outside when she comes?"

"What difference does it make? We'll wait and see."

It made a difference. "Did you finish fixing the door at their house?" He nodded.

Yesterday while Bebe cleaned the house where the Pinheads would live, Jack and Foley chewed bologna sandwiches and argued. They were supposed to be rescreening that porch and door. Maybe Jack thought if it weren't freshly tight, Rosie would crawl out the edge and run around foaming at the mouth. Mostly they argued. Their hammers would bang awhile, then stop. On her knees at kitchen cabinets, Bebe could hear Jack say, "An eighteenth-century man?" He sounded insulted.

"I mean you're a sucker for reason and the great chain of being." Foley laughed.

"And what are you a sucker for?"

"I'm not a sucker." More hammering. "Pass the tacks down here. Bebe, now, she's a Romantic. You two are a funny combination."

"She's romantic about John Garfield and Rock Hudson."

(That's not so, Bebe thought. She couldn't abide Rock Hudson.)

"I don't mean Romantic in that sense."

She missed sentences while she spread shelf paper in the closet and stuck it down with masking tape. Passing through the rooms, she only caught snatches.

"I left school because I was learning one thing at the expense of something else."

"What else?"

Foley didn't know.

"Is it bothering you today? How many fingers?" She heard Jack laugh.

Again: "Is this tight enough? . . . The funny thing to me, Mr. Sellars, is that you seem to be headed in Bebe's same direction. I read what you wrote in my book. You both want something to last but nothing does."

"Memories last," Jack grunted.

After a while Foley said, "Memories don't last for me like they do for your generation."

"You haven't had time to get any good ones yet."

"Let me finish. It's part of the generation gap. For instance, you people are still hung up on families. We're into communities and cooperative groups."

"Communes?" said Jack, making the word a condemnation.

"O.K., even communes. The young people have to work together to build a better present world right here in the time we live. The past is no good for us now; it's another age and another way of thinking. Bebe still thinks it does somebody good for me to mail home a postcard."

Bebe held her breath to catch Jack's answer. "Bebe thinks it would do your mother some good."

No, she thought. Foley, too.

"I'm trying to point out the difference between the father image and the brotherhood image. The father image is dead for my generation."

How ignorant he was, she thought.

Soon Jack came into the toilet, zipped loose so hard you'd think his fly was two feet long, and peed with a great rush into the bowl she had just disinfected. He was talking to himself, imitating Foley in a high and prissy voice that Foley didn't have. "His father image is dead. For Christ's sake. *His* father." The toilet lid slammed. "The colleges," Jack said with an angry stare at Bebe, "have just cut these children *loose* in the world!" He left the urine for Bebe to flush, which showed Foley's deep effect on him since he had an old maid's neat toilet habits. At great speed she could hear Jack's hammer tapping outside. A new argument. She caught the louder parts.

Foley's voice: "I never said that. I said there was no such thing as time except as man invented it. Did you know one effect of LSD is to raise the body temperature and that alone contracts the sense of time? Tranquilizers slow it down."

No hammers now. "You take that stuff?"

"If I wanted to, I would."

"Well, don't." Silence. "What about the sun and moon and stars? They set up the days and seasons. People just gave time a name."

"Ah, but people have always imagined a world without time."

"The sun, moon, and stars," Jack insisted. "I'm talking about those physical facts, not what people imagine. Night and day."

"They called it eternity. Anyway, the physical time you talk about is running out." There followed some boring harangue about the second law of thermodynamics, which seemed to be unpleasant news to Jack, so Bebe stopped listening. Soon the porch door slammed and they walked into the sea oats, arguing, the work forgotten. Bebe nailed up half that screen herself.

In the night Jack woke her with a good shake. She reached

out but it was not the dream bothering him. "It must be the middle of the night," she said.

Jack sat up in bed. "Foley Dickinson might be a worse liar than Willis is."

"What does he lie about?"

"Foley's no atheist!" Jack said, fairly chortling.

"Jack, are you drunk?"

"He just knows all the good reasons he ought to be. What a big joke on Foley! What a big joke on the university!" Bebe yawned. Jack fell back on the pillow, laughing. "And he called *you* a Romantic. I can't wait to tell him."

Bebe said sleepily, "Don't tell him."

"Why not?"

"Because. Listen, they're coming tomorrow and you're going to have a headache from no sleep."

"I never," Jack lied, "get headaches." He lay down chuckling.

Now he sat across from Foley at breakfast and, from his quick grin, must have remembered the secret he had discovered and Foley had not.

"Good eggs," Foley said. "Good coffee." Bebe liked feeding him. He enjoyed everything.

"Want to go up to Willis's after breakfast, Foley?"

Bebe said Willis had already promised to deliver their order early, with extras on applesauce and every item on George Bennett's list. Then she saw Jack wanted to keep arguing with Foley, who had taken his mind off the Pinheads' coming. "Bring us some beer, then, and light bulbs," she said.

Though it was raining, they decided to ride double on Foley's motorcycle. "You better wear my helmet," Foley said.

They went down the steps, Jack teasing, "See that? It's the road. Stay on it. I don't want your next absence to be me."

She had not heard Jack talk so much in a long time, much

less laugh, and was almost jealous. Sex, though, beat conversation. Living was better than anybody's thoughts about it.

Bebe fed the dog, then—lazily—slid their dishes into soapy water. She went through the motions of cleaning the kitchen. Funny how, after eighteen years, she couldn't feel housework was really her *job,* but only something temporary that must be done until better things turned up. That—even now—she might invent something or be discovered by Hollywood. That her name could any day be read off some millionaire's will.

She scoured the sink and polished both chrome faucets, humming the hymn from Mamie's funeral. *When we've been there ten thousand years / Bright shining as the sun / We'll have more time to sing God's praise / Than when we first begun.*

The funeral had almost been a happy occasion. For one thing, the Loftins looked so funny trying to keep up a hundred death customs, scared of forgetting an important one, that they ran around like a flock of hens; and the undertaker was trying to keep his rituals straight on a parallel line with theirs; while the preacher from Hebron had his own routines to complete; and only Mamie seemed to feel easy about it all, and to lie in her coffin wearing a silly smirk the mortuary had drawn there with Revlon lipstick. That thing in the box was so clearly not Mamie at all, but a yellowed mockery she had left behind to illustrate her amusement, that Bebe dismissed the corpse after first shock of seeing it dressed in a pink silk nightgown Mitzi Gaynor might have worn. What the family had really come to mourn, and could not, was the part of Mamie none of them knew, the life and memories they had come a generation too late to grasp, so that only Mamie was really old enough to have wept for the real Mamie, and her corpse looked somewhat comical.

Bebe sang the hymn now, happily, with much weight on the part about singing the praise of God. Zorro, shut into the broom closet by mistake, began to yap. She let him loose and he ran barking to the back door. A minute later Bebe, too, heard tires roll across the backyard and an ugly car horn, then a second, louder blast. She drew back the curtains and watched a gray Oldsmobile park on Jack's centipede grass. The rain had ended and the car roof was half dry. She could see a driver, two passengers in the back.

Her question was answered. She was the one who had to go out to meet them.

Bebe stepped out the back door onto the platform where her mop hung drying in the sun. And there they were: the nurse with her head stuck out the driver's window, a mean look on her face, and behind her a woman and boy, drowsing, a quick impression of broadness and lank hair.

Bebe, who had squared her shoulders to confront the Pinheads, burst out laughing because—of all things to think!—it hit her that Blake and Otis could visit Pickle Beach after all since the nurse's face gleamed with the rich color of fudge under her starched cap. The sun glared off steel-rimmed glasses she must have borrowed from her granny.

"Mr. Jack Sellars, please," she called in a nearly bass voice. She didn't smile. Her skin might be fudge but the voice was vinegar. As if Bebe looked deaf and stupid, she suddenly yelled, *"Sellars!"*

She looked so irritated Bebe half forgot she was a Sellars, too, and said in confusion, "He isn't here."

The nurse growled, "He's supposed to be," and turned off the motor. She said to the vague forms in the backseat, "Not here, wouldn't you know it?" Thrust her head out again. "Isn't this his house?"

Bebe started slowly down the high steps, flattening her hair with one hand because the nurse's flared outward like a thornbush. "He's just gone up the road to the grocery store; ought to be back in a few minutes. I'm Mrs. Sellars." Should she hold out her hand? The nurse drew back before she could decide. She reached the car and the woman and boy leaned forward on the backseat. A quick glimpse of ugliness. Real physical ugliness. Then Rosie pressed her face flat to the back window glass, mashing her features out of shape, making her nose a pale snout, and looked like a piglet. Behind her the boy hid his face in her brown dress.

Bebe said to the nurse, "That's your house down the beach, beyond the trailer. I can show you."

The nurse nodded and motioned Bebe to get in. The hot car smelled of sweat and vanilla. "You can drive right to the door. The key's in it." The very roots of Bebe's hair seemed to be listening to the Pinheads chuckle behind her. Yes, they chuckled.

The nurse said coldly, "I'm Miss Whitaker," and drove rapidly past Foley's trailer to turn off where Bebe pointed. She parked by the prefab shell and stared.

"It's pine paneled."

Miss Whitaker closed her thick eyelids. "I wouldn't be surprised."

"Can I help carry in the bags?"

"Not yet." Stepping from the car, she propped on the open door and gazed through tall weeds to the water. Her uniform was so heavily starched it seemed more bent than wrinkled. "*You!*" she bawled, and thrust her wide body inside half over the seat. "You stay right here. Don't even move!" Her bright glasses flared at Bebe like a pair of flashlights. "I'll have to lock the car."

"I'd be glad to watch . . . Well. All right." Bebe wished she had worn more than a flowered robe over her sweaty slip. Miss Whitaker locked both car doors. Bebe couldn't bring herself to look at the two in the backseat, Rosie and what's-his-name. She just couldn't. "We left the house open, not knowing what time you'd come." Miss Whitaker followed her into the main room with its open kitchenette on one end and a linoleum-topped serving bar. The pine walls were yellow as squash. "Two bedrooms on the far end. A connecting bath."

"I see." She jerked off her round glasses as if she desired to see less.

"There's a screen porch."

"Yes." Her gaze was on the flooring of streaked pastels, with a tan patch worn at the sink. "Is it clean?"

"I cleaned up good yesterday."

Miss Whitaker checked the latch on both doors, picked up a vase of beach poppies and set that on a high shelf. "How about food?"

"The store should deliver it anytime."

Bebe got more and more nervous, watching her move critically through the house, lift a clamshell ashtray and set it down again. Miss Whitaker was the first mean Negro she'd ever met. She hadn't shown the first smile or spoken a single thanks. It made Bebe feel as if the nurse were really Blake Wilkie, and Bebe had kerosene spilled on her hands.

Partly to excuse her, Bebe said, "You must be tired."

She made a *tock* sound with her pink tongue. "My tired is just starting. Is the water drinkable?"

"It's fair. Did they . . . give you any trouble?"

"What do you mean by trouble?" She popped her glasses back on her broad nose and stared straight at Bebe. Not Phibby's sliding look, which flicked across the face and moved on. Bebe had no idea what she'd meant by the word *trouble* and began to button and rebutton her robe. The nurse finally said, "We'd better unload the trunk first." Bebe almost answered, "Yes, ma'am."

While they carried in boxes and suitcases, the Pinheads crowded their faces into the rear window, their low laughter rumbling like thunder from many miles away. At the edge of Bebe's eye, their faces blurred behind the glass. Broad faces and hanks of brown hair—that's all she allowed herself to notice. One of them scrabbled a set of fingers up and down the car window, up and down. Fat fingers, moist on the tips, with short nails. Bitten. What did a Pinhead have to be nervous about? The luggage was heavy. Something inside might clank like a chain. She followed Miss Whitaker's white cotton stockings, flour white over her solid legs, and tried to imagine nursing two Pinhead Negro patients and wearing black stockings for the job.

Miss Whitaker let Bebe carry the heavy stuff. "The refrigerator was turned on for you last night; should be good and cold by now." She only marched by and waggled her starched cap. "I made up the beds." Another nod.

When everything had been unloaded and Miss Whitaker's bags placed in the choice front bedroom where she would catch the breeze, she told Bebe (just like that) to go home and leave the rest to her.

"When Jack comes—"

Tock with that tongue. "I'll call if we need him. Or is there a telephone?"

"Only in the main house."

"Well, that's a mess," Miss Whitaker snapped.

Bebe showed her the brass ship's bell she could ring. "One of us is always there. And there's a boy staying next door in the trailer."

"It'll have to do."

"Just ring if you need anything."

Miss Whitaker hurried Bebe to the porch. "Fine, fine."

"The boy's name is Foley Dickinson. Nobody else is at the beach right now." Somehow Bebe was already outside while Miss Whitaker nodded her bushy head, latched the screen, and tried it a few times. Then she rushed inside the house without another word. Bebe had to tramp home through the thick hot sand. Didn't even get to ask if she was the same nurse from last year or a new one.

Zorro was barking, trying to paw open the porch door. Fearing he'd bother Miss Whitaker, Bebe stood on the steps telling him to calm down. He would not. Bebe could see that gray car, two fat people and a white uniform going inside the house and probably hooking that screen behind them. Could Rosie unlatch doors? Would she remember being here before? Bebe wondered if either of the Pinheads could swim.

"Oh, come on, Zorro, but stay with me." The pup ran ahead over the damp sand, still pocked with raindrops. In the sunlight each crater was slowly drying and would crumble away. Toward the surf, Bebe crossed that line of bottles and Dixie cups and gum wrappers Foley liked to call the giant ring around the giant tub. Bebe sat beyond the wet sand to guess how high each wave would come. She felt let down. Since May they had waited for the Pinheads to come, and here they were, big deal, with Miss Medical Grouch. Must have a bedside manner that scared people back to health, witch doctor style. Not like the nurse Bebe had the morning she woke up in the hospital with her ovaries cut out, wondering where they were. Did hospitals throw tonsils and ovaries into the town garbage with old chewing gum and cans? She lay there alone. A buzzer hung on a black rubber rope by her head so she gouged the button. They sent some virgin in the tenth grade who was scared of her, red-haired, with restless green eyes and freckles. "How you feel?" she recited, and showed her milk teeth. It seemed important to her that Bebe lie and claim excellent health. Right then her chest fell in, and she whimpered, "My ovaries hurt." The child looked so embarrassed. Such a red, speckled face! Bebe was choking in that bed. "Damn it, my ovaries hurt!"

The girl went to the hall and called somebody to give Bebe a shot and make her hush.

"So they hurt—I wouldn't be surprised," Miss Whitaker would have said.

At the Pinheads' house the brass bell suddenly began to clang. Bebe crossed from damp to hot sand which burned her bare feet and arrived flying to look through the screen.

Miss Whitaker hung the bell on its hook. "Did you get plenty of applesauce?"

"Plenty," Bebe said. Her own temper rose. But the Pinhead boy came onto the porch before she could say more and at last she was staring into his face, which looked a bit Hawaiian. His black hair had been cut around the rim of a bowl and he even had stringy bangs. His black eyes were lifted at the corners by the pressure of pudgy cheeks. She thought of the coolies who built the Burma Road. "Hello," Bebe said.

He stepped back. She was not sure whether he was looking at her or not.

"I put it in the living room," Miss Whitaker told him, pointing. He caught his lower lip with his fingers and pulled it. "I'll show you in a minute."

When Zorro barked between Bebe's ankles, it startled them all, but the boy was terrified and fell backward into the living room and out of sight. "He is down on the floor again," groaned Miss Whitaker.

Bebe grabbed Zorro against her chest and even muzzled him with one hand. "I'm sorry."

Miss Whitaker was already going indoors. "Keep that dog at home," she said.

Bebe called, "He's just a pup and if they got used to each other, maybe . . ." She could hear nothing inside the house except, in a minute, a closing bedroom door. She put Zorro down and he ran home as fast as he could. Jack must be there.

Rounding Foley's trailer she met him coming in search of her, and told him the Pinheads were here. "How are they?" he asked, eyeing their silent house.

"The nurse is crabby." He waited. "The other two seemed . . . They seemed happy."

"Happy?" Jack let Bebe climb their steps ahead of him.

"They kept laughing. The boy's scared of Zorro. Foley come with you?"

"He's downstairs putting in a new spark plug. How'd they look? Do they talk?"

"Not to me they don't. The boy pulls his mouth." She showed him with her own and the act repelled him. She added, "It wasn't disgusting, exactly."

"Willis is over there now with groceries."

"He better watch out. Miss Whitaker might bite off his other fingers."

"Was there something wrong with the house that got her going?"

"She's just the bossy type."

"Has to be, I guess, to do that job." He stood over Bebe in the swing. "Is the boy full grown?"

"He's the same size as his mother. But they're both short and fat. Mashed down, in a way."

"Mashed down," he repeated. He absently pushed the chain with one hand. "George said neither one had ever been violent. They were laughing, huh?"

"See there? Willis is leaving." The pickup scattered sand gunning out of the Pinheads' yard and threw up a new supply turning swiftly into theirs. Jack and Bebe started through the house. Willis was talking loudly outside in the yard and when they reached the kitchen he was coming up the stairs at top volume. "Have you seen her? That nurse is a nigger! Jack? They have sent us a nigger nurse!"

Jack's mouth dropped and Bebe said, "Didn't I mention that?"

"Ugly as a mud fence and mean as sin!" Willis almost exploded into the kitchen and swiped Bebe's arm with his partial fist. "They're going to give you two a life membership in the N-double-A-C-P!" Even his scalp was red, he was so excited. "That woman has set in Hell and played in the ashes. Told me I sold off-brands. Get that! Off-brands!" He laughed and took an excited jab toward Jack's chin, which was still hanging loose, and bobbed around the kitchen like a prizefighter. "Her name is Miss Whitaker and if she finds one blood spot in one egg she won't pay for the whole carton! She wanted me to know that right off. She will have butter instead of margarine, thank you, and the chicken cut up in advance!"

"Aw, sit down, Willis," Bebe said.

Willis helped himself to coffee and then set the cup on the windowsill, too stimulated to drink it. "I'm planning to bring that woman's order late at night and put it in the back door and run. She sent back the hamburger. Too much fat! How fresh is my milk, she wants to know! Asked me what farmer grows my leaf lettuce and did I know if any of his family was disease carriers! Wait'll I tell Polly that! She grew every piece herself."

Jack said, "What about the Pinheads?"

Willis opened and shut the refrigerator. "They were out on the porch so I didn't see them much. Sitting on the floor like kids, you know? With their legs spread? Rolling this ball back and forth." He added, "I saw more of the ball than them since it kept passing by that open door. That's all I looked at while that woman reamed me out."

"Cream's on the table, Willis," said Bebe, pointing.

"Didn't see it." Now he couldn't find his coffee. Bebe handed the cup off the sill while Jack pulled up a chair.

"She didn't need to see me or anything, did she?"

"Listen, Jack, I wouldn't go if she did!"

All day they waited for Miss Whitaker to ring her brass bell and complain, but it was so quiet up the beach you couldn't tell anybody was there. Bebe barbecued chicken and Foley enjoyed his but Jack mostly sucked off the sauce. In the afternoon, Jack sat by the trailer reading late entries in Foley's journal and keeping an eye on the Pinheads' house besides.

Indoors, Bebe wrote Grace Fetner that she had arrived home safely and was just fine.

The afternoon passed without a sound from the Pinheads' house. Three or four times Jack wandered in and said to Bebe, "I guess I ought to walk over there," but time passed and he didn't go. Bebe warned him if he woke Miss Whitaker from a nap she would take his head clean off.

Just before supper he called her to the porch and showed her three small figures up the beach. One, in a white dress, had set a chair on the dune and arranged herself the way Lincoln sat in all the pictures of his monument. The other two stood knee deep in the water. They carried a striped beachball. Probably they chuckled; Bebe could halfway hear them even at this distance, so far away she couldn't tell Rosie from her son.

For a long time Jack and Bebe stood on the porch watching them throw the bright ball in the waning light, or squat and set it lightly on the water so it floated out to be carried back on a new wave. Just before dark, Miss Whitaker rose and whistled through her fingers the way people call dogs, and they quit playing in the water and followed her into the house.

"The one carrying the ball," said Jack, "must be the mother."

That night it took Bebe three sheets of paper to work out

just the message she wanted to write and exactly how to say it. Then she addressed a postcard showing the sand and sea and their fuzzy house at Pickle Beach to:

Mr. and Mrs. Dickinson
Dentist or Orthodontist office
Hagerstown, Maryland

On the back she copied the message neatly. "Your son Foley has been visiting with our family for some days now. He is a very nice boy and in good health and wants you not to worry. Sincerely, Mrs. J. S. Sellars."

Then it occurred to her they might jump on a plane and come here and make a big scene about taking Foley home and sending him to a head doctor, though Bebe wouldn't blame them much. There was no printing on the card to show which beach it was. She stuck it inside her letter to Mama and asked her in a P.S. to mail it from Greenway so that postmark would be on it.

There wasn't a bit of need to mention this to anybody at Pickle Beach, so Bebe didn't.

11

Jack Sellars

June 20–23

Nobody ever looked as good as Bebe did, climbing off that bus Thursday night, sleepy, her hair tangled. She said, "There you are!" and lit up in some way Jack could hardly describe. He drove home with his arm around her, speeding, feeling young, and they left the suitcase in the car overnight and said their real hellos in bed as grownups should.

Jack fell asleep still joined to her; sometime in the night they came loose without knowing. Once he half woke and Bebe's earlobe looked like a raindrop near his eye; he remembered touching his tongue to it and drifting away again on the full taste and feel of her.

In the morning she whispered, "How you doing, honey?" She tickled his tailbone. "You miss me?" He pretended to be asleep. "Jack?"

Suddenly he slid over and laid himself on her body just for the good feel it gave his body all the way down. Toads sit in puddles and drink water through their skins; he felt that way about having Bebe home. He tried then to make the speech he had been preparing. "If it wasn't for you, Bebe," but she laughed under him.

"If it wasn't for me you'd jerk off in your hand a lot."

"That and other things," Jack said. "I'm glad you're home."

"Me, too." She crossed both arms on his back so he could feel her pulse tap softly on his ribs. "If people come back to earth more than once, Jack, let's you come back as Bebe and I'll come back as you, and we'll get married all over again."

There were worse things than being simpleminded. Jack nodded his head against her warm shoulder. "I won't be a very good wife."

Bebe said, "I ain't choosy. Now roll off before you mash me flat."

Foley took to her right away, perhaps because she took him over.

"Close your mouth when you chew," Bebe ordered, and Foley did. "If I had a son your age," she declared, "I wouldn't give him penny *one* for a dangerous motorcycle. Suicycle, that's more like it. Murdercycle."

She scolded and clucked. By Friday night Foley even offered—he *offered*—to let Bebe read his journals, but she said books weren't her speed.

She made him sit under a lamp so she could examine his eyes while he explained. "I don't see a thing." She frowned.

He laughed and said that was his problem, too.

"Roll toward the ceiling. Um. Look down." He told her about the doctor. "Hold still," she said, and put plain eyewash in them that she bought off the drugstore shelf. "Keep still," she said while it spilled from his eye and down his face. Jack sat on the hearth and watched Foley's bottled tears run down. "Now listen," she said, sponging his cheek. "What worries you, Foley?"

He told her how big and impersonal college felt, and how the cities were decaying. There wasn't any job he really wanted to do for the rest of his life. There might be race war. Kennedy got shot down by a maniac just when he might have changed the country. The war in Vietnam was immoral and because of DDT the bluebirds were nearly extinct.

"Uh huh," she said, raising the eyedropper again. "What else?"

Adults didn't understand their own children. People could turn into Nazis over how long a guy wore his own hair. Marijuana should probably be legalized but he had friends who got on heroin and now were inside a living death. The business-industrial complex and the war machine had thwarted the Constitution. Jordan and Israel were a powder keg and Red China belonged in the United Nations.

"Besides that?" Bebe said softly.

For a long time while Foley sat in the dark to rest his eyes on the spacious night, they murmured on the porch. Jack was distracted by their steady hum. He asked Foley if he could try the BSA one time.

"Sure," Foley said. "They do feel better, Bebe. What kind of medicine was that?"

"Go on," she said.

On the edge of the asphalt paving, Jack rode the motorcycle slowly, letting the clutch out too fast, throwing his pelvis out of joint on the kickstart. He got hot and sweaty. When he came in for water Foley had worked up to existentialism, which Bebe probably thought was infectious.

"Jean-Paul Sartre," he was saying soberly.

"John-Paul Selfish, it sounds like to me," Bebe said. "Have you written your mama all the time you've been gone?"

Jack went out smiling and this time got the BSA to carry him through the cool wind like the point of a knife and again, but briefly, he envied Foley the freedom to take off on a whim and ride around the countryside. I've been there already, he thought.

Friday night Foley built a fire on the beach and they roasted hot dogs. Jack ate so many Bebe said he was lumpy with wieners like a cornshuck mattress, then had to explain to Foley what that was. Long after supper they sat smoking cigarettes and drinking beer by the fire. The ocean shone with mystery. There was a long white road across it toward the moon.

"You don't even have a girl?"

"Not right now," Foley said. "But don't look worried, Bebe. I've had plenty of girls."

"Which one did you like best?" Foley wouldn't choose. He taught Bebe some Boston University dance and Bebe shook herself up and down and sideways in the moonlight until she spilled beer all over herself. "Come try it, Jack!" He was too sore from kicking the motorcycle over. He asked Foley if it was something like the twist and got a groan at how out of date he was.

Bebe dropped to the sand and put her hand over Jack's watch just as he lifted it. "Don't look," she begged. "It isn't late."

It was but he promised; in fact, he took the watch off and stuffed it in his pocket and stared into the flames while Bebe sang (not very well) with her face wistful as a girl's. Her small voice was not quite grown up, either, and she sighed like a teenager who still expected adventure and romance to come to her, maybe Tyrone Power to float in on a log.

Foley didn't know her songs and she didn't care who Rod McKuen or Leonard Cohen were.

"Time after time / I'll tell myself that I'm / So lucky. . . ." She'd stop to see if Foley could join in. "Frank Sinatra," she'd explain, impatient. "In that movie *It Happened in Brooklyn.* Didn't you see that?" Swaying, she sang until the words ran out. She stood on the sand and showed him how Sinatra used to drape on his microphone when he starred on the "Hit

Parade." Foley knew who Sinatra was. She was glad to hear that, at least.

Then an old Crosby tune, "Sunday, Monday, or Always."

Foley called it sentimental trash. He bragged about acid rock, but couldn't sing any for her. He winked at Jack. "The songs Bebe likes have to be sung through a mouthful of powdered sugar." He listed bands with funny names. The Grateful Dead. Steppenwolf and Grand Funk. Stark Naked and the Car Thieves. He said modern lyrics dealt with modern problems.

"It's all the same," said Bebe, waving her hand, singing on.

She showed him Alice Faye from *Alexander's Ragtime Band.* All wasted on Foley—though he paraded with her, even stumbled behind her trying to learn to throw his ass the way Carmen Miranda did with a fruit basket balanced on her head. But he ruined everything by laughing out loud when she sang, "This world is not my home / I'm just a-passing through. . . ."

"The Briarhoppers sang it on the radio," Bebe explained. "I used to listen all the time."

He was off again, roaring. "The who? The what?"

"Briarhoppers. Listen, Foley Dickinson, they were famous."

"And you laugh at *our* bands." He didn't know any hymn she tried, and said he was Episcopalian. Bebe had grown up on hymns, by radio and at Hebron and under the summer tents spread in old pastures near the mill. She sang him Troy's favorite about the dark trials which took place under the eye of God and would be better understood by and by.

"You must be a Southern Baptist," Foley said.

"I'm not anything anymore."

Jack said that made her a nihilist, another new word he had learned from Foley. But when Foley defined it, she shook her head, said she was an everything-ist.

In the sand the three played ticktacktoe and soon they were

running—even Jack—up and down the beach dragging with their toes huge drawings and letters beside the dark water. *Chicken Little was right,* Foley scraped in the dirt with his foot. *This lampshade made in Belsen.* Bebe drew giant flowers and birds with wide wings. Jack could not resist showing Foley he knew things in writing he did not know in speech, and with a stick began listing the Latin for certain plants: *Dionaea muscipula,* the Venus flytrap, and *Pontederia cordata,* pickerelweed. He listed *Protozoa, Coelenterata, Echinodermata.*

"Listen, I studied biology," crowed Foley, and wrote *Mollusca, Arthropoda, Chordata.*

Amphibia, Jack scrawled.

Mammalia, wrote Foley. He added *Oculus, oculorum. Videre.*

Jack was running out of words and did not know the ones Foley was writing now. He scribbled *Gynmospermae* and *Angiospermae.*

Foley didn't even notice. He was staring at his last scrawled entry in the sand, *Deus absconditus.* He scraped it out with his heel.

He and Jack fished in the moonlight while Bebe threw driftwood on the fire and sang to herself, or sometimes danced slowly with her shadow. The few fish they caught she made them throw in the ocean again.

By the time they waved good night to Foley, Bebe was full of beer and sentiment and old music. She was also out of breath from trying to tell Jack a long story about Mary Ruth Fetner and how Versie Loftin could talk to bees.

"Come on," Jack said, and patted her sandy rear.

"Oh, that was good!" Bebe giggled. "And you did some singing, too."

"Didn't," said Jack. "You know I can't carry a tune."

"I heard you humming, though." She sighed over the sweetness of her final song and went on wailing it in a loud voice up the dune toward the house: "His *eye!* is on the Spar *row!* And I know *he!* watch-*chez! me!*"

Jack tightened his arm around her. Maybe he loved Bebe best when she was a little limp and misty, just a bit drunk, talking about Ethel Waters as if they were first cousins, whispering, laughing for nothing.

On their bed she dropped sideways and lay with her feet still touching the floor. "That's a nice boy," she murmured.

"He's all right. Hope he stays awhile."

"He has got some ignorant ideas," she said owlishly. "Ig-nor-*ant.*"

Jack lifted her feet onto the bed and covered her. She looked wide-eyed at the ceiling. "I meant to undress," she told it. "Well." She fell asleep.

Saturday morning, the Pinheads came while Jack was at Buncombe's store. All day Jack dreaded facing them. Things were going so well at the beach that when he examined it, he felt uneasy again and the brown thrasher flew in his head and blinked a distrustful eye. From what Bebe said, the nurse was no kin at all to Ethel Waters.

He knew he ought to walk over and at least introduce himself to the nurse, if only for good manners. He didn't go. For a while he worked under the house with cacti and succulents he hoped to overwinter in beds on the lee side of the house. Some would bloom like orchids, tough desert dwellers though they were. The bishop's cap and strawberry cactus dated to the Cretaceous age of forty million years ago. He'd have to tell Foley that. His biggest problem in raising cactus was to keep Bebe from watering them to death.

At twilight he saw the Pinheads for the first time up the beach. He could see little except their squat size and similarity, and that their hands hung down too far and made them look prehistoric.

Sunday morning when he woke, the house was full of a funny smell. He rose in bed on his elbows and sniffed the air, then called loudly, "Whatever that is for breakfast, I don't want it."

Bebe said it was Rice Krispie candy, which woke him in a hurry. "I don't want that, either."

"It's not for you, silly. Your memory's not an inch long."

"What am I supposed to remember?" Jack sat up and coughed. Too many cigarettes last night.

"Bible school."

"Do what?"

"Polly's bringing the Bible school class here for a picnic today; have you forgot? She asked you weeks ago."

He had forgotten. The sea's floor dropped too sharply near the Buncombes' and that current was too swift. "Well, that's kind of a mess with the Pinheads here."

"Polly knows they're here."

Sitting wide-legged on the bed, he said good morning to his hernia by sliding his fingers cautiously down, but it was still mended. Someday he expected to wake and find it lying again like a marble in his groin. The first time it grew fast and painfully, the inside of Jack leaking out into a ball. In Columbia at the VA hospital they said it was irreducible and might strangulate and advised surgery. Now Jack had a patch there to hold his inside inside.

"Who in the hell, Bebe," he called, "wants to eat that marshmallow stuff?" He pulled on his pants, thinking how Bebe went to a hospital to have organs out while he went to get his pushed in and sewed down. All doctors could do was cope with decisions the body made. I'm getting sick, said the body. I'm breaking or bleeding or starting to grow in the wrong place and what are you going to do about it?

Bebe offered him a gluey piece of candy that smelled gagging sweet, like gardenia. "So the Pinheads are here. Big deal. So's Foley and he can help lifeguard."

"Get that stuff out of my sight." Jack found a shirt with the scorched shape of an iron on the pocket. "Look what you've done."

"I know it," she said. "I am really sloppy sometimes."

He stretched. "No wonder Pauline said she'd see us Sunday. I thought she meant you'd finally promised to go to church."

"Not me," Bebe said. "You want to warn Miss Whitaker there's a crowd of kids coming and some might wander up her way?"

Jack dreaded it. "You really think they'll bother her?"

"Old Grouch might bother them," said Bebe.

In an hour he was carrying a foil-wrapped plate of sticky candy along the beach because Bebe thought the Pinheads might enjoy it. She'd held Zorro's collar and propped open the door so Jack could get down the steps without spilling. "You don't look much like Red Riding Hood," she giggled.

In the shade by his trailer, Foley lay on a towel wearing the sunglasses Jack had bought. He was tan and looked healthier, maybe had gained weight. He was writing in his journal. Jack waved but forced himself to press on to the Pinheads' house.

Pinhead. Only a word to describe how a mystery looked from outside, he thought. The rain falls down by gravity; why does the rain fall? Jack had believed when he started reading books he would get wisdom, but all he found was names. Hernia, Mr. Sellars. Yes, but why is my intestine coming out into the air?

Jack walked by Miss Whitaker's gray car, balanced the

candy, and knocked on the door. He was about to see with his own eyes what the word *Pinhead* stood for. Nobody came. He knocked again. A piece of Rice Krispie candy fell off the plate and rolled in the sand.

Rounding the house, he found Miss Whitaker on the porch blowing cigarette smoke and acting deaf. "I know how hard it is to hear the back door," he began. "I'm Jack Sellars." He put his hand on the knob. She kept on rocking. "You people get settled all right?" Silent, she blew smoke through the screen over his head. "My wife sent you some candy."

She got up slowly to unlatch the screen. She'd been chain-smoking, stubbing butts in a china bowl half full of sand. "I don't do much cooking and they love sweets." He thought the twist at her mouth might even be a smile. She was a big square woman with a chunky face and pores like pockmarks in her wide nose. "Come in, Mr. Sellars." Jack sat gingerly in the rocker Foley had painted and spread his hands over the two daisies he'd also drawn on the armrests. The striped beachball had rolled itself under Miss Whitaker's rocker and bobbled a little below the rungs.

"If that bathroom sink stops up again, you let me know," said Jack. "They're still in bed?"

"They sleep a lot." She carried the covered plate inside.

The porch had already been swept and through one window he saw Miss Whitaker's bed so tightly made a sergeant could bounce quarters on it. She came back, uniform rattling, and stood in the doorway as if displeased to see him still there. "The FM on that radio doesn't work."

"Somebody broke it." About 160 pounds, but he couldn't guess her age.

She decided to sit down. "Is the beach always this quiet?"

"I'm afraid not. That's one thing I came to talk about."

Miss Whitaker put on her glasses and waited.

"It sure is hot." His throat felt dry.

"You want a drink of water?" She sighed. "All right." In a minute she stuck a cold glass in his hand. "That refrigerator takes all day to make ice. Now. What is it, Mr. Sellars?" She dropped with a thud into the rocker and he was afraid she would bear down on the Pinheads' ball and pop it and they might spring screaming from their beds.

"There's a bunch of kids coming to the beach this afternoon. They might get noisy."

"Is that all? We are not bothered by any noise."

He was surprised at the "we" and decided it was professional only, as in "Time for our pill." He really wanted to tell her to keep the Pinheads inside while Polly's Methodists were here.

She surprised him further with a sudden question. "Are my patients kin to you?"

"Certainly not! I never even laid eyes on them!"

"O.K.," she said.

"What makes you ask that?" For a minute he was afraid, up close, there might be a physical resemblance.

"Mr. Bennett said I was to keep them out of your way. He made a big point of how touchy you were." She fixed him with her glittering glasses. "Are you touchy, Mr. Sellars?"

"George and I had a little business disagreement, that's all." If she thought him touchy, why didn't she volunteer to keep them locked in? He tried easing back to the subject. "Have you met the boy in the trailer?"

She said reluctantly, "Nice young man."

That crack in her armor encouraged Jack to say, "He's going to act as lifeguard. This is a church class, most of them six and seven years old. We'll try to keep them below Foley's trailer."

"Rosie likes children," Miss Whitaker mused.

He pictured Rosie loping down the beach to play ball with

the crowd. "Well now. She might rather stay inside while they're running around."

"I don't see why." She wore two glass rings on each hand. "Rosie's shy but she likes to watch people. I wish we had a TV in the house; she enjoys that."

"Is that so?" said Jack. The ice water made him sweat. "She get much out of it?"

"That's hard to tell." Miss Whitaker pumped her rocking chair with broad white oxfords and the beachball trembled.

"You do this kind of nursing much?"

"No," she said. "I'm in maternity."

He leaned forward to set his glass on a table. "I think it would be better if you people stayed inside while the kids are here."

She stopped her rhythmic chair and seemed about to rise. "Because of their infirmity? Or mine?"

"I beg your pardon?"

"Because they're feebleminded or because I'm black?"

Christ, one of those! He said, "Now listen, all I meant—"

"Which of us are you asking to stay in our place?"

"It's just that children can be real cruel. They might say things."

"Which do you think they would holler—'Dummy'? Or 'Nigger'?" She leaped up, waved her arm toward Foley's towel, and bellowed his full name like a gospel singer. Ships at sea could have heard her. He came across the sand carrying his ledger under one arm.

"I didn't want anything to scare the children, either," Jack added.

How Miss Whitaker laughed, a roar from her belly. "If it wasn't for children and hippies, I would give up on this world. Foley Dickinson?"

"Good morning again," Foley said, poised in the weeds and bright blanket flowers.

"What was it you said this morning about open housing?" she called.

Foley called he could take it or leave it, which seemed to be the right answer.

"Is black beautiful?"

"Well, in your case it has to strain some," he said.

She laughed again. "This boy doesn't have our hangups, Mr. Sellars."

Just then Jack heard them. Inside the house he heard bare feet hit the floor and a blurbling noise like hot bubbles in a deep vat. They seemed to be scuttling across the floors like dwarfs and trolls in fairy stories. Jack was sixteen before he read any fairy stories. He stole the book.

Miss Whitaker swung her shiny glasses toward Jack. "These two patients here," she said, "have scrubbed me with a washrag to see what color was underneath. You know what they did when that didn't work? They scrubbed each other. They thought they might have a brown layer on themselves." Cords tightened on her neck. Inside the house the noises went on.

Jack said, "If you'll hand me the candy I'll come back and we can start all over. You act like a . . . a . . ."

"Paranoid," said Foley, "but even they have enemies." He swept off an imaginary hat. "If we knew who the head Klansman was around here, ma'am, we would go burn a watermelon in his yard."

"Told you he was a nice boy. You ought to adopt him," said Miss Whitaker. She cocked her broad head to listen. "Are they up?"

Jack wouldn't turn for fear of seeing Rumpelstiltskin and his mother through the window glass. "I never meant one thing about Negroes," he said in a loud voice.

She scraped the chair and beachball out of her way. "Don't say *nigra;* I can't stand that." She went inside to the whines and whispers. Maybe she had to lead them both to the toilet like little children.

Foley said, "She's all right; let it go."

"That's no chip on her shoulder—it's the whole woodblock." Jack still hadn't seen the Pinheads and wasn't about to wait around now. Coming out the door, he said, "She works in maternity. It's a wonder she don't scare the babies back *in*."

Foley fell into step beside him. Jack said, "That woman is hateful."

"She had good teachers." Zorro ran to meet them. "You know what I wish my eyes would do? Turn everybody the same color—that would have some value." He scooped up the puppy. "How do you like this green dog?"

The Methodist children arrived after lunch and ran on the beach like crabs, with Pauline trying to keep count. They were noisy, all right, and colorful. Maybe Rosie was watching out her window and couldn't tell it from a TV show. Bebe stayed indoors to store their bottled drinks while Jack and Foley stood guard in the surf. "Don't go out too far!" Jack called.

"Comes Bebe," Foley said. "In a hurry, too."

Jack saw her bounce down the steps in that red bathing suit she said was too tight. Her face was down. She headed toward them at a run. "That a car under my house, Foley?" Jack asked.

He squinted. "Believe it is. Those eyedrops . . . I can't get over it. I feel better. . . ."

But Jack didn't hear, having started to trot toward Bebe. "You can just tend to him!" she cried angrily while he was still ten feet away. "Because I am not going to do it! He's your friend and he's brought his wife this time and she's got her snoot stuck out over God knows what and I have promised Polly to help with these children!"

"Who?" said Jack, but he knew.

"He parked under the house and I just went straight out the door and if Zorro bites him I don't give a damn." Bebe passed him and Foley, who had loped up to see what was wrong. "Let him get hydrophobia for all I care. I have got more things to do than pay him attention."

"It's all right, Bebe," Jack said.

She dug her foot in the sand. "You have left off your sunglasses," she said to Foley bitterly. "You have got no sense at all sometimes. Are you going to be lifeguard or not? I have just seen one child nearly drown in a pond no bigger than a tennis court and I am not in a mood to be scared like that again." Foley followed her toward the surf, where children were screaming and splashing, while Jack plodded to the house to find a key for Mickey McCane and pretend he was glad to see him.

Willis's clock was telling time loudly to an empty room. Jack heard Mickey knocking.

And for the first time in weeks the old uneasiness rolled in him. Here they all were at a crowded beach by the thunderous ocean, carried here by accidents of one kind or another, the way a man whose name he could never remember dealt one jack on a blanket twenty-five years ago and George Bennett said, "Hot damn! Full house!" The recruit said he'd have to locate his deed to his beach lot and sign it over; George said tomorrow morning would be fine. "Write me an IOU, though, while the others watch." The recruit wrote out his gambling debt on a small piece of paper and committed them all.

"Are you coming or not?" Mickey called at the back door. He was laughing.

12

Bebe Sellars

June 23

Bebe was slow storing Pauline's bottled drinks and mixing lemonade. Because of Randy she felt nervous to have ten children in the water at once, and be responsible for their safety. In most of her daydream movies, death was postponed or averted, and often she rescued young men from crashed airplanes or pressed her thumb on a severed artery.

In a favorite fantasy, Bebe had the role of a young guerrilla leader fighting cruel Nazis, who survived with her brave partisans on the rocky Balkan slopes and committed brilliant sabotage which tore up property instead of people. She was as beautiful as Ingrid Bergman and wise as Pilar. In a classic early scene she would lie, belly down, behind boulders while a man showed her how to shoot a rifle and asked if she could now kill a man. "Mechanically, yes," she would say, sighting into the green valley. "Emotionally, I don't know."

Bebe was proud of that dialogue. Once this had been a long dramatic speech; by now she had pruned it until everything was in those six words and the intense way she spoke them.

She tasted the lemonade and the flavor was exactly the right mixture of tart and sweet.

Sand crunched under the house as wheels rolled over it. Blocking Zorro with the broom, Bebe stepped out to see a taillight winking red in the shade near Jack's cactus plants. A woman was climbing out of the car, rear first, but Mickey McCane had already stuck his head into view at the spot where—were she wearing a dress—he could have seen clear up the skirt. He stepped closer. Bebe looked silently down on his smile, crew cut, the wink he held down a long time with his left eye. He said nothing. The woman was facing away, looking for her purse. Mickey ran his tongue slowly over his upper lip. He wore a look Bebe had not seen since Edward G. Robinson, in *Key Largo,* said something soft in Lauren Bacall's ear that only she heard, and instantly she tried to beat him with both fists.

The woman's nasal voice echoed under the pilings. ". . . get away, just the two of us, you said, and this place is depressing. Why not a nice hotel?"

Not answering, Mickey walked under the steps, lifted his hand, and wrapped four fingers where Bebe could see them on the corner of one riser. Slowly he rubbed the wood as if it were a woman's skin.

Big deal. Bebe slammed the door behind her, ran through the house and outside to Jack. Her heart felt swollen. She watched her knees pump like cloverleaf rolls, one with a toothmark scar—the one Mickey touched in the car that time. She got the scar in an unimportant wreck. She was dating a boy who hadn't been driving long and he drove by mistake off Connor Street into the Fetners' front yard, through the wisteria, and crushed his fender on the porch rail. He lost a cup of blood from his nose and the ashtray bit out a hole in Bebe's knee. Walt Fetner stormed down in his underwear and ran him off with the first thing he could find, which happened to be a handle which had rusted off a toy wagon.

When she told Jack Mickey McCane was here, he went to the house and left Bebe, Pauline, and Foley to count the ten children playing in the water. Polly wound and unwound on one finger the brass locket chain she was keeping for one of the girls. "I've *got* it!" Polly said every time the girl started out of the breakers, frowning.

Bebe's bathing suit already felt gritty. "Look how red that child is. She's going to peel."

"She likes peeling," Polly said. She said that girl peeled acres of herself the whole week of summer Bible school, even during prayers. Once she called over a toddler and said, "Open your mouth and close your eyes and I will give you a nice surprise," and then popped several sheets of her own skin onto his tongue.

Foley saw Bebe making a head count and said softly, "There are ten, Bebe, still ten."

Bebe was tense. From the corner of her eye she saw Mickey McCane appear at his trailer door with a pair of binoculars and point them at her red bathing suit. The bastard. Deliberately she puffed out her stomach.

"You got my locket, Miz Buncombe?"

"I've got it, Phoebe, see?" The heart swung brightly in midair. "That child is the worst pest," Polly grumbled. She suddenly jumped off her plaid blanket. Quickly Bebe counted them: Ten.

Then she saw Foley, too, was staring up the beach and Mickey's binoculars had shifted toward three people, elbows out, posed in the foam before the Pinheads' house. The dark one wore a white swimsuit. The two round ones were wrapped in towels.

"I knew it," Bebe said. "Miss Whitaker got insulted. She'll stand there all day like a statue just to prove she can."

Polly whispered, "Bebe, you think they might come this

way? Children this age . . . they might point. They might make fun."

Miss Whitaker might swoop down like a gull and carry one off in her beak if he did. "They haven't even moved," said Bebe. In a way, Bebe was glad to see the three planted so solidly in the water, minding their own business. Miss Whitaker might be taking revenge but the Pinheads wouldn't know what revenge was, and couldn't care, so they splashed in the water just because water felt good and the sun was warm and being alive on a summer's day was good. They never suspected the ocean could drown them and—if it should—would go down in the dark water curiously, expecting bright shells on its underside.

"They better not make fun," Bebe said, watching the ocean gently roll around their innocence.

Foley leaned on the ice chest to cool his red back. To prove it wasn't lost, Polly held up the locket for the hundredth time. She whispered to Bebe, "I wish they would move instead of just standing there."

Foley launched into a long speech about unreasonable fears of the mentally retarded.

"They make me nervous," Polly said. "Willis says that nurse is dark as a blacksnake and mean as a cottonmouth."

Bebe could see Mickey hurrying from his trailer toward them. He called, "Who in the hell is that?" and pointed at the threesome standing so still in the ocean's edge.

"You tell him, Foley, you know so damn much." Bebe ran away down the beach and when she glanced back from the far groin all of them looked like sticks set upright in the sand: Polly and Mickey and Foley in a little triangle, a smaller one up the shore in the water's edge, and the tops of the children barely showing above the water as it came steadily rolling in. Bebe counted them: Ten.

13

Mickey McCane

June 23

Jesus, but Bebe looked good on those high steps in her red bathing suit! Tits so solid you couldn't put a fingermark in them no matter how you squeezed. Mickey wanted Eunice to see what a real woman was like and he nearly breathed out loud, "Get a load of the ass on Bebe Sellars!"

Eunice crawled from the car whining and claiming her leg veins hurt from sitting so long. "Is this it?" She knocked a dirt dauber's nest off a post. "This is the place you've been raving about?"

She couldn't see Bebe. Mickey reached overhead to grab a stairstep close to Bebe's foot and tried to say with one look how much he felt for her.

Bebe wheeled and went inside for their key, probably because Eunice was so embarrassing and she felt sorry for him being married to her. Mickey said to his wife in a low voice, "I have leaned over backward to do what that pansy doctor said; will you quit bitching?" He bounced laughing up the stairs and pounded on the door.

Jack answered. Bebe would rather not see him in a crowd, he guessed. Mickey called Eunice inside to see the big clock on the mantel. Eunice liked old things. "Does it keep good time?"

Jack said, "Keeps loud time."

In the car again with the trailer key, Mickey poked Eunice's tan arm before turning on the engine. "Well, you were the quiet one; what's the matter with you?"

"Why should I answer that?" Eunice said. "You'll tell me. You always do."

Mickey scratched off, angry, and reparked behind the trailer he had rented for a week. If it wasn't for him, Eunice would still be counting words in want ads for the *Angier Daily News*—and when she got the monthly weeps she acted as if marriage had kept her from being top writer for AP-UPI.

He yanked the handbrake. "Listen, Sugarbunch, you spoil your own vacation if you want to. No skin off my ass."

Somehow Eunice had worked up a crazy idea about staying in a big hotel where maids would make the beds every day while she was downstairs eating breakfast. Mickey slid out of the car. "I can have a good time anyplace. You ought to try it." He unlocked the trailer.

"This is no vacation," she nagged. "It's not what you promised. You know it's not."

"You want to sit in that hot car all the time, it's all right with me." He went inside and turned on the air-conditioner.

After a while she straggled in and sat on their suitcase in the middle of the floor. "Some second honeymoon."

Some secondhand bride. He brought in the grocery bags. She'd never had to lift over ten pounds when he was around, but that Bebe, with some color and female shape to her, wouldn't even let Mickey carry her china barrel. Eunice sighed and started unpacking food.

"What do you need with all those guns?"

"Might shoot some rabbits." Last year Mickey hunted them in weedy marshes near Carolina Beach by the inland waterway. Runty brown things with a small tail that had a bluish cast. "I don't know why Jack didn't buy a beagle while he was at it." Jack did nothing but sprout seeds in a box; no wonder Bebe was bored. "Did you see his long-legged black dog?"

"Can you hunt rabbits this time of year?"

That was Eunice down to the ground. When's the season? Did you buy a license? She thought each rule was serious. To her, every shotgun shell Mickey bought took milk off the table.

He shook out his prized camouflage suit and hung it alongside the brooms. Even if he was only out walking and target shooting, Mickey liked to dress in its mottled green and brown jungle pattern. Cheaper ones were sold by army surplus, but they didn't last. He had owned this suit three years.

One spring, near Angier, Mickey walked up on a boy and girl screwing on Raven Rock by the Cape Fear River, where the Tuscarora used to camp. (And do their own screwing, he guessed.) He'd seen the same girl in his laundromat. He hid under laurel thickets to watch the boy bang her good and the sound of her single squeal at the high point vibrated him like a jolt of hot current. That's one time Mickey wished the suit had extra zippers. It was hard to play pocket-tool through layers of waterproofing. Next time that girl came in carrying her clothes basket, Mickey called her behind the dryer and asked about the bruise she got at Raven Rock. "Was it here?" he said, touching. "Was it over here?" She just stood there looking sick. "I know your secrets," Mickey said.

Eunice closed the top cabinet. "And what am I supposed to do while you're hunting rabbits?"

"There's other people here." He unpacked his saltwater fiberglass rod, the one that sang in his hand.

Eunice looked through the window at the crowd on the beach. "I left my own boys to come down here with a dozen kids."

"None of them live here." Mickey was certain Bebe had wanted to keep her figure too much to get pregnant. He doubted Jack had ever earned much money for her, either. That house in Durham . . . some contractor got rich. She deserved better.

Eunice said she was going to change clothes, so Mickey swung her heavy bag onto the bed. Her frown lines deepened. She waited while he unlocked it and dropped the key in his pocket. "I might as well swim as long as I'm here," she said.

"Don't put yourself out." He decided to unlock his tackle box. Its contents made him know how women felt, counting their jewels. He fingered those crowded trays of metal squids, bucktails, eels, doodlebugs, plastic seaworms with wobble plates, bugeyes, treble-hooked plugs. He had nicknames for some.

"Which suit would you wear?" Eunice held up a blue one and one with yellow flowers.

He thought about Bebe's body above him on those stairs. "Doesn't matter."

Naturally Eunice squeezed into the narrow toilet to undress. Scared to death he might lay her across the dinette and climb her one time. Ought to do it, too, one night before she could get that flat round box out of her drawer and opened, that rubber thing folded and shoved in. She acted as if it hurt even to touch that precious crack of hers. Dr. Culver said two children was plenty for a woman with Eunice's nerves. Mickey wouldn't let her take pills since he'd heard they made some women grow beards, so it had been rubber over her or over him since they got married. Some nights the bed even smelled of rubber and that took his edge off, often after he had stood by the lavatory working up to sex for twenty or thirty minutes.

Not wanting children, Mickey would bet Bebe wore one of those permanent coils and could just drop down anywhere, any time of day, and spread her legs and be ready. She walked like a woman who was a little damp and open and ready all the time.

Eunice edged out wearing the yellow flowers, too bright and out of place blooming on her dry body. "I'm ready to go outside and you're still fooling with those fishhooks," she complained.

Mickey wrapped his Shakespeare reel in cloth and put the box away. Walking behind her, he popped the elastic in her suit, but do you think she would laugh?

By the door he tried out his new binoculars. He hoped, with them, to spot the places fish were rushing bait on the surface. Mickey knew one man who swore he could smell different fish. Melons meant bluefish, he claimed, and striped bass smelled like thyme. Mickey thought he was being cute. "Smelled like time!" he hooted, and the smartass spelled it.

"I forgot my sunburn cream," said Eunice, turning back.

Mickey trained the binoculars on Bebe, talking to some tall, blond-haired boy. Sometimes, he thought, women who don't know they're being watched will scratch themselves or pull up their clothes to look for chiggers. In the laundromat he had watched a woman take off her brassiere while her blouse was still on. Unhooked the back, worked a strap over one elbow, pulled the whole thing out the other sleeve and dropped it in the washing machine with her other clothes. He couldn't get over that.

Bebe looked tired. She had probably missed him. Mickey swept the sea with his glasses. A fin? A floating board. Then he trained them up the beach and some animal sprang up and pressed its face on his eyeball.

"Jesus Christ!" Mickey let the glasses drop on their strap. Three figures stood in the water's edge. He began focusing the lens. The first was a nigger—he'd never expected to see that at Pickle Beach. A maid, he guessed, too lazy to stay inside and mop. But the other two!

He'd never seen anything like it! They looked like gorillas!

First a young one, pudgy, with his head out of shape. Thick-necked with a tongue that stayed partly out of his mouth.

And a grown female, but husky, her narrow eyes hidden by high white cheeks and a stack of coarse hair that strung down her head on all sides.

He thought he was dreaming. "Eunice! Come out here a minute!"

She carried her sun cream to him, spreading it thickly on her arms. "Wipe off your hand. Now take a long look to the right. What do you see?"

Eunice nodded and swung the tubes over the trailer at a low cloud. "Not there!" With one hand Mickey jerked her head up the beach till she had to be looking straight at them. She quit breathing; not a yellow flower moved in or out. She fingered the focus knob.

Mickey hurried down the dune to ask Bebe who in the hell those people were, but somebody must have called her from beyond the far groin. Pauline told him. He met Eunice on the beach and told her to swim or something; he wanted the binoculars again.

"Poor things," Eunice said.

He tried first, with his naked eye, to get the whole picture. The female and young one had started to pitch a beachball, taking turns. They squatted with the ball between their thick thighs and then, two-handed, scooped upward and heaved it overhead. They looked double-jointed.

He called to his wife, "They are feebleminded. I told you, remember? They're not even supposed to be here yet." She was already in the water. He hung the spyglasses around his neck and hunkered on the sand to watch the Pinheads remove their towels.

The boy—he was nearly grown—had a skull flat in the back matted with black horsehair. There were cracks in his tongue. Mickey swept the lens to the female's stubby hands, too small and wide for those meaty arms, thick with hair. Her top row of teeth did not meet the bottom row. She might have been five feet tall; the boy was less. She wore a tank suit, black, and under it there were . . . not tits, exactly. Dugs. He'd heard them called dugs. Out of her suit, hair curled at the crotch.

Mickey jerked his glasses left. The boy's crotch was hairy, too, with a lumpy look. He pictured a handful of genitals, different from his own. He felt sick.

Mickey felt heavy pressure to piss, which happened to him a lot. He'd gone to a doctor—not Culver—but he said the plumbing was fine and did he sleep enough? "I'm not sure why your blood pressure's so high." Mickey told him he was a go-getter.

The black woman must be their keeper. Mickey found her broad face in the glass. She was big and could overpower anybody. Each time the striped ball flew straight up and fell straight down, she clapped her pink palms, but she never smiled. A guard from the funny farm.

He called to Eunice, "Have you ever seen anything so ugly?" She laid a tan finger across her tan mouth. He said louder, "I picked this week on purpose. George said he wouldn't send them till July." The yellow flowers were only wet to the waist, she was so timid. "Jack didn't tell me the beach was full of freaks, and integrated, too. I ought to get my money back."

That made Eunice slide one hand in the water, watching. She hoped they might move to Myrtle Beach.

"Think I'll walk around, take a look."

"Look at them, you mean." Eunice fell backward in the

water and floated off, cool as a corpse. Close to the dunes, swinging the glasses on their strap, Mickey strolled up the beach toward the nurse and the crazies. The nurse kept one eye on him but the others didn't even see him come and pass; maybe their eyes were bad, narrow and turned up that way, and so much hair in the way. The female's back was turned. One of her thick arms lay on the young one's neck. It looked like patches of hair on her shoulders but Mickey wasn't sure.

He got a low back pain. There wasn't one bush tall enough to step behind. He climbed the dune faster through nettles and sea oats. Towels hung by the college boy's trailer and more outside the house where the freaks lived. Behind the dune, Mickey tried to empty his bladder but hardly an ounce dribbled out. He thought the hot sun had something to do with that.

At the southern edge of the beach he reached a tidal creek. Fiddler crabs scattered and grabbed at the roots of tall grass on the bank. He looked at one of the ugly bastards magnified.

Then Mickey laid his binoculars on the sand, took out his pocket comb, and ran it nervously over his short black hair. Any minute, he thought, Bebe would have the sense to turn around and walk south down the beach to meet him. He knew she wanted that. He moved nearer the mouth of the creek so she could see him from a distance. Soon crabs edged out of their holes and he threw shells to make them scurry. They got used to it, though, until even a hot cigarette didn't bother them much. Mickey slid off his shoes and scratched the bottoms of both feet. He was ticklish on the toes.

Until today, Mickey had only seen one loony up close, a colored man, must have been seventy. Thanks to old Lyndon Johnson, everybody in Angier thought he could use the public laundromat these days, even a thing like that. Nitch Lassiter—he had a harelip besides—would come in and pull up a chair to the front-loading Bendix to watch the wet clothes go around; couldn't tell it from television. Mickey ran Nitch off a hundred times. He'd shamble down the alley to see if the A & P was throwing away old lettuce. Mickey was scared of him but concealed it. Nitch couldn't remember anything five minutes; how do you know what somebody will do who can't remember not to? Maybe Nitch had something to do with messing up his washing machines that night.

Mickey rested on his elbows. The sand made them sore. He looked as far as the binoculars would reach but Bebe was still out of sight. She might be walking the other way by the road so nobody could see her. She'd run to him. Mickey ought to be ready when she came running beside the stream. He began to exercise his will so when she hurried to him his sex would leap boldly at her.

A marsh stink the wind blew up his nose spoiled his concentration. He thought about Bebe. When he walked behind her a roundness flipped above her hipbone, first left, then right. He wanted his hand there when it rolled up the next time. Some stocky black-haired women he had wanted by force and surprise, but Bebe he wanted slow, all night long. Mickey laid his hand lightly on his fly, but the moment subsided when she did not come, the way a fire goes out without fuel.

He waited by that creek till it got to be four o'clock and Eunice went inside their trailer. Four-thirty and the picnic kids packed and left and that college boy cleaned up napkins and burned the trash. At five the Pinheads kicked their ball over the dune and the nurse carried her chair inside. Mickey watched her through the glasses and her ass was solid steel.

Still he thought Bebe would come. He took a few swipes at his prick but no real man made it that way by himself and why didn't she hurry up? The paper plates and cups burned red beside the water, then the ashes smoked and the boy buried them in sand. Once a car passed and he thought Bebe might be leaning out a window looking for him, but it turned inland toward the bridge. He used his shoe heel to tap some crab holes shut and pass the time. The college boy went inside.

Finally Mickey hung the binoculars around his neck and stood up. Pickle Beach looked empty. Things were getting that yellow color, late in the day. The pages of old letters have that color. He really didn't like walking on the beach after dark. The night sky got so big here and bore down on you so.

But he walked slow in case Bebe was hiding somewhere. Eunice was indoors, probably washing her hair or her pants—she washed her pants so much you could have a safe bandage anytime. Sure enough, when Mickey got there a pair was blowing on the clothesline.

Next door the lights were already burning though the sun still glowed red over the creek. Maybe the Pinheads were afraid of the dark? A greasy smell blew from the trailer; Eunice was browning a hamburger to slap in a bun with store-bought slaw. The shades in those lighted rooms of the Pinheads' house were pulled nearly shut.

Mickey got to wondering who slept with whom in that house. If a boy that age slept with his mother and they neither one had good sense . . . well? Who knew what they might do? The idea made pins and needles on his neck.

He ducked under Eunice's clothesline. With the noise the ocean made, a mowing machine could drive through the yard and nobody know. Quietly, he slipped to a lighted window with the shade not fully drawn. He could see a slice of bedroom cut across drawer handles and chairbacks. Then, like a moth passing a windshield, somebody walked naked across the room and out of sight. The pink shape moved so fast and so sideways, all he could see was navel and ass; couldn't tell which one it was except it sure as hell wasn't the nurse. He twisted his face to one side against the sill to see where all that pink skin had took itself.

Nack nack. The sudden noise made Mickey jump and his foot bent wrong in the sand. Eunice stood in the trailer behind him, rapping a spoon on the window glass. All her teeth showed. When he limped inside she didn't say a word. She knew better. She just dropped that oily meat on a bun and passed the ketchup. Mickey wasn't hungry. He ate too fast and swallowed too much air.

Pauline Buncombe

June 23

At evening services, Pauline sat in the third row of the Methodist church. She had to sit in the third row because the preacher made everybody in the thin Sunday night crowd move forward so they almost felt huddled together at one end of a cavern. Sunday nights they were studying the Book of Job and at Wednesday prayer meetings, Genesis. Pauline liked Genesis better.

She had gone home dissatisfied the previous Sunday night. The subject of Job appeared to be unjustified suffering and nobody in all forty-two chapters was sure what the answer was except God, and He didn't tell.

Job argued with his friends that when evil befell a man it was not always a punishment for sin, and there the discussion broke off. He capitulated. God's righteousness, so Job understood, could not be detected in the regular world as God ruled it—that's how things were. What Job did: he gave in. It was as though Job had demanded of the Universe, "Why?" and the Universe said, "Because."

Pauline found this outlook gloomy and was not cheered when the prologue hinted Job's pain was meant to test his faith. If *Job* wasn't faithful with his reputation known all the way to Heaven, who then could ever be? In the end, of course, God blessed Job more richly than before, but it sounded to Polly like a sop or an afterthought.

So tonight she was tense in her pew and sat with ballpoint pen poised over verses already heavily underlined. The preacher summarized the arguments of Eliphaz, Bildad, Zophar, and Elihu, some of which sounded pretty convincing. Job replied to each and, afterward, God spoke out of the whirlwind (rather sarcastically, Polly thought), asking Job if he could explain how the world originated, could understand the instincts of animals; could he even take over and run the earth himself? And Job gave in. Not because of the words which the whirlwind spoke, not those, but because "mine eye seeth thee." Polly was disappointed at this weak conclusion. Until that moment Job had been more blunt than patient. Then he folded. Had she missed something?

She listened carefully so the preacher could explain what she had overlooked in her study. But the point of the story lay in that moment of acceptance: "Though He slay me, yet will I trust in Him." How was such trust possible? She would need harder Bible study. Maybe she ought to commute to Wilmington and take a course in the Old Testament.

Leaving the church, Pauline stopped in the vestibule and said to the preacher out of one corner of her mouth, "I'll be glad when it's Wednesday and we get back to Adam and Eve."

Mickey McCane

June 23

Mickey hurried along the darkening beach. His stomach was knotted with gas pains but he had to know where Bebe was. The lights from her house threw yellow squares on the dune; he stopped in one and tried to stand in the middle of the gold. His stomach hurt. His mother would have called it "rifting"; she meant belching and burping—he didn't know where she got that word. Mickey knocked on the door and rifted.

"Hello, Mickey." Jack didn't even smile. There was a good smell, better than hamburger. He might be getting an ulcer but the doctor said baking soda would help; doctors were too busy making money to care.

Jack pushed the door, holding a slice of bread in one hand and making sure Mickey saw it. "Just finishing some deviled crabs. Want some?"

"I've already got indigestion, thank you." He examined Jack's face. Jack had probably kept Bebe from coming but there was no way to tell.

Mickey followed him to the kitchen. He had never seen Bebe in an apron before, and it didn't suit her. She ought to wear all black silk. By the refrigerator stood the college kid with his hair grown out like a queer's.

"We didn't get introduced this afternoon." The boy stepped forward. "Foley Dickinson."

Mickey gave the boy's hand a real grinder till his eyebrows shot up.

"I'll finish the last ones while they're hot." Jack sat down to his plate. They left Mickey to pull his own chair into the kitchen and find a place for it.

Jack was scraping the shell. "Got these early this morning as fast as I could drop a line into the creek. Got some oysters, too." He showed Mickey a blister on his palm, or maybe he only meant the Dickinson boy to see it. "How's Eunice like the beach?"

"What has shocked us both," Mickey began firmly, "is having those freaks right next door. I never thought from what Willis said they would be so . . . Well, I'm asking what happens if they get loose?" He bent so Bebe could see him petting her black dog. The pup laid his ears back and Bebe put him outside the back door.

She gave Jack two more hot crabs, baked in their shells with crumbs and red powder on top. She hadn't spoken the first word. That proved Mickey's effect on her. Mickey understood women, who looked for strength and confidence in a man. They liked to believe they couldn't help themselves and that sex happened to them like a storm or a flash flood. If his daddy had learned this lesson young, he might have kept his wife at home. Mickey held his gaze on Bebe to watch her response. The dog whined to be let in.

He forced his attention back to Jack.

". . . not really as bad as I expected," he was saying. "That nurse is a hard case, though." To Bebe, "Thank you, honey." That really galled Mickey, the way he said that so deliberately.

The Foley boy took a crab, too. "Miss Whitaker put herself through nurse's training being a maid and a cook and it took her ten years."

"I didn't know that," said Bebe, filling his coffee cup, not looking at Mickey, who had heartburn all over his chest.

He lit a cigarette and blew smoke slowly but the ring broke

in midair. "You are sure right, Jack. George hired his old army buddy to do the dirty work. He's got you looking after two freaks and besides that he's integrated the beach. What next?" He could have added: There goes your business. He'd seen it happen at his laundromat. Lyndon Johnson only said one smart thing his whole time in office; he said, "Throw your bread on the waters and the sharks will get it."

"I've seen the boy up close," Bebe finally said, directly to Mickey. "He's a baby, that's all. A baby."

"A gorilla is more like it."

"They won't get loose," Jack said, and seemed to allow the food Bebe had cooked for him to linger on his tongue. "I can't see they're bothering anybody."

"The way they walk around? Stark naked?"

Foley said how could he know that? And Bebe gave him a funny look, probably from associations with the word *naked.* She poured her own coffee. She didn't give any to Mickey.

He shifted in his chair for fear his stomach would growl aloud, like an animal. "Even if they weren't freaks, you've still got a nigger woman out on the beach in plain sight and too big to miss. People will drive straight on, Jack. They're on vacation to get away from that. Jesus, they're everywhere you turn. You don't know *who* uses the public toilets anymore!"

The queer said quietly, "I never did know, did you?" Mickey looked at him closer. He sounded like the crowd that took over Columbia last month.

Bebe cleared plates and Jack let Zorro in. The Lab ran between Mickey's feet and started pawing at the chairs, trying to reach the food on the table. Mickey stepped on his hind foot and made Zorro get down. "You better start getting him in shape before he gets any bigger. A Lab's a stubborn dog. You've got to train him young. I'd rather have hounds myself, or a good beagle."

"I don't plan to hunt him," said Jack.

Mickey made the queer meet his stare. "People leave home to get away from problems, not to see niggers, that's all I meant." That boy's hair hung to his jaw. Why wasn't he in the army? "All spring when I came home tired, I'd turn on the TV and there was nothing but one race riot after another. I'd sit down to relax and there was the latest race riot. They must have had two hundred different riots on the six o'clock news." The boy, he was glad to see, was paying attention. "And when a decent taxpayer works all year and takes one week off, there sits one on the beach."

"A race riot?" said the boy.

Thought he was smart. Bebe dumped dishes in the sink and turned on the water, loud. Foley said, "King's death was on TV, too. Kennedy's death."

"King is what set it off. Any excuse would do." Mickey measured the boy—maybe twenty years old, tall, muscles too stringy. "You must be about draft age?"

"About." Whatever that meant.

"The army will make a man of you. That's where I met Jack, did he tell you?"

"I enlisted in thirty-nine," said Jack, pushing Zorro away from his chair but not very hard, "and stayed in there ten years. I just got used to the army, I think." He shook his head. "Ten years."

"It's a great life." Mickey meant that. In the army, everything looked planned and well organized on the surface, but underneath that lid it was a crazy place. Once you got used to nothing making sense, it provided freedom. Your worst suspicions were confirmed and that made you grow up, made you fit to live in the world. When they sent more gas than the airplanes could burn, you dumped it in the sea so nobody would cut down your quota. There was probably old gas of Mickey's in this Atlantic Ocean right outside.

"I was the best shot in my outfit," Mickey said, glancing at Bebe. She wiped the table with a wet rag, swabbing practically around his elbows.

"The army taught me how to beat the odds, stay alive. You live with an enemy always out of sight; that's good training." He'd have to say one thing—Foley had a polite smile and knew how to listen to his elders. "Once you live through the bullshit at basic, you understand how the system works." Nothing, in fact, had worked for him quite as well as the war, where the enemies were all dressed alike and could be easily identified. Mickey decided to step on the black dog's foot for Jack and it yelped and moved off. They've got to learn who's boss. The boy watched him with real interest as if he might draw Mickey's picture when he went home. Bebe went into the bedroom and stayed awhile with the door closed, because she was nervous to have him in her house, just as he'd hoped.

Like a sissy, Foley gathered the last of Bebe's saucers and put them in the sink. There was a rattle on the roof.

"Little shower," Jack said, standing up and stretching. "Won't last long." He led the way to the living room and Mickey had to carry his own chair back. The room felt cold with Bebe gone. "How are things at the laundromat?" Jack turned to Foley and described the mess in the washing machines and the kid said he ought to write that down. Mickey could see rain blowing through the porch screen, darkening the chairs and swing. Jack lit torn papers under the fireplace logs.

Mickey froze in his chair. He was on the verge of breaking wind and anxious to get it done before Bebe reentered the room. He bore down but nothing happened.

"Warm things up a little," said Jack absently.

The kid lifted a ledger off the mantel and flipped pages as if he owned the place. Mickey waited for Jack to call him down. Foley put the book back, though. They pulled their chairs closer to the fire and propped their shoes on the hearth. Mickey had liked that as a kid and would let the soles get so hot they would hurt when he walked. Zorro scratched furiously on Bebe's closed bedroom door. "That is one spoiled dog," Mickey said.

Jack and Foley started talking politics. Mickey might vote for Reagan if the Republicans picked him, since he could win; but otherwise he'd vote for Wallace even though he couldn't win. He was planning to stand up for what he believed.

Bebe came out of the bedroom. She had taken off her apron and changed to a long-sleeved high-necked dress because of the damp air. It was an orange dress. She sat next to a bookcase that matched it. As soon as Bebe was settled in her chair, Mickey handed her a card he'd got at the Cotton Club. STOP SEGREGATION, it said. TAKE A NIGGER HOME TO LUNCH. Without a blink she said Foley collected different sayings like that and passed it to him. Damned if he didn't stick it in his pocket!

Mickey told a few clean jokes and watched Bebe slowly relax. Her eyes were dreamy and he thought she might be imagining things that were due to happen to her and to Mickey, seeing them move in some tiny distant landscape as he often saw himself. Bebe didn't look forty. Her blond hair touched her shoulders and there were no broken veins in her legs. She caught Mickey watching and asked, "Could I call Eunice and ask her to come over?"

"She's bound to be in bed. Never has had much energy." He was glad when Jack finally brought out some drinks. Even the kid took one. Mickey felt better and the gas had subsided, although he was careful not to belch in front of Bebe.

Slumped across her sandals, Zorro went to sleep. Mickey doubted Bebe understood it was vital to train pups young. Maybe she even thought him mean, but he had feelings. Women liked men to have feelings.

So he told a true story that happened at home in Harnett County.

"There was a farm woman had her first baby and it wasn't white, but not real dark, either. Gypsy skin. But the hair grew out kinky and you could tell the truth by the shape of its nose and mouth. People claim to tell Negro blood by fingernails but that's not reliable. This story happened fifteen, twenty years ago. The mother acted like nothing was wrong. She'd say, 'Isn't it nice he's got curly hair?' And everybody looked over her head at each other. Well, the farmer, her husband, was about to go out of his mind. He asked her and asked her. She swore that baby was his. He didn't know what to think. Was she lying? Had she slept with a workman or one of his tobacco tenants? He asked her some more and she even swore it on the Bible: No. And all the time that baby was getting darker. She kept it inside in the summertime and still it got darker. Got six months old, got ten. Got a year and got darker. Everybody in Harnett County was talking. But what if she really hadn't slept with some black buck? Why, then there might be color in the farmer's own blood! That made all his brothers nervous and nobody would even say it out loud. They had kids already, every one with brown hair and eyes and good suntans. So they told the farmer: Throw that woman out; she's no good; it couldn't possibly be your kid. The farmer accused her some more and she swore on the Bible some more. He started drinking. One day he went into the barn and bit down on the barrel of his shotgun and blew off the top of his head. And they never did know for sure, his family. About that baby."

Mickey shook his head at the end. "That's the worst thing I know of that ever happened in Harnett County." The others were staring. "I was still in school when I heard it and I never forgot it." He reached to scratch Zorro's back, but the pup rolled over and Bebe scraped her shoe away.

Bebe's eyes were wide and she sucked in a long breath. "What happened to the baby?"

At first he couldn't remember. "Oh, the woman took him away someplace; I mean she had to. Moved to Raleigh or Norfolk or some other big city and people said she lived down in colored town with that half-white baby. But the family never got over it. It broke them every one."

Foley got up from his chair, set his unfinished drink on the hearth, and grabbed one of those ledgers. He walked out the kitchen door and down those high steps without so much as a good night, kiss my ass, or anything.

Jack coughed. "He's got to check his motorcycle every night." He emptied his drink.

Mickey didn't much like rye; at the Cotton Club, gin was the thing to drink. Bebe looked so sad he told another joke but she forgot to laugh.

She said in a soft voice, "How did Miss Whitaker like that candy?"

"She liked it, she liked it," Jack said. "How about oysters? You think she'd like some oysters?"

"I'll carry her some tomorrow."

It got so quiet that when the clock went off and played three-fourths of a tune, everybody jumped, even the dog. The rain had stopped. Jack was poking his ice with one finger so Mickey gave Bebe a long sexy look and, very slowly, licked his bottom lip. Right then, with his luck, a belch rammed up in his throat so suddenly he jumped to his feet so nobody would notice when it rumbled out. He hurried to the kitchen and took a swallow of water straight from the spigot.

It might help him to get outside. He came back asking why didn't Jack target shoot with him on the beach? "We'll even teach Bebe how."

"I don't know. I haven't handled a gun in twenty years."

"It'll scare the Pinheads," Bebe objected.

"Listen, you can't let people like that run your life that aren't even people. The rain's quit; let me bring over the handgun and we'll go a few rounds." Jack and Bebe eyed each other. Mickey said, "It's good for the dog just in case you ever hunt him. There's nothing worse than a gun-shy dog." They were still looking at each other. He couldn't stand it. He noticed Jack's eyes were so blue they would have been better on a woman. "I can still outshoot you any day, Jack Sellars."

"Wouldn't doubt it. All right," he said, almost wearily. He finished his drink and said they'd meet Mickey on the beach. Mickey hurried to the trailer and woke Eunice dragging his gun case out of the closet. "Never mind, never mind," he said when she mumbled. He loaded the pistol and decided to take the binoculars, too, and a paper target. He ran past the Pinheads' house to the beach. Bebe was already there, alone, staring across the white spillway between the shore and a low moon. She had thrown a sweater around her and stood wide-legged and barefoot in the sand. The damp air lifted her hair straight up so it seemed to hang about her head like a cloud. Mickey ran toward her, the binoculars thumping his chest.

"Jack's putting out the fire so the sparks won't blow," she said sharply before he could speak. "He'll be right here."

"Let him take his time." Mickey got beside her so their hips would touch. "I want to see you, Bebe."

"Cut it out." She stepped on the wetter sand and looked across that lighted tunnel to the sky. "Is that a ship out there?"

He saw nothing but the log he had spotted earlier, drifting. "I want to see you by yourself."

She took another step. "I'll bet your own laundry water washes out near here," she said. "I guess you empty into the Cape Fear River?"

"Quit changing the subject." Mickey tried to laugh. "I admit it was hard to get over what you said, the powder puff business, but I'm over it, Bebe. I was pushing you hard and you just struck out. You want me and I want you and you like it. You might not even want to like it, but you do."

"Not anymore," said Bebe. "If Eve had had time to get acquainted with the snake, she'd have taken up peaches. Now will you let me alone?"

He couldn't help touching her, just once, and that was all it took. His pants nearly unzipped themselves.

She rose on her toes and took a long rabbit hop into the water's edge, where he couldn't follow unless he wanted to walk in shoes and all. "I saw in the paper last week," she snapped, "that laundries in this state cause more pollution than mills and sewage plants put together, and Foley says it's so."

The door to their house slammed. "Sugarbunch," said Mickey, and either she shook her arm loose or pushed somehow or even meant to hit him; and the binocular strap slid down his arm. The spyglasses dropped, lens down, onto the only goddamn Coke bottle the picnic kids had left on the whole beach. He heard the glass crack.

Coming down the dune with the dog, Jack said, "What'll we shoot at? Watch that thing, Mickey!" The pistol had leaped toward Bebe, now swung at Jack. Mickey managed to push its barrel toward the sand to point where his ruined glasses lay. In the cool air he started to sweat. "I said, what will we shoot at?"

"How about Bebe's dog?" Mickey forced a laugh.

Jack propped a conch shell on a stick and drove the wooden

stob into the wet sand. In the moonlight the shell's white mouth gleamed. He was still close by when Mickey cut down and blew it to pieces.

Bebe cried out. Jack didn't move except to pick at his shirt-sleeve. In a minute he said, "Those pieces flew all over me, Mickey."

"You try it." Mickey held the gun to Bebe but she would not. She said the noise had already stopped up one ear. Jack fired next over the water.

"That way," said Bebe, "you never even know what you might have hit." She stopped Zorro from chewing on the binoculars and held him in her arms.

"Call out that college boy," said Mickey, "and let's see what are his chances to live through Vietnam." He had the worst taste in his throat, as if his stomach had suddenly emptied up instead of down. Thanks to Bebe, his whole groin ached. He set up the target but Jack shot at a patch of seaweed washed on the sand. He still had a good eye and steady hand. Bebe complained that now both her ears were going deaf.

"Please stop," she said. Mickey shot up the pasteboard target because that bitch wasn't going to tell him what to do. She paced in the sand till he ran out of bullets, sticking her fingers in one ear, then the other. "That's weird," she told Jack. "I can't hear what you two say but I can hear my clothes rustle. I can hear my jaws click."

When they were saying good night, turning to leave, Mickey got behind Bebe and gave her the hardest pinch he could and held it and drove in his fingernail. She wouldn't even say ouch, wouldn't look at him but at Jack, at *Jack,* while she told him, "You should have worn a sweater, too." She waited without a flicker or a wince until he had to let her go. Mickey wheeled and shot a crab he saw moving on the dune. They carried the dog inside and turned out the lights.

The minute their house went dark, Mickey cleared his throat and spat what tasted like pure acid and thought about going home to Eunice instead of Bebe, going home to Eunice for the rest of his life, and finally dying in Eunice's bed with nobody to come to his funeral but Eunice. Not that he wanted Bebe anymore—bitch! But he'd always need other women; he was highly sexed on his mother's side. He would go right on buying them when the need arose. He saw that his life would go on the way it had the first forty-one years, and spat out bile again.

Mickey tried his binoculars but the stars were only a rush of milky light. In the dark he couldn't tell if one lens or both had broken. He picked up the Coke bottle and sailed it over the beach, walking home.

Highly sexed on his mama's side. The times Mama was home she'd soak in the bathtub and talk to him through the door in her husky voice. "I ought to go to Persia," she'd say. "I hear they've got more men than women in Persia."

He wondered if that was true. When Mickey was in first grade and the teacher asked for home addresses, he said his mother lived in Persia.

Between Foley's trailer and the freak house, something rolled in the shallow surf. At first he thought it was a dead man and he jerked up his broken glasses, but all he could see was something huge and black. Mickey ran toward it. Closer, he saw it was only a length of rotted timber, maybe the very board he had seen floating earlier out from shore. Took a long time to wash in here.

Quickly he turned away and kept walking, not wanting anybody to think a chunk of wood could fool him. He wouldn't want the Pinheads or that nurse to think that.

When Mama left home she might stay gone a year. But she did come back, just as he told Eunice; she always came home. There'd be then a week of fighting in his house, real fighting, with chairs broken and bruises made. After that a few quiet months. Some nights Mickey would eat hot dogs with his parents in a café and both would let him taste their beer.

Then Dad would go. He'd set out for work one day and just keep walking. He could never last as long as she did, though. Six weeks or seven, he'd be back. No fight. He'd try to start one. She wouldn't say a word, combing her straight black hair, biding her time. The day he came back, she'd start planning where to travel next, with whom, how, pinching back cash. When she got everything ready, she'd take off without a word. Mickey might come home from school and the house would be empty. Or he'd wake up in the morning to hear the silence, go slowly downstairs with dread, and find her kitchen cold.

Both parents had one funny habit. Mickey never knew if they set it up together or each one hit on it by himself.

The times Dad was gone, Mama would say, "You know, Mickey, he's my second husband and a little bit crazy. I only come back because of you, to make sure he didn't hurt you. He's jealous that I had you by another man. Your *real* daddy, now! Shoo! What a man!"

And then, the year Persia was in Houston or Milwaukee, Dad would say at least a hundred times, "Oh, Mickey! If your own mother had lived! A second wife—it's never the same! She must be nuts. She'd have to be to run off all the time like this. Wouldn't you say she's nuts? Your real mother must be turning in her grave!"

Of course he figured out neither one had ever been married before. He finally figured it out.

When a match was struck among the tall grasses on a dune, Mickey's head jerked around by itself. The flame went out and left a hot coal hanging in the night air. That hippie was smoking and spying on the dunes, watching him shoot, watching him chase down a log on the beach. "Dickinson? That you?"

He didn't answer. One time, thought Mickey, he won't answer me and I'll cut down on a beer can and nip him by mistake.

He hefted the pistol and held it so moonlight could glint on its pearl handle. He yelled, "I'm *talking* to you!"

The clouds shifted. Mickey could see him sitting back with his legs bent, in tall weeds that still had raindrops on them. He looked like one of those Confucius types, the ones that stand on their heads to the East. The boy said finally, "I was just watching the stars."

There's no need to watch them at the beach when they seem to fall on your shoulders. Mickey could almost feel their points prick his skull.

"Don't wave that thing," Foley said when Mickey pointed out the Big Dipper. "I've heard Pete Seeger sing about the drinking gourd. Slaves used to follow it north when they ran away."

Mickey climbed the dune to look down on him. With all that hair, you could take him for a woman. "You're from the North, right?" Foley said Maryland. He sounded more North than that. "I bet you think everybody down here rides around Saturday nights and throws firecrackers at pickaninnies." No answer. Mickey poked the pistol butt in Foley's shoulder. "Want to shoot once?" He said not. "Old Jack hasn't lost his touch."

"I was watching," Foley said.

How much had Foley seen? Bebe? Had he seen that bitch hit him and break his glasses? Again Mickey got the sulfur taste in his throat.

He said, "Here you are riding around trying to understand this country, but you are going to go home without understanding the South."

"You're about right."

"Well, ask me something. I have lived here all my life."

Foley went on smoking. "You might not be typical," he said. "The Sellars might be typical."

Mickey was not going to be canceled by that bitch and her husband. He stood there and thought through what would be safe to tell a Northerner. He had already told the worst story he ever heard in Harnett County. He thought he might convince Foley that whites would look after the colored down here, since they understood them, while Northerners didn't.

"We just had a speaker at the Cotton Club," he began, and had to stop. "What's that missionary's name in Africa?"

Foley said Africa was full of missionaries.

"No, the famous old guy with the hospital that just died."

"Schweitzer?"

"That's the one. This speaker knew all about Schweitzer. And he wasn't some ignorant man; he had more degrees than you'll ever get, and he told us what Schweitzer said and it really hit the nail on the head. He said no white should hate the Africans or any other colored. Said the colored should be looked on as our younger brothers." Mickey bent down and lit a cigarette of his own so Foley could see him smile. "Schweitzer had lived with them and knew them. I thought that said it all, kid. It's something Northerners haven't learned yet. The younger brother. That's what Schweitzer said."

"I hope not," said Foley. The match had gone out but in the dark he said a funny thing; he said, "Mr. McCane, I can see you just as clear as clear can be."

Mickey was angry but, to tell the truth, Foley had hurt his feelings, too. You try to make friends with people and they kick you in the teeth; why is that? He stuck the gun in his belt and walked away.

"Good night, Mr. McCane."

Wouldn't answer him.

Yes, Bebe meant to hit him. Foley Dickinson must have seen it, seen Mickey just stand there and take it. Mickey tramped past the trailer and cut a diagonal across the next yard. What real man would take that off a woman?

The lights were off in the freaks' house where they maybe slept naked, that woman and her no-brain son, together for all anybody knew, and feeling each other. That made Mickey sick to his stomach and he crossed the yard slowly in case there might be something to see, or a shadow on the window shade. Jesus, for all he knew the nurse got in the same bed and played games of her own.

He didn't know why Bebe was so suddenly a bitch. Somebody had turned her against him.

He thought for a minute somebody moaned inside the Pinheads' house and he froze and listened, but could only hear the sea.

People like that, the government ought to put them to sleep.

14

Bebe Sellars

June 24

Poor Eunice McCane, a dishrag woman. Bebe sat by her in the second folding chair. Between them lay a bedspreadful of guns.

Her face was turning red in the glare. "Mickey takes them every place he can," she said, watching him pepper an old log on the beach. "He carries guns the way some men carry pocket change."

The hot sun was halfway up the sky. "Are you a good shot, too?"

"Not me. He tried teaching me but all I ever learned was names. That little one he's got he calls a plinker or a varmint gun." She took up the beige wool she was knitting into squares.

A twenty-two, Bebe thought. Earl and Troy used one to shoot rats at the Greenway dump. They took her once but she couldn't see the fun of standing in garbage and shooting at every shadow with a naked tail. She learned one thing—rats scream. Not squeak, either, but scream when they're hit. Bebe went to sit in the car after she heard that.

These aluminum chairs made her forearms sweat and gave

the skin a bitter, metal smell. Mickey said, "You try now, Foley."

Foley sighted a long time before squeezing off a shot that made splinters fly. His eyesight, Bebe thought, was improving. Mickey held the gun toward her.

"Your turn, Bebe." He made it sound like a threat. Today his face was different. No flirting. He seemed angry. His gaze was like boiling water. Bebe shook her head. She wanted to keep an eye on the Pinheads' house. Jack had carried them oysters.

Foley loaded and shot again. Both wore swim trunks. Mickey kept touching his hairy chest. He even looked good but Foley looked better. Bebe would like to rub sun oil over his young skin, but not from desire, only liking. There was no way to like Mickey, no way at all. She could still go to bed with him in some risk-hungry mood when peril was briefly attractive. Might have, at twenty. Now she knew even that sweetest of spasms, from him, would carry the next day's shame; the best moment be stained in advance with regret.

She saw Jack leave the Pinheads' house. He stopped to hold Mickey's gun at his eye but shook his head and didn't shoot, coming on to Bebe, smiling.

Last night Bebe had told him everything. The moment on the porch, how Mickey had the hots, the powder puff, everything. She showed him the darkening bruise where Mickey's thumbnail had cut a half-moon into her skin.

Jack wanted to have it out with Mickey then and there. "I didn't know how bad it really was."

Bebe didn't want a big fight. "After this, just tell him Pickle Beach is full every time he wants to come. Let it alone for now. His wife is with him, Jack."

"I hit George Bennett for a lot less."

"Did it change him?" Bebe said. "Let's just keep out of his way."

Jack wasn't sure. His finger slid between her breasts, a good sign, and she lay back lazy as a cat. He said, "Remember that other fisherman from Angier? Right before you went home?"

"I *am* home," Bebe said quietly.

"Wade talked about Mickey. He's already been bankrupt twice. Eunice bailed him out. And Eunice pays to keep his old man in a nursing home."

"Big deal," Bebe said. She was old-fashioned and thought Grandpa ought to lie in the front bedroom and die in plain sight with his children standing round.

"I'm asking—is he just mean or did circumstances make him mean?"

For once, Bebe wished Jack would talk less. "Everybody's got troubles and they don't all turn out mean."

"Besides that"—Jack laid one leg over hers and whispered in her ear—"Eunice is cold-blooded. The whole Cotton Club has talked that over."

"Wasn't it good of Mickey to take that up with them!" Bebe pushed her hips against him once.

"I'm told she would never like this," whispered Jack. "Or this. She'd move right away from this."

Now as Jack dropped to the sand, Bebe gave him a significant look so he could judge Eunice McCane for himself. She said (with her eyes): Could you be potent with this? Jack's eyes answered: Mickey chose her.

Eunice said, "Did you get to see those poor retarded people?"

"They're not so bad up close."

"Told you so," Bebe said.

"When I got there, Rosie was in this rocking chair and the boy in her lap, big as he is." Jack touched Bebe's ankle, then wrapped his hand there like a warm bracelet. "She was singing to him. I couldn't understand any words but maybe he did."

"How about Miss Whitaker?"

"She smiled, she really did. First time I've been able to tell she had a tooth in her mouth. Must be the oysters."

No. It's the beach, Bebe thought. After a few days here you slowed to the ocean's rhythm. Things fell into place on a scale that matched this endless sea and sky. Both were so big that they measured the people who came. The sea was very blue today, very radiant in the hot sun. How long the ocean had been there, how much longer it would stay than they ever could. Beside the ocean, people turned back into what they always were.

Between shots Mickey called Jack to take a look at that BAR on the bedspread. Out of the pile Jack lifted a long rifle with a narrow scope on top. The stock was decorated. Jack hefted it in one hand. "How much does a gun like this set you back?"

Set *Eunice* back, Bebe thought.

Carrying his plinker like a soldier in a parade, Mickey squatted to lay it carefully on the bedspread and take the bigger one from Jack. "I knew an ex-GI would jump at that name, but it's a different gun. Cost me nearly two hundred. Browning just put this out last year. It's for hunting big game." He snapped out a clip and showed Jack four rifle bullets.

"I didn't know you had any big game in Harnett County."

Bebe said, "What were you planning to shoot down here? A whale?" He slid the clip back with a grating noise.

Jack swung the heavy gun to his shoulder. "The barrel feels too long."

"Twenty-two inches. Look through that scope. It's shockproofed and double weatherproofed. Look at that hand-checkered wood and the way they've finished that metal. That's one sweet gun, let me tell you. Try it out over the water."

Jack shook his head. "Too much gun for me."

"Eunice, come fire this little Remington one time, show them what you can do. Bebe can't stand it; it stops up her ears."

Eunice didn't want to shoot. She pulled her pale eyebrows

together and wouldn't reach for the plinker. "You know I can't hit anything." But she sat up in the webbed chair. "You go ahead, Mickey."

"I'll load for you. Come on; I want Bebe to see I can teach anybody to shoot. I'm a good teacher." He said toward Bebe bitterly, "I could have taught you if you'd let me."

"Mickey, I'd rather not." Eunice was standing.

"Goddamn it, you just like to be begged." Quickly he put on a smile for the others. "Now carry it like I showed you."

Slouching, Eunice walked to the mark. They called to Foley to quit poking in the log and move back.

"Farther than that!" warned Eunice. She shot and missed. Bebe had always wondered where the world's missed bullets land, whether animals out minding their own business got hit and killed by some. That reminded her of Zorro, who had run under the house to escape the noise.

Mickey yelled again that it was Bebe's turn. Again she shook her head.

In a quiet cold voice, Jack said, "She doesn't want to."

"Sure she does. At heart she does."

"I said she didn't want to."

Bebe jumped from her chair, wanting no trouble. "I can shoot his stupid gun one time. Big deal." She felt too happy to let Mickey bother her anymore and once on her feet and running, she ran straight past Mickey and his stupid gun, into the sea, splashing cool water over her shorts and shirt. It clung to her skin.

"Quit clowning and come on," yelled Mickey.

Just to show he had no hold over her, Bebe ran out again, even across his line of fire down the beach and—feeling so free—took a big leap and jumped over Foley where he was stretched in the sand. She fell beside him, panting. "Too old to cut up like that." Or too old not to.

Off by themselves the two McCanes waited. Mickey held the gun high. She got her breath back. "Foley, you ought to go home and get yourself a girlfriend."

"After Chicago, maybe."

"And don't you take Mickey up on that rabbit hunting trip."

"Told him I was a vegetarian. You might as well shoot one time. He won't let you alone till you do." Foley pointed to the target. "It's an old timber off a ship with a big spike in one end."

"That's what I'll aim at, then. That spike."

Mickey gritted his teeth as he handed her the Remington. "See if you can hold it steady." He reached around to guide it to her eye, then flattened his body to her back. She didn't care; she was wet back there. "Higher," he said. "Brace it on your cheek." Eunice made marks with a knitting needle in the sand. Mickey said, "Settle down, Bebe, and stop laughing."

She couldn't help it; the fool still thought he had power over her. The gun wagged up and down until she saw his serious, angry face. Eunice walked away.

"Shoot to the middle, a little bit low. You'll probably jerk."

He rubbed against her. "Stand back," she said.

He laid his chin on her left shoulder, saying furiously, "Even now I could give you one more chance."

"You make me sick," Bebe said, trying to get the gun to hold still.

At her ear he said, almost spat, "You broke my glasses."

Bebe shot and missed everything. The noise flying inside her head scared her or maybe it was Mickey's face. She let the others, at their distance, see her pleasant smile but through her teeth she was saying in the ugliest tone she could, "I have told Jack everything that happened and maybe now you'll let me alone."

Mickey jerked the Remington out of her hands and dropped

it. He stood holding the BAR. From the look on his face he could club her with it.

Bebe wheeled and right then the Pinheads filed out toward the beach with Miss Whitaker, who surprised everyone by a friendly wave. Bebe waved back; Jack waved; Foley jumped to his feet and waved. Even Eunice flapped her hand once in the air.

And the long gun rose in Mickey's hand. "Jesus!" He laid his face almost tenderly on the stock. He swung the barrel up the beach and followed the Pinheads and Miss Whitaker just as if they were quail.

Bebe said, "Don't do that."

Eunice was coming, trailing wool behind her, "You told me never to point that thing unless I meant to shoot."

He was barely leading them with his big game rifle. Bebe slapped the cold barrel aside. "Don't scare them, Mickey."

He stood perfectly still. Then he said with an effort, "I'm just using the scope to see them better. Some cheap whore broke my binoculars. Besides, they've not got sense enough to be scared."

"You're scaring me, then."

Over the gunsight he squinted at Bebe. The scope looked like a black handle stuck in his eye. "Yes," he said. "Maybe I should." A pause. "Maybe it's time."

15

Mickey McCane

June 24 (Night)–June 25

Mickey couldn't sleep. Their small air-conditioner had run so hard it almost set itself on fire, so after dark when the seabreeze cooled, he'd switched it off and opened every door and window. He needed that fresh air. He was about to choke, perhaps from humidity. The moon which lit the screen door was almost full. Mickey rolled in the narrow bunk. The trailer seemed twice as long at night, and looked crowded. He might have been lying in a damn troop train grinding its way to the front lines. He felt itchy from sleeplessness.

He got out of his bunk and wormed beside Eunice into hers. She sighed away to one side. He gave her the knee. "You awake?"

Her breath was too deep so he knew she was faking. Years ago, when Mickey couldn't sleep, his mama would come in the bedroom (if she happened to be home) and lie on the covers beside him and tell him to draw breath as deep as he could and count five before letting it out. "I'll stay till you're sound asleep," she'd promise, but Mickey's practice breathing fooled her and she always left too soon, and he would lie there breathing deep in the dark room, trying to hear if the front door had closed behind her, if a taxi had pulled to the curb. He had to teach himself ways to go to sleep, tricks to play on his own body.

"Wake up, Eunice." He slid down and right away both feet stuck into the open air. He hated a cramped bed. Eunice's spine was lined up with his nose. "Turn over," he said. Sometimes anger would pour heat into his prick.

But she wouldn't. Hell, he didn't much care. His skin crackled with energy but both feet were cold in the damp breeze. A medic once told him people died from the foot up, that a coldness rose like water till it hit the heart. He knew when Dad had his heart attack he claimed both feet felt numb and very big. He kept rolling his eyes at Mickey and his jaw ground back and forth. "Where's your mother?" he kept moaning. Mickey should have said, "Which mother?" Anyway, she was dead by then in a boardinghouse fire in Nashville. The smoke got in her lungs and she died and went to Persia.

Mickey sat up and yanked the sheet. How could any man sleep after what that bitch had said? First Bebe broke his glasses, then ran her mouth to her husband! And she laughed; everybody on the beach heard her laugh. Those Pinheads up the beach—even they heard it.

He poked Eunice until, with a sigh, she rolled to face him. She even slid a hand on his neck when she found his mouth so near her breasts, and he caught one nipple in his teeth. Often that worked for him. Sometimes, though, he could suckle all night and still not raise a thing. Eunice, no patience as usual, reached down to touch him. A minute before he'd been getting there. Just the thought of her tan fingers sliding inside his thigh made him shrivel.

He jerked back and hissed, "There's nothing you won't do, is there, Eunice? Nothing!"

Suddenly the trailer door rattled. Somebody raked a dime or a long fingernail across the screen. Mickey hadn't rolled out so fast since his army days. He dropped to his hands and knees by the bed, naked.

"You fall out?"

"Be quiet. There's somebody messing with the door."

Eunice said she hadn't heard a thing. He caught her shoulder. "There it went again—surely you heard that?"

"I don't hear a thing but the wind and the water."

But Mickey knew by his own fear something was out there. His heart boomed all over his body. He could see clearly the block of gray light where the screen door was, so whoever it was must be down by the steps, hiding off to one side. He told Eunice for Christ's sake to shut up. She rolled to the wall. "Hear that?" She said nothing. He grabbed a handful of her nightgown. "You hear it?"

"You told me to shut up. No, I don't hear anything."

"You think it might be Bebe's dog?"

"Will you take my word there's not a thing out there but the ocean?"

"That dog is black and hard to see." It was something worse, though. Something that had traveled a long way to find Mickey.

"Go back to bed."

He crawled between their bunks along the scratchy rug. At first, like Eunice, all he could hear was the crash of the waves. Then it seemed he could pick out a separate rumble. His own stomach growled. Jesus! Outside, by the door! It must be the Pinhead woman. He knew it as well as he knew his own name. She was squatting by the trailer, her knees wide apart, waiting with her bulk throwing a big square shadow on the sand. Mickey could not see her yet knew she was there.

Behind him Eunice mumbled, "Are you in bed?"

"Yes," he said, and crawled on down the trailer. The nurse must be sound asleep. Left a door unlocked. And this . . . this halfway woman had got loose like a wild animal to wait for him outside his door with her hands dragging on each side and that black hair hiding her face.

God knew what she wanted! She probably didn't know. There wasn't much dangerous she could pick up off the ground—no rocks—but he remembered those thick arms; they could crush a man. Mickey had the feeling if he went back to bed she might creep down the trailer and just crawl on top of him without a word and lie there so he'd have to look up at her wet mouth and shaggy hair. He was shaking all over. Had to calm down, by God, and defend himself.

The guns were on a bench in the dinette. Just Mickey's luck: the one his hand found in the dark was the varmint gun, only a .22. Might scare her away, though. He was almost certain when the shot went off she'd flip backward and scream like that ape in the Tarzan pictures. Or maybe she'd just stand up and spread her arms and come forward and draw him slowly against her wide chest.

He loaded the rifle easily in the dark. He could even do it better that way, by touch. The clicking noise made Eunice call, "Mickey?" He sat still, half under the dinette table, until she went back to sleep.

Sliding to the door, he crouched low in the moonlight. He could see the rim of the dune, surprisingly bright, and nothing on the sand between the hill and trailer. Mickey couldn't tell if the loud noise in both ears was the Pinhead's breath or his own. Once he stood up he'd be able to see the wide ocean, which sometimes looked like a solid wall, and could turn swiftly to where she waited. He would know her, even in the dark, by that round fringe of black hair. His mama wore hers that way, too, with a headache band.

Mickey took a deep breath, counted five, getting ready. With the gun barrel he lifted the hook on the door. He was careful. She might bite down on his throat.

He threw himself forward, yelling, burst open the screen, and jumped flatfooted on the sand to wheel with the rifle trained on her . . . on her dugs.

Nothing.

"Hey, you!" He raced after her all the way around the trailer, came back to the open door and stood there, trembling. Maybe she'd crawled underneath on her belly and rolled up in the dark.

He couldn't see a thing. Not a sign. He lay down on the sand himself to see even the dark spots by the concrete blocks. Once more, rifle cocked, he circled the trailer.

When he came around the second time Eunice was waiting on the steps with both hands pressed against her ribs. "For God's sake, Mickey! I didn't know what was going on!"

He said, "She was out here!"

Eunice said, "Who? What's the matter with you?"

Next door the house was dark but he heard a window slide up. To help her sneak back in, he guessed. He was shaking all over, so clammy the gun felt wet.

"Come back to bed, Mickey; you're naked as a jaybird." Far away a dog barked and Eunice pointed toward the sound. "You hear that? That's Bebe's dog in Bebe's house. You must have been dreaming the whole thing, noise and all."

Out her front bedroom window the nurse called, "What in the hell is going on?"

"Don't you cuss *me!*" Mickey shouted. "Just don't you cuss me! You keep those two freaks locked up where they belong." He even shook the Remington.

Miss Whitaker moved away, then came back to the window. "You are out of your mind, Mr. McCane. They're both in bed and sound asleep. They won't be asleep long if you're going to stand out here yelling."

"They're in bed *now!* Sure they are! *Now!*"

"They've been in bed the whole time and both doors are locked."

"*Now* they're locked!" he cried.

Miss Whitaker said, "I want you to know I've seen plenty of men without clothes before and it's not worth losing sleep." She shut the window and pulled down the shade.

"You through now?" Eunice said. "You done yet?" She went inside the trailer.

Mickey looked down at himself. The beach light was so queer. His skin was stony gray, his groin so black it looked like a cave. He was naked as a baby and cold as a baby must feel when he comes into the world.

Inside, Mickey laid the gun on the bench again and crawled into his own bunk, his heartbeat still very loud and his hands shaking. He curled up and tried to warm his fingers between his legs.

In the dark Eunice asked, "Did you unload that gun?"

"I will." But he got up and carried it back, still loaded, and laid it on the floor right by his bunk. He wasn't as stupid as women were. He didn't believe every fool thing he was told. He had learned that early in life. Mickey decided to say that to Eunice. "I want you to know I don't believe every fool thing I'm told."

"Oh, Mickey," she whispered. "Mickey. Mickey."

Alone, he strained to hear noises that meant the Pinhead woman might come back and slip inside this time and touch him. In the morning he'd show everybody her footprints beside the door and that would do it; the nurse would have to move them out of the house and off this beach. Somebody ought to slap a suit on Jack Sellars for letting dangerous people loose in a public place. What if he'd been some old man or sick? What if he'd dropped dead with a heart attack? One smart lawyer and Jack could lose everything. Everything. He rolled a long time in bed, trying to get warm.

The cold shaking kept him awake. Once he got up quietly and looked out all the windows, tiptoeing so Eunice wouldn't ask stupid questions. The sea looked higher up the beach than he'd ever known it to come. He even took out his binoculars to check the high tide mark, forgetting that bitch had broken them. He unclipped the BAR rifle scope in the dark and used that instead. Yes, the tide was very high—maybe the full moon had something to do with it. Or maybe some terrible earthquake had happened way out to sea in the very depths, and the shock waves were sweeping toward them and would drag Pickle Beach away.

He stared at the sea so long through that scope his right eye got numb and it made him dizzy. Back in bed, he put the scope under his pillow and reached down to touch the cool gun by the bunk. No. That wouldn't do. He got up and swapped the Remington for the big game rifle. For a long time he tossed. Then the dozing started.

Mickey hardly ever dreamed except as a kid, but no wonder he did that night after the Pinhead woman had almost succeeded in coming to his bed and touching his face with her animal one. A scare like that would make anybody dream.

He dreamed he was in a ship's engine room, working hard, in front of an open coal-fired boiler like the ones in old trains. He was covered with sweat and had taken off his shirt. The engine room was crowded with workers but Mickey had the biggest shovel; he was the main one. He talked to some foreign Arab boy, who told him they were running a holy submarine and had to keep piling on the coal because it was rising very fast now, against tons of water pressure. Jesus was on board that very submarine and He was headed for the surface. Their job was to get Him there in time for Judgment Day. Mickey thought it was funny that Jesus was rising out of the middle of the earth up through the water instead of coming down through the sky like everybody expected. That must be His little joke. They threw in coal until the captain came down to give them a pep talk. The captain was very old and white-haired and wore big rubber boots because his feet were cold. Mickey kept pouring on the steam. He wanted the credit for getting Him there. The Arab said the Virgin Mary was on board, too; they had docked for her at an Eastern port and she had been carried on board in a box with a silken canopy. "Have you seen her?" Only from a distance, the Arab said. She had a veil. Mickey wanted very much to see her without the veil but when he asked, the captain said he never would. He had some nerve saying that, hot and tired as Mickey was.

Before they got the submarine stoked up enough to break out of the water, Mickey woke very early in the morning, worn out, tangled in the sweaty sheet. He was lying on his stomach with both hands underneath and his arm muscles cramped.

In the dim light he saw Eunice asleep on her bunk with her mouth open. It was like waking up frightened as a boy and finding the world turned wrong. Turned so lamps were set even with his head and it felt he was looking down at the ceiling instead of up. In the trailer this morning, everything had been pulled out as long as a tube. Mickey's feet were farther off from his head than usual and the door seemed a long hike from his bed.

The door! The footprints! He dressed quickly and hurried outside. The sand was smooth. Mickey bent down in search of one mark anywhere and found only his own trail. Somebody must have smoothed out every footprint that should have been there. The Pinhead woman did come back, he thought, and patted her marks out by hand. He walked around the Pinheads' house as quietly as he could and tried both doors but they were locked. *Now* they were locked.

At the edge of the morning sea a fishing boat moved out of Southport and a little nearer, one of those plastic sailboats that looked like toys. Mickey remembered the holy submarine. What made him dream that? He was glad his dreams were rare.

He lit his first cigarette and swallowed too much smoke. He gagged but all he could vomit up was foamy spit and he let that fly in the Pinheads' yard. Since it might be Jack's rye that tore up his stomach, he went in and drank a ginger ale.

Mickey decided to walk to the creek and figure out what was going on. Bebe might have something to do with it. He took the little Remington off the floor and shouldered it, then hung the Browning automatic hunting rifle on the other shoulder. He stood beside the closet for a while because something vital was missing. Yes. The jungle suit. Mickey put that on top of his other clothes and camouflaged himself so the Pinhead woman couldn't find him.

Then he walked outside and stood on the dune with that ginger ale prickle all over his skin trying to think. What else? Ammunition. He went into the trailer again and collected all he'd brought for those two guns. It seemed important to divide up the bullets left and right so each pocket had the proper load for the rifle hanging on that side. He didn't know why he might need so many. They were heavy and made him walk awkwardly.

One other thing. In the trailer the third time he got the rifle scope out of his bunk, where it had slipped way down the mattress. He walked slowly up the beach in the gray light.

How his mama had hated guns! When Mickey was twelve he saved up to buy a Daisy air rifle, saving some of the price straight from her pocketbook. She took that gun away and hid it. Each time Mickey found it and shot off a BB or so, she would hide it in a new place. He stopped in the sand and smiled.

Once he found the gun crammed in the laundry hamper, along with Mama's lace pants with their funny sticky smell. The day Mickey shot a robin, Mama stuck the rifle up her bedroom chimney and he spent days cleaning soot out of the barrel. After that he learned to hide the gun himself, mostly by tying it to the coiled springs on his bed. He liked to lie there at night and know his weapon was a secret underneath. Sometimes, even when she had been gone to Persia for months, she would manage to hide his gun by some long-distance magic. It would vanish from under his bed. He knew by then that if she was gone, he could find it again in her underwear drawer, where it somehow traveled.

If she could see him now! Guns on both sides! That BAR was so heavy it pulled Mickey off balance on the thick sand. Once he even tripped on an empty inner tube and fell and slid sideways down a dry hill the wind had built last night. He lay there with his eyes shut. The sun glinting off the ocean made them water. Mickey used the two gun stocks like crutches and pushed himself up. There was sand all over his jungle suit now.

At last he stood at the mouth of the tidal creek looking at a reef near to shore. At low tide there, you could probably lift out sand clams with a trowel. They bury themselves and spit out water, which makes a little keyhole on top. With the rifle scope Mickey sighted at the passing blue and white sail he had seen before and fired the Remington a few times since it was well out of range. He was glad to find the scope saw almost as well as binoculars. The light was too strong on the water, though. And after he used it too long the right side of his head seemed to shrink.

He waded through shallow water up the creek bed. He kept on his shoes because of the sharp oyster beds in the slimy mud. Bet there were shrimp, too, if he just had one other person to help him drag the seine. Any person. He'd had to do everything by himself, always. He stopped in the water and thought about that. But it has made me strong if they ever ask something hard.

The creek bottom was full of unexpected holes and once he wet the rifle stocks stepping into one. Mickey chose a sandy bend and climbed ashore where, for a while, he ran around stamping at the tiny crabs. How quickly they tumbled into their holes! Dancing this way and that made him dizzy. He sat on the bank with the heavy rifle and blew shell holes in crabs that were underground.

His mouth had the queer taste of dried ginger ale. Mickey raked his fingernails across its sweet skim on his tongue. That made him remember the Harnett farmer who went to the barn and stuck his own gun in his mouth, and he made himself look down the silver barrel. No. He looked at the beautiful shining spiral. No, he would never do that. No matter what happened. Some people would like it if he did. He was no fool.

If I ever did shoot myself, Mickey thought, I'd leave this note addressed to the old folks' home. I'd write: From now on send my dad's bill to his first wife when you find her.

He heard a car driving along the road. He ran over the hills of sand full tilt to catch it before it turned inland because he wanted to tell something to the blackheaded woman who was driving, but when he got closer he saw her exhaust disappearing toward the bridge. He walked back slowly, panting, and told her the story anyway.

"This is another sad story that came out of World War Two. God, it could make any dogface cry! And this half-ass chaplain used to go around telling it—everybody hated that man—but sometimes I'd follow after him just to hear him tell it once more to the next platoon. This is the story.

"Are you listening?" Mickey sat by the creek again and made the crabs listen.

"The chaplain would start off saying we never did love enough, that was the steadiest sin in the world and so on; you know how chaplains will talk."

The crabs knew.

"Then he'd say there was this Christian woman sent her only son off to the war across the Pacific to fight Japan, to Bataan and Corregidor; and she loved that boy better than she loved her own life. No matter how far away he got, she loved him. She worried and she prayed about him; he was her only son. The son got wounded in the war but he wrote her from the hospital that it was nothing much; he'd be coming home soon, and if she could see the poor fellow in the next bed, she'd know how lucky he was. His mama fell down on her knees and thanked God she would soon be together with her only son. And a month later on the way home he telephoned her from a hotel in San Francisco. Said he'd be home in two days and which train to meet. Said he was bringing a friend with him who had been in the next bed in the hospital, and that poor boy just dreaded to go to his own home at all. Could he bring the friend home awhile? That mama said sure, and thank God they were both alive! Then her only son said, 'There's just one thing, Mama. He got wounded bad and he's blind.' She said, 'Poor thing, bring him on.' Her son said, 'And he's sick a lot and he lost both legs at the knee. It'll mean so much to know he can live with us awhile.' Then the mother said slowly into the telephone that if the buddy was *that* bad off, he'd need special treatment. They couldn't take care of all that just in their own house. She said, 'Even if he's your best friend in the world, you've got your own life to lead and I've got mine. What can a boy like that do? He'll get to be a burden on you.' Her son said all right, he wouldn't bring him. And he never came home. They found him dead on the sidewalk where he'd jumped out of that San Francisco hotel. He was blind and both legs were cut off at the knee."

Jesus! Mickey couldn't stand that awful story! He was nearly crying just thinking about it. Men don't cry. He used to beg the chaplain: Don't tell that awful story! But he'd go to every meeting just to hear if he would. He'd say, "Mickey, I never guessed you were so sensitive."

Jesus! Anybody would be sensitive to a goddamn mother like the one in that awful story.

Mickey blew his nose and jumped up to go to the trailer and see if maybe he could eat something. Too bad he didn't have one single person to help carry that heavy stuff. He stayed out of the water this time and followed the creek bank. The tide was going out and the sea would suck most of the creek out of the land and into itself.

Near the creek's mouth, Mickey thought he heard some woman calling, but it couldn't be Eunice this far away. He'd heard a man often married a woman that reminded him of his mother. Not so—his mother was short and broad and had straight black hair that grew in a round cap on her head. He listened again for the woman's voice. Nobody would be able to see him in his hunting suit. He doubted the Pinhead woman could say his name or anybody's name. "Mickey?" Could the wind sound like somebody's name? He spun around, searching.

Gulls were diving at the sand reef where the creek emptied and filled, making their short hoarse screams. Didn't sound like "Mickey." He looked through the rifle scope but could not tell what they were scavenging. From this point, Mickey could see all of Pickle Beach for what it was—six dingy boxes washed up on the shore. The empty shell home with an empty trailer parked in front were closest to where he stood. Farther northwest was his trailer and the Pinheads' house and then Foley's trailer. Even farther away the Sellars' house had the highest roof with the crossed lines of the only TV antenna. Ugly. Nothing good could happen here.

Both guns were heavy. The morning sun got hotter. Mickey let the Remington drag and clipped the scope back on the BAR for fear he might drop and lose it in the sand. Underfoot there were egg cases and speckled conch shells, but nothing worth picking up.

Somebody stood in the water near Mickey's trailer. Eunice must have got her butt stirring early. If that bitch hadn't ruined his binoculars, he could take a good look. But he needed to rest anyway—that jungle suit made him sweat so. He dropped to one knee and swung up the Browning to look through its scope. It wasn't Eunice. Jesus.

His back hurt but Mickey couldn't stop to piss now. He edged closer down the beach. Since he'd left the Remington where it fell in the hot sand, he started getting rid of its shells, too, behind him in a metal trail, one at a time.

Why didn't somebody sterilize them years ago? Some people shouldn't have children. Children need mothers that live in a real house and love them.

He looked again. Bebe was out there, too, saying something to the nurse, and she even waved to the Pinheads, but they probably didn't have sense enough to wave back. How could she do that?

Mickey's eye swept the beach and he began to run toward an oil drum which had been used by somebody for a cookstove. It felt good to rest the heavy rifle there while he rolled his arm around to loosen the shoulder socket. Then he knelt and looked through the scope but Bebe had disappeared. The nurse sat on the dune, busy sewing on buttons or something. By itself the gun leaped seaward and Mickey tilted his head.

And there they were. The Pinhead woman was looking straight at his trailer door and he knew she would like to slip inside and wait in his bed for him. She stuck out her hand. Mickey flinched; he thought she was pointing out his face across all that distance, but then her no-brain son laid his hand inside hers. They fell back side by side in the water's edge with their feet pointing out to sea.

The rifle scope had an excellent lens. He could pick out any parts of them he wanted.

The female had her legs spread wide, and the boy had his. Every wave rolled in and churned over their round bellies. The son was laughing.

"Now let me tell you," Mickey said aloud to the black-haired woman in the passing car, "that is a filthy sight." He could see how good it felt washing that way between their legs. His stomach got hard and heavy.

Mickey rubbed the ring the scope had indented around his eye. He drove in the right lid with the heel of his hand. Why did he have to be the chosen one? It should have been done years ago! Why was it Mickey McCane sent out on this beach with a full clip in his gun? He didn't want to. Bebe would understand that since she had almost changed everything for him. Nothing made sense in this life for a long time, he thought, but it all moves you at last to the place where a justice has got to be done. He was not here by accident. Even the gun had pressed itself cold in his hand.

Mickey's right arm was cramped. He might have a blister on the palm. He steadied the BAR and rubbed his face deep in its carved stock. How could any Pinhead give a damn for any other Pinhead? Was that fair? When so many are left out and cheated and have to do everything by themselves?

Right in his scope the female Pinhead was wiping both thighs with her wet hands. Her black hair hung evenly around that ugly face. She dribbled water down the boy's head and he laughed at her with his tongue half out of his mouth and tried to catch hold of her dripping hand. It was so filthy.

Mickey got him on the first shot. He thought the bullet went into his ear and lifted him up by the brain and carried him five feet away down the surf.

The female jumped up with her hands high in the air and her mouth wide open. She yelled. She tried to scream . . . she said . . . Riley? Clyde?

Mickey thought: My God, she has given that thing a normal name!

He let her have two in the chest. That left him with one in the clip and he might have fired that, too, but she fell down beside the other one in the red ocean then, and there was no good angle for the shot.

The nurse got to the water's edge where they lay just about the same time Mickey reached the surf on his part of the beach and they stared at each other down the long edge of the endless sea. The nurse was screaming in a high nigger voice and throwing one hand toward him. Mickey heaved his gun far out in the water so nobody could hide it from him anymore.

He wanted to watch whether the seagulls would dive after it or not, but he didn't have time, and he ran easily with long free steps over the dunes to the asphalt road, and across that and down the high bank into the matted pickerelweed swamp, where he knew he could hide in his jungle suit until the world was ready for him.

16

Bebe Sellars

June 25

While Jack and Foley finished their pancakes, Bebe walked Zorro under the house so he could excrete everything before riding in the car. At every moment she could see, hear, and smell the sea. If I lived in a desert, she thought, and somebody told me about the ocean I wouldn't even believe it.

That reminded her to sneak a little water to Jack's cacti while Zorro was squatting in the gray sand. She couldn't get over that funny word, cacti. Foley said: *Dominus, Domini, Dominum.* Sometimes Foley couldn't resist showing off, like college boys in the café bragging about a taste for *escargots,* when all they meant was snails. She guessed he'd outgrow it.

The dog was finished. Jack was to carry him to the vet this morning because of those watery stools; hookworm, Willis said.

"He's ready," Bebe called up the stairs. "I'm putting him in the car." Both came out the back door but she said, "Foley, why don't you stay here and help me with the dishes?" She wanted to talk to him about going home to Maryland.

"I was planning to go with Mr. Sellars to the vet," he complained.

"How many men does it take to deworm one dog?"

After Jack drove away with the pup, she stationed Foley by the dishrack with a towel and started on the importance of going home so you could appreciate the full length of your life thus far and not get hung up on the separate parts. She saw Foley was amused at her arguments. "Think how your mother feels, you on the road with bad eyesight."

"That's a lot better now," he said.

"Does she know that? Did you ever write her?"

"Where do the cups go? I'm not going to some shrink and lie down on a couch and tell him about playing doctor with the neighborhood kids, Bebe."

"Right-hand cabinet." She sloshed soapy water over the plates. "Big deal," she said. "I am not talking about little things like that." Without looking at her hands she scrubbed syrup off, watching instead the birdbath below her window where some rusty sparrow was washing the mites from his wing feathers. She was trying to talk about the whole shebang, his life and everybody's life, and whether he'd wind up saying yes or no to that. Bebe sighed. It was simpler to stick to the practical details.

"You don't know how lucky you are, Foley, with a family that loves you and can send you to school. Think how they worry. Think how you'd feel if your son was running around waiting for his whole country to come to an end."

The living room clock chimed: nine-thirty. That chimney must act like an echo chamber.

She was beginning to get on Foley's nerves. He put the cups away with much clanking. A dozen times Bebe had tried to have this talk and Foley had sidestepped. He believed, said

Jack, in passive resistance. All that resisting was what got him into trouble in the first place.

He said to her, peacefully, "I can't live the life my parents would pick for me, Bebe. We hardly agree on anything. A philosophy, the goals of society, things like that." He handed back a fork with food in the tines to be washed again. "All his life my father's been in some kind of . . . of penal servitude. To people's crooked teeth, of all things."

"So ask him about it. Ask him. Ask him what else goes on in his head."

"All I'd get back is a list. His mortgage, his taxes, his wife and his children. I'm not going to live by some list."

Oh, Foley. Foley! Yes you are, Bebe thought. Honey, you will. And parts of it you won't ever get checked off. And still there was more to living than that. "Ask what was on your daddy's list he didn't get."

His polite smile. No comment. "Foley, when your daddy was your age, what do you think he was like?" Bebe wiped the table.

How he laughed! "Oh, boy, I can tell you that! He was true blue and foursquare. He saved all his money and talked respectfully to older people even if they were stupid. Notice that, Bebe. Even if they *were* stupid. He listened to wiser heads and set goals for himself. He wore his hair short and his chin up, looked ahead, and stood on his own two feet."

The talk wasn't working. She raked crumbs into her open hand. All Bebe knew was that everybody had to go home, work back down that old road they came by, hold it open, make some kind of peace—or else memories would bang around loose in them. Home came to them, then, and it hurt. And meantime the wheel was turning and the great blue ocean rolled. . . . She drew a deep breath. "Foley," she told him carefully, dropping the crumbs in the trash, "when you have children of your own . . ."

Well. That did it. Foley threw the towel over his face and stood there masked, laughing and shaking all over. With his head in a sack that way, he looked like a horsethief who might be hung if he'd once stop laughing and hold still. In the movies the judge never had this much trouble with Andy Hardy. Had Bebe ever listened to such advice herself? No. She got furious because she was going to Hollywood and would wear her hair in a platinum pompadour like Ginger Rogers.

She slapped her dishcloth on a rack. "I'm going to ask Miss Whitaker if they'd like some pound cake; you just stay in here and laugh."

The Pinheads were playing in the water. Bebe closed the porch door behind her. She was thinking of how to start over with Foley and tell him about Greenway this last time and how it meant something, even now, to know her ajuga was spreading at Hebron every time it rained.

Miss Whitaker sat in a chair on the dune mending a white stocking. "They'd like the cake," she said to Bebe, who stood by her watching the Pinheads lie back in the water's edge while it washed them and floated out their hair.

"Rosie really loves that boy," she said, and Miss Whitaker nodded her bushy black head. Foley could learn something if he would just step on the porch now and look at the Pinheads bobbing their feet in the sea. If only he'd open his eyes! She glanced toward her house in case he might be seeing them, really, for once; but spotted instead the grocery truck parking at the side. "I'll send Foley with the cake," she said. Rosie made a noise at her in the water. "Morning, Rosie! Nice day," Bebe called. They waved. Way up the beach she saw a tiny figure all alone on the sand.

She did not look forward to a visit from Pauline. That picnic had left Polly with plans to enlist Bebe as a regular helper in the Sunday school. Pauline had been calling her on the telephone and calling her. Even the preacher called once. Inside a church, Bebe thought, she might smother.

She told Foley that when she got indoors. Naturally he couldn't help teasing, and shook his finger in the air. "Why, Bebe! You don't know how lucky you are to have a friend like Pauline who cares about the future of your soul. Why, think how she worries! Think how you'd feel if you had a good friend—"

"Just close up your mouth before Pauline hears you," she said. "She is right outside. I get you. Big deal. Lay off."

Up the high stairs Pauline Buncombe carried a pasteboard box of so many home-grown tomatoes they were going to rot on Bebe's windowsill before she could use them all. A blue piece of folded paper was stuck with them inside the box. It might be the Sermon on the Mount or maybe this time the Barren Fig Tree or the One Lost Sheep. Bebe opened the door.

Polly said, "Aren't these pretty? They're Big Boy tomatoes, best I've ever grown, and not a disease carrier has laid his hand on a one, in case you're asked. Morning, Foley. Bebe, you think we might get more rain? Willis says his back hurts and that's usually rain."

If it rained, maybe Mickey would go home early and let everybody alone. "Is he wearing his back brace?" said Bebe.

"Yes, and he grumbled all night."

Bebe lifted the coffeepot and shook it. Pauline said yes. Getting out cups, Bebe twisted sideways and tried reading the title stuck down among the tomatoes. "In the beginning" was what it said. She ought to lend that to Foley.

"You were just wonderful to all the children. And thank you, Foley, for being our lifeguard." Pauline blew into her cup. "I hardly got a wink of sleep with Willis's hot water bottle falling on me all the time."

Bebe had slept as deeply as Jack, relieved now that she had told him about Mickey. Never once, she thought, had Jack considered the possibility Mickey might tempt her, that she might be curious to know how it would feel to lie down under cruelty. Jack thinks I'm better than I am; might as well take that compliment and hush. The beach was changing Jack. He hadn't dreamed the river dream for a long time now.

Bebe cut the pound cake in half and began to root around in a cabinet for wrapping paper. "After a while, Foley, Miss Whitaker wants this cake." He poured his own coffee and sat across from Pauline, who said, "I saw Jack driving that dog past about nine o'clock and the way he was having to wrestle on that front seat, it'll cause a wreck someday." Now she shifted in her chair, got her face ready to deliver her speech. "I want you to come to our study group, Bebe. Either one, Wednesday or Sunday night. Did you read that outline Willis brought?"

"I forgot," Bebe said. She had stuck the first small folder under the clock.

"On Sundays it's Job," Polly said. "Job is hard."

"Well, that lets me out," said Bebe. She would not look at Foley, who enjoyed seeing her on the receiving end.

Sudden inspiration. Pauline patted Foley on the hand. "And why don't you come with her?"

"He can run me up on his motorcycle," Bebe said.

Foley hid his mouth with the cup for a minute, then asked politely, "And what are you studying, Mrs. Buncombe?"

How was that for a straight man! Frog never did better for Gene Autry, nor Gabby Hayes for any cowboy hero.

"Hand it to me out of the box, Bebe. Genesis on Wednesday nights. Our theme is In the Beginning *God.*" She said God's name very loud. "That's what we have to remember." Unfolding the flier, she held up the front page so Foley could read the title. "Being college trained, you'd like it, Foley. Our preacher's real modern—I mean he can consider evolution and everything. You don't have to think that seven days is seven *days.* He tells us to think about Genesis as a metaphor."

Foley nodded to show that he knew what a metaphor was. Well, Bebe didn't. She didn't miss knowing. She decided to unload those overripe tomatoes and not say a word.

Pauline turned to the second blue page. "That's the main thought, those first four words in the Bible. 'In the beginning, *God.*' "

Foley asked her what were the last words in the Bible. The question flustered Pauline. She turned the folder thoughtfully but there was nothing printed about it there. Bebe gave him a stare.

"I'm not too sure but I can guess, since the last book, Revelation, is about the end of the world. That's what its title means, Apocalypse, the end of the world." Pauline was a serious student of the Bible and kept notes in the margins, and now she looked smug at the good fruit her hard work had borne.

"The word comes from Greek," Foley said, "and means the lifting of the veil."

Pauline's eyebrows flew up; she had something new for her margins. "Which veil?"

"The veil so you can see the truth, I guess."

Bebe said quickly, "Your family must go to church, Foley. I bet your mama even prays for you."

He smiled but concentrated on Pauline. "And the last words in Apocalypse, I think, ask Jesus to hurry up and come quickly. That was written in the first century A.D. and I guess He wasn't quite as quick as they had in mind. I guess the veil didn't get lifted."

Pauline frowned wrinkles deep in her wind-burned forehead. "I'm not sure. Bebe? Where's your Bible?"

She *would* ask. Bebe was ashamed to admit she had stuck it someplace in an orange crate with all Jack's other books. She was no reader. She said in a hurry, "He's right. That's it. That's how the whole Bible ends."

Not satisfied, Pauline tapped the title page of her folder. "Anyway, we're studying Genesis, not Revelation. I had no idea you were such a Bible student, Foley Dickinson. That gives me hope you'll straighten out after all." Her voice grew more confident. "I do think there's a great hunger for God among the young people and that's why so many have turned to drugs."

Foley didn't answer. She added more sugar to her coffee. "The fact you're so well informed is all the more reason you ought to come Wednesday nights with Bebe. Since you studied the Bible in college."

"High school," said Foley. "The Hagerstown churches paid a little old lady to give an elective in Bible literature and when you took that course instead of study hall you got an extra credit."

"We ought to try that here," said Pauline thoughtfully, "in the Brunswick County schools. Many children just don't read the Bible anymore." She handed him the blue paper. "Look over this, Foley. You might find it deeper than what you studied in high school."

Bebe saw he was beginning to enjoy himself and that the smile was in danger of turning to a sneer. Not reading, but turning the paper in his hands, Foley blocked steam off his cup. "What I always thought about Genesis," he said, still tickled in that superior way, "is that God put His money on the wrong man." Pauline was really shocked and gave Bebe a stare that said so.

"What if"—Foley grinned—"He'd been better pleased with Cain's offering of fruits and nuts and vegetables instead of

Abel's blood sacrifice? With living plants instead of dead animals? That might have changed the history of the Western world."

She almost spluttered. "You'll find that explained right there on page three, Foley Dickinson. It's a prophecy of blood sacrifice for sin."

One corner of his mouth turned up. "It's a prophecy, all right. We've been wiping out sin with blood ever since instead of trying peace and nonviolence."

"All but your generation. Right?" said Bebe.

"He might better come Sundays for Job," snapped Pauline. "You've got violence inside you, too, Foley Dickinson. All of us have." He shook his head.

Suddenly Bebe discovered how angry Foley made her, baiting Pauline, and she said in her meanest voice, "Go on to Chicago, Foley Dickinson!" He was surprised and set down his cup. "You ride right on and you be sure to play smart aleck everywhere you go, hear? Talk down to everybody. Do it in Latin. Mock people's religion!" Foley's smile was stuck under his nose as if he'd forgotten it was there. "You know what's wrong with you, little stuck-up boy? You don't think you'll ever do anything dumb or mean or ugly. You don't think you'll fail or be ashamed or have something in your past you can't stand to look at! You think taxes and laws will solve everything. Well, let me tell you something!"

(Oh, Bebe thought. What if I cry? Foley won't but what if I do?)

"Let me tell you that the whole world . . . the whole world . . ." She couldn't remember what she'd wanted to tell him. Her voice got tangled in her throat and wouldn't come out. She turned to the sink and opened both faucets for no good reason. She thought about Jack and a death that happened and herself, and a birth that didn't, and all of them. All of them.

Foley shook his head. His long hair, almost the color of her own, slapped his two cheeks as he stepped beside her. "Bebe?"

Might know she'd cry! So simpleminded she could cry over nothing at all on a day she began feeling swell, just swell. Bebe started popping Pauline's tomatoes, one at a time, on the windowsill, bruising them near the stem. He was so young. She wouldn't want to be that young again. So much to live through yet and so much of it hard. Hard to let anybody else have what you wanted and didn't get, or had one time and lost. Hard to remember but nobody could ever forget. Some days it was even hard to love people the way they needed loving, and be satisfied with whatever love you happened to get back.

Foley touched her shoulder. She couldn't seem to say anything sensible and what popped out was, "You've got to ease up on people."

"I will," he said, "and I'm really sorry."

"Don't be sorry. That isn't it. Say yes."

"I'm still sorry. What can I do to make up?"

Bebe forced herself to laugh. "You can go home and be good to your mother, that's what." Now Foley laughed behind her and Pauline laughed, relieved.

Foley said he'd do that. "I'll be sitting in Chicago listening to one dull speech after another and I'll be so bored I'll get up like the prodigal son and go home, I really will. I'll tell my mother there was a woman I met at Pickerel Beach and she gave me good advice."

Bebe reached to her shoulder where he had put his fingers, and mashed them. When the time came, she knew, he would not remember. She got her throat cleared out. "Pauline, I never saw such big tomatoes." She slid a split one out of sight behind the curtain, then stopped there with the juice wetting her fingers.

Somebody was screaming on the beach.

Screaming closer, screaming up the steps, crashing open the

screen door, screaming on the porch and all the way across her living room.

Miss Whitaker was screaming in the doorway with her glasses down on one cheek. She screamed at them all. It blew Bebe like a great wind. She never had heard such a scream.

Foley was the first to move. He pushed the nurse out of the way and she fell against the refrigerator and wouldn't stop screaming. Bebe heard him run out of the house, the screen door banging. Bebe ran after him.

Over the sand he was racing. Bebe ran fast to get away from that terrible scream in her house. Where were they going at such speed? She pounded behind him across the dune. Now that she was safely outside she could admit to herself how the woman looked screaming in the doorway with that red gristle stuck to the starch on her skirt, but while it was happening . . .

Not slowing down, Foley hollered loud, "*Go back!*"

No. The scream was too loud to go back. Bebe topped the dune and took three more hard thuds on the sand. She saw . . . washed in a pile on the beach there was . . . half in the water . . . one leg that's all right and the arm was still white but oh Lord it was so red there and something had gnawed out his whole head it's Rosie's face down in the water couldn't get to him she got close she tried to touch she is getting that red all in her mouth. . . .

"*Go back!*" Foley yelled. Water flew up around his running feet. He bent by the boy in the surf, moved over, squatted beside Rosie and lifted her mouth out of the bloody water. He looked at their house. Then he stood in the surf and stared at Mickey's trailer. Bebe had to stop running. She might be on fire.

Foley sprang onto the sand and ran crouching along the beach, bent low till the dragging hand grabbed up a Coke bottle with green light inside it and he lifted that high as a torch on his way to the trailer. He stopped by a low pile of shells. He slammed the bottle into them and the glass bottom broke off jagged and sharp. He kicked out the trailer screen and disappeared inside.

Somebody else was running now. No matter what came up behind her, Bebe couldn't move or do anything but wait on it to come.

Pauline said in a weak voice at her back, "I called the sheriff. . . . Are they both? Yes. The nurse said they were."

It was strange that Bebe could answer just as calm in a time like that: "She shouldn't be screaming all by herself in that empty house."

"You come, too, Bebe. Mickey's gone crazy. He might shoot any one of us now. Come on."

Foley stepped out of the trailer alone, his broken bottle still high and shaking in his right hand. Pauline said, "Come on, Bebe. We've got no protection out here. Look yonder, Foley's coming, too."

The three of them kept from looking at the water's edge where, in rhythm, they shivered and trembled, lay still, and were again disturbed. Bebe wouldn't look at the surf but still she could see how lazily their black hair floated up and down and was stained.

Pauline called to Foley, "The law is coming. And an ambulance." She wrapped her arm around Bebe, cold as a rubber hose.

When Foley fell into step beside them, Bebe told him to get on his motorcycle and go after Jack but she couldn't even remember where the vet lived anymore; Pauline had to tell him that. Foley was staring at the sharp bottle in his hand; on purpose he cut his own thumb with its edge and then seemed surprised to see blood welling out through his skin.

From as far away as the steps, Bebe could hear Miss

Whitaker crying deeply from somewhere inside the house. You just can't keep screaming that loud for very long.

Willis's clock tore up the wall and bells echoed up the chimney to prove it was noon. Under the sun in its zenith, all were out looking for him: the Brunswick County sheriff and Jack and Willis and Foley and deputies and highway patrolmen, and maybe strangers.

Miss Whitaker had given herself a shot and lay on Bebe's bed asleep, and Zorro slept near her white shoes. Bebe wouldn't take a shot or even a tranquilizing pill; she was numb enough from events.

Bebe tiptoed into the bedroom. Miss Whitaker barked, "Who's there?" With her glasses off, her whole face looked tired.

"It's Bebe." Time was, a white woman had to stop and remind herself to say Mrs. Sellars. What a lot of work that was.

Miss Whitaker tried to sit up. "We can't leave them out in the water."

"That's all been done. I went out and sat in your chair till the ambulance came; you were there, remember?" She didn't, although she stood right by the bodies and waited knee deep in the water, and then was in charge of seeing them decently covered with their arms arranged on their wide chests. For a long time she fooled with Rosie's hands, trying to cross them and hide her wounds.

Bebe pushed her back onto the pillow. "I did what you said but Eunice McCane won't come. She just sits on her steps at the trailer. I think she believes he'll try to get to her and maybe he will. There's a deputy hid in the trailer in case he does."

Miss Whitaker dropped an arm across her eyes. "Has he got any other gun besides the one I saw him throw?"

"Not except maybe a twenty-two."

"They were harmless." She choked. "They were both so harmless."

Bebe left the room because the nurse had told all this before: how they couldn't stand to be out of each other's sight, and how each would wait and whimper outside the closed bathroom door till the other came. How they were always patting and stroking the inside of each other's arms. How they liked rolling the ball. How, in the morning if Rosie woke first, she would walk over and touch Michael lightly on the face.

Miss Whitaker called, "Are the doors locked? Has that man always been crazy?"

"It's all right. Go to sleep."

Since she had asked, Bebe had to walk through the house and double-check every door, and the window latches next. To be really afraid, in the bones—it made her whole body hurt. Earl told her once about an old maid that couldn't go to bed at night until she had looked for prowlers everywhere through her whole house and, last of all, rammed an ice pick through every keyhole.

Tightening one window lock, she saw Eunice McCane on the beach near the trailer with wind whipping back her skirt and her hair. Had she really been surprised? Nobody could tell. She was staring over the water, the one direction he couldn't have gone.

On Bebe's mantelpiece lay a loaded pistol. Jack had stacked her cups in crazy towers to place it there, the holly inside the angel and the saucers crooked, just in case, after showing her how the cylinder was full and how she should take the safety off and how to cock the hammer.

"Now if you have to use it," he'd said, "wait till he's close and aim at his middle." He tried to put the pistol into her hands. Bebe asked him where that thing came from and he said it was one of Mickey's guns. She couldn't touch it then, so he left it right over the hearth in plain sight. "I'll tie Zorro downstairs so he'll bark," Jack said. Bebe wouldn't have that. He could bark in the house just as well. "You lock every door," Jack called, going down the stairs to join the manhunt. Bebe watched him from the kitchen window. He yelled by the birdbath, "Just stay out of sight and shoot out and shoot through."

Then all the men set off, in cars, in two directions. By now roadblocks were set up everywhere. Willis said they might bring in bloodhounds. He was riding in the sheriff's car, having showed off his hand and described a runaway convict he cornered, years ago. Eunice thought Mickey was dressed in a white shirt and denim pants. She had given them an old photograph out of his wallet, which was still in the trailer, with a long fold down the face that separated his eyes.

Bebe stared at that gun butt behind an overturned cup. Jack had come close to asking her outright if she could kill Mickey if she had to, and Bebe came close to answering like a movie: *Mechanically, yes. Emotionally, I don't know.*

Willis's clock had let fifteen more minutes go by and chimed about it. She remembered the pint of brandy in the linen closet they bought for hurricanes, or times when pneumonia would have to be warded off. She might as well take one drink straight from the bottle.

She carried the brandy to the living room window and lifted the bottle to her lips. Then, throwing her head back to drink, she saw him through the dusty glass. Across the highway he was coming slowly out of the swamp, walking that dry ridge where George had dredged out a drainage ditch last year. No, that couldn't be Mickey. It was a soldier in some kind of combat suit with a camouflage pattern in the cloth. Maybe they had sent to Camp LeJeune for a posse of marines. The hot brandy stung her mouth like orange rind and burned going down.

When she heard the linen closet close, Miss Whitaker called out, "Who's at the door?"

"Nobody. Everything's fine," Bebe said. "They've called in the military police." Nothing to do, then, but pace up and down the room and wait for the clock bells to ring on the half hour.

Next time she looked, the camouflaged man was much closer. Bebe couldn't have found him at all if she hadn't known to follow the ridge where she had last seen him. His uniform blended perfectly with the reeds and marsh grasses. There could be a hundred more in the swamp by now, dressed like that, searching, but she could see only one coming that way. Usually her vision was very good. She scanned the green field and waited for its pattern to move. The man went out of her sight now, below the highway bank. He was climbing the weedy slope. A head without a helmet came into view. He stood on the roadside staring at this house. Oh, my God.

Bebe ran to the mantel and scattered cups getting hold of the pistol. Could she hit him out the living room window? He wasn't very far away. How far does a pistol shoot? He held up one hand with the palm toward Bebe in a wave of some kind or a blessing. She believed he was making some speech she couldn't hear through the closed and locked window. The gun trembled in her hand. What happens when you shoot through window glass? Which way do the pieces go?

Now Zorro was growling and sitting up at Miss Whitaker's feet.

And the man waited motionless on the sandy shoulder of the road as if he expected an answer to what he had said. Could he see Bebe, maybe, in the high window with his own gun shaking in her two hands?

Where was that stupid deputy? She was ready. He would run out of the trailer and bring his own gun as soon as he heard this shot. It was hard to cock the pistol—it left her fingers weak. She decided to brace her wrists on the back of a wooden chair. She held the gun steady.

He had spread his arms wide as if he might reach out for a woman or wait for a cross to be shoved up behind him. Aim at his middle was what Jack had said. That was where Bebe aimed.

17

Jack Sellars

June 25

At one o'clock Jack used his key on the kitchen door and came in calling for Bebe. He let out a long breath when she answered. She sounded weak and sick; everybody felt sick.

Jack washed his hands at the sink, saying through the doorway, "We've had no luck. The men are still out. They found both his guns so he can't be armed—one in the water, and one close by the creek. Maybe he stole a boat." He grabbed a towel. "What makes a man crack up like that, all of a sudden, with no warning? God only knows."

Bebe said softly, "Yes. That's right."

He came into the living room drying his wrists. She was sitting on the hearth drinking straight from the brandy bottle and the pistol lay by her on the bricks, not where Jack had left it. He opened his hand and the towel floated down.

In a weary voice she said, "He's in the swamp. I saw him. He came out at noon and went back."

Jack started running around the room, grabbed up the gun, tried to look out every window at once. He could see nothing but pickerelweeds and marsh grass, green and level from the highway to the farthest pines.

"Why didn't you shoot? The guy in the trailer would have heard. Bebe? Why didn't you shoot?"

She looked at the pistol he was waving in the air and shook her head. "I didn't know how," she said.

Jack dropped the gun on an orange crate. In a minute he'd go tell the sheriff where Mickey was but right then what he needed was to put his arms around her and rub his face in her yellow hair. He said, "I love you, Bebe."

"Yes, you do," she said calmly. Her face was against his shoulder and, beyond, she rested her eyes on the boundless sea.